The Wrong Men

The Wrong Men

Rob Barron

The Book Guild

First published in Great Britain in 2026 by
The Book Guild Ltd
Unit E2 Airfield Business Park,
Harrison Road, Market Harborough,
Leicestershire. LE16 7UL
Tel: 0116 2792299
www.bookguild.co.uk
Email: info@bookguild.co.uk

The manufacturer's authorised representative in the EU
for product safety is Authorised Rep Compliance Ltd,
71 Lower Baggot Street, Dublin D02 P593 Ireland (www.arccompliance.com)

Typeset in 10.5pt Garamond Pro

Printed and bound in Great Britain by CMP UK

ISBN 978 1835743 829

British Library Cataloguing in Publication Data.
A catalogue record for this book is available from the British Library.

To Juliet, Rosa and Daniel.

What was Johnny Jewell listening to in December 1979?

1

December 1979, York District Hospital

The hospital lay quiet under a dark, starry sky, a slumbering giant hemmed in by car parks, clipped lawns, and residential streets, all glistening with the first signs of a hard frost. Inside, hundreds of shadowy rooms were connected by a sprawling network of brightly lit corridors. Some rooms never slept, housing weary staff who kept watch under harsh strip lighting, monitoring patients and umbilically connected equipment. Alert for any beep or ping, any erratic dial, any change of breathing, they maintained their vigil throughout the night, waiting for the death rattle, or one of the multitude of crises that often prefigured it.

Those still awake and alert were the slowed heartbeat of the sleeping giant, unmoved by its occasional stirrings and twitchings through the night. In the dead stillness, porters in pairs or singly occasionally passed along corridors, pushing trolleys, carrying bin liners, disappearing from pools of light into darkness and reappearing again. Lifts wheezed. Lights pinked. Wall clocks ticked.

The end of one long, dazzling corridor on the ground floor ended in a T-junction. To the right was the mortuary. To the left, the car park and the nurses' home. To turn outside was to catch one's breath against the icy cold of a late-December night and flinch at the sudden hiss of steam from boiler pipes. The covered walkways and car park were studded with low lighting for safety, but the squat block of the nurses' home was enveloped in darkness. All except for one window on the ground floor, a yellow square against the black. It was facing the car park and an adjoining, detached one-storey building. The central metallic chimney of that building seeped a thin plume of smoke into the night sky, and there was a constant low growl from inside. The hospital incinerator burned steadily throughout the night.

A curtain shivered. A door opened. A trolley squeaked. The flagstones prated. But no one saw and no one heard. The incinerator rumbled on.

*

The phone rang again. Johnny lifted his head with a jerk and banged it on the shelf above him.

"What…?" he spluttered, feeling the top of his head to assess the damage and soothe the pain. He swung his legs from under the lacy blanket and sat up. The room was hidden in darkness, but on the far wall, the clock washed away the last whispers of his dream and brought him back to reality. 3 a.m.

The phone kept ringing, angry and insistent.

"Alright, alright," he muttered, stretching out to pick up the receiver and silence the noise that was drilling a hole in his skull.

He composed himself and picked it up, just in time to save it from screaming out at him again.

"Porters," he said. His tone, picked up from repeated observation of his colleagues, oozed bored indifference.

The voice at the other end crackled through the airwaves.

"Were you asleep?" It was a woman's voice, faintly amused. "I've been bleeping you lazy bastards for ages."

"No, of course not," he protested. "I was in the middle of something."

"Yeah right. Is that Johnny, the new lad? Good-looking, scruffy, studenty type? Someone told me you were on duty tonight."

"Yeah, that's right. Who are you?"

"Gloria, ward thirty-six."

"OK. So, what do you want, Gloria?"

There was a pause. Johnny waited and the pause grew. He frowned and tried to decipher the sounds from the receiver, muffled as if a hand had been placed over it. Then Gloria's voice returned, drained of its previous lightness. She cleared her throat and spoke, flat and colourless.

"We've got a customer for Rose Cottage. Ward thirty-six. Chop-chop."

"Gloria, are you—" Johnny began.

The phone went dead.

He shook his head and reached for the light switch above the sofa. Spitting and crackling, the strip lights overhead coughed uncertainly into life. For a moment, the light seemed to be making up its mind whether it could be bothered and then the room was flooded with a harsh, white glare. His hand automatically went to his head again and he shielded his eyes from this fresh assault.

The room was better in darkness. A few fraying armchairs, a Formica table, a microwave, kettle and a fridge. The only luxuries were the two sofas, sagging and stained, on opposite sides of the room. He looked across to the other, expecting to see the still form of his colleague for the night beginning to stir under his blanket. It would not have been a surprise if Gordon had deliberately ignored the phone, waiting for Johnny to deal with it. Nor if he had slept serenely through it. But the sofa was empty, the regulation hospital blanket in a crumpled heap on the floor.

Where the hell is he? Johnny thought. *As soon as there's some bloody work to do, he disappears.*

There was nothing for it but to go on his own, and hope that Gordon had picked up the request on his walkie-talkie and was already on his way. At the door, he stopped to check he had everything. He felt the pockets of his overall. The walkie-talkie, packet of cigarettes and lighter were stowed in one, his battered copy of *Bleak House* in the other. Yes, he was good to go. He stepped out into the corridor and closed the door behind him.

2

The hospital corridors were eerily quiet at that time of night, frozen under the death-ray sheen of the brutal strip lighting. Some of the lonelier byways were shadowy, studded with safety lamps to save money. Most of the inhabitants were upstairs, asleep in the wards, but there were still pockets of sentient human activity: the reception staff, medics and porters ghosting their way around the building, and the random collection of drunks and stab victims in A&E that were slumped over crumpled copies of yesterday's papers.

It was Johnny's favourite time to be at work. The night shift was generally quieter, apart from the horror of casualty, and there were plenty of opportunities to find a secluded spot and settle down with a book, or to snatch some sleep, always with a walkie-talkie by his side, in case of emergencies. The downside was that it was also PCT: peak corpse time. Since working as a porter, he had begun to realise that the overwhelming characteristic of hospitals was that they were places where people came to die. And die they did. Usually between 3 and 4 a.m., seemingly to spite those people who were asleep and whose responsibility it was to prepare and dispatch the body on its last journey. People like Johnny.

And people like Gordon. Or Dr Death, as the other staff called him behind his back, because of his strange obsession with dead bodies. Of all of the duties a hospital porter had to deal with, taking a body to the mortuary was the one they hated the most. All of them except Gordon. It was always a two-man job, and it was universally acknowledged that the worst thing that could happen to you as a porter was to be on a body with Gordon. The first time it had happened to Johnny, he was relieved that the task was not as visceral as he had feared. The body was neatly swaddled in a white cloth but his relief evaporated as soon as they got the trolley into the service lift. Gordon sealed the lift, and to Johnny's horror, opened up the trolley, and started to poke around inside, trying to find a gap in the shroud. He turned, and catching the expression of disbelief on Johnny's face, protested, "What? Don't be weird, it's interesting, innit? Death is all around us, Johnny; it's not healthy to pretend it's not there. You should embrace it."

"Yeah, man, whatever," Johnny mumbled. He backed down, not wanting to have an argument with someone on his first day. No one had told him at the interview that he would have to embrace anything, and he began to wonder what exactly he had got himself into. Perhaps he should have taken that job in the abattoir after all.

So, where was Gordon now, when a new customer presented itself for his services? He would be furious to miss out on a nice juicy stiff during the middle of an otherwise uneventful night shift. Johnny frowned as he turned the corner of the corridor leading to ward thirty-six. He never thought he'd be desperate for Gordon to show up for a job in the morgue, but it wasn't something he was keen to do on his own. He turned the corner to the ward, activating security before pushing the door to enter. In the half-light, the sad institutional Christmas decorations draped around the nurses' desk and Blu-Tacked to the walls appeared almost jolly, the multicoloured lights winking intermittently into the gloom. Under a cone of yellow lamplight, a figure looked up from her files.

"At bloody last. I know he's dead, but there's no need to keep him waiting. Carry on like this and we'll 'ave two for yer."

"Why? Someone else on the edge?" Johnny replied. He recognised Gloria now, her face, half in shadows, half-lit by the glow from the desk lamp. She seemed to have recovered her playful mood.

"Dr Death looked in at Mrs P from Poppleton earlier on. I could tell from the look in his eye that she's not long for this world."

They spoke in subdued voices, not out of any respect for the living or the dead, but for fear of waking any of the patients on the ward. The night shift was only tolerable if, once asleep, held down by a variety of chemical coshes, they stayed asleep.

"Where is he then?"

"Room five, just down the road. He's all done for you, squeaky clean, with my very own fair hands."

She held them up for inspection, her red fingernails glowing under the lamp.

"No, not the stiff – Gordon. Where's Gordon?" A look of alarm flashed across Johnny's face. "He's not still in there with him, is he?"

"Bloody hell, is he not with you then? God, that's all we need. Dr Death has gone AWOL. He's only good for one bloody thing and he can't even be here to do that. Wait till I get my hands on him; he'll wish he were never born"

Johnny looked again at the pale hands and flashing red nails. He gulped. She could definitely do some damage with those, he thought.

"I'd love you to get your hands on me, Gloria. You only have to ask."

They both whirled round. Striding down the corridor towards them, a grin spreading across his face, was Gordon, the strip lighting sparkling in the greasy sheen of his forehead. He was a little flushed and breathless, but every time Johnny had seen him, he had looked like that. He wore a little canvas bag strung diagonally over his shoulder, the strap tight, a beige chevron across his porter's overall.

"Bloody hell, Gordon, don't sneak up like that. You nearly gave me heart failure."

"What a shame, my sweet. I could've given yer artificial resus. A bit of mouth-to-mouth and chest compressions. Just like the old days. I've got better since then, though. I went on a course last week."

He rubbed his hands together and cracked his knuckles, flexing and stretching his fingers. He stared directly at Gloria and slowly licked his lips.

"Or is that what you'd rather Johnny did? Eh? Come on, what's this young lad got that I haven't, eh?"

Gloria rolled her eyes. "There aren't enough hours in the day for that one, sunshine. But anyway, where the bloody hell have you been? Up to no good by the look of it; you're usually as miserable as sin."

Gordon suddenly looked shifty, but then recomposed his features into a picture of innocence.

"I don't know what you're talking about, Gloria; I'm always a little ray of sunshine, you know that. It's important to be happy in your work. You should think on that, love. No point being a slave to it, 'cos one day, you'll be dead."

A cloud passed across her face. She pursed her lips and began to shuffle her papers at the desk. "Speaking of which, it's time you lazy buggers did some work. Room five. Go on, chop-chop, I've got work to do, you know."

Her patience had clearly run thin. Johnny and Gordon

exchanged a glance and with raised eyebrows between them, they turned to deal with the body, pushing the trolley further down the corridor. It stopped outside room five as Gordon negotiated entry to avoid banging against the doorjamb. Johnny looked back towards the desk. Gloria was still there, alone, her head in her hands, picked out by a warm stripe of yellow light, surrounded by darkness. He was confused. One minute, she was full of life and attitude; the next, she seemed defeated somehow, as if the other version of her was an act for everyone else's benefit. He was about to ask her if she was alright when he felt a tug on the trolley and was pulled into the room. He felt a surge of sympathy for her. No sleep for the nurses on nights, yet she kept smiling, despite the pressure. Let her have a moment or two when the mask slips, he thought. She deserves it. They all do.

3

The room was faintly illuminated with a night light, and the presence of shrouded figures in two other beds sharpened their attempts to be quiet. They gingerly slipped behind the curtain surrounding bed four, dragging the trolley with them. There on top of the bed lay the freshly swaddled corpse. Johnny felt the familiar shiver of apprehension run over his skin. Yes, he was still very new to this job, but he was sure that this was something that he would never get used to. Gordon, on the other hand, could barely contain his excitement. But for the time of night and the other lightly dozing patients, he would have burst into a cheery whistle.

With a nod to Johnny to take the feet, he grasped the neatly folded head end, and again wordlessly, they swung the corpse up off the bed and into the bowels of the metal box. Johnny had been expecting a heavy load and heaved rather too energetically, almost overshooting the open box.

"Steady on Johnny, man," hissed Gordon. "You nearly had 'im in the corridor. You're not tossing the bloody caber, you know."

"Sorry, sorry," Johnny stammered, "I didn't expect him to be so light. Light as a feather, there's nothing to him."

"Aye, that's cancer for you."

With the iron lid closed and the lacy blanket in place, they steered the death trolley through the curtains and out into the main corridor. Gloria was still at her station, phone in hand, a frown on her face. As they glided past her, Gordon with his thumbs up as if successfully accomplishing a tricky domestic task, she asked them, "You haven't seen Sutherland on your travels, have you? I've been trying to get hold of him to come and check on Mrs P, but he's not answering."

Gordon brought the trolley to an abrupt halt.

"Sutherland? No, we ain't seen 'im. What do you want him for anyway?"

Gloria's expression was withering. "I've just told you. He's the consultant on duty; I need him. This is a hospital, Gordon."

Gordon hesitated. For a moment, he looked preoccupied, but then he roused himself. "Well, no, we haven't seen him."

"Yes, so you said. Oh well, I'll just have to get the new Junior. Poor lass, she's rushed off her feet."

"My heart bleeds for her on her salary. Come on, let's get this over with so we can go and get a cup of tea."

Johnny took his cue and continued pulling the trolley towards the door and out into the corridor. Once outside, with the door closed, he slowed it down again and stopped, turning back to face Gordon, who asked, "Well?"

Johnny nodded back towards the ward they had just left. "Bloody hell, that Gloria is something else. Wouldn't like to get on the wrong side of her. Wouldn't mind getting on the right side of her, though. Very attractive woman."

Gordon burst out laughing and shook his head. "You'd be punching well above your weight there, Johnny lad. Gloria would eat you alive and spit the bones out."

Male pride dented, Johnny responded, his voice dripping with sarcasm, "And you'd know, would you, Gordon?"

"There's more to Gloria than meets the eye, you mark my words. We go back a long way, me and her, a long way. Take my advice. Leave well alone there."

Johnny opened his mouth, but had no reply.

Gordon filled the gap, irritably. "Let's get on with it, Johnny. We haven't got all night."

Johnny set off with the trolley. He picked up pace as he moved towards the lift, propelled from the back by Gordon. He turned back again.

"Come on Gordon, slow down, man. He's in no rush, you know."

"No, but I am."

"What for? What are you hurrying towards? You're not usually so desperate for a cup of canteen tea. And where exactly were you earlier?"

"Why are you so interested, all of a sudden? None of your business – I just had stuff to deal with, that's all. Keep your nose out."

"Alright, alright, I was only asking. I just thought I was going to have to do the body on my own."

He was looking back towards Gordon as he spoke and caught the look of alarm that flashed across his face.

"Look out," Gordon shouted, pulling back on the trolley. It was too late. A white-coated figure, laden with a tower of packages, suddenly emerged from a door on their left. Johnny crashed into her as he turned to face the way he was walking. The newcomer was sent flying and stumbled to her knees as the tower toppled and scattered across the corridor.

"Shit, sorry," Johnny said. He kneeled down, laying a hand on the shoulder of the person on the floor. "Are you alright?"

She turned to look up at him. It was a young woman, a doctor judging by the stethoscope around her neck.

"Ow," she said, in a soft Scottish accent, rubbing her shoulder, "you need to watch where you're going."

"I'm really sorry, honestly, I didn't see you. Here, let me help you up."

Johnny scrambled to his feet and offered her his hand. She reached out and he pulled her up towards him. She dusted down her white scrubs and looked around at the bedpans that were scattered across the corridor.

"I've made a right mess here," Johnny said and he began to pick them up.

Gordon shifted awkwardly. "Johnny, we've got a delivery to make."

Johnny looked up from the floor and Gordon raised his eyebrows and looked pointedly at the trolley.

"Sorry, Gordon. Look, you go on. I'll meet you at the mortuary when I'm done here. I won't be long and it's only fair."

The doctor smiled at him. "There's no need really, I can manage."

"No, no," Johnny jumped in, "it was my fault, after all."

He returned the smile. Now that he had got a proper look at her, he felt he would much rather spend some time with her than with Gordon.

Gordon seemed to recognise the look. He snorted, looked first at Johnny and then the woman, and began to push the trolley down the corridor.

"Take your time. I'll see you down there."

They watched him go, his figure receding into the distance. Johnny turned back to her and knelt down on the floor in front of her.

"It won't take a minute to collect all of this stuff up." He smiled, reaching to the sides to scoop the bedpans round between them. They began to stack them into a tower once again, building it up in the space between them. Johnny reached behind him and scooped some more bedpans into his orbit. He noticed an open packet of syringes in the middle, picked them up and handed them to the doctor.

"These must be yours."

She blinked at them, unsure, then took them from him and stuffed them into her pocket.

"Thanks. Must have dropped them. Don't want to leave these lying about."

They continued clearing up until the floor was clear, their hands weaving a complex choreography as they reached and stretched for the furthermost bedpans.

"Thanks." She smiled. "It's nice of you to help."

"Well, it was my fault. But why is a doctor collecting bedpans? I'd have thought that was well below your dignity."

She laughed. "Dignity? Oh, I haven't got much of that at the best of times. Gloria asked me and I had a minute, so you know."

"Really? Well, you look pretty dignified to me. I mean…"

She suddenly leant forward, her head dipping past his own, a breeze of perfume momentarily scrambling his brain. She popped up again, sitting up straight and holding his book between her fingertips.

"Dickens. That's not standard issue for porters these days, is it?"

She held up the book in front of her. Johnny felt a little embarrassed, as if he'd been caught doing something he shouldn't.

He shrugged. "Gets a bit boring on nights. There's usually time to kill. Anything's better than talking to Gordon."

She laughed. "The guy that just left? He's the weird one, right?"

Johnny hesitated. "Well… I'm not sure what you mean…"

"It's alright, I've heard all about his interest in the bodies.

Everyone knows. I've only been here three weeks and I know all about him."

Johnny shrugged. "He's alright. Not as weird as the stories make out. Anyway, we're all weird in one way or another. Everyone's got something going on."

The woman went to speak, but then paused. Johnny was suddenly aware that they were very close together, their knees almost touching on the floor, and that she was looking at him intently. He felt a little foolish and worried that he had plunged into intense conversation too soon. She smiled again, but there was a hint of sadness in her voice.

"Yeah, I think you're right about that. Everyone's got something going on."

Then she seemed to shake herself free and started again. This time, her voice and smile radiated warmth.

"We're straight into the big conversations. What's your name, anyway?"

"Johnny," he replied. He was strangely relieved to have an easy question to answer. There was something vaguely unsettling about this encounter. Doctors usually didn't give porters the time of day, regardless of what was in their pockets.

"When do you get a break? Do you want to have a coffee in the canteen before your shift finishes? You could be my first friend here."

"Yeah, OK." He glanced at his watch. "About five? We should be done by then."

"OK. I'll buy you a bacon sarnie, for helping me out. If I'm not there, I'm standing you up. No, it all depends on the bleep, obviously, but it's been pretty quiet so far tonight."

"Sod's law says that there'll be a major incident then, just before I'm due to clock off. Listen, I'd better go; I don't like to leave Gordon alone with the body for too long, if you know what I mean."

"Sounds interesting. You can tell me all about it in the canteen. See you later."

She turned the full radiance of her smile on him. He seemed to see her properly for the first time. She was beautiful. Tall and slim, with hazel eyes and glossy, black, spiky hair. She had a lovely, warm, open face and there was a faint cloud of perfume that travelled with her. The white coat and stethoscope only served to underline her attractiveness. But more than that was the aura of energy that seemed to surround her. The end of a night shift usually promoted a dead-eyed exhaustion. This girl positively shimmered with life, as if she were running on adrenaline after some kind of sparkling success.

They stared at each other in the doorway for a second too long, before Johnny shook himself free.

"OK, bye then."

As he turned to go, she called after him. "Johnny?"

He whirled round a little too eagerly. "Yeah?"

"Your book. You forgot your book."

She passed the paperback to him and their fingertips touched as he took it from her. He gulped, turned away and went down the corridor to meet Gordon. As he walked away, he immediately began to berate himself. He felt sure he had gone a little red during that conversation. Then he stopped and cursed himself again. Her name! He hadn't even asked her name. What a loser! Full of these recriminations and more, he continued towards the lift, clinging on to one fixed point in the maelstrom of his thoughts, the only thing he was absolutely sure of.

She was drop-dead gorgeous.

4

Not even the prospect of interrupting Dr Death, alone in a lift with a corpse, could dampen Johnny's spirits as he walked down the corridor floating on a cushion of air. For the first time since starting this job, it was not the end of a night shift he was looking forward to, but a meeting over coffee at 5 a.m. Admittedly, the canteen of York District Hospital in the dead of night was not the most romantic of venues, but that doctor was something special.

He went up to the door of the lift, pressed the button and slipped inside. The doors slid shut and when he jabbed the basement button, the lift sighed into action, smoothly elevating his stomach as it made its descent. It juddered to a halt and the door opened with a wheezing sigh. The basement corridor outside was gloomy, an eerie, half-lit passageway that ended in a T-junction. The left turn led to the mortuary, the right to the incinerator.

He shook himself and pressed on, shouting out in advance of the corner, "Gordon? Gordon, where the bloody hell are you?", expecting to find him with the trolley lid up waiting outside the door of the mortuary. But when he took his first pace into the main corridor, under the arrowed sign, it was empty. There was no sign of Gordon, nor of a trolley, just a gloomy, deserted passage, the ticking of the electric wall clock and the insistent hum of the neon night light. But then, towards the end of the corridor, he noticed the door of the mortuary was wide open and harsh, white light spilled out through it.

Oh, there he is, thought Johnny. *He's started without me.*

Relieved finally that he wasn't on his own down in the bowels of the hospital, he strode towards the wide-open door with a spring in his step. He shouted down towards the morgue, partly to give Gordon notice he was about to come in.

"Hey, Gordon, I thought you were going to wait in the lift, man. The trouble with you is that you just love your job too much."

He went straight into the glaring strip lighting of the mortuary, a smile on his face, ready to bat back and forth Gordon's excuses and unlikely explanations.

"Well, what—"

Johnny's artificial banter froze on his lips. The mortuary was completely empty. His eyes darted around the room, taking in the four-tier bank of fridges all along one wall, and the pneumatic trolley stationed at the end, ready and waiting to jack up the next body to the correct height.

Nobody. His mind raced. Why had the door been open? Where was Gordon? What was taking him so long? The whirl of questions served only to ratchet up the tension in his mind, as he realised that the only company he had in this humming, creaking, bare room were the swaddled inhabitants of the fridges in front of him. Behind the orderly ranks of stainless-steel doors lay racks of neatly arranged corpses, only a few feet away from him. In a horror film, this would be the point where they all, as one, raised themselves from the dead and, zombie-like, began to open the doors of each of the fridges that housed them, before overpowering him. His heart pounded and he looked back towards the door to the corridor, as if he were ensuring his means of escape was still unblocked. He smiled to himself and made a conscious effort to rein in his imagination.

Then, from the corridor outside came an eerie creaking sound, rhythmically repeated every few seconds. His imagination momentarily reasserted itself as the sound ripped through the quiet stillness in the mortuary, and his breath caught in his throat. Then he realised. The trolley. This must be Gordon at last.

As the sound began to get steadily nearer, he leant his head out around the door to get a view of the length of the passage.

"Christ man, are you trying to give me a heart attack? Where the hell have you been?"

It was Gordon, head bowed, his portly frame pushing the trolley, still with its lacy blanket draped over the edges. With every revolution of its wheels came a painful squeaking sound. He looked up.

"Eh? Oh, sorry. I was… er… busy." His eyes flicked downwards.

"Busy? Gordon, you are seriously weird, you know that? I've been waiting here on my own for ages. Well, not quite on my own, if you know what I mean. Johnny and the Stiffs. Good name for a band, but not a lot of fun apart from that."

"Alright, alright, they're not going to get out of the fridges and come for you, man. I've not been that long. Don't make such a fuss, you big girl's blouse."

Johnny stood to one side to allow Gordon to push the trolley through the doorway.

"And anyway, how come you came here and then went off again?" Johnny was on the attack and was not going to let Gordon off the hook too easily.

Gordon stopped dead in his tracks, the trolley straddling the doorway.

"What do you mean, 'been here and went off again'? I haven't been here. I've just arrived. What are you on about?"

It was Johnny's turn to look puzzled.

"Then why was the door open when I got here? Wide open. I came in expecting to find you here and there was nobody. Just me and the stiffs."

"And there was no one in here?"

"No, Gordon, no one."

"But that can't be right. I..."

He trailed off, shaking his head. Suddenly, he looked as if the troubles of the world were on his shoulders.

"What's up, Gordon? Are you alright? It was just the door, I'm sure."

Gordon looked up as if suddenly realising where he was for the first time.

"Hmm? What? Come on, let's get this one in. We can worry about the door when we've done it."

He wheeled the trolley into the middle of the room and pulled the blanket away.

"Get the lift," he instructed Johnny. "If I remember right, the next space is on the top deck."

Johnny smiled ruefully as he pulled the lift trolley away from the wall. Gordon always knew exactly what the state of play with the fridges was: how many bodies, who they were, where they stopped, where the next free berth was. He had probably already been there earlier in the shift to check, just in case.

"Right," Gordon continued, "let's get him on the lift. You take that end." He had opened the trolley and indicated the end of the corpse nearest Johnny. Johnny leant in and grabbed hold of the end of the swaddling.

"Got him? Right after three. One, two, three."

They both heaved and the body, slightly buckling in the

middle, came out easily. In the same swing, they deposited it on the adjacent lift.

"Now, you start pumping, high as it'll go. I'll check the gaps."

He moved to the line of fridge doors, and counted down from one end. When he was satisfied, he reached for the door handle and pulled it open. This was the bit of the job that Johnny really hated the most, the tiers of swaddled bodies like mummies, revealed to the living. It was like the corpses' having the last laugh, with their unmistakeable message: *it's only a question of time for you, and don't you forget it.* Gordon, however, was immune to this kind of fanciful thinking around the dead. Johnny had done this a few times with him, and he was always unmoved, as if he was simply delivering a parcel.

The cry when it came took Johnny completely by surprise. Gordon called out and staggered backwards, crashing against the lift. The trolley wobbled alarmingly and the swaddled body they had just loaded on to it fell until it was hanging half-on, half-off, the head end colliding with Gordon's cowering, crouching figure. Instantly, he leaped up and screamed at the top of his voice.

Johnny was baffled. "Gordon, what the fuck are you playing at? You're never normally like this in here, it's just..."

He stopped as Gordon frantically pawed at his sleeve. He pointed upwards at the open door of the fridge.

"Look! Look at that, Johnny!" he managed to gasp. "He's dead."

"Of course he's bloody dead; this is the mortuary, what—"

Gordon grabbed at him again. "No, no, look."

Johnny followed the direction of his trembling finger. He walked over to the door of the fridge. There, on the middle deck, standing out among all of the swaddled bodies, was a man, laid flat on his back with his head nearest the door, a stethoscope sticking in his ears and the brilliant white of his doctor's coat disfigured by a small, vivid, red stain that had dribbled from his head to his shoulders. Sticking directly out of his forehead, standing vertically, was a scalpel. A lanyard hung from his head. Johnny, summoning unknown reserves of calm, reached out and lifted it slightly into the light, so he could read it more easily.

"Dr Gerald Sutherland, Consultant."

5

Johnny took one final look towards the doors of the canteen, stubbed out his cigarette and drained the last mouthful of coffee. She wasn't coming, that was clear. He didn't know why he'd thought that she would. It was a couple of hours later than they had arranged, but after the events of the night, the minute he was dismissed by the detectives in charge of the investigation, he suddenly found himself ravenously hungry and in desperate need of a bacon roll.

There had been a lot of hanging around waiting to be interviewed after the police had arrived, and there had even been a few calls they had to attend to. The work of the hospital went on, despite the fact that a senior consultant had been found murdered, so he'd had to transfer a patient to intensive care and they had both had to pick up the waste from theatre to take to the incinerator. Thankfully, there had been no further bodies. Not even Gordon would have welcomed that.

When they had got to the bottom of the corridor and turned towards the incinerator, they had both stopped and looked back down the passageway leading to the mortuary. The corridor was flooded with harsh strip lighting and the area outside the door to the morgue was taped off as a crime scene.

A single policeman stood outside the tape perimeter on guard. He seemed just about to step forward and warn them off when he suddenly had to step aside, as a trolley bearing a body bag was wheeled out. Johnny and Gordon exchanged silent glances as the trolley passed within a couple of feet of them.

Johnny suddenly realised what was going on. "Of course. I hadn't thought about that. They can't use our mortuary, 'cos it's a crime scene. I wonder where they'll take it. Him."

"They'll probably send him to the pathologists for a post-mortem. That's what usually happens in cases like this. But no point worrying about that now. The sooner we get this done, the sooner we can go."

He nodded at the bags they had picked up from the operating theatres, a random selection of tissue and body parts from the previous sessions of surgery. It was a sobering reminder of the realities of working in a hospital. All of those layers of finer feelings, morality, spirituality, ideas of the afterlife, turned into fairy stories after you had worked a few shifts dealing with the realities of human existence. The post-operation theatre run was the quickest reminder that, when everything else was stripped away, we were no more than a collection of bones, fluids, tissues and organs, sealed neatly in a bag of skin. What was wondrous was the fact that, for long periods of time, this improbable arrangement actually worked. Until it didn't.

"Listen, do you mind if I get off? You can do that on your own, can't you?"

Gordon suddenly looked shifty. It was unlike him to try and slide out of work while there was any chance another body might need dealing with.

"No, no, that's OK, Gordon. It's been a tricky shift to say the least. You go, I'll finish off here. The day shift'll be here any minute."

"Thanks, Johnny, you're a pal. You're not a bad lad for a student, you know."

Johnny watched him turn and go, untouched by the unsolicited compliment. There was something more pressing on his mind, something that had been troubling him ever since the first moments after they had discovered Sutherland's body.

"Hey, Gordon. Wait a minute."

Gordon turned back. "Yeah, what is it?"

"How was it? In your interview, I mean. What did they ask you?"

A cloud passed over Gordon's face. He paused. "Well, they were checking timings, and what we had done on the shift and if there had been anything unusual. Just that sort of stuff. Took my fingerprints as well."

"Me too. They did everyone who was on shift and in the vicinity, apparently. Just to rule people out, I think."

Gordon nodded and took a quick glance around. "Why, what did they ask you?" He reached out and took hold of Johnny's elbow and continued in a lower voice, his eyes darting all around the corridor. "You didn't say anything, did you?"

Johnny pulled his arm away and took a step backwards. "No, of course not. They asked the same kind of things as they did you by the sound of it. It's funny how they always manage to make you feel guilty, even when you've done nothing wrong. The main guy asking the questions, Grayson, I think his name was, he seemed a bit bored by the whole thing. He kept going on about when we got there and what else had happened on the shift. Was more like getting told off at school rather than a murder inquiry."

The mention of the word "murder" sent a chill across the conversation, as if they both suddenly appreciated the reality of what had happened to them that night. They exchanged a guilty, furtive glance.

As Gordon finally turned to go, Johnny blurted out, "But why, Gordon?"

"'Why?'" he repeated with a touch of irritation. "What do you mean, why?"

"Why did you ask me to say we had been together for the whole shift and that we went down there together? Where were you? What were you doing? Why can't you tell the police the truth? I've just lied to them in a murder inquiry, and I'm not quite sure why I did that. It doesn't make an awful lot of sense to me right now."

Gordon closed the gap between them both and dropped his voice almost to a whisper, looking around as he spoke. "Look, everything will be fine if you just stop making a fuss about it, alright? I just had a bit of business to do during the shift. You know, people to talk to, things to do, that sort of thing?"

"What things to do? You're not making much sense, Gordon, to be honest. You were gone a few times last night. You could have been up to anything."

"I was up to something, Johnny. But not murder, for God's sake. This is York District Hospital. Real life, not a whodunnit on the telly."

Johnny's expression remained unconvinced.

"Look, I can't tell you any more, for your own sake. It's a bit dodgy, and the people involved are not very fussy, if you know what I mean. Listen…" He moved closer and laid his hand on Johnny's arm. "Listen, leave it with me for a day or two until I've boxed it all off, and I'll tell you all about it. I've just got to get the timing right, OK?"

Johnny thought for a moment. "Yeah, alright. But I need to know, Gordon. It's not fair otherwise."

"Yeah, yeah, it'll be fine. We're on the same shift for the next couple of nights, aren't we?"

"Yeah, we finish on Friday morning. Then I'm on nights again, starting Sunday."

"Yeah, me too. Perfect. Listen, I'll try and sort it tomorrow, yeah? Saturday at the latest." He glanced down again at his watch. "And now, I really have to go. Got to get home, alright? See you tomorrow, yeah?"

This was clearly a rhetorical question because he had already turned and was moving away down the corridor without waiting for a reply.

Shaking his head, Johnny turned and carried on towards the incinerator room.

And now, in the bleak surroundings of the hospital canteen, Johnny was troubled by two things. What had Gordon been up to that meant he'd asked Johnny to lie for him? And had this unfortunate murder blown things for him and that gorgeous doctor? He'd spent half an hour facing the only entrance while he lingered over those questions and there had been no sign of her. He caught himself with those thoughts circulating around his mind in an endless loop and he smiled at his own stupidity. Someone was dead, for God's sake. The problems of his imaginary love life seemed a little self-indulgent in the circumstances, particularly when the key word was "imaginary". He didn't even know her name and she was probably just being polite after he had helped her out earlier. In fact, he wouldn't be surprised if he never saw her again.

"Hello, what are you smiling at? Thinking of me or the dead body?"

The interruption wrenched him out of his introspection. He looked up, startled. It was her. Christ, had he been sitting there gormlessly, staring into space with his mouth open, dribbling and smiling?

"What? Oh, hello, I thought I'd missed you."

"Yeah, well, it's been that kind of night. Are you finished then?"

"Yeah, the shift went over a bit because of the police, but the early shift are in now."

"Mind if I join you? I've finished as well and I'm knackered so I'm going to crash, but I need a coffee first to unwind. Do you want another?"

"Oh, yeah, thanks. White, no sugar."

He watched her walk over to the counter. It was beginning to get busy now, as the early shifts had started to drift in along with those who had finished nights and needed to offload before heading off home. The whole place was agog with the news of what had happened to Sutherland, and there were knots of people scattered around tables gossiping and sharing what they knew.

She came back with a tray, manoeuvring it high and low as she negotiated the arrangement of tables. She set it down gently in the middle of the table and sat down, smiling.

"Very bad for your reputation, you know, sharing a table with a lowly porter," he said, reaching out and taking the coffee. "Thanks, by the way."

She shrugged. "I don't honestly think my reputation is at stake. They already think I'm a bit of a weirdo."

He looked again. She had a little CND badge tucked under her name badge. Her face seemed tired and a little drawn, and just for a second, Johnny caught a hint of sadness in her eyes. She forced a smile and sipped her own coffee.

"Not that I give a toss about that. They're probably right."

"You allowed to wear that badge?" He nodded at her badge.

"It's small. Nobody seems to have noticed yet," she replied with a smile. "Are you allowed to wear yours?"

"Huh?" He looked down in the direction of her glance and remembered his Rock Against Racism badge. "Oh, that. I don't think they care about what the porters wear. As long as they're OK to get covered in shit every day. So, what happened to you last night? Have you been interviewed by the police?"

"Yeah. I can't believe what happened. I'd seen him earlier on the shift. Sutherland, I mean."

"God, how weird. Was he alright when you saw him?"

"Yeah, I think so. He was exactly what they're all like. Bit rude, bit full of himself, bit flirty."

"Flirty?"

"Yeah, you know. Typical bloody middle-aged man. Think they're God's gift and that women are gagging for it? Pathetic really, but harmless. I've had worse. Most consultants in this hospital seem to think women are only there to make tea and adore them."

"And now he's dead." Johnny shook his head.

"Someone said you found him."

"Me and Dr Death, yeah. It was when we were doing that body. Just after I met you. It was weird. Horrible, actually."

He recounted the events in the mortuary, leaving out the part about Gordon asking him to back up his story, before asking her about her experience. Helen had always said it was good to ask questions, particularly with women.

"Have you been interviewed by the police yet? What did they ask you?"

"Oh, you know. They just rattled through where I was during the shift and whether I knew him. You know, stuff like that."

"Did you say he'd helped you earlier?"

"Yeah, but I kinda played down him leching over me. I didn't want them coming up with some PC-plod theory about violence against women. They'd take one look at my CND badge, find out I've been on Reclaim the Night marches, and suddenly, I'd be their prime suspect. Angry Feminist Revenge, you know?"

Johnny laughed nervously. "Yeah, absolutely." He hadn't really any idea what she was talking about, but her perfume and hair had convinced him to agree with everything she said. He knew that this approach would only get him so far before she realised he had nothing of interest or value to say, but right there and then, it was all he had. One step at a time. He could work on being fascinating later.

6

She yawned and rubbed her eyes. Johnny stopped mid-sentence. *Shit, I'm boring her to death and she's just being polite.* He glanced up at the clock on the far side of the canteen. Nine o'clock. Before he knew it, before he could do anything about it, he was dragged into a yawn of his own, one of those yawns that left you feeling even more tired than you were at the beginning.

"Sorry," he said, immediately after it had subsided, "I'm shattered."

"Me too," she replied. "It's been a long night. Time for bed."

There was a pause. Johnny blinked and scrambled around his brain to come up with some words that could reasonably fill the gap. She smiled at him and his sense of panic grew.

"You in the nurses' home?" He was relieved that he managed not to stumble over his words.

"Yeah," she replied. "You should see it. It's a real palace."

He gathered his cigarettes and lighter and fiddled around, replacing plates and cups on the tray.

"Shall I walk over with you? My bike is in the shed right next to you."

He stood up, scraping his chair along the lino floor. She looked back at him, still sitting down. Why wasn't she moving? Maybe she didn't want to walk back with him. Maybe she thought he was trying to get an invite to her room for coffee or something. He jumped in to fill the gap again.

"I mean, if that's alright with you. You going back to your room now?"

She looked puzzled, and then suddenly stood up, her hands reaching for her tray.

"Yeah. If I don't get to bed soon, I'll be in no fit state for my shift tonight. I'll end up killing someone. Medical negligence case. It'll be all over *News of the World*."

He laughed, a little too loudly. "You'd probably get away with it, while they're all looking for who bumped Sutherland off."

She didn't reply and he moved off towards the exit with his tray. He was pleased to be on his feet, moving, doing something. Walking in single file at least meant that he didn't have to own his last stupid comment. They slotted their trays in the metal trolley and walked to the exit, threading their way through the lines of tables. He could feel everyone's eyes on them as they left. He could imagine their thoughts. Even though a consultant had been murdered there that night, they had eyes for only one thing. A doctor and a porter, eh? Well, I never. Never mind, she's new, she'll soon learn.

He smiled wryly as he followed her out. *They're probably right as well. She will learn – so I might as well enjoy it while I can, and not expect too much.*

He was so lost in this train of thought that he didn't realise she was talking to him.

"Hey, Mr Porter. You gone to sleep on me already?"

"Hmm?" he stammered, confused. "Asleep?"

"I've been talking to you like an idiot, getting no response. You really know how to make a girl feel special."

She turned her smile on him as she spoke. He melted.

"God, sorry. I really must be tired."

He cursed himself. It had all been going so well. She was so easy to talk to, they had just lost half an hour chatting in the canteen before he had begun to feel a little nervous. He just had to maintain the pretence of being a charming, thoughtful young man for a little bit longer and then he could get home, collapse in to bed and recharge his batteries, ready for his next encounter with the beautiful doctor.

They were at the bike sheds now. She stopped opposite him. He summoned one last effort of will to produce a light, friendly, interested, but not threatening, sign-off. Relationships were such hard work.

"Well, that was really nice. We should have more murders at work if it always means we make new friends. You on tonight?"

"Yeah, start at six."

"Shall we try and meet up again? Breakfast?"

"Sounds good, Mr Porter. See you then."

She walked away and Johnny unlocked his bike and wrestled it out of the rack. He mounted and was just about to push off towards the main road when she called out, "Hey, Johnny."

He turned to see her.

"Yeah?" he called.

"Don't you want to know my name, then? Might be useful in the future, you know."

He could feel himself going red. Shit, what a loser.

"Yeah, of course. Sorry. What's your name?"

"Juliet."

He opened his mouth to speak, but she held up her hand to stop him. "Don't say anything about Romeo."

"That's a lovely name. See you tomorrow, Juliet."

"Bye, Mr Porter."

He set off on his bike. By the time he had left the hospital grounds and was hammering along Gillygate, he had a broad fixed smile on his face. He couldn't feel the icy wind at all.

Juliet. She was called Juliet.

7

The room wrapped them in a comforting silence. After the manic activity Grayson had negotiated in the corridors, this was like walking into a church. It didn't seem appropriate somehow, given what was still lying on a table somewhere in a police mortuary. That scene was a world away from the polished parquet, thick Turkish rugs, leather sofas and fragrant fresh flowers that furnished this room. From his seat, he could see a view of a clipped lawn and mature shrubbery that was shrouded in the remnants of the early-morning, freezing fog.

He turned his attention back to the man sitting opposite him. Balding, with thin streaks of snowy white hair stretched across a pink expanse of scalp, matching his ruddy complexion. His tweed jacket and tattersall shirt completed the picture of a man who would not look out of place at a meeting of the local hunt. Arthur Edwards, Hospital Secretary.

His companion broke the silence. "Bad business all round, Simon. Especially at Christmas. And here, in my hospital."

"Too cruel anywhere, Arthur, as Banquo said to Lady Macbeth."

Edwards shot him a weary look. "Not Shakespeare, please Simon. Things are bad enough without you showing off."

"Sorry. Did it for A level. You can never get rid of it after that."

Edwards smiled. "Goodness, you make Shakespeare sound like Herpes, Simon."

"Well, you'd know more about that than me. But let's get down to business. What can you tell me about Gerald Sutherland?"

"Senior consultant. Well-established figure in the hospital. Been here for over twenty years, I think. You'll want to look at the records for that sort of detail, I suppose."

"Well, yes. I was wanting something more than I could easily find in his file. What was he like? Are you surprised he's been murdered?"

Edwards hesitated. "His file?" he began, uncertainly, a cloud passing over his face. "Well, I…"

The door opened after a polite knock, and a grey-haired woman came in with a tray of coffee and biscuits. The cups, Edwards' best porcelain, rattled with a brittle musicality. The sound, gentle though it was, disturbed the cushioned quiet of the room, and Grayson's questions were lost.

"Coffee," she announced, setting the tray down on the low table.

"Thank you, Janice." Edwards smiled at her.

"Anything else?" she asked, hovering.

"No, that will be all," he said.

She returned his smile and glided out. The door closed behind her, shutting out the brief glimpse they had had of purposeful activity in the corridor. In the room, sealed and comfortable, calm was restored once more. Edwards poured the coffee and Grayson tried again.

"Were you surprised? About Sutherland's death."

Edwards took a sip of his coffee before replying.

"Well, a murder is going to be a surprise, isn't it? Might be a routine occurrence in your line of work, but I assure you, it's not in mine."

"Let me put it another way, Arthur. Did he have any enemies among the staff?"

"Enemies? No, I wouldn't say that. But he wasn't what you'd call a popular man. A bit arrogant. A bit old school."

Grayson saw an opportunity.

"Bit like you then, Arthur. Old school." Before Edwards had a chance to protest, Grayson pressed on. "Was he a friend of yours?"

Edwards blinked nervously, processing the question. "I saw him socially. You know, the usual round of North Yorkshire events. Rotary Club. Highly thought of in the Party."

"And the Masons?"

Edwards put his cup back in the saucer and narrowed his eyes. "Let's not go there Simon. Look, Sutherland was an awkward cuss, but he was a damn fine surgeon and an asset to this hospital. I don't want you stirring up any unnecessary trouble. This could be awkward – bad publicity and so on. There are enough deaths in hospitals without adding murder to the mix. I hope I can count on you for your discretion. A light touch, Simon."

"A light touch?"

"Listen, I'm having lunch with the Chief Super next week. A Christmas social. Would be nice to have a result by then, so I can put in a good word for you. Time you had a promotion, don't you think? You've got my full cooperation. Anything you need, just ask, old man."

Grayson sipped his coffee and let the silence grow.

Edwards stood up. "So, I'll let you get on with it. The Friends Meeting Room has been allocated for your incident room. Janice will direct you. If you need anything else, just ask her."

"Thanks. The team have made a start on preliminary

interviews, just to rule people out and establish timings and movements, that sort of thing. I'll go down to the incident room now and get established."

He drained his coffee, stood up and allowed Edwards to shepherd him to the door, where a smile, and a firm handshake propelled him over the threshold.

"Oh, and Simon. Keep me posted, won't you? If anything comes up that I should hear about first. You know what I mean."

He nodded as he was handed over to Janice in the corridor. She made polite conversation as she led him to The Friends Meeting Room. Grayson smiled and made bland appropriate responses, but he wasn't really listening. He was still thinking about the meeting with Arthur Edwards. A light touch, eh? Edwards was worried about something coming out, that much was clear, but just then, he had no idea what it could be. He'd soon find out though, and then things could get very sticky.

*

Jacko shivered under the canopy of the walkway and looked around him. To his right, the corridor to the mortuary and the main hospital building. To his left, the car park and in the distance, the nurses' home. This must be the place, even though there was no sign. This would be his third interview of the day already. He reached for his ID and rapped sharply on the door in front of him. He was about to knock again when the door opened outwards and a gust of warm air billowed out into his face, accompanied by a roar.

Jacko held his ID out in front of him.

"DC Reg Jackson, North Yorkshire Police."

The man facing him was tall and well built, wearing a brown overall. He stared at Jacko for a moment, on the verge of irritability.

"Is this about the murder then?"

"That's right, sir. Are you Dave Henderson?"

The man scowled. "Yeah."

"Can I come in, Mr Henderson? I just need to ask you a few questions."

The man hesitated but then stepped aside to let Jacko through. In the middle of the room, stretching back to the rear wall, was a huge, iron cabinet with a central pipe leading up to the ceiling. There was a large, central door and a complicated-looking control panel. Jacko took in the rest of the space and noted a closed door in the far corner, a desk under a noticeboard, and a battered sofa and chair combination. On the left-hand side of the room was a pile of plastic bags, like bin liners, coded with various colours.

Henderson nodded at the sofa.

"You'd better sit down. I hope this is not going to take long. I'm right busy this morning."

Jacko settled himself in the chair and took out his notebook and pen.

"No, it'll only take five minutes of your time. Nice and warm in here, isn't it?"

"Aye, it's not bad in the winter. Different story come summer, mind."

"So, Dave. What does your job entail then?"

"I'm in charge of incinerator." He jabbed his thumb towards the roaring spaceship in the middle of the room. "I have to burn all the hospital waste, like. Body parts from operating theatre. Medical waste from wards. Paper and whatnot from offices. Even stuff from canteen sometimes. Those bags over there are due in next."

"Is it just you then?"

"Too bloody right. There was a lad wi' me up until last year, but he got fed up of it and just upped and left. Can't get a replacement. Some of the porters pick up a bit of overtime to give me a break, but that's it."

"Does it keep on going through the night, then?"

"No, we don't run at night. I keep her fired up at the minimum level to save having to light her every day, but there's no one on duty after five. I usually come in at seven in the morning to clear the backlog."

"So, you weren't here when Mr Sutherland was murdered, then?"

"If it were after five o'clock, then no. There's no one here after that. Can't say I'm sorry, though."

"About Sutherland, you mean?"

"Aye. Right bastard he were. Full of himself, like most of 'em here. Thought he were God's gift. Had an eye for the ladies if you know what I mean."

Jacko nodded over towards his noticeboard. "Seems like he wasn't the only one, Dave lad. Very nice."

Henderson turned. The noticeboard had a couple of grubby sheets of paper pinned to it, and a few photographs, but the majority of the space was taken up with lurid colour pictures of naked women, pouting and thrusting pneumatic breasts upwards. Acres of unnatural, stretched, tanned skin, like animals that had been fattened for market.

"Aye well. There's nowt wrong wi' looking, is there? Sutherland would have been better off if he'd stopped at looking."

Jacob smiled at him and winked. "No, I quite agree. It's only natural to look."

They both stared at the pictures for a moment longer. Finally, Jacko roused himself and stood up.

"Well, I won't trouble you any more. I'll let you get back on with your work." He glanced again at the pictures and gave Henderson another wink.

Henderson scrambled to his feet and showed Jacko to the door. At the threshold, Jacko turned to him.

"Thanks for your help, Dave. Oh, by the way, do you work at the weekend? Just in case we need to ask anything else?"

A flash of irritation passed across Henderson's face.

"Between nine and five, yeah, I do. Can't think I'd be able to tell you any more, though."

"No, you're probably right. Thanks again, Dave. Mind how you go."

Henderson closed the door and retreated back into his lair. Jacko looked back at the closed door. The roar of the fire was sealed away inside and a chill wind blew across from the car park. He put his notebook away and smiled to himself. Ordinary bloke, got on with his job and who liked beautiful women. Nothing wrong with that.

8

By the time Johnny had reached Lendal Bridge, he'd lost all feeling in his fingers, and had had to start methodically removing one hand from the handle bars at a time and stuffing it inside his pocket for a minute, before swapping to do the same with the other. Not for the first time, he promised himself he'd buy a pair of gloves before his shift that night.

The Ouse was shrouded in a freezing fog that cast a grey, muffling blanket over the city. Normally, his cycle home after a night shift was done in total darkness, long before the rush hour had started, through deserted streets studded with amber streetlights. Johnny usually loved the ride home like that, when York seemed to be frozen in some kind of tableau, its ancient stones still sleeping, before the hordes of shift workers and later, tourists, rudely shook it awake to claim it as their own. Because of the shenanigans with the police, he was much later than usual, and the wintry sunlight of early morning exposed the endless traffic jams, noise and bustle.

A solitary ride in the dark would have been perfect for him to think again about the strange events of last night's shift, but that would have to wait. Now, all he wanted to do was to warm his hands on a cup of tea, and burrow down deep into his bed and sleep. That thought kept him going as he swung round in front of the station, and then out, under the shadow of Micklegate Bar and onto the main road west towards the Knavesmire. In the thin light, the huge advertising hoarding by Blossom Street blared its message to rush-hour traffic: *Help Us Stop The Ripper from Killing Again.* It was in brutalist black and white, set apart from the usual colourful billboards, like a punch in the face. Johnny never knew whether it did any good, only that it gave him a sinking feeling in his stomach twice a day.

A minute later, he swung his leg over the crossbar and freewheeled as the bike came to a smooth halt outside his house. He opened the door and negotiated his way past bottles of milk, a few items of post and the morning paper lying on the mat. He stowed the bike in the hall, slotting it into the space between the other three bikes that were there. Whose was missing? Probably Jaggers. He'd already be at work by now, sitting at his desk in a centrally heated office just outside Walmgate Bar, bored out of his brain with only another seven hours to go before the sweet release of five o'clock. Still, central heating was a bonus. Their house was freezing, and it had already been a hard winter, with the prospect of a few more months of hoar frost, snow and biting winds.

He went back to collect the paper, post and milk bottles, and made his way to the kitchen at the back of the house. The door was closed, but its glass pane was warm with yellow light and the familiar sound of Radio 4 drifted through into the corridor. Someone was in and someone was up, that much was obvious. He struggled to open the door and keep hold of the paper, post and milk at the same time. Finally, he nudged it open and the door swung inwards.

There was a glorious blast of warm air as he stepped down into the kitchen.

"Crikey, where've you been? You're about two hours later than usual."

He looked up as he edged his way to the huge kitchen table, where he deposited three pints of milk and the rest of his stuff.

"Oh, hi Helen. I didn't expect to see you. You not working today?"

"No, day in lieu. Told you yesterday. But anyway, I asked first. Where've you been?"

Helen sat at the far end of the kitchen, close to the oven. She had her hands, in fingerless mittens, clamped around a gently steaming cup of tea. She appeared to be wearing several layers of woollens, finishing with an enormous baggy pullover of broad red and black stripes, in homage to Dennis the Menace.

Johnny slumped down into the nearest chair with a groan.

Helen snorted. "Dear God, Johnny, that's the sort of noise my grandad makes when he sits down. Why are you late? You're usually out of the door on the dot at six."

Johnny smiled knowingly at her. "No, Helen, my sweet. That's the sort of noise you make when you've been up all night involved in a murder investigation."

Her jaw dropped, just as Johnny had intended.

"A murder?" She smiled uncertainly. "You are joking, aren't you?"

"Nope. I've been talking to the police and everything. The mortuary is all taped off, just like on the telly. I found the body, as it goes."

"That must have been awful. What happened?"

"Nah, it was pretty cool, actually. It was one of the consultants, a guy called Sutherland. Me and Dr Death were doing a body in the morgue, and he was in the fridge. Just like that. It was amazing; he had a scalpel sticking out of the top of his skull."

Helen gave him a withering look, her sympathy draining away as quickly as it had come. "Amazing? Really? Not for Mr Sutherland, eh?"

Johnny suddenly felt rather silly. Helen had an uncanny ability to turn a spotlight on his more juvenile qualities, and even he had to admit, he gave her plenty of opportunities to practise.

"Any tea in that?" he said, nodding at the old, brown pot in front of her, chipped and stained.

She pushed it towards him.

"Help yourself."

He poured a cup of tea and added some milk.

"It's just that it was quite exciting, you know. Pretty creepy as well."

Helen thawed a little. "You were on with Dr Death then? He's the weird one, right? Nothing to do with him, I suppose?"

Johnny hesitated. "Nah. I mean, he is a weirdo, but he doesn't need to go killing people. There's enough bodies for him in the morgue as it is."

Helen narrowed her eyes. "You took a bit too long to answer that question. You thought about it too, admit it."

He laughed. "Yeah, alright, I did for about a nanosecond, but it's definitely not him. He's harmless really."

"Well, if it's not him, it's someone else. Someone you work with. You should be careful, Johnny."

"Not necessarily. The hospital is full of people wandering about. The security guys get more sleep on the night shift than the porters do. Could be anyone."

"Great," she scoffed, "I feel very reassured. No security."

Johnny took another gulp of his tea and beamed at her. "Helen, I had no idea that you cared so much about my safety. That's lovely, it really is."

She scowled back at him. "Don't flatter yourself. Would be hard to pay the rent without you."

He finished his tea and stood up.

"But I'm shattered. I really need to get some sleep." He turned to go and Helen called back to him.

"So, did the police keep you all this time? Seems a bit excessive."

"No, that was the other thing about the shift. I met someone interesting and we had breakfast and chatted about the murder thing."

Helen forced a smile. "You've made a friend. Bless. Shall I invite them round for tea? Who are they?"

"One of the doctors, actually. She's new."

"She must be," Helen replied sourly. "What's her name? Moriarty? Dr Crippen?"

Johnny was at the door now. He beamed at her.

"Juliet. Her name's Juliet. Hey, I'm going now. See you later. I've gotta sleep."

He shut the door behind him.

At the table, Helen watched his blurred outline through the door window disappear.

"Juliet," she muttered. "I might have known."

9

Johnny awoke with a start several hours later, the gloom of a late-December afternoon filling his room. The street lamps outside were already lit, their amber globes visible through his window. He shivered under the duvet. It was the thing above all others he did not like about working nights: the way that his waking hours were permanently in the dark. A week of nights always left him tired and pale, like a ghost.

Gritting his teeth, he leaped out of bed and in a frenzy of activity, pulled on his clothes, fighting the icy edge to the still air. He made his way downstairs and headed to the kitchen, where the yellow light still blazed into the corridor through the glass. He had no idea who was in. Jaggers, Kate and Mark were probably still at work, or at the university. That left Helen. But when he went into the kitchen, it was deserted. He saw, in the middle of the table, a note left on a sheet of hole-punched A4.

It was Helen's handwriting, with its unmistakable, large, even letters, in black felt pen. He picked it up and read it.

Johnny – don't forget to sort out the barrel of beer for the party on your way to work. See you later. Have a good shift. Don't murder anyone!
Hel x

He smiled but then saw the time on the kitchen clock. 5 p.m. He grabbed his coat, checked his wallet and keys, and headed for his bike. The front door slammed behind him, and he set off, accelerating towards the traffic crossing the end of his street.

He crested a hill, and then the bike swung into a long descent. He freewheeled, leaning back, enjoying the speed as it began to pick up. A quick stop to arrange the beer delivery and then, in no time at all, he swept into the hospital grounds and locked up his bike as usual. It was pitch-black and the whole site was studded with walkways and street lights. Above, the cloud cover was beginning to break up and in the gaps, the beginnings of a starry night could be seen.

He shivered. If that kept up, it was going to be an even colder night than before. And he still hadn't bought those gloves, he thought ruefully, rubbing his hands together as he made his way to the porters' restroom. He pushed open the door and walked in.

"Here he is. Our very own intellectual."

"Hey, Johnny. Still on that Dickens then? Ask me if you need any help with it."

"Good evening, JJ. Cutting it a bit fine, aren't you? We thought you were going to let down your old mates."

Johnny blinked in the glare of the neon strip lighting. The banter he'd been greeted with was undercut by the smiles that accompanied it. It was a familiar crew: Pat, in a state of undress at his locker, his sunbed tan set off by a skimpy pair of briefs and a gold medallion. Throughout the conversation that followed, Pat busied himself with his preparations. He slipped into t-shirt, tracksuit bottoms and his white overall. He turned back to the mirror inside his locker door, and carefully combed his thick, curly, black hair.

Then there was Les: blond, short and tubby, with a red face and a goatee beard and moustache. He was already dressed for the shift, with his white overall set off by a lapel badge that read: *NUPE Shop Steward*. The third member of the team was Gordon, Dr Death himself. His smile faded almost at once to be replaced by a shifty downward glance. Johnny clocked it immediately. There was unfinished business and they would have to have a little chat at some point before the end of the shift.

"Alright, gents," he said. He looked at his watch. "Right on time. I can even get in a trip to the canteen, if I get a wriggle on."

This provoked groans of disapproval. He ignored them.

"Oh, and Pat?" he continued.

"Yeah."

"Don't call me JJ. I've told you before. My name's Johnny."

Pat smiled at him. "Yeah, I know. Sorry, JJ." He turned to the others and winked.

Johnny sighed, but there was something about this pantomime that they went through at the beginning of nearly every shift that he found vaguely comforting.

Pat continued, pocketing his little victory. "Hey, Gordon was saying that you and he found the body last night. In the morgue, wasn't it?"

"That's right. We were doing a body and Sutherland was there when Gordon opened up the fridge. It was pretty weird."

"You must have thought all your birthdays had come at once, eh Gordon?"

"Yes, very funny, Pat. It was not very nice, actually." Gordon looked away and began to fiddle with his walkie-talkie.

"Come on, Gordon, man. You've not said a bloody word about it, and usually, you can't stop talking about the stiffs. Anyone would think you had something to hide, eh lads?" Les nudged Pat, and winked at him and then Johnny.

Johnny intervened. "Are the police still here? Didn't see any signs when I came in. Did they interview you lot last night as well?"

"Yeah, they're still around," Les answered. "The mortuary's all locked off. We've got to use Clifton if we get any bodies tonight. They're using the Friends Meeting Room as an incident room. And yeah, they talked to all of us."

"Do you think they've got any ideas about who did it?" asked Johnny.

"Plod? Nah, they're clueless, as usual. Mind you, they've got plenty to choose from, haven't they?"

"What do you mean?" asked Johnny.

"Well, he was a bit of a twat, wasn't he? Treated people like muck. Not many people are shedding a tear for him."

"Come on, Les," said Pat, "that's hardly a reason for murder, is it? If being a twat is all it takes, there wouldn't be many doctors left."

"Nor porters, come to that."

There was a pause, as they all contemplated doctor twats and porter twats. It was a sobering calculation each of them went through, but their ruminations were interrupted by the door opening again. The last member of the shift crew had arrived. He shuffled into the room, head down, already in his work clothes. He was a tall, lanky, stooping figure with enormous feet that seemed to slap the lino as he walked. He looked late fifties, early sixties, with a beak of a nose that sprouted tufts of greying hair from cavernous nostrils. This matched the thinning hair at his temples, but the crowning aspect of his appearance was the ginger toupee that bridged the grey temples, as if a tomcat had settled down to sleep on the top of his head while he'd been asleep.

"Sidney. Good of you to come," said Les.

Sid looked up, distracted. He seemed rather surprised to see the others there, and took a second or two to orientate himself to this new reality.

"Evening," he said eventually, taking in everyone in the room. His greeting was delivered in a voice so gloomy that it cast a shadow, sucking the life and energy out of all there. He focused his attention on Les.

"Good of *you* to come, Leslie. Has your statutory sick leave come to an end? Must be, what, six or seven weeks since we saw you last?"

"Yes, I'm very well, thanks for asking, Sid. It just so happened that my return to health coincided with the end of my union-agreed days off sick. Anyroad, enough of all of that. Time to get this show on the road." He looked at the sheet of paper he had in his hand. "Right. Johnny and Sid, you're on the dinner run. Gordon and Pat, you're doing laundry, and that leaves me floating and on call. Everyone alright with that?"

It was a question that did not expect an answer. There were a few nods and grunts of agreement. Johnny tried to catch Gordon's eye, but he was having none of it.

"Right then," Les finished off, "let's get on with it."

Sid shuffled over. "Come on then, Johnny lad. It's the express meals on wheels service for us."

They walked into the corridor. There was a small truck waiting for them where it had been left by the last shift. It was an unusual vehicle: a cross between a milk float and a bumper car from the fairground. They clambered on board, Sid taking the driving seat in a mark of his seniority. He turned the key in the ignition and they moved off with a whine, down the brightly lit corridor towards the canteen.

They made steady progress down the main ground-floor corridor, which stretched the length of the building. There had been the usual corporate attempt to celebrate Christmas. The windows had been stencilled with fake snow piles, and at intervals, there were a variety of decorations: tinsel, balloons and Father Christmas figures. In the entrance foyer, in front of the main reception desk, a large real Christmas tree had been stationed, and the reception area itself was peak Christmas. The further from this epicentre, the more variable the Christmas iconography became. By the time one reached the dark shadows of the service lifts, there was a permanent state of February. Cold, gloomy, bleak, with no hint of celebration to cheer the mood.

Sid parked the truck and they loaded the trolleys into the lift, processing the delivery, one ward at a time. They had to go back to the canteen to pick up the second load, and went through the same procedure as before.

It was getting on for six forty by the time they arrived at the final ward. Sid parked the truck in the corridor and waited while Johnny pushed the trolley into the ward. He left it just inside the door and called down to the nurses' desk.

"Dinners!"

He turned to go. It was time for a cup of tea in the restroom before going back to pick up all the empty trolleys. A voice stopped him in his tracks.

"Johnny! Johnny, love."

He turned. It was Gloria, her red lipstick like a beacon from four yards away. She beckoned to him.

Christ, that was all he needed. A bit of *Carry On* innuendo with Gloria. He forced a smile and went over to see what she wanted.

She smiled at him and laid her hand on his. "I'm glad you're on tonight, Johnny," she said. Her voice was quieter than normal and her eyes flicked left and right along the ward corridor. She leant closer to him. He could smell her perfume. "Listen, I heard that it was you that found the body this morning. Was Gordon with you then?"

"Yeah. He saw it first when he opened up the fridge. Saw him, I mean."

"Oh, Johnny, love, that must have been awful."

"Yeah. The whole thing's been a bit weird."

"Did the police talk to you last night?"

He nodded. "What about you?"

"They had us all in. Where were we, what time, did I see him, was there anyone unusual hanging round, what was Sutherland like? On and on they went."

"And was there? Anyone unusual around?"

She laughed. "Only Gordon. And he's more pathetic than unusual."

Johnny looked at her again. She was, he had to admit, a very attractive woman, particularly when she smiled. Probably in her forties, though Johnny would be the first to admit that, like for many twenty-two year olds, everyone over the age of thirty five was just uniformly old to him. She had shoulder-length, blonde hair, brown eyes and a slim figure. She knew she was sexy, but it seemed to him that she used that as some kind of a weapon, so that she was the one in control. He found it faintly unnerving.

He considered her again and wondered whether she was trying to tell him something about Gordon. He decided to change tack. "And what was Sutherland like?"

She scowled. "Vile. He tried it on with me, you know. One night shift. He never did it again."

Johnny took in her red fingernails, her chest and then her face, her lip curled in absolute disdain. *No*, he thought, *I bet he didn't.*

The door to the ward cracked open a fraction. Sid's ginger toupee appeared first, in the gap, followed by the rest of him.

"Stop flirting, Johnny. Come on, we've got stuff to do."

"Coming." He turned back to Gloria. "Sorry, gotta go."

She smiled at him. "No problem. But Johnny, if you get a spare five minutes, and you can get rid of Lurch there, come back up. When it's quiet, eh? You need to tell me what happened with Dr Death last night."

He frowned. "What?"

"Off you go, or he'll faint with hunger."

He rejoined Sid in the corridor and they continued with their deliveries. The truck wheezed its way down the corridor, past the tinsel and glitter Merry Christmas signs. Johnny was oblivious to it all. He couldn't stop thinking about Gordon and last night. And now Gloria. What did she want to know about last night? Or maybe, he thought, it was more about what she wanted to tell.

10

The Friends Meeting Room was thick with cigarette smoke. Half a dozen desks had been set up, each one carrying a phone, an ashtray and the beginnings of a pile of cardboard folders. To one side of the room was a fridge, a kettle and a sink, to the other, a set of noticeboards with a growing collection of photos and names pinned to them.

"OK, listen up everyone. Let's go through what we've got so far."

DCI Simon Grayson prowled the space in front of the boards, every now and then jabbing his finger at something on them to emphasise his point. He scanned the team in front of him, each at their own desk, coffee mugs and cigarettes in hand. DC Reg "Jacko" Jackson, in his mid-forties, a beer belly straining against his nylon shirt and kipper tie combination. He was, thought Grayson, a better copper than he appeared, which had its uses.

DC Paula Marsh, twenty-seven, tall, slim with shoulder-length, brown hair, her outfit suggesting that her clothes had been assembled and worn with some flair and precision. She was shiny and new, fresh out of the packet. He was reserving judgement on her.

DS Clive Brooks, thirty-two, sat up ramrod straight at his desk, which stood out from the rest, an oasis of neat order in a sea of grubby chaos. That sense of order was also reflected in his appearance. Neatly trimmed moustache, newly trimmed, shoulder-length, dark hair, sharp, expensive suit and a breeze of clinical cologne. Brooks, with eight years under his belt, was the rising star of North Yorkshire Police. He'd started well and had got better. He had no intention of being in the same place, at the same rank, with the same people in a year's time. Grayson was also reserving judgement on him. Talented, yes, but trustworthy? Well, that was an entirely different question.

Yes, not a bad team. Not bad at all.

"The victim. Gerald Sutherland, fifty-two years old. Single, with no particular partner, and no children. Lived in a very posh Victorian villa down by the river. What was it again?"

His eyes raked the team.

Paula Marsh piped up when he caught her eye. "New Walk Terrace, guv."

"Yes, New Walk Terrace. Very nice. Thanks, Paula. Has had several lodgers in the last few years. Have we got anything on his current crop?"

Paula answered again. She glanced down at her notes, balancing her cigarette on the ashtray. "Not yet, guv. There was no one in when we called. We've got the deceased's keys, but we need a warrant to go in. I was going to call back later and give it another go."

"Alright. But if there's no one in again, it'd be a crying shame not to use those keys, eh? A quick in and out."

"A quick in and out, eh Paula?" smirked Jackson. "That'll be a new experience for you."

Paula did not miss a beat. "But not for you, Reg, eh? At least, that's what Mrs Jacko told me."

Jacko's face crumpled like an old balloon. Rousing himself, he spat back, "Shut it, Paula. Fuck's sake, no sense of humour you lot."

Grayson held up his hands. Paula was going to be a problem, he could see that.

"Alright, alright. Ladies, please. Mind on the job, if you don't mind."

"His mind's always on the fucking job," Paula muttered, just loud enough to be heard.

"Paula, that's enough, darling," said Grayson, his patience beginning to fray. "Just make sure you check out the property and the lodgers tonight."

"Sir."

Grayson turned back to the board, and then to the team. "The body was found this morning by two porters who were doing a routine delivery of a body from one of the wards. Death on the ward during the night. They seemed harmless enough, but let's keep an open mind on that. The older one, Simpson, he's got a bit of a thing about bodies, apparently, but that's just gossip at this stage. The young lad, Jewell, he's a classic lefty waster. Was at the university until last year, and has only been at the hospital since October. Clever sod, but seems like a nice lad."

"Has he got any form, guv? The weirdo?" asked Clive.

"Not as far as we know, but that's a good call, Clive. Check him out for anything on record. It might be harmless gossip, but it could be something more."

"Sir."

"Have we covered everyone who was on shift last night? Everyone in the vicinity, that is?"

"Just about, guv."

"What about the incinerator? That's just round the corner from the mortuary. And Sutherland's office?"

Jacko examined his notebook. "I chatted with the incinerator chap. Dave Henderson. Sound as a pound, I reckon. Didn't like Sutherland, but he reckoned no one did. Doesn't work nights, so he wasn't in at the time of death. He's out of the frame. Said sometimes, a couple of the porters fill in for him, because he's they're short-staffed."

"And what about the forensics, Jacko? Anything back yet?"

"No dabs on the scalpel, or the body. Obviously been handled by someone who knew what they were doing. The rest of the morgue is covered in them, as you'd expect, so they're not much use."

"What about cause of death?"

"Nothing back on that yet. And the time of death is a bit tricky, because of the fridge, but Williams reckoned between eight and midnight last night."

"Midnight?"

"That's what he said."

"Interesting. According to that young doctor, that was when she last saw him. They did a patient together. No one else we've spoken to saw him after that."

"So that doctor." Paula paused and consulted her notes. "Juliet Fulton. She was the last person to see him alive. Apparently."

"Something not right about that. We're looking at a very narrow window there. We'll talk to her again tomorrow then. Double-check those timings. Jacko, I need you to find out about Sutherland's next of kin. You'll need to talk to them. Try and build up a picture of what he was like. Clive, you do the same with his colleagues here in the hospital. We need to know who his friends were, what he did with himself, whether he had any enemies, that sort of thing."

"Guv."

"Anything else?" He scanned the team. "No? OK, good. We'll start again tomorrow, eight-thirty sharp."

They each stood up, shuffled their papers together, and moved towards the door.

"Time for a beer before you get home?" Jacko asked at the door.

Grayson checked his watch. "Aye, a quick one," he replied. He looked back into the room. Paula was still at her desk, going over her notes. "Fancy a drink, Paula?"

She looked up. "Hm? Oh, no thanks, sir. I've got a few things to do before I finish off."

Jacko raised his eyebrows at Brooks behind Grayson's back.

"Well, don't be too late, and make sure you lock up when you go."

"Yes, guv."

"Oh and Paula?"

"Sir?"

"Don't forget New Walk Terrace. Don't be knocking them up out of bed, eh?"

"Yes, guv."

Brooks and Jacko chorused, "Night, Paula."

"Night."

The three men closed the door, and from the corridor, as they walked away towards the pub, there came peals of laughter. In the incident room, Paula bent over her desk and carried on annotating her files.

11

It was midnight. The regular jobs had all been finished, and the last half of the shift would be marked only by emergencies and call outs, if anything. Or, in the porters' dream world, uninterrupted sleep. There was often some action in the next hour, as the fallout from a night of drinking in York found its way, via A&E, to the hospital, but after that, a blanket of quiet would usually descend on the dimly lit corridors. In that netherworld, porters on the night shift, apart from those assigned to casualty, would drift off singly to find their preferred bunks for the night, each one clutching their bleep, just in case.

Everyone had their favourite spot. Some just bedded down on the sofas in the restroom. Others found a trolley, in a lonely anteroom off a gloomy passageway in the bowels of the building. The more senior porters, like Les, fancied themselves deserving of something finer. He took great delight in reserving the leather chesterfield in the boardroom for himself. It was the room used by hospital management and senior clinicians for meetings, but at night, it was deserted, secure behind the always locked door. But it was one of the peculiarities of the job of a porter in a busy hospital, that no door was ever locked to them. They had the keys, and the invisibility, and the round-the-clock access, to be able to get into any room on the site should they need to. Or want to, which came to much the same thing. And when they had completed whatever pressing task that had presented itself, they could lock the door again, and no one would ever know that they had been there.

Les took his walkie-talkie with him, in the same way everyone else did, but there was an unspoken understanding that he would never have it switched on. Once he had settled himself for the night, not even a terrorist incident or a jumbo jet crashing onto York Minster could wake him.

Johnny had settled himself down on a corner of one of the sofas in the restroom. The fluorescent overhead lights had been switched off, and the room was dark and restful, lit only by two small lamps. One cast a pool of light on Johnny's lap and *Bleak House*, and the other was on the floor at the end of the second sofa, where Sidney, snug under a lacy blanket, had lapsed into regular gentle snoring, his ginger toupee rising and falling in the corona of light from the lamp.

He put the book down and sighed. Jarndyce and Jarndyce had little appeal. The prospect of sleep had less. He had hoped to corner Dr Death by now to try and get something that was closer to the truth from him. He also needed to go back to ward thirty-six and have that chat with Gloria. She seemed very interested in Gordon's movements last night. He had the distinct impression that she wanted to talk to someone about Gordon as much as listen. What did she know? And why was Gordon avoiding him? They'd agreed to talk again, but he'd only caught one glimpse of him all shift. It was clear that Johnny would have to take matters into his own hands, or he ran the risk of not seeing him for a week or more. Luckily, he had a plan, a plan that he knew was foolproof.

Both of these issues filled the space that Jarndyce and Jarndyce had vacated. But more insistent than them, the issue that kept jostling for position, elbowing everything else out of the way, was that doctor.

Finally, he could stand it no more. It was time for decisive action. He eased himself from the sofa, wincing when the ancient wooden struts creaked, betraying his movement to the world. He looked over at Sidney and breathed a sigh of relief when his snoring continued uninterrupted.

He pocketed his Dickens and his bleep, and stole through the gloom to the door. He closed the door behind him without even a faint click and picked up speed down the corridor. As he threaded his way through the network of passageways, he turned over in his mind what he was going to do next. He'd head first to ward thirty-six and kill two birds with one stone. A chat with Gloria to see what the state of play was with potential deaths that evening. If anyone was in the frame to shuffle off this mortal coil, she would know about it and be already making preparations. Although their own mortuary was still out of commission, and any bodies would have to be stored at Clifton, it would still be down to them to prepare the body for transport. And that should be Dr Death and Pat, according to the rota. It would take physical injury to stop Gordon getting his hands on a corpse, but thankfully, Pat was easier to persuade. A quick chat with him earlier had been enough to persuade him to go missing if a call came in. The prospect of a cigarette in the canteen would always trump a trip to the morgue with Gordon. And then he, Johnny, could just appear casually at the ward as Gordon's partner.

He might be surprised, but Gordon must know that they had to have that chat sometime. Better get it out of the way, surely? And then he could, in a quiet corner somewhere, grill him about where he'd been the night before. He'd already admitted that he'd been up to something, but up to what exactly? And then he could see whether his answers matched up to whatever he was going to find out from Gloria. All of that would be interesting, and the whole thing had already livened up a humdrum night shift, but his main concern was Juliet. While he was pursuing the first two threads, which required him to be out and about the wards, he was quite likely to come across the beautiful doctor. She had said she was on nights again, so he was bound to come across her sooner or later. Maybe, with some cunning questions to Gloria, it would be sooner.

As he turned the corner to another deserted corridor, he was jolted out of his daydream, realising for the first time exactly where he was. Maybe it was time for a change of plan. He'd forgotten that his route to ward thirty-six would take him down this particular corridor. To the untutored eye, it appeared the same as all the others: gloomy, lit only by dimmed night lights, but Johnny recognised it immediately as the corridor that housed the sexual health clinic. During the day, it was busy, populated by sheepish-looking young men, shuffling into side rooms, heads down and collars up, but now it was entirely deserted, and off the beaten track. And it was those two qualities that made it so attractive to Gordon. It was, Johnny remembered with a hint of a smile, Dr Death's preferred spot for a night-shift kip. Maybe, just maybe, this is where Gordon was hiding, getting his head down for a few hours.

He gave a quick look both ways down the corridor, and then slipped into the room like a shadow. It was dark inside and he didn't want to risk turning the lights on. He wanted a quiet chat with Gordon, not to give him a heart attack by ripping him from his sleep with fluorescent light flooding the room. In the gloom, he could make out a trolley, a desk, some cupboards for the paperwork and specimen bags and a sink. Damn! Nobody.

But then, as his eyes became accustomed to the darkness, he saw the curtain at the back of the room. He crept across and took a peek behind it. Nobody again, only another trolley with a set of blankets on it. Oh well. It was always going to be a long shot. He would just carry on to ward thirty-six, and check out who was in the frame for the mortuary.

But then, just as he was about to turn towards the door, the silence was broken by the sound of approaching footsteps and whispered conversation. In a flash, Johnny dived behind the curtain and clambered up onto the trolley. He didn't want his feet to be seen at the bottom of the curtain, but he immediately began to regret that decision when the plastic-lined mattress creaked alarmingly as he shifted his weight on it. But there was nothing he could do about it now. The door swung open and two people, men by their voices, came into the room. Johnny froze and willed himself to stay stock still and silent, as the conversation continued.

"...we're going to have to tone it down a bit, that's all. The place is crawling with coppers."

It was Dr Death. Johnny could barely breathe, and his heart hammered in his chest. He concentrated completely on staying absolutely still. Any movement would cause the plastic-covered mattress to squeak its betrayal.

Another voice joined in, a man, but not one that Johnny recognised.

"Listen, Gordon, that's your problem, not ours. We still need you to make the delivery, as we agreed. There are people who are expecting it and they are not very understanding. I wouldn't advise you to piss them off, because they're not too fussy about how they behave."

Gordon's voice took on a desperate note. "I've already lied to them about last night. I just need to keep my head down, just until they've gone. Surely your clients can understand that, can't they? When everything's gone back to normal, I can get the stuff, as much as they want."

"You're not listening. See what happened to Sutherland last night? Let that be a warning." The voice took on a warmer, friendlier tone. "Look, you've got keys to get anywhere in the hospital, and you can be here when it's deserted. Just keep your cool, and choose your time. I need it tomorrow."

"Tomorrow?" Gordon almost shouted, but then immediately lowered his voice. "And why the hell did you have to do that to Sutherland? I know he was a prick, but Jesus, that's made everything worse."

"Sutherland has got nothing to do with us. We're not that stupid."

"But you just said—"

"Just trying to frighten you off. But that doesn't mean we were involved. We assumed it was because he can't keep his dick in his scrubs, that's all. Tomorrow, alright?"

Behind the curtain, Johnny was beginning to lose all feeling in his legs. He was praying for this secret meeting to finish so that he could get up and stretch. He slowly moved his right hand to massage his leg when he felt the walkie-talkie in his pocket. Shit! If that went off now, he was done for. With sweating, trembling fingers, he reached for it and agonisingly pulled it, inch by inch from his pocket.

By this stage, he could hardly follow the conversation a couple of metres away from him on the other side of the curtain because of the roaring sound of his own breathing and the hammering of his heart. He licked his lips and swallowed, making one last effort with the switch after wiping his sweaty fingers on his overall. There was a tiny click as he managed to switch it off, and he waited in an agony of expectation for the curtain to be ripped back and the violence to begin.

Nothing.

He tuned back into the conversation. Dr Death was still talking.

"…had no choice. He knew I'd slipped away when we were called to do a body. I had to make sure he didn't let on to the police, didn't I?"

Johnny had forgotten about the pain in his leg, his walkie-talkie and the sweat trickling into his eyes. Everything was subordinated to the task of listening to every word that Gordon was saying.

"What the fuck, Gordon? What exactly did you tell him?"

"Just that I was meeting someone because I was up to something. Said I'd explain it all to him."

"What? You said what?"

"I had to say fucking something, didn't I?" Gordon hissed. "It'd be disastrous if he went to the police because he thought I was involved."

"And what, exactly, are you going to tell him, Sherlock? Amaze me."

"I dunno, for fuck's sake. I'll make up some shit."

From behind the curtain, Johnny heard a slap, a scuffle, and a strangled cry. The second voice came again, strangely quiet this time.

"That's just a taster, Gordon. Now, what's this guy's name?"

"It's the new lad, Johnny, the student. Johnny Jewell."

Behind the curtain, Johnny closed his eyes, still stinging with sweat, and grimaced. A bad night had just got a lot worse.

12

When the door closed, Johnny waited for thirty seconds or so before lowering himself from the trolley and sticking his head into the corridor. He jerked it back in again with such force, he felt sure he must have given himself whiplash. He tried it again, more slowly. There they were still, Dr Death and his partner in crime walking away from him to the end of the corridor. He didn't recognise the second man. He was a couple of inches taller than Gordon and was wearing a brown overall with the collar up, and a dark woolly hat jammed down on his head. They disappeared round the corner.

Johnny leant back against the doorjamb, closed his eyes and exhaled in a puffing sigh, as if he were releasing pressure from a balloon. What the hell had he just heard? Who was that other guy and why did he want to know his name? And what on earth was he going to do now? His heart was still racing and his mind was scrambled, but he knew that he needed to talk to someone about all of this before he either lost it completely or, horror of horrors, he accidentally stumbled across Gordon's mate on his own in a dark and deserted corridor somewhere in the hospital. The very thought of that stoked up his fears once again.

But he couldn't spend the rest of the shift hidden away in here, just hoping that in the morning, everything would be miraculously OK. Gloria, that's who he had to talk to, and then Juliet. Even just for a friendly face. He slipped out into the corridor again, and made his way to ward thirty-six, navigating crossroads stealthily, always ready to shrink against the wall or crouch behind a cabinet at any sign of trouble. By the time he got there, his nerves were shot to pieces.

He took a deep breath and went into the ward. All the patients had been asleep for a couple of hours now. The lights were low and routine tasks were few and far between, so it was not unusual for the ward to appear deserted. He could see, illuminated by the light from the desk lamp, the hunched figure of Gloria.

She looked up at the noise of the door opening and was about to speak when Johnny hurried towards her, a finger across his lips. She frowned and waited. When Johnny got to the desk, she spoke in a low voice.

"Why all the secrecy? What's up? I've bleeped you a couple of times, you know."

Johnny looked up and down the ward.

"Is anyone else on with you?"

"Just a couple of the girls. It's been a quiet night."

"Where are they?"

"They're just looking in on the patients – regular ward round. Why?"

"Is there somewhere we can go, just for five minutes?"

She smiled at him. "Ooh, Johnny love, I thought you'd never ask. You're a bit of dark horse, aren't you?"

"No, Gloria, be serious. There's no need for all of that. We need to talk. About Gordon."

The smile left her face instantly. "Come on. We can use a side room. I won't be missed for five minutes, and I can keep an eye on the desk."

She came out from behind her reception area and led him to a door just around the corner. They both went in and she closed the door behind them, leaving a crack with a view of the desk. The room was a jumble of bedpans and boxes, in darkness except for the shaft of light that came through the crack. Their voices matched the gloom.

"Come on then. What about Gordon? What's the daft bugger done this time?"

Johnny's face fell. "I thought you were going to tell me."

She looked puzzled. "No, love. I just wanted to know what happened when you found the body. You know what he's like. And there's all kinds of rumours flying around about why Sutherland was murdered."

"What kind of rumours?"

"Well, he was a randy sod, for one thing. I told you before, I had to fend him off a few times. That's alright, I can look after myself, but he was very handsy with the younger nurses as well. And a bit more than that, if you know what I mean."

"Just the nurses?"

"No, doctors too, by all accounts. That new lass had a bit of a tussle with him. Even the cleaners, he wasn't fussy."

"The new doctor? Juliet?"

Gloria raised her eyebrows. "Juliet, eh? We are very cosy then, aren't we? Fast work, Johnny lad. Bit out of your league though, I'd have thought."

Pride conquered caution and he raised his voice. "Cheeky sod! And anyway, she's just a friend. But Sutherland tried it on with her, did he?"

"So she said. But she's got a bit of fight about her, that one. I don't think he bothered her again."

"Did no one ever report him?"

Gloria snorted. "Report him? Who to? All the older men in charge who've probably slapped him on the back and bought him another drink when he was telling them all tales of getting his end away with a pretty young nurse? Johnny love, you've got a lot to learn about the ways of the world."

When he thought back over the events of the previous twenty-four hours, he had to agree with her. But there must be something else. He could quite believe that Sutherland was a dirty old man, he wasn't that naive, but what about Gordon and the mystery stranger?

"And Gordon? Is he involved in anything dodgy? I know he's got a thing about the bodies, but I don't mean that. Last night, he disappeared when we were supposed to do that body. Couldn't get any sense out of him when I asked him where he'd been." There was a pause. Johnny lowered his voice even further. "Is he dealing drugs or something?"

In the darkness of the room, a chevron of light fell across Gloria's face, from the doorjamb. Johnny looked urgently at her for her reaction. He wasn't sure whether he was being paranoid about Gordon. After all, Gordon was just a middle-aged, slightly weird but otherwise mainstream guy. Even saying out loud his suspicion made Johnny feel more than a little foolish. *Gordon, a drug dealer? Don't be daft, Johnny.* That was what he was half-expecting Gloria to say. It was certainly what he wanted her to say.

But in the pause that was slightly too long, a hint of a shadow passed across Gloria's face, and he realised that it didn't really matter what she said. For some reason, instinct or natural suspicion, he wasn't going to believe anything she said.

"Dr Death, a drug dealer? Don't be daft, Johnny."

The sentence hung in the air between them. Johnny swallowed and dredged up a smile.

"No, you're probably right. I'm just trying to explain where he disappeared to last night, that's all. But I'm putting two and two together and making them come to five."

"Five hundred, more like."

"But who killed him, then? And why did they do it in such a weird way? You know with the scalpel and leaving him in the fridge."

"How should I know? That's the bloody police's job, isn't it, not ours," Gloria snapped with irritation.

Johnny could see that he wasn't going to get anything more out of her. He shrugged. "Suppose not," he muttered.

She opened the door a fraction wider.

"Listen, I'd better get back on the desk, before anyone notices. And you'd better get back to work. Don't forget to switch your walkie-talkie on."

They both slipped back into the corridor and went back to the reception desk, which was still deserted.

"Do you reckon there'll be any bodies tonight?" asked Johnny.

"Dunno about the other wards. Mrs P from Poppleton is still clinging on, but she'll have stopped taking sugar before the night's out, I reckon. Why? You're not turning into Dr Death mark two, are you?"

He smiled and shook his head. "Nah, not yet. Just planning the rest of my shift, that's all." He turned to go. "See you later."

"Johnny?"

"Yeah?"

She looked around and lowered her voice.

"You should maybe keep your head down and stop asking so many questions, now. Leave it to the police, eh?"

He nodded. "OK," he said.

As he walked away from her, he felt that the cloud hanging over him had just got a little darker.

The door closed behind him and Gloria was left in the pool of light at her desk, staring at the door.

13

Johnny trudged along the corridors, oblivious to the cheery Christmas messages, glitter and tinsel that came and went at intervals out of the gloom. A couple of times, he caught sight of someone going about their business at the end of a passageway or through a plate glass window, ghostly figures caught passing through pockets of neon in a sea of darkness. Each time, he caught his breath, looked over his shoulder and shrank against the wall. He really needed to have that conversation with Gordon, but after what he'd heard from behind that curtain, what on earth was he going to say?

Before he knew it, he found himself outside the porters' restroom. He hesitated, looked in both directions down the corridor, and then decided. He'd just pop in and check to see if Sid was still fast asleep. If he was, he'd carry on to the canteen to get a coffee and a snack. For one thing, he was starving, for a second, he needed to stop and think somewhere that was relatively safe, and for a third, if he was lucky, he might just come across Juliet on a break.

He opened the door a little, expecting to find the room in darkness, with Sid still snoring underneath his blanket. Instead, it was flooded in harsh fluorescent light that spilled out into the corridor. Two faces turned to look at him. His jaw dropped.

"Eh up, Johnny, where've you been, lad?"

Sid's gloomy tone was completely at odds with the smile that lit up his face. Something had cheered him up. Usually, an air of despondency seeped from him, like a chilling, Dickensian fog, but now he seemed almost jolly.

"Alright, Sid," he replied. "Oh, you know, I've just been out and about. Couldn't sleep."

"Not like you Johnny," came the second voice. Gordon had a bright, brittle tone that screamed guilt to Johnny's ears. "You can usually sleep through an earthquake. You got something on your mind? Been up to no good?"

Johnny forced a smile. "Up to no good? Not me, Gordon. What about you?"

He started. "What do you mean?" His eyes flicked from side to side.

"Where've you been? Haven't seen you or Pat all night."

"Oh!" Gordon's relief was palpable. He was not a very good liar. He continued, slightly more confident now. "It's been a pretty quiet night. Pat's gone down to casualty. He's got his eye on one of the student nurses down there. I've just been chatting to Sid about his show."

Sid leant forward eagerly. He had a newspaper of some description in his hand, opened at a page that was ringed with circles done in blue biro. A second paper stuck out of the pocket of his overall.

"It's all going very well, Johnny. You need to make the date in your diary for next July. A day concert at the racecourse. I've planned the line-up and I've already had some promising replies from agents." He tapped the side of his nose. "Top quality acts, Johnny. International names, most of 'em. Can't say too much at the moment – it's all a bit delicate, if you know what I mean – but let's just say, 'Sweet Caroline', eh?" He held up his hand. "But let's not get ahead of ourselves, just yet. Mum's the word."

Johnny caught the smirk on Gordon's face, but he didn't have the heart to join in. Sid was so convinced this was going to happen, it seemed cruel to make fun of him, when it was the only thing that lifted his perpetual gloom.

"You got any proper music acts yet? Modern stuff, you know. You need some punk, Sid, or Two Tone. That 'll bring the students in."

Sid snorted his scorn. "Punk! I'm not having that rubbish. I've got a reputation to protect in the business. No, Johnny lad, it's just noise. My event will be quality. Pure quality."

He stopped, subsiding into a delightful daydream about his role as impresario, the mastermind behind this festival of showbiz superstars. The conversation was over, and Sid turned his attention back to *The Stage*. He ringed another advert with his biro and then removed the second paper from his pocket and carefully unrolled it. It was a copy of *Variety*. He opened it up at the small ads, and began to scour it, his forefinger tracing details of auditions and casting opportunities.

Johnny turned back to Gordon and they exchanged a raised-eyebrow look between them. Just as Johnny was about to suggest that they slope off to the canteen for a bit of privacy, their walkie-talkies went off in unison. They ignored them.

Eventually, Sid laid down *Variety* with a heavy sigh. "Porters," he droned into the handset, his downward cadence communicating a lethal cocktail of annoyance and despair.

The device crackled back into life. "We need a porter down in casualty, please"

There was a pause. The three of them exchanged glances, back and forth, each waiting for one of the others to crack.

Sid gave a sigh of epic proportions and intoned into his walkie-talkie, "Then you must have one, I suppose."

He hauled himself to his feet, and, pocketing his copy of *Variety*, just in case, shuffled to the door in silence, and then into the corridor, shutting the door behind him.

"So, what exactly is the thing with Sid?" asked Johnny, more to delay the real conversation than from any pressing desire to know the answer. Although he had only worked there for a few weeks, he had learnt enough to realise that the porters were an extraordinary bunch of outsiders and misfits, such that Sid's eccentric behaviour barely merited a mention.

"Oh, he's harmless enough, poor old soul, but a bit weird. He just lives in a fantasy world of his own most of the time. Sometimes, he visits the rest of us, down here on planet Earth, but mainly, he thinks he's in showbiz. He tells stories about all of the famous stars he knows, and the shows he's done, but it's all bollocks. Obviously."

It came to something, thought Johnny, when someone as deranged as Gordon, Dr Death himself, could describe a colleague as "a bit weird".

"And the racecourse concert?"

"Just humour him. He'll drop it soon enough, and then he'll move on to some other tale, just as daft."

Johnny nodded and a silence fell between them. He waited to see what Gordon would do.

Eventually, Gordon cracked.

"So, about last night," he began.

"Ah, I was wondering when you were going to get to that. Have you been avoiding me, Gordon?"

"No! Course not."

"I need an explanation, man. And it needs to be good enough to convince me not to go to the police."

Johnny could hardly believe what he was hearing himself

say, but he'd had enough of dancing round the subject, even after the earlier conversation he'd overheard. It was dangerous, but worth a punt.

"The police? Woah, calm down! Johnny man, there's no need for the police."

"That's down to you, isn't it? Come on, let's have it."

Gordon hesitated, on the verge of a revelation.

Johnny tried to gently push him on. "Let's cut to the chase. Are you dealing drugs? It's the only thing that makes any sense."

"Drugs? No, I…"

Gordon trailed off, eyes cast down, before his face lit up. "Alright smartarse. Yes, I am doing a spot of dealing. But just a bit of dope, some weed, and a tiny bit of speed. That's all. I had to meet my supplier last night; that's where I was. That's why I couldn't have you talking to the police. They'd ask too many awkward questions."

Johnny stared at him, unconvinced. "How the hell did you get into that? No offence, but you'd stand out like a sore thumb in some of the student pubs I used to go to."

"Someone I know from school. He is a serious player, but I just do bits and pieces. He does it to help me out with cash. And the fact that I look normal, unlike you scruffy student layabout types, is an advantage as far as he's concerned."

"But what the fuck is your supplier, a serious player according to you, coming into the hospital for? Doesn't make sense."

Gordon shook his head. "This has been a normal night shift, yeah?"

"Yeah"

"Who have you seen round and about?"

"No one. Been as quiet as the grave."

"Exactly! It's always like that, after about 2 a.m. isn't it? No security, no one wandering round except for us. And we've got keys that let us go anywhere. It's perfect."

A growing sense of relief was beginning to wash over Johnny. It kind of made sense. And it might mean that the lunkhead in the clap clinic wouldn't do serious physical damage to him. At least not if Gordon could report back that he'd lapped up the story.

"So you had nothing to do with Sutherland?"

"Sutherland? Jesus wept, I've got nowt to do with him. You'd be better off looking at some of the women he's tried it on with."

"But why was he in the fridge like that, with the weird scalpel thing?"

"Fuck knows. Revenge? Someone a bit kinky? I don't know. Just leave it to the police."

There didn't seem much more to say about it. And the idea of Gordon being a dealer was nagging away at him. Was he telling the truth?

Then an idea occurred to him. "This dope that you sell then, Gordon."

He was immediately wary. "What about it?"

Johnny shuffled awkwardly in his seat. "Can you get me some?"

A huge grin split Gordon's face. He shook his head. "I might have known. You don't give a toss about the murder. You just wanna score."

"Yeah, whatever. But can you?"

"Course I can, Johnny mate. Got some nice Lebanese, a bit of Black. Maybe some homegrown if you're short of cash. Just name it."

"It's just that we're having a party tomorrow, and it'd be good to have some blow to celebrate Christmas, you know."

"Yes, very traditional. Very festive. Tell you what I'll do. I'll get the stuff, if you give me an invite. Then I'll deliver it personally. Cash on delivery, like. Couple of days off work, would be nice to have a bit of a party. Particularly when I'm working Christmas."

The rest of their conversation passed in a blur. By the end of it, when Dr Death went off for a last couple of hours of sleep before the end of the shift, Johnny had given him his address, told him what time to turn up, and had agreed that he could bring a few mates along with him.

When Gordon had slipped away into the corridor, Johnny was left alone in the shadowy restroom. His relief at Gordon's explanation had not survived long. His heart sank. How on earth had this happened? From being a potential murderer who was dobbing him in it with his nasty accomplices, Gordon was now in the role of mate, someone who went to the same parties as him. Even worse, he was the friendly neighbourhood dope dealer. Suddenly, the world of twenty-four hours earlier, when Gordon was just plain old weirdo Dr Death, a tubby, middle-aged, slightly balding, lonely misfit, seemed very appealing. Since then, a ritualistic murder had occurred, Johnny was an object of interest to a local gangster, and he had lied to the police in a murder inquiry.

Worst of all, Gordon had somehow mysteriously morphed into being his friend.

14

The rest of the shift passed by in a blur. The rush of drunken lads in casualty had long been cleared, and evidently, Mrs P of Poppleton had maintained her iron grip on life in ward thirty-six, as there had been no call for a customer for Rose Cottage. It was the quietest Johnny had ever known it on nights. Normally, this would be the signal for the porters to hunker down in their favourite sleeping spot. Everyone else took advantage of the opportunity, but Johnny could not clear his mind of the evening's events. He took refuge in *Bleak House*, pleased to be able to escape his worries for a time before they inevitably came creeping back, furtive and insistent. He interspersed his reading sessions with regular patrols around the corridors and the wards, taking in the canteen. He even made sure he deliberately walked past the corridor that led to the mortuary, just to check that it was still all taped off. The corridor was in total darkness, but he could still make out the police crime scene tape across the door. Even the entrance to the corridor had tape strung across it, like the tinsel that glittered over much of the rest of the building, so he couldn't sneak down and take a closer look.

Probably just as well. He'd already got himself into hot water by asking too many questions about the murder because of Gordon's strange behaviour. At least now he had a plausible explanation of what Dr Death had been up to. He turned back to retrace his steps, checking his watch first. 5 a.m. One more hour to go before the end of the shift and he still hadn't come across Juliet, which was the real reason for his repeated laps of the hospital corridors. And this was his last shift until Sunday, two days from now. It would be bloody typical, he thought, if that first meeting, which seemed to hold so much promise for the future, was just going to fade away without any development. The deathly quiet of the dim corridors during the night shift, which he usually enjoyed so much, were becoming the backdrop to his own increasingly gloomy thoughts. What on earth was he doing with his life anyway, stuck in this ridiculous job, filling time? Juliet had promised to be a delightful distraction. The prospect of that dribbling down the plughole merely underlined the emptiness of his current situation.

He turned the corner deep in thought. A familiar voice wrenched him back into the here and now.

"There you are, Mr Porter. I've been looking all over for you. You avoiding me?"

"Juliet!" he exclaimed. "Where've you been? I was starting to worry."

She frowned. "Worry? Why, what's happened?"

He looked around and lowered his voice. "Nothing. Just that, there's stuff to talk about. And we said we'd meet up for coffee."

"Sounds like you've had a heavy shift, Johnny."

He smiled. "Yeah, you could say that. Listen, can you finish your shift now? We could start breakfast early."

"No, sorry. I've just been bleeped."

His face fell, and he cursed himself for betraying his disappointment.

"But listen, I'll be done at six. I'll meet you at the canteen and we can talk then."

He looked at her properly, framed in the halo of the dimmed fluorescent strips in this quiet part of the hospital. She was tall, with a white overall over her blue scrubs. She had a stethoscope around her neck and a bleep clipped to her breast pocket. Her hair was a stylish, spiky shock of glossy jet black, and her face was even featured, with a warm smile, showing her white, regular teeth. There was a tiredness in her hazel eyes that gave her an enticing air of vulnerability, underneath her facade of brisk capability. The faint scent of some unidentified woody vanilla perfume clung to her. Johnny felt himself falling from a great height, like a jolt in a dream, and he realised he was staring gormlessly at her in silence. He was suddenly very aware that he was on the edge of making a fool of himself with this woman who he barely knew. He shook himself free of the spell and forced himself to speak.

"Yeah, OK, great."

He wished he hadn't said a word after such a meaningless contribution, but then managed something a little more normal.

"I'll walk with you to the lift, and then I'll go on to the restroom, if that's alright."

They continued down the corridor, Juliet setting a fast pace in response to her bleeped summons. Johnny was used to seeing doctors all over the hospital, power-walking their way to their next patient. Very often, they broke into a run, if the call was urgent.

She had time for one question before she had to turn off for the ward.

"Has something happened on the shift? Did you get to talk to the weirdo guy, Dr Death? You seem a bit on edge."

"Yeah, I did. It's been a stressful night. Listen, I'll tell you all about it later; you've got to go."

They stopped momentarily at the lifts to the wards. She pressed the button to summon the lift and then turned back to him, laying a hand on his arm.

"OK, see you later. But Johnny, be careful, yeah?"

She pulled away and stepped into the lift. The doors closed and the lift wheezed upwards, out of sight.

15

He looked up at the clock on the wall of the restroom yet again. Sid was still gently snoring under his blanket, so he had just settled himself quietly in the corner with his book and waited for the end of the shift. He saw all of the words on the page, but couldn't recall anything of what he had read, his mind returning again and again to the events of the shift. Soon the day shift would start arriving, ready to begin the familiar daily schedule again: breakfast run, laundry, lunches, specimens, path lab, theatre waste for the mortuary, and the regular transfer of patients and supplies to and from outpatient clinics.

He replaced his walkie-talkie in the charge cradle, packed his bag and began to get changed. It was a little early, but he wanted to get a flyer. As soon as the clock showed 6 a.m., he'd be out of there, on his way to the canteen to meet Juliet. The clock dragged its way round to six painfully slowly, and then he was gone, exchanging the usual hellos and goodbyes on autopilot. Gordon had not reappeared since he had left a couple of hours earlier to grab some sleep, but that was not so unusual as to provoke suspicions on Johnny's part.

To his surprise, when he turned the corner, there she was, checking her watch and shuffling from foot to foot outside the canteen. She looked up and saw him and her face, which had been clouded with anxiety, blossomed with a smile.

"Oh, hi. You're here." She raised her eyebrows. "Well, I mean obviously you're here. And obviously, you know you're here, so..." She trailed off.

Johnny burst out laughing. "You sound like someone who's had a long shift as well. I thought you'd be waiting inside, like before. Don't you wanna get anything?"

"No. Listen, do you mind coming back to mine? We've got stuff to talk about. We can have breakfast, and it's just more private. I don't want the entire hospital gossiping about us having breakfast together in the canteen."

"Yeah, great," he replied, thinking, *You don't want to be seen with me, 'cos I'm a porter and you're a doctor.*

"It's just this way."

She led the way down the corridor, towards the lifts. Their walk started in silence which continued until they were inside the lift. She pressed the button for the ground floor and the awkwardness began to grow.

"So was it a heavy shift, then?" Johnny started, just to break the silence. "Seemed a bit quiet to me."

"It was pretty standard, actually. A few call-outs. Nothing too bad. I think the murder thing is starting to sink in, that's all."

"Yeah, me too."

He didn't want to go into any more details until they were safely inside her room, so he moved the chat onto other things. He was beginning to run out of small talk, and didn't know her well enough to be able to embrace amicable silence, so it was with some relief that they reached the walkway outside that led past the bike sheds to the nurses' home.

They were just about to turn off towards it when Johnny caught sight of Gordon, on the other side of the bike sheds. He was deep in conversation with another figure, who was swaddled in a coat, scarf and woolly hat against the freezing weather. He instinctively grabbed hold of Juliet's arm and pulled her deeper into the doorway leading to the main building.

"What—" Juliet protested.

"Shh!" he hissed. "Look."

He nodded towards Gordon, away in the distance.

"Isn't that Dr Death?" said Juliet.

"Yeah, but who's the other guy?"

"Dunno. He looks kind of familiar, even under all of his winter clothes."

"Someone from the hospital, you mean?"

She thought for a moment. "Yeah, but I can't put my finger on who, exactly. But listen, why are we skulking around in the shadows like this?"

"The last thing I need is another conversation with Gordon. Let's just wait for a minute until they go, and I'll explain when we get to your room."

They didn't have long to wait. Their conversation seemed to get a little heated. Voices were raised, though not enough to make out what was being said, and there was some finger jabbing on both sides. It ended with both of them stalking off in opposite directions, Gordon to unlock his bike, and the other man towards the car park. Johnny and Juliet exchanged a look and when the coast was clear, emerged from the doorway and carried on to the nurses' home.

"What was all that about?" Juliet asked. "Was that anything to do with you? What happened when you spoke to him?"

"Look, let's just get to yours, yeah?"

She did not reply, but fumbled in her pocket for her keys. She opened the main entrance to her block and they went through, leaving the heavy door to swing back and lock itself. There was an immediate embrace of warm air and she went down the corridor, which was a spartan arrangement of bare, grey breeze blocks. At the far end, she stopped and let them into her room.

"Welcome to my little palace," she said as she shut the door behind her. "Come on, I'll make coffee and some breakfast."

She dumped her coat and bag on the bed, and switched on a kettle on the other side of the room.

"You want any toast? It's all I've got, so please yourself."

He nodded. "Toast and coffee would be great. Thanks."

He took in the room in a glance. It didn't take long.

"Don't you have any sort of kitchen here?"

"There's a communal kitchen on each floor, but really these are just places to crash after a night shift. The canteen's just over in the hospital, so a kettle and a toaster are all you need. How do you take your coffee?"

"Milk, no sugar."

She finished it off and passed it to him, indicating the free chair. "Have a seat."

He settled himself down, putting the coffee on her bedside table. The room reminded him of student halls, all breeze blocks and Baby Bellings, with room for a bed, a desk and a wardrobe and nothing more. There was something unfamiliar though, something that jarred when he remembered his own room in Derwent College, and the many other rooms in all of the colleges that he'd drank coffee in, smoked joints in, listened to new records in, and, very occasionally, had drunken sex in, more or less successfully.

That last thought broke the spell, as he was once again aware that he was sitting about a metre away from someone who oozed sex appeal, was sitting on her bed, and who appeared to like him. But then, the room was so small, he was about a metre away from everything in it, so that really didn't signify much at all.

"I don't get how you're here. I thought this was a nurses' home."

She laughed. "It is, obviously. But there are some rooms reserved for trainee doctors like me. So that doctors who are here for their training have a base when they start. Most of them move out when they get settled, apparently. Or that's what my colleagues have told me, anyway."

As he listened, Johnny worked out what was unfamiliar and why. The room was completely bare. There were no posters on the walls, no family photos on the desk, no knick-knacks or ornaments at all. It was a room that gave no clue about its inhabitant. The only extraneous items were a couple of cardboard boxes stowed away underneath the bed.

She noticed his eyes sweep around the room.

"I know. It's a dump, but it's a temporary dump. Or at least that's the plan. I've only been here a month or so; I just can't face unpacking everything."

"How come you're here? Like, where are you from?"

Even as he said it, he realised he knew nothing about her.

"Me? I'm from Edinburgh. I started training in Leeds, and then I transferred here."

"You moved from Leeds? Funny, most people go the other way. York's tiny in comparison. You've got to go to Leeds for all the best gigs. We saw The Clash last year."

"So did we. But like, you managed it, didn't you? People in York aren't under house arrest."

He laughed. "No, suppose not."

They were both smiling, and he was struck by the physical sensation brought about by liking her more and more. It was like a rising tide of warmth, a suffusion of serotonin. She liked The Clash. She wore a leather jacket. She was funny. And, oh yeah, she was gorgeous. But one thing nagged away at him. What did she mean by "we"?

"Don't suppose you know of anywhere to live, do you? I mean, this'll do for now, but once I've found my feet, in the new year, I'll need somewhere a bit more permanent."

Johnny looked around the bare room again. "You'll need somewhere a bit more fun. This must be a bit like solitary confinement."

She shrugged, a little embarrassed. "Yeah, well…" She trailed off once again. "Anyway, what about you? Where are you from, and all of that stuff?"

"Listen, can we do all that stuff later? I need to talk to you about last night." Johnny began to relate the events of the previous night, but this time, he included the details about Gordon disappearing, and him lying to the police about being with him all shift. Then he described the conversation he'd overheard between Gordon and the mystery man.

With each successive, improbable detail, Juliet's eyes got wider and her jaw dropped lower. "So you really think he's a drug dealer then?"

"Yeah, I do. But not like he described. That was just to explain what he'd been doing the night before, that would stop me asking questions. They were talking about something a lot more serious than dealing a bit of dope to students. Gordon was scared stiff of that guy, whoever he was. And I reckon that was the guy in the bike sheds just now."

"I wish I could remember who that was. I've definitely seen him before, here in the hospital."

"I don't wanna know who he is. I'm worried he's going to come and find me on his own. He asked Gordon for my name."

"And what did Gordon say?"

"He told him."

"No! What a bastard. He grassed you up good and proper. What are…?" She stopped mid-sentence, her brow furrowed.

"You don't think this guy would hurt you, do you? Maybe you should go to the police and change your story."

"Admit I lied, you mean? In a murder investigation. That's going to go down well, isn't it? Nah, I'll keep that up my sleeve as the nuclear option."

She reached out and took his hand. "Johnny, promise me you'll be careful. Don't go and get yourself killed. You're my only friend here."

Her hand in his, warm and alive, scrambled his reptilian brain for a moment, but then he pulled himself together. He squeezed her hand.

"Maybe we could form a partnership."

She smiled at him. "That's very formal. Do you want to ask my father's permission?"

"No, I mean, try and work together to find out what happened to Sutherland. You get to the bottom of who the mystery man is. I'll try and get more out of Gordon. He's coming to our party tonight with some dope. That'll be a good opportunity to ask more questions."

She perked up. It was as if someone had turned on a switch. "Party? What party?"

"We're having a Christmas party tonight. I had to invite Gordon to it and to he said he'd sell me some dope."

"Dr Death? But he's about forty, isn't he?"

They both contemplated the horror of being old, and then, the worse horror of being old, but acting inappropriately, like selling drugs and going to parties. Eventually, Juliet shook herself free from the appalling spectacle of Gordon at a wild party. She put his hand to one side and said, "This is truly shocking."

"What?" he said. "What's the matter?"

"You're having a party and you haven't invited me. Shocking."

"Of course I'm going to invite you. Give me a chance; I've only known you a day."

"Well, I might not be able to come. I'm very busy."

"Well, can you come?"

"Course I can come. The only party I've been to since I've been here has been the weekly Friday gathering here in the communal kitchen. Organised by Glenys, the small girl from Tang Hall. Pot noodle and a warm glass of Blue Nun. The only drugs on offer are paracetamol. Maybe ibuprofen this Saturday, as it's Christmas."

"No wonder you moved from Leeds. You've come for the glitzy social life."

"You'd think we'd be able to do better for drugs here. This is a hospital, after all. I mean…"

She stopped mid-sentence, her hand instinctively going to her face in shock. And then her expression began to thaw and a smile of triumph broke through the clouds.

"Of course. That's who it was."

"What? Who what was?" Johnny had no idea what she was talking about.

"The guy with Dr Death. The guy covering his face by the bike sheds."

"The guy threatening Gordon in the sex clinic? The nasty piece of work who wants to do me some damage, you mean?"

She widened her eyes and nodded.

"Well?" insisted Johnny, about to burst with frustration. "Who is it?"

"It's Mike Hutchinson."

"Who?"

"Hutchinson. He's only in charge of the hospital pharmacy, that's all. Every drug known to medical science passes through his hands in this building."

A silence fell as the implications of what Juliet had said percolated between them.

Finally, Johnny passed judgement. "Fucking hell. Fuck. King. Hell."

16

"Diamorphine? That's definite, is it?"

"Yes, guv. Massive overdose. And there's more. His hands and ankles had been tied before his death. But even more interesting, his arms show signs of regular injections."

"So, this wasn't a one-off then?"

Brooks shook his head. "Nope. Sutherland was a heroin addict."

Grayson stopped for a moment, taking in what he'd just learnt. He hadn't been expecting anything much out of the ordinary from this briefing. Cause of death from forensics and maybe something from Sutherland's house, but not much more than that. It had been a slow start to the day, a dark, cold December morning that threatened snow later, and the team had dribbled in, attending to the business of coffee, breakfast and nicotine, before settling down at their desks. The conversation was concerned only with Christmas, shifts and holiday plans. The air had not crackled with energy nor expectation, and Grayson, surveying his team sprawled out in front of him in a drab room already full of cigarette smoke, had prepared himself for a long, dull trudge through this case.

"And what about the scalpel?"

Brooks smirked, noticing that all of the team had begun to lean forward a little, their interest piqued by his first contribution.

"Well, that's interesting, guv."

"Interesting?" Grayson interrupted. "I'll be the judge of that, Clive. Go on, interest us."

"The scalpel didn't penetrate the skull. It was inserted through the scalp down the top of the head, so it would stand up straight when the body was horizontal in the fridge. It wouldn't have been able to go through the bone, without a lot of force, and even then, the blade would probably have broken. According to Arkwright."

"So it was put there for show then?" Paula Marsh leant forward as she spoke.

"To make us think… well, what, exactly?"

"That the murder was the work of a weirdo, who was out for some kind of revenge." Jacko delivered the explanation as if Paula was a particularly dim child.

She persisted. "But does that suggest some planning? Or someone who would have a scalpel to hand?"

"This is a hospital. Presumably, there's a lot of them about. Scalpels."

Underneath her calm exterior, Paula seethed.

Grayson intervened before the spat took root. "Would Sutherland routinely carry one? Seems unlikely outside of the theatre."

"Ah, I checked that, guv," said Brooks. "Apparently, it was a little superstition of his. He always had that particular one with him in his white coat. And the only prints on it are his."

"Murdered with his own scalpel, eh? Or made to look like that at any rate."

"But why bother? Was it a spur of the moment thing? Risky if it was. Would have taken some time to do it. And why put the body in the fridge? There are bodies taken down there every day more or less. It's not as if it was hiding the body, is it?"

Grayson paused again, frowning.

"What about the prints in the morgue? Have they come back yet?"

Brooks continued. "Yes, guv. There are prints all over it, obviously, but nothing on the trolley or the body. The two porters..." He glanced down at his notebook. "Yeah, Jewell and Simpson. Their prints are all over the fridge door and the door to the mortuary, as you'd expect."

"We need to talk to those two again. Jacko?"

"They've just finished a night shift and they're not back on until Sunday."

"Get their addresses from personnel and pay 'em a visit. And anything on the weirdo, Simpson, yet?"

"I'm going to follow that up straight after briefing, guv."

"Good. Paula, New Walk Terrace? Anything?"

"Yeah, I went round. There were a couple of nurses there."

Grayson raised his eyebrows.

"A couple of nurses? What, like on tap? Just in case?"

"One of 'em lives there, guv. Lodger. The other was round for a few drinks. Both work here." She looked down at her notebook. "Both young, both blonde, both pretty," she said.

Jacko looked at the other two men. "Let's not be nasty about pretty, blonde young women. They're our favourite kind, eh guv?"

"That's enough, Jacko. This is a murder inquiry," Grayson barked back. He was going to have to do something about those two. Already, he was tired, walking the line between feminism and team building. It was a struggle he couldn't win, so he'd best just be straight and slap down each of them in turn. And he didn't have time to waste in managing the internal mechanisms of his team.

"They didn't seem too cut up about Sutherland's death, guv," Paula continued.

"Surprised?"

"Oh yeah, it was news to them, but that's about all. Apparently, there's been a stream of different lodgers there"

"Get a list and check them out. Any bad feeling, any grudges, that sort of thing. Why have so many of them left? Was it rent in kind? What we've heard so far about Sutherland from the hospital is that he had a reputation for abusing his position as far as female staff are concerned. A few half-hearted complaints, investigated and dismissed, but the hospital might be a bit lax with the senior members of staff. They wouldn't be the first."

"Senior male members of staff, sir," said Paula, her eyes flicking towards Jacko.

"Usually, DC Marsh, usually. But not always. Let's keep an open mind, eh?" Grayson replied.

"Some women are like that, eh guv? Despite what Queen Victoria thought." Jacko smirked.

Paula set her jaw, her lips in a thin, straight line. "Something else, sir."

"Well, out with it, Paula."

"I had a chance for a little nosey around, sir. In his bedroom. In the bedside table, there was a pile of drug paraphernalia: syringes, wraps, mirrors. Absolutely ties in with the forensics. The other one said she would stay, didn't want her mate to be there on her own, after the news."

Grayson nodded. "Great work, Paula. Well done. Let's get back round there today, with a full forensic team. And we need the names of the two women; we'll interview them formally today as well. What about next of kin, Jacko?"

"Very few of them, from what we can see. Mother died about twenty years ago, but they were divorced by then. Father lives in South London. Beckenham. He's about seventy-five, but fit as a fiddle, apparently. He's coming up on the train. Be here at lunchtime. We'll have someone at the station to meet him."

Brooks snorted. "VIP treatment."

"He might be fit as a fiddle, Clive, but he's an old guy who's lost his only son. I think we can run to picking him up from the station. Any siblings?" Grayson was keen to cut to the chase and establish the facts.

"No, only child. Was a younger sister, but she died when she was a kid."

"OK, thanks Reg, good work," said Grayson. He turned back to DS Brooks. "So, Clive. What did you find out from his colleagues here?"

"Pretty much ties in with what Paula was saying. I've got a few more people to talk to, but there's a clear picture emerging that he wasn't very popular, especially with women. Some of his colleagues had a grudging respect for him, but that seemed more to do with a bit of jealousy and admiration for his womanising, shall we say."

Paula sighed heavily. "Despite the fact that all the women we've talked to despised him. Is that really what men aspire to?"

"No, it's not, Paula," Brooks replied. "To be honest, it doesn't really make sense. Doesn't ring true. We need to talk to them again."

"Do that today, Clive," said Grayson. "Any clearer picture of time of death?"

"Yeah," Jacko replied. "I spoke to Dr Williams earlier. His report has just come through. After the PM, he revised the time of death to a window between 11 p.m. and 1 a.m."

"1 a.m. the absolute latest?"

"You know what Williams is like. He doesn't understand 'absolute', only percentages. But he was as definite as he ever is."

"So, one thing is crystal clear," Grayson pronounced with a grim smile.

"One thing? Better than usual then. What is it?"

"We need to talk to that young doctor again. Dr Fulton."

17

By the time Johnny woke, it was already early afternoon. He stretched and checked the clock. 1 p.m. There was a brief moment of panic, until he remembered that he didn't have to go to work for two days. He snuggled back down under the duvet and luxuriated in the warmth and the prospect of free time in front of him. Normally, in this situation, he would have fallen back to sleep for another couple of hours, but his mind was ticking, churning over thoughts about the party, about Sutherland, and about Juliet.

Their chat in her room earlier had worked out perfectly. The conversation felt effortless. He had invited her to the party, and she seemed excited to come along. They had chewed over what they knew about the murder, in particular, her recognition of Hutchinson from the hospital pharmacy. She seemed to really like him. She had wanted to know about him and his family and where he was from and all of that stuff. Afterwards, Johnny had been worried that maybe he hadn't asked enough questions about her, but when he had tried, she had stuck with some basic facts before declaring herself shattered and in need of sleep. Before he knew it, he had found himself in the corridor walking to the bike sheds, despatched with a friendly kiss and a see you later.

Reluctantly, he dragged his attention away from Juliet, back to the here and now. He poked his head outside of the duvet and shivered as he registered the reality of a freezing winter's day in a largely unheated house. Plumes of breath rose above the duvet as he surveyed the room. His clothes were where they had been scattered after the night shift, and the chill in the air was accentuated by the strange, bleached light in the room. That could only mean one thing. He dragged the duvet with him as he went to the window and opened the curtains a crack.

He had to narrow his eyes as the bright whiteness of the outside world flooded his gloomy room. His eyes gradually became accustomed to the light, and his spirits soared, instinctively, as he took in the sight. Snow. The usual grimy street scene, with its miscellaneous parked cars, dustbins and grey, mean, skinny trees, was gone, hidden under a brilliant-white covering of snow. And this wasn't a disappointing, thin dusting, already turning to slush. It was bona fide, four inches of plump, crisp, creaking snow.

He gritted his teeth, abandoned the duvet and raced to put on his clothes, before thundering down to the kitchen. If anything, the corridors of the house were even colder than his room.

He burst into the room, teeth chattering. Four faces turned to see his entrance.

"Christ, it's cold!" he exclaimed, and he hurried further into the room, shutting the door tight behind him.

The four were sitting around the kitchen table that was covered in the debris of domestic life: plates and cups, jars of Marmite, honey and jam, an industrial wedge of cheddar and a chipped teapot.

"Shit, you're early. Didn't expect to see you before teatime," said Jaggers, who was in mid-roll of a cigarette. He was slightly overweight, with dark, curly hair, a beige-green flak jacket and a huge pair of Doc Martens boots that were prominently on display as he sat with his feet up on the adjacent chair.

"Couldn't sleep," said Johnny as he rummaged around on the table for something to eat.

"Too excited for Christmas?" asked Helen.

"Funny. Excited about the snow, at any rate. That must have all come down while I was in bed. It was only just starting when I arrived this morning."

"Hey," said Jaggers, a gleam in his eye, "we should go sledging in the park. Brilliant."

"Sledging? The park's as flat as a pancake, Jaggers. The laws of physics do apply, you know," said Kate. She was sitting with her legs, encased in jeans and slipper socks, draped over Mark's legs on the chair next to her. Mark, with his John Lennon glasses and stubbled chin, was still immersed in *The Guardian* sports pages, and had barely noticed Johnny's entrance.

"Well, snowballing at least," said Jaggers, looking round the table.

There was no response to the suggestion.

"Jesus, man, you lot are no fun. When was the last time it snowed? Real, proper snow, guys. Come on. Hey, Mark? What do you say?"

Mark looked up from the paper absentmindedly. "Huh?"

"Snowballing, Mark. It's proper Charles Dickens out there."

"Too much to do, Jaggers. We've got to get ready for the party tonight, remember," said Mark.

"Like what?" asked Jaggers scornfully. He nodded at the side of the kitchen. There were cases of wine piled up next to the fridge. "We've got the drink, and we've made the tapes; that's all we need worry about."

"I know this is rather bourgeois for you, Mr Marxism, but the house is still a tip," said Helen. "We're going to have to clean. And tart up some of the Christmas decorations as well."

Jaggers raised his hands. "I can go with cleaning. I'll even help. But Christmas decorations are a bridge too far."

"Even ironic ones?"

"Especially ironic ones. I want nothing to do with it; they're a capitalist plot to—"

Jaggers got no further with his analysis of the opium of the people. There was a sudden outburst from Mark. He sat up holding *The Guardian*.

"Shit. Look at this. There's another one."

He spread the paper flat on the table in front of them and read the headline. "Latest Yorkshire Ripper victim: university student, aged twenty."

All of the oxygen was sucked out of the room. Their conversation about the Christmas party seemed to belong to a different era, one that left them feeling unfairly ashamed for indulging in escapist pleasure.

"Where was it?" asked Kate.

"Leeds. Yesterday," said Mark.

They all exchanged looks.

"Leeds? Fuck."

No one said it, but they were all thinking it. A student, brutally attacked and murdered less than twenty miles away: it all seemed far too close to them and their world. They could have their party that night, and then wake up the next morning with a hangover, before going home for Christmas with their parents. They would be a little bored at home, a little on their best behaviour, but at least Kate and Helen would be safe. And then they would have to come back to their own lives in the real world of non-Christmas, where the streets of York were cold, wet, and dangerous, and where women could not walk on their own after dark.

*

There had been no further talk of snowballing. They had lost themselves in cleaning and cooking, activities that absorbed them and produced something tangible at the end: a clean kitchen floor, a hall covered with holly and tinsel, a tray of mince pies. By the time dusk began to gather, on what was the shortest day of the year, their collective effort started to falter, and the group splintered. Each one of them followed an individual path: Johnny retreated to his room, treating himself to the gas heater and his records, lying on his bed as *London Calling* ripped from the stereo. Mark was in Kate's room reading, while she was knitting and listening to the radio. Jaggers had stripped down his bike in the hall, and having cleaned and oiled each part, was now putting the whole thing back together again. Helen sat at the kitchen table with a pile of oranges and cloves, a chopping board and large, glass bowl. A recipe book was propped open in front of her. There was an air, underlined by the gathering darkness and glinting fairy lights and tinsel, hanging over the whole house, of calmness, of quiet reflection, of unspoken appreciation, of domesticity.

It was broken by a hammering on the front door, insistent and demanding. They all heard it, except for Johnny at the top of the house, cocooned by The Clash. Jaggers put down the front wheel of his bike, wiped his hands on an oily rag, and made his way to the door, navigating the debris his efforts had produced. He opened it and there on the doorstep were two people, in their twenties or thirties, he reckoned. A man who was very well groomed in a smart suit and tie and overcoat, and a woman, younger probably. The man held something out in front of him and smiled pleasantly at Jaggers.

"I'm looking for a Mr Jewell. John Jewell. Is he in?"

Jaggers looked a little puzzled. For a second, he had a feeling of dread, thinking that they had been visited by Jehovah's Witnesses. "Johnny? Yeah, Johnny's here." He frowned, taking in the two visitors again. "What's it all about?"

"Police, sir. DS Brooks, and this is DC Marsh. We need to speak to Mr Jewell, sir. Can we come in?"

"Police?" Jaggers' confusion thickened. "Sorry, why do you want Johnny?"

The man's smile returned. "If we could just come in and speak to Mr Jewell, please sir."

Jaggers met the smile with a studied, neutral expression. "I'll just go and get him. If you wouldn't mind waiting here, I'll only be a sec."

It wasn't a question that expected an answer. He shut the door in their face, turned and ran up the stairs, two steps at a time, until he arrived at the top floor outside Johnny's room. *London Calling* was deafening at that range and he didn't bother to shout through 'The Guns of Brixton'. Instead, he battered at the door and opened it at the same time.

"Police, Johnny. For you. Downstairs."

Johnny sat bolt upright, reached across to the stereo and turned it right down, having caught one of Jaggers' words.

"Police? On the phone?"

"No, you muppet, they're here. They wanna talk to you. Hurry up, I've left them freezing their bollocks off outside."

Johnny leaped off the bed and brushed himself down.

"Thanks, Jaggers, that'll have put 'em in a good mood."

He dashed past and thundered down the stairs.

Jaggers shouted after him, "You've got to let these bastards know who's boss."

As he continued headlong down the stairs, Johnny muttered, "They know who's boss, Jaggers, and it's definitely not us."

He opened the door and flashed an apologetic smile at Brooks and Marsh, who were stamping their feet in the snow on the doorstep, with frayed, thin smiles.

"Sorry, bit of a misunderstanding. Is this about the stuff at the hospital?"

DS Brooks was blankly neutral. “Mr Jewell? Yes, it is, sir. If we could just come in?”

“Of course. Sorry. Come in, come in.”

Johnny felt that there must be a middle way between Jaggers’ class war and his own fawning obsequiousness when dealing with the police, and he cursed himself for failing so abjectly to achieve it. He held open the door and welcomed the two officers inside. They squeezed past him, eyes laser-like as they went down the corridor towards the kitchen. Johnny closed the door behind them, and with a sinking feeling, followed them into the heart of the house.

18

Over at the nurses' home, snow had begun to fall again from the darkening sky. Grayson looked back from the narrow window of charcoal and white, and turned his attention to Juliet Fulton, who was perched on the corner of her bed. The glare of the overhead light flooded the room, in contrast to the gloom outside, and emphasised the spartan pokiness of her accommodation.

"So you can see, Dr Fulton, we've got a bit of a problem, now we've refined the time of death. According to what you told us last time, you were with Sutherland barely minutes before he was killed."

She smiled sweetly at him. "Well, not exactly, Inspector. That's not really how it works, as I'm sure you know. He could just as easily have been killed forty-five minutes after he left me, couldn't he? And that might be a bit of a creepy thing to think about, but it's not suspicious."

Grayson returned her smile. She was a cool customer, no doubt about that. A little bit arrogant, a little bit too sure of herself, but that wasn't a crime, it was just annoying. And, even more annoying, she was right.

"Tell me again what was going on when you saw him."

"He was the consultant on duty, and I'm just a junior, so part of his job is to be available if I need some advice. Like a second opinion."

"And had you come across him earlier on the shift?"

"Just once. It had been quite a quiet night. He helped me early on with a patient who had been in theatre earlier in the day. And then round about midnight, I bleeped him to have a look at an old boy I'd examined. Suspected heart attack, but he'd been stabilised and seemed to be responding well. It was a bit tricky because he was also being treated for dementia and his behaviour was a bit erratic. Sutherland came and dealt with that and then he left about half-twelve. That was it. Check it with Gloria. She was there."

"Gloria?"

"Gloria Simpson. Senior nurse on duty."

"And how did he seem to you?"

"What do you mean? He was the same as normal."

"I didn't know him, Dr Fulton. What was normal for him?"

She hesitated before finally giving Grayson what he wanted. "I'm new here, Chief Inspector, but I'd been warned about him. He was a flirt. And a bit of a bully. I'd seen him earlier treating one of the nurses like dirt. He'd already asked me out, and the second time, he was a bit of a groper." She shuddered. "Urgh. Vile."

"Are you saying he assaulted you, Dr Fulton?"

"No. I mean, yes. Well, sort of. Nobody else would call it assault. It would just be dismissed as a bit of fun. Anyway, I kept the patient firmly between him and me, and in the end, he gave up. He said he'd see me later. More like a threat than a farewell, if you know what I mean. And then he left."

"Where did he go?"

"Don't know. I imagine he went to the consultants' common room. They hang out there when they're on call, try and get some sleep if it's quiet."

Grayson thought for a moment and let a silence grow as he took in the doctor and her room. He'd already clocked the badges: *reclaim the night*, and, *a woman needs a man like a fish needs a bicycle*. That last one made him smile, despite himself. He could imagine Lisa quoting that one. Fulton's clothes were young and alternative, but then some of his younger staff off duty would never be mistaken for police officers, and he was experienced enough to know that people were endlessly unpredictable and more than the sum of their accoutrements. Even so, he made a mental note. Might be worth running a check on her, just to see whether anything came up.

And then her room. There was just nothing there, as if she was expecting to be gone in a week or two.

"How long have you lived here, Dr Fulton?"

She frowned, as if the question was unexpected. "Oh, about a month, I think. Why? Is that important?"

"Well, it's not the kind of place I'd expect a doctor to be. It's a bit basic. And you don't seem to have made your mark on it, if you don't mind me saying so."

She laughed. "No, not very girly of me, sorry."

She noticed the thin, straight line of his mouth didn't flicker at all.

"Like I said, I've just moved here. Transferred from Leeds General. I'm looking for somewhere else more permanent."

Grayson fixed her with a raking stare and let a moment of silence grow between them. Fulton held his eye with an air of icy calm. He flicked open his notebook, and made a note: *Check with Gloria Simpson.* He looked at her again, smiling, and added, *Beef burgers, chips, peas.* But she didn't know that. Keep her guessing for now, and at the very least, he'd manage to bring home the right stuff for tea tonight.

*

The snow was thicker by the time Brooks and Marsh trudged back to their car, and the darkness had brought with it an edge of frost to the night air.

"So what do you think, Paula?" Brooks asked, looking back at the yellow lights of Johnny's house.

"Well, on one level, they're just a bunch of typical student wasters getting ready for a Christmas party. Harmless enough. And Jewell seems like a nice kid. Nicer than the first guy. He was a bit of an arse."

"He might have been nice, but he wasn't telling us everything, I'm pretty sure of that. He was on the verge of telling us something, but then thought better of it."

"Did you clock the smell?"

"Student house?"

"Weed. Stank of it."

"Same thing, surely."

"Funny. Not all students are dope heads, you know."

Brooks thought for a moment. "Might be worth another look, though. Have a word with the lads in the Drug Squad. Mount a little raid tonight. What do you think?"

Paula shook her head. "Come on, Clive, we've got more pressing things to deal with than busting a few lefty dopeheads."

"But they don't know that. Put the fear of God into 'em. I'm sure that Jewell lad will spill the beans if he thinks we're going to do him for possession." He tossed the keys to Marsh. "You drive, Paula. I've got things to think about."

"Oh yeah," she scoffed, opening the car. "Like what?"

"Like what to wear for the party. Come on, let's get back to the hospital. We need to talk to the boss."

19

Johnny glanced down at his watch. Ten-fifteen, and The Acorn was doing its job, gently oiling its clientele before ejecting them back onto the streets at last orders. There they would join the rest of the drunken punters who created the undertow of violence that seemed to permeate the streets of central York every Thursday, Friday and Saturday night, regardless of the weather. Thursday was payday, and the brown envelopes fuelled the copious flow of drink for a few days before they were empty and the drinkers were forced indoors in front of the telly until Thursday came round again. Tonight, the weather was bleak. The snow had stopped a few hours earlier to be replaced by the beginning of a hard freeze, but it would take more than that to dampen the spirits of York's drinkers. It was the last Friday before Christmas, so the usual suspects had been joined by work socials and office parties. It was hard to judge whether this would make the streets more or less toxic than usual, but whichever way it panned out, Johnny was grateful he wasn't one of the porters dealing with the aftermath on tonight's night shift.

That, however, wasn't the thing that preoccupied him. He looked around. His friends had taken over one end of the pub: tables and standing room. The invites had made it clear that the party would start at about eleven at their house, but that everyone was invited to The Acorn, a little way down Micklegate, from about eight-thirty, just to get things going. The Acorn was taking its festive responsibilities seriously. The pub was liberally festooned with glitter and tinsel, but their Christmas tree was underwhelming, a tiny artificial version that stood on the end of the bar. Stan, the landlord, had calculated that this created more space for drinkers to stand and more drinkers meant more profit. The hubbub of conversation vied with a relentless soundtrack of Christmas singles, and the queue at the bar was two or three deep in places.

On the face of it, everything was going well, but Johnny was uneasy. He was waiting for two people in particular to turn up, and he couldn't settle until they did. Juliet and Gordon. His order finally arrived on a round tin tray, and he held it high as he turned away and forced his way through the crush towards the corner table where his house mates were holding court. There was a certain prosaic straightforwardness about his tray of drinks: five pints of Sam Smiths, with a regulation quarter inch of spillage slopping around in the bottom. It was a pleasing contrast to the snowballs, gin and tonics and port and lemons of the Christmas revellers.

He pushed his way through the crush to the table, where his housemates were anxiously staring at their empty glasses. He deposited the tray on the table and sank into his chair.

"At bloody last. Did you go to The Grapes for these? There's a bar over there, you know." Jaggers had seized his pint before he had finished the sentence. The others followed suit.

"It's chocka, man. You're lucky I wasn't longer," Johnny protested.

"Very lucky." Helen smiled sweetly at him. "We really missed you when you were gone."

She patted his thigh and left her hand resting on his leg while taking a sip of her pint. The others sniggered. Johnny thought about a witty reply but accepted defeat gracefully. Helen always had a way of taking the mick that was only just on the right side of belittling, and he was often left wondering what, exactly he had done to deserve her scorn. The barbs were delivered affectionately enough and she always moved on quickly, but for Johnny, the sting lingered rather longer than it should have.

"So, I reckon we've got time for this and another before we have to get back," said Jaggers. He gestured around the pub vaguely. "There's a lot of people here. It's all building up nicely."

Mark took in the crush of people Jaggers had waved towards.

"We even know some of them, as well. That might help the party atmosphere."

Jaggers frowned, sucking on his roll-up. "What do you mean? Just about everyone's here who we invited."

"They're not the problem. I reckon that apart from the Radio 2 listeners enjoying their one night out of the year, there's about twenty lads on the lash in here, all looking for somewhere to move on to. And they're not so far gone to have missed out that there's a party at the top of Micklegate. These guys can smell a bit of after-hours action a mile off. There'll be a queue following us up the hill at closing time."

Through clouds of smoke, Jaggers looked afresh at the drinkers on the other side of the room.

"You might be right. And they could be trouble."

He ground the damp end of his roll-up in the ashtray.

"Some nice-looking girls with 'em, though. As long as they bring summat to drink with 'em, they're more than welcome. It is Christmas, after all."

Mark summoned a wry smile. "You're all heart, Jaggers, you really are."

The night rolled on. The drinks flowed and so did the conversation. They even took turns to give up their seats around the table to make forays into the scrum of people in the pub whenever they spotted someone else who had turned up for the party. For the rest of the house, the Christmas holiday was really upon them now; work had finished, and the prospect of at least a week off was like lifting a lid, and they were all determined to enjoy their last day or two in York before making the trip home. They had banished the grim news from Leeds of earlier and were clinging on to a sense of togetherness and fun. All except Johnny.

In between the jokes and the drinks and the earnest conversations, he was on edge, his eyes constantly flicking towards the doors. For one thing, he hadn't finished work. So much so, he was actually working over Christmas itself, a phenomenon that Jaggers in particular couldn't seem to get his head around.

"So, you actually have to go in on Christmas Day then? How does that work?"

"Jaggers, people still get ill over Christmas. They have to be looked after, fed and watered. They're not just all dumped back on to the streets for three days and expected to get the bus home. There's people working on Christmas Day all over the country in one thing and another."

Jaggers shook his head. "And, what, then you just come home when you're finished, on your own, like? Nobody'll be in the house, you know."

He looked at Johnny with narrowed eyes, as if he were expecting him to suddenly crack and say, *Nah! Only joking, mate.*

When this did not happen, he wandered off, back into the fray, still shaking his head. Johnny watched his progress for a split second before his gaze was dragged, yet again, in the direction of the pub door. Helen plonked herself down in Jaggers' seat, only just ahead of Kate, who had been waiting patiently for an opportunity to slip back into her home group. She punched Johnny on the arm.

"Ow! Careful, Helen man, that hurt." He rubbed the top of his arm, grimacing.

"Well, you are still with us after all. We thought you'd been taken by aliens," she said.

"What are you on about?"

"I've been watching you, matey. Hardly a minute goes by without you staring at the door. You can't help yourself. Who are you expecting?"

Johnny frowned and took refuge in his pint. He was playing for time.

"Whoever it is, I wish they'd just bloody turn up and put us all out of our misery. It's been like trying to have a conversation with a goldfish."

He looked down again before finally deciding to take the plunge.

"Sorry. It's just that I've got myself in a bit of a situation. You know, the thing at work."

Helen sat forward, alert. "The murder, you mean. You make it sound like an HR issue."

He laughed, but not as if he meant it. "That's how weird it is, I suppose. Yes, the murder."

"Well what is this 'situation'? You haven't done anything silly, have you?"

"Thanks for the vote of confidence."

She laid her hand on his arm again. "Johnny, stop messing about. What have you done?"

He hesitated, took a quick look at her and then stared at his pint again. "It's Dr Death."

"What about him?"

He hesitated again. Helen's patience was beginning to wear thin. She was just about to tell him to spit it out or shut the fuck up, when it all tumbled out. "I've invited him to the party. It just sort of happened. I dunno how."

She stared at him and then burst out laughing.

"Is that all? Jesus, Johnny you had me really worried for a minute there. Look, I know he's a weirdo, but it's just a party. It'll be over before you know it. Nobody'll mind that you invited a pervert with a fixation on dead bodies to the party. Might even catch on."

He shook his head. "There's more. Much more. He..." He trailed off.

Helen stood up and collected her coat and purse. "Johnny, you're doing my head in. Come on, let's go back home and be there to start it off. We can talk on the way."

Johnny mumbled agreement as he stood up and followed her, as she elbowed her way through the crush and out onto the street. Behind them, Jaggers, Mark and Kate watched them go, eyebrows raised, glances exchanged.

"Do you think anything is going on with those two?" asked Mark.

Kate shook her head. "Nothing more than usual. Helen hiding behind sarcasm and Johnny with a bag over his head. He's hopeless. If he found her naked in his room, he'd think she was looking for her washing."

Jaggers looked from one to the other, baffled.

"How come you two know all of this stuff and I don't?" he asked. "I thought they were just friends."

Kate reached over and stroked his hand. "That's because you've only ever been in a relationship with your bike, Jaggers."

His face fell and Kate was immediately struck by guilt.

"There, there, Jaggers. Don't worry, it's a very nice bike." Kate's guilt did not last long. "And speaking of long-term successful relationships, it's your round." She passed him her empty glass.

20

Johnny closed the door behind him and stepped into the lane that led to Micklegate. The cold air was a slap in the face after the cosy warmth of The Acorn, and it stopped him in his tracks.

"Jesus, it's cold."

The snow had frozen into jagged troughs underfoot and he had to pick his way carefully to catch up with Helen, who had marched further down the street. At the last moment, he slipped and fell into her arms. She grabbed hold of him while he steadied himself.

"Careful!" she exclaimed. "We've got things to talk about before you throw yourself at me."

She linked arms with him and they turned at the end of the lane to walk up the hill towards the city walls. Despite the weather, there were a lot of people on the street, in pairs and groups, all intent on getting out of the cold and into the next pub. Most were going down the hill towards the river and the town centre. The traffic in the other direction was sparse, but that would change in the next half an hour as The Acorn chucked out, sending a long line of people in search of Johnny's party.

They clung to each other as they crunched their way through the frozen snow underfoot, glad of their heavy overcoats and scarves.

"Come on then," Helen began as they settled into a rhythm of walking, "what have you done this time?"

Johnny told his tale, falteringly at first but picking up speed as Helen egged him on. By the time they reached the city walls, he had finished.

"So, basically, I've invited someone who's probably a sex offender to our party, to deal us some dope. He won't know anyone and he'll stand out like a sore thumb. He's about forty, he looks weird and is a bit smelly. The last thing I want is for him to think he's my mate. Or anybody else at the party to think that, to be honest."

Helen stopped under the ancient stones of Micklegate Bar. She took a step back and looked at Johnny as if for the first time.

"My God, Johnny, the only thing you're concerned about is that this guy is not cool enough to be seen with at our party. You're worrying about your street cred."

Johnny's face fell. "No, I'm not. Jesus, I'm not that shallow. Give me some credit."

He looked what he hoped was a mixture of hurt and insulted, but when he saw Helen's face begin to crack a hint of a smile, he couldn't keep it up. His own smile elbowed his serious expression from his face and they both burst out laughing.

"Alright, alright. Maybe I was a bit. But honestly, Helen, the minute you see him, you'll know what I mean."

They finally recovered their composure from the giggling fit that had overwhelmed them and started out again towards home. As they stepped out from under the city wall, away from the crowded warren of streets that made up most of the city of York, they were immediately aware of the huge, black, velvet hemisphere of the night sky above them. The sky was clear and studded with stars, though an ominous bank of clouds was piled up to the west. The snow underfoot was thicker here and they laboured slowly along the street, clouds of breath above their heads.

"The thing that you should be worried about doesn't seem to worry you at all," Helen continued.

"What's that?"

"Why did he lie, this Gordon bloke? And then, why on earth did you repeat the lie to the police when they first interviewed you? I don't get it."

"I told you, he lied because of his dealing in the hospital. He didn't have anything to do with Sutherland; he was just selling some gear while he was on his shift. That's why he disappeared for a while."

She thought for a moment, just as they turned the corner to their road.

"You know, if the police don't catch someone soon, you're going to have to tell them about this. You know that, don't you? And that's an offence, as far as I'm aware, lying to the police."

"I'm going to have to keep my fingers crossed that they do catch someone then."

They had arrived outside the house. Helen reached for Johnny's hand and took it in hers. The street was still and quiet, layered with snow. In the windows stretching down the street, fairy lights twinkled, mirroring the stars above them, set against an inky-black backdrop. The icy air gave every moment an edge of significance and this was a moment that had settled between them.

"Johnny—" she began.

"It's not just Gordon," he interrupted.

"What do you mean?"

"That girl, Juliet, the doctor I told you about. I invited her as well. I thought she'd be in the pub."

Helen let go of his hand. "Juliet?"

"Yeah, you know, the person I—"

"I know who she is, Johnny," she snapped. "I just—"

From across the street, a voice called out.

"Eh, Johnny lad. I thought you were never coming, man. I've been freezing to death out here waiting for you. No sign of a party, though. I were just about to go home."

Johnny looked up, startled. A figure came out from a side road. He was not wearing a coat and he trembled as he spoke. As he came closer, it was clear that he was wearing blue suede shoes, bootlace tie and zoot suit with hair oiled back, Elvis style. In an incongruous touch, a small, grubby canvas haversack was over his shoulder, the strap diagonally across his suit.

"Gordon. Hello. Er, we were just getting the party going now. Come on in. This is Helen. Helen, this is Gordon."

He sprang forward, his hand pointing out like a jouster's lance.

"Hello Helen, love. Very pleased to meet you."

He grabbed her hand and started pumping it before she could speak. Johnny watched this happening, not knowing quite how to make it stop. He was just about to open the door to let them all in when there was the sound of a car pulling up. They all looked in the road. A taxi had stopped, engine running and exhaust fumes billowing into the frosty air. The door swung open and a young woman with black leather biker jacket, beret and her trademark red mohair jumper glided out and paid the driver. She looked up, her face radiating warmth, style and glamour.

"Hello, Johnny. I'm not late, am I?"

Johnny felt he was drowning in a tsunami of social awkwardness and embarrassment.

"Er, Helen. This is Juliet. Juliet, Helen."

Helen looked up, her hand still held in Gordon's. She blinked in the dark, screwing her eyes against the street light on the other side of the road.

"Oh," she stammered, "what are you doing here?" Then she stopped abruptly, embarrassed. It was like saying hello to someone off the telly when you bump into them on the street and think they are a hard-to-place old friend. "Sorry, I..." Helen trailed off.

The woman facing her smiled uncertainly.

Where on earth had Helen seen her before?

21

There was a moment of silence that hung between them, and four pairs of eyes darted back and forth. It was Helen who had the skills and presence of mind to break the silence.

Helen released herself from Gordon's energetic handshaking, smiled sweetly at Juliet and said, "Hello Juliet. Welcome to the party. I'm Helen. Shall we go in?"

She turned immediately without waiting for a reply, and slipped her key in the lock. With a gentle push, it opened and she led the way inside, switching the hall light on as she did so. She did not look back, striding imperiously down the hall towards the kitchen. The others followed her, still silent, still awkward, as if they were waiting further instructions. Helen called to Johnny, at the back of the queue, "The drinks are in here. Do help yourselves; we've got just about everything. Johnny, do you want to get the music going? So people don't have to talk if they don't want to."

Her tone managed to add an extra frisson of ice to an already freezing interior.

"And maybe you could turn the heater off in the front room? It's pretty warm now, and there'll be enough bodies soon to keep that going."

Johnny ducked into the first door off the corridor, grateful for a practical task to be tackled. The room, usually a rather shabby, nondescript space in daylight, had been transformed by some artfully arranged fairy lights, hand-made decorations and the flickering gas fire, into an inviting winter grotto. The fire hissed relentlessly, the blue-orange flames casting warm, dancing shadows on the walls. Johnny bent down and turned the knob. The flames died back immediately, the hissing drained away and the room got a little darker.

Gordon had followed him in, the lights gleaming in the darkness and bouncing off his slicked-back hair.

"You got money to burn then? Wish I could afford to keep my heating on when I'm not in."

"Well, it is a special occasion. And it's not as expensive as you might think."

Johnny pointed down at the base of the gas filament. It was a ten pence in the slot affair, the rogue landlord's usual defence against impoverished tenants who would disappear before paying their final bill. This landlord had not reckoned on the ingenuity of the cash-strapped ex-students currently in residence. The bottom of the slot machine had been unscrewed, and was currently home to a single coin that was endlessly recycled.

"Bloody hell, Johnny. Not as green as you're cabbage looking, eh? Good on yer, lad." His eyes gleamed with admiration. "That means you've got a bob or two to spare when it comes to tonight's business, eh? Shall we get it out of the way, before the crowds arrive? What do you say?"

Johnny considered the situation. He had a lot of explaining to do with Helen as far as Juliet was concerned. Although he didn't really know why. Helen was always rather spiky with him, no matter what he did. He couldn't do right for doing wrong, sometimes. And Gordon, in his ridiculous outfit, was another hindrance. If he could buy some dope from him, get him alone and ask him a few more questions, well then maybe he could just abandon him and get stuck into the party. Once he'd got that out of the way, then he could find Juliet and, if all went well, make some kind of a move. It was a party, for God's sake! Plenty of opportunities to snuggle down in a dark corner with a drink and a spliff, and let intimate conversation segue into a kiss. And then, surely, one thing would lead to another.

"Johnny! Are you there? What are you smiling at, you gormless bugger?"

"Huh? Oh nothing, nothing. Sorry, miles away."

"So, business then."

A furious knocking on the front door interrupted them and the hum of conversation and laughter carried through from the street. Evidently, the party was about to kick off in earnest.

"Yeah, let's go up to my room and get it over with. The place will be heaving before too long."

"You're not going to let them in, then?" Gordon asked with a backwards glance at the door as Johnny led the way to the stairs.

"Nah, Helen will deal with that. I don't wanna get caught in the influx."

He considered that explanation enough and zipped up the stairs, two at a time, diving into his room. Gordon, wheezing, lumbered after him. Johnny, with a careful look back down the stairs, heard the hammering on the door get more insistent. He slipped back inside and closed the door behind him.

Inside, the air was iced. Johnny made his way over to the gas fire. He knelt down, turned the knob and, fumbling with the outsize matches, tried to light the hissing stream of gas. The first match broke and he scrambled for a second, scratching two or three times without success. Eventually, with a dull crump that sent a shock wave across the room, the match lit and the gas stream exploded into life.

Gordon jumped back in alarm. "Careful, Johnny lad," he said, "You won't have any eyebrows left if you carry on at that rate."

"Yeah," Johnny acknowledged, "sorry, it's a bit temperamental. You need to develop the knack. Anyway, come in, have a seat."

He gestured to an inflatable armchair in lurid-green plastic to the side of the fire. Gordon looked dubiously at it and lowered himself down into it, the plastic screeching hideously as he manoeuvred his backside into a stable position. Every movement produced a reprise of the first noise with an array of permutations: farting, scraping, screeching. Once settled, he held onto the sides as if he were in a dodgem car.

"Bloody hell, what kind of chair is this? I'll need a fucking winch to get me up out of this. I'm not as young as I was, you know."

"Stop moaning, Gordon, and start dealing. The sooner the business is done, the sooner you can sit down on a proper chair."

Johnny went across to the door and turned the key in the lock, before going back to perch on the edge of his bed. When he looked, Gordon's expression veered between concern and disbelief.

"Is that really necessary?"

"Don't worry, I'm not the mystery killer. I just don't want anyone walking in on us while you're selling me some weed, that's all."

Gordon was not convinced. "How come you've got a lock on the door anyway? You living with a bunch of criminals, or what?"

"All the rooms have got locks. Apparently, the house used to be a brothel before we moved in. Every bedroom was for a different girl. I suppose the pimp wanted to control everything and make sure nobody ran off with the takings. Dunno. Anyway, the locks are still on the doors."

Gordon looked around the room, taking everything in. A lascivious smile spread across his face as if he were imagining what the room had witnessed in the past. Everything seemed to be low and close to the floor. Gordon perched uncertainly, his backside only six inches from the carpet wobbling on the inflatable, green plastic of the chair. Johnny's bed was just a mattress, covered in an oriental patterned throw he'd sourced from a head shop on Micklegate, along with a series of other knick-knacks. The air, beginning to warm up now, was heavily scented by incense and Johnny lit a joss stick as he spoke. There was a desk by the window, and the walls, plain magnolia, were covered by bookshelves and an eclectic selection of posters: Great Art reproductions coexisted peacefully with punk and two-tone bands and calls to agitprop action.

The lighting in the room was warm and intimate. A table lamp on a bedside unit, and another on the other side of the room, carried a red bulb with a lacy throw over the metal skeleton of a shade holder. That, and the flickering light from the gas fire, cast a soft focus over everything in the room.

"This is very cosy," Gordon remarked as his eyes rapidly scanned the room. "And it's all very clean. Looks like a French tart's boudoir. Smells like one too. You on a promise tonight, you old dog?"

Johnny was mortified. The last thing he wanted was to have a ladsy chat with weirdo Gordon, as if they were mates or something. The fact was, Gordon was closer to the truth than Johnny was comfortable with. He had hoovered the carpet and changed his sheets. He'd also braved the icy reaches of the bathroom to have a bath and splash on some aftershave. Just in case.

He hesitated for a fraction too long. Before he could answer, Gordon exploded with delight.

"You are, aren't you? Bloody hell, yer jammy sod. I've read all about this. Four or five of you sharing. Lads and lasses all together. Sharing what though, eh? Must be a lot of bed hopping when these cold nights draw in, eh? Bit of comfort?"

"Jesus wept, Gordon. Control yourself, man. It's nothing like that so you can keep your sicko fantasies to yourself. We're all just friends, OK?"

Gordon held his hands up, his smile undiminished.

"Alright, alright. Have it your own way. Just making conversation."

"Let's just get on with it, shall we? Then we can go back downstairs and have another drink."

Gordon nodded and removed the canvas rucksack from around his neck. He rummaged inside it, taking out a camera so he could explore the bag more comfortably.

"Blimey, Gordon, that's a nice little camera. SLR, isn't it? Didn't know you were into photography."

Gordon continued to rummage while giving Johnny an arch look with raised eyebrows.

"There's a lot you don't know about me. I'm a man of many talents. Got my own dark room at home."

"I always wondered what was in that bag you carry at work. The lads used to joke it was specimens from theatre."

"Did they? Well, there you go. Don't take any notice of what that lot say. Shit for brains, the lot of them."

He finally found what he'd been looking for in the bag and began to bring out some small plastic bags and a set of scales.

"Now," he began, "what was it you were after?"

*

Down in the kitchen, Helen's reservoir of good manners was becoming dangerously depleted. Being left alone with Johnny's fantasy doctor while he disappeared was bad enough and it was with some relief that she had to make her excuses to answer the front door for the arrival of the first guests. But once they had piled in and coats had been stowed and drinks provided, she was once again aware that Juliet, if that was her name, knew no one and was awkwardly nursing her glass of wine standing alone in the corner with a fixed, glassy smile on her face.

Helen caught sight of her across the crowded room and stopped suddenly, as if someone had just given her a shake. There had been a glimmer of recognition outside, but in the darkness, the moment had passed. Here, illuminated by the corner light in the kitchen, there was no doubt about it. Helen had seen her before, and quite recently as well. But where? She racked her brains. The memory hovered just out of reach and wouldn't come into focus. *Best not force it,* she thought. *It'll come back to me if I ignore it.*

Instead, she looked back at her as she made her way across the kitchen. She was annoyingly beautiful and Helen had several other compelling reasons why she should just ignore her, but the fleeting shadow of vulnerability that flashed across her face when she thought no one was watching had called out to her better nature. She began to navigate a passage through the crowd, holding her own glass of wine and the rest of the bottle high as she did so. She was able to scrutinise Juliet as she came. By the time she arrived in front of her, she had taken in her outfit and appraised it. The process had done nothing for her mood. She was the coolest, most stylish person there. No wonder Johnny was so obviously smitten.

"Hi, Juliet. Sorry to abandon you. The host's duties are never done, you know."

Juliet looked up, as if startled from a daydream. "Oh, no problem. Listen, don't feel you have to look after me. I know you've probably got loads of people you want to talk to."

"No, don't worry. I don't imagine you know anyone here. Well, apart from Johnny, that is. I don't know where he's got to. He should be looking after you really." She smiled again, before adding a postscript with just the right amount of acid in it: "He's not very reliable, I'm afraid."

Juliet returned the smile. "Oh. Isn't he?"

Helen cursed herself. *Don't do that. It's not her fault. Or his. Just be normal and help the girl out.*

"No. I mean, he's lovely really, he just gets easily distracted."

There was a pause and the rising hubbub of background conversation washed in to fill it. They both shifted awkwardly.

"So," Helen began again, her voice bright and brittle, "you work with Johnny at the hospital?"

"Oh, he mentioned that, did he?"

"Yeah. He told us all about the murder. Sounds horrible."

"Yeah, must have been for him. He found the body, you know. Him and Doc... er Gordon, one of the other porters."

"He's here tonight. He was outside with you. You couldn't miss him in that outfit."

"Yeah, I saw that. I was a bit surprised. He doesn't look anything like that at work. You know, he's strictly man at C&A there. Beige acrylic cardigan as standard. And I didn't think he was a mate of Johnny's or anything."

"No, I don't think he is. I think Johnny wanted to talk to him about what's gone on at work away from everyone else."

Juliet looked puzzled momentarily then quickly rearranged her features into a more neutral expression.

"Really? I'm surprised at that. Has something else happened then?"

"No, I don't think so. I just don't think Johnny was convinced by his story."

The frown reappeared on Juliet's face.

"So have you been OK at work after all this? I mean they haven't caught anyone yet, so whoever it is is still out there. Might be someone you work with. It's really scary if you ask me."

Juliet took a sip of her wine. "I don't want to think about it. The police are all over the hospital. I'm just going to carry on working and keep my head down. It'll all be over before too long."

Helen took this as her cue to change the subject. "So", she said brightly, "Johnny was saying you haven't been in York long. You were in Leeds, weren't you?"

"Yes, that's right. Moved here about a month ago after I transferred to the district hospital to finish my training."

"What went wrong in Leeds, then?"

A ripple of annoyance flashed across Juliet's face and then disappeared.

"Wrong? Nothing went wrong."

"Oh, sorry, I just thought that…"

Helen trailed off, not knowing what to say. She knew what she wanted to say – *don't be so prickly, you icy bitch* – but she thought, on reflection, that probably wasn't her best icebreaker. And definitely not sisterly. She was just about to launch into another conversational gambit when they were spared further awkwardness. Over the noise of the music in the front room came the sound of the front door opening and a large crowd piling into the house. She looked up and there were Jaggers, Kate and Mark with a crowd of friends just in from the pub.

They clocked each other and the newcomers made their way to the kitchen to get drinks and touch base with the advance party. Jaggers was the first to make his way through the scrum. By the time he got to her, he was already holding a pint from the barrel and a lit roll-up.

"It's looking good, Hel. Good thing you and Johnny came back early." He looked around the kitchen. "Where is his lordship, by the way?"

Helen had bever been so glad to see Jaggers. She almost hugged him.

"He's upstairs with Dr Death. He'll be down in a minute."

"Dr Death? The weird guy? What's he doing here? This I have to see."

Juliet laughed out loud. "Does everybody know about him then? Is nothing secret here?"

Helen intervened before Jaggers could answer the question. "Sorry. Juliet, this is Jaggers. He lives here. Jaggers, this is Juliet. She's a doctor at the hospital."

His face blossomed as he was able to look more closely at her. He had noticed her with Helen as he came across, but confined himself to the merest flick of the eyes. Now he could stare with impunity. Helen, never surprised by men's capacity to disappoint, saw with weary familiarity another normally well-behaved example of the species roll over in the face of the heady combination of beauty, intelligence and sex appeal.

"Is she really?" said Jaggers, beaming as if this were tremendous news. "Well, I never. Tell me all about it. And let me get you another drink."

Helen, already invisible, slipped away and left them to it. That was quite enough polite duty for one night.

22

Up in Johnny's room, the deal had been concluded. A small plastic bag of grass had been exchanged for some crisp five-pound notes. Gordon counted it carefully twice, enjoying the cool smoothness of the new notes, freshly removed from Johnny's bank the day before. The smile on his face faded seconds later.

"I was expecting you to buy more than this, you know, Johnny. Hardly worth my while coming out for this."

"Sorry to disappoint, but I'm pretty sure I didn't give you that idea. I'm an occasional smoker, not a dope fiend. Anyway, I thought you were coming as much for the night out as the prospect of business."

"Aye, mebbe," Gordon conceded. "I'll have a drink or two and a nose around. There's bound to be a few people here who'd like to score. That might make it worth my while."

Johnny bristled. "I'd rather you didn't go touting for business here, if you don't mind. Do it outside if you must, but not in the house."

"What, out in the snow? It's brass monkeys out there, man."

"It's up to you. If you want to sell more, you won't feel the cold."

Gordon's face fell a little further.

"Listen, you definitely won't feel the cold if you have a little smoke first. Shall we sample the goods?"

Johnny reached for the rizlas and began to construct the chassis of a joint with the ease of a veteran, removing three papers before deftly assembling them. Gordon eyed the procedure with some distaste.

"Not for me. I just sell the stuff, that's all. I'd prefer a drink, if it's all the same to you. I'll leave the illegal drugs to you hippies. We could go downstairs and make a start on that barrel. And you could introduce me to your friends." He leant across to Johnny and patted him on the leg. He lowered his voice conspiratorially. "That lass, Helen, the one you were with outside? She's a lovely little thing, isn't she? You could maybe put in a good word for me there."

Johnny opened his mouth to speak, but he hovered over a choice between amusement, horror and indignation, and in the end could choose none. He stared at Gordon, his mouth still open as if he were about to speak. He took in the high sheen of sweat on his forehead, the rolls of fat at his neck that meant his bootlace tie was strained like a thread around a rolled joint of pork, and the faint aroma of old sweat and unwashed underpants. He made to speak and then stopped again, reminded of Gordon's reputation when it came to the inhabitants of the hospital morgue. All told, it was not a promising list of qualities in a suitor.

He closed his mouth and shook his head. Gordon looked back at him, a hopeful smile on his damp face.

"No, sorry Gordon, I don't think that's going to work."

He looked hurt. "Why not? What's wrong with me?"

Again there was a pause. Johnny finally chose compassion.

"Nothing, Gordon, nothing. It's just that she's interested in someone else. Might already be a done deal, if you know what I mean. You'd be wasting your time there."

Gordon appeared to be considering this carefully. "Her loss, obviously."

This was Johnny's attempt to finally close down the appalling vista of possibility that had opened up in front of him in a kind way. There was one more detail he had up his sleeve to clinch the deal. "Anyway," he began cheerfully, "I've got drink here. No need to go downstairs just yet, eh?"

He reached down by the side of the bed and produced two bottles of Old Brewery ale and held them up for inspection. Gordon's face lit up as he watched Johnny open the bottles and pass one with a glass over to him. He poured it, creating a considerable foamy head, and then held it up to the light, revolving it with his fingertips. Finally, he took a long, deep gulp, smacking his lips as he brought the glass down again.

"Give me that any day over your daft drugs."

Johnny took a sip of his own beer and lit the joint.

"Each to his own, Gordon. But now you've got a beer and you're sitting comfortably, we really do need to have a chat."

He breathed out a lungful of smoke that drifted around him, stained a diabolical red in the light from the side lamp. Outside the room, two floors below, the noise of the party was steadily increasing as more people piled in and the music was turned up. Some had begun to venture upstairs in search of a quiet, secluded room where they could chat and smoke a spliff or two in peace. Johnny was keen to use this moment to pump Gordon a little harder for information.

"A chat? What about?" asked Gordon disingenuously.

"Come on Gordon," Johnny sneered, "don't play dumb. You know what about. Sutherland, of course."

Gordon shifted uncomfortably in his green inflatable, which signalled his every move with a squeak or a scrape.

"We went through that on the shift earlier. I was just meeting—"

Johnny cut him off. "Yes, I know, you were just meeting with the mysterious Mr Big, your drug supplier. Or so you said. It's just a bit of a coincidence that you go missing just before Sutherland's body is found. Were you supplying stuff to him as well?"

"What?" stammered Gordon. "No, of course not. Why say that?"

"Because he was an addict. Heroin."

Gordon looked dumbfounded. He even stopped wriggling on his chair. "An addict? How the hell did you find that out? You've only been at the hospital for five minutes."

Johnny took another sip of his beer and then another toke on the joint, biding his time, watching Gordon's face intently.

"The police, actually. Remember them? You know, the boys in blue you lied to a couple of days ago."

"Have you been to see them, Johnny? What the fuck did you do that for? We talked about this at work. I thought you got it. I…"

He trailed off and looked down, shaking his head. He looked broken, but Johnny did not soften the terseness of his reply.

"They came to me. Here. Today. And I'm feeling like a fucking idiot for lying to them. I'm telling you Gordon, I'm not sure how much longer I can keep this up."

"They've been in the house? Why didn't you tell me, man? Do you think they'll come to mine?" Gordon looked around wildly as if they might still be lurking in the wardrobe.

"Probably already there, Gordon old chum."

There was a frantic screech from the inflatable chair as Gordon struggled to lever himself up out of it. His face had taken on the pallor of a raw sausage.

As suddenly as he had managed to conjure it, Johnny's sarcasm drained away. It seemed too cruel somehow.

"Gordon. Gordon, man. Sit down. It's alright, there's no need to panic. We just need to talk this through so we're clear. And you need to think about what you said to the police in the first place and what you might have to tell them now."

The change of tone seemed to work. The air had left Gordon like a sagging balloon and he sank back down into the chair. He was defeated, but that was a step in the right direction away from hysterical.

He managed to speak again. "What did they ask you? Are they onto something in particular, or are they just digging?"

Johnny took another drag on his joint before answering.

"The time of death is awkward for you. The time when you went AWOL straddles the window exactly. And the heroin thing means they are going to look closely at suppliers of drugs."

He stopped and looked pointedly at Gordon through the cloud of blue-grey smoke. Gordon seemed in a world of his own, deep in thought. Johnny wasn't even sure that he had heard what he just said. He held up his carefully constructed joint between his finger and thumb as if for inspection.

"Does anyone spring to mind?"

Even when he was trying hard to be sympathetic, Johnny found sarcasm so hard to resist.

The message finally filtered through. Gordon sat up, sending the chair into another paroxysm of screeching.

"You mean me? I've got nothing to do with heroin and that kind of serious shit. That's way above my level. I told you, an old school pal just does me a favour so I can make a bit of money on the side."

"And what about Mike Hutchinson? Where does he come into it exactly?"

Gordon looked baffled. "Hutchinson? The pharmacy guy? What's he got to do with anything?" His frown gradually blossomed into a sunrise of realisation. A halting understanding broke out on his face. “The drugs, you mean? Has he been robbing from the hospital? Fuck me, was it him supplying Sutherland?”

“You tell me, Gordon, old son.”

Gordon lapsed back into bafflement.

“Oh come on, don’t play the innocent. You’re not that dim. I saw you with him on last night’s shift. I heard you, for fuck’s sake. You’re both up to your neck in this.”

“Heard us?” Gordon was incredulous. “Heard who? What are you on about?”

“I heard you talking. In the clap clinic, you know, where you kip down. I wasn’t going to mention it, ’cos he sounded like a bit of a maniac, but you keep feeding me a load of old bullshit. We can’t go on like this, Gordon. It’s time for the truth.”

“But where were you?”

“Behind the curtain. I heard the whole thing.”

Gordon rubbed his chin as he stared into space, trying to process what he’d just heard. And then he decided. With a superhuman effort, driven by adrenaline, he leaped out of the chair and got to his feet, grabbing his shoulder bag.

“Come on Gordon, man. Admit it. You were there, weren’t you? Now what the fuck is going on?”

He’d reached the door by this time and was fiddling with the key to unlock it. He turned back to Johnny. “I’ve heard enough, I’m going. If the police are coming to my gaff, there’s stuff I need to do.”

“But Gordon—”

“No, Johnny, that’s enough,” Gordon snapped back. “If you were there, you’ll know that these people are fucking crazy. You’re supposed to be a clever lad. For fuck’s sake, start acting like it. Stay out of it and leave it to the police. If you keep asking questions, there’s no telling what they might do. To me and to you.”

He opened the door, allowing the noise of the party to burst in, adding detail to the thumping bass lines that had been rumbling through the floor into the room. At the threshold, he swung round again and fixed Johnny with a hard stare.

"Oh, and another thing. You need to get your facts right. You might have been skulking in the clap clinic, spying on me, but you've put two and two together and come up with four hundred."

Johnny looked quizzical. "What do you mean?"

"I might have been there. So might you. But I'll tell you something for certain. Bloody Mike Hutchinson wasn't."

23

Johnny slumped back down on the corner of his bed. His mind was racing. What on earth had just happened? He needed a moment or two on his own to think before he could go back downstairs. And needing to think meant no more weed. He pinched the end of the joint to save it for later and lit a Silk Cut instead. He took a long drink from his beer glass and pulled on the cigarette. As he exhaled, he could feel himself settling into a state of greater calm. Each second of expelling the smoke from his lungs eased him more securely into the present moment.

The music and chatter downstairs seemed to fade further into the background as he replayed the conversation with Dr Death. The gamble he had taken had backfired. It seemed at the time that he had been holding all the cards, and that once Gordon realised that he knew Gordon wasn't telling the complete truth, then he would just crumble and tell him everything. What a brilliant idea that had been. Instead of crumbling, Gordon had panicked, and in the end, couldn't get out of the house fast enough. All of his fantasies of a student party and chatting to that nice Helen had evaporated. The idea that the police might be on the verge of coming to see him at home seemed to completely freak him out. Presumably, he had the bulk of the stash his old school friend provided him with hidden away there somewhere. If the police found that, he'd be in big trouble. No slap on the wrist for supplying; he'd be looking at being sent down. And they would make the connection with Sutherland as well, given his addiction and the way he had died. No wonder he was panicking.

He took another drag on his cigarette. Unless there was something else in his house he didn't want anyone to find. Johnny shivered and shook his head. Given what everyone said about him, he didn't like to think too deeply about what Gordon might have ferreted away under the floorboards at home. And by the sound of it, he was also petrified of his suppliers, who didn't seem like the kind of people who would be too fussy about physical violence.

His mind drifted back to the conversation he had overheard in the clap clinic. The guy with Gordon was seriously scary. And Juliet was convinced it was Hutchinson from the pharmacy. It all made perfect sense. Until Gordon threw a bucket of cold water over that theory. What did he say? Mike Hutchinson wasn't there. It was spontaneous and credible. Johnny was sure that Gordon was telling the truth, about that at least. But then, Juliet had been so sure as well. They couldn't both be right, could they?

Juliet! He sat up with a start. He hadn't said two words to her since meeting in the street outside, and the business with Gordon had taken longer than he'd thought. Juliet had been stuck downstairs with a whole pile of people she didn't know. He wouldn't be surprised if she'd just slipped quietly away in a huff. He ground his cigarette out in the ashtray and stood up. Just before he left the room, he went over to the window, cracked the curtains and looked out into the snowbound, wintry street below. The sky was clear, and the winking stars set against the black sent a shiver through his bones.

He stared out for a moment more. Perhaps he shouldn't have smoked that joint on his own, after all. He was just about to shut the curtain and rejoin the rest of the human race down in the party below when he caught sight of two familiar figures huddled in intense conversation in the street just outside his front door. He moved closer to the pane of glass and peered down at them, trying to make out their faces. He had to stop to rub a window in the misted glass his breath had created. It was Gordon and Juliet, deep in conversation, their heated words sending plumes of vapour into the night sky. Johnny rubbed the glass again, as if what he was seeing couldn't possibly be true, that in some way, the blurred outlines could not be trusted.

They looked so incongruous together: Gordon, a middle-aged man wearing a Teddy-boy outfit, shivering with the cold, and Juliet, young, dark and glossy with beret, leather and mohair. They couldn't possibly be connected, could they? But the urgent hand that Juliet laid on Gordon's arm indicated a different story. And then, as the glass began to mist over again, he threw her hand aside and stomped off down the road, crunching his way through the frozen snow ridges. Juliet watched him go and then turned back to the front door.

Johnny stepped back from the window and let the curtain fall back into place. Now was not the time to start pondering the significance of what he'd just seen. If he sat back down again and started to ponder anything, even the colour of the walls, he'd disappear into a dope-fuelled trance and still be there staring at the walls half an hour later. No, this was the time for action. It was time to rejoin the party. He had to talk to Juliet.

24

With each step Johnny took down the stairs, he got a little closer to the real world of people and things, leaving the inside of his head, where nothing could be relied upon, further away. Outside of his room, the noise of the party – the throb of the bass, the bubble of conversation – was much louder. On the first landing, sitting on the top step, he encountered a couple he didn't recognise, interlocked in a passionate embrace. He carefully navigated a route around them, apologising for any interruption, as he went. They ignored him.

Making his way down the final staircase was like slowly lowering himself into a warm bath, as the heat from the kitchen and the accumulated crush of people in the front room outperformed any central heating system. He glanced across to the kitchen and through the mass of people, saw the condensation trickling down the black, bare windows with harsh flashes of reflected light, cold and garish. A glance the other way allowed him to see the heaving, swaying mass of dancers in the front room. He allowed himself a half-smile. At least Jaggers' tapes were going down well.

He popped his head around the corner, just to check whether Juliet was in there. The noise and heat were overwhelming. A few people were screaming at their dance partners, smiling inanely while trying to deliver chat-up lines through the wall of sound, but the funk of James Brown defeated them and they joined the rest of the crowd and lost themselves in the groove instead. Johnny was about to slip away, back into the corridor, when he noticed Jaggers in the far corner, dancing with an unselfconscious abandon, whirling his arms and legs in such a way to seriously endanger the life and limb of anyone in his orbit. This included a tiny slip of a girl whose accompanying dance resembled a sparrow quivering in the cold. Every now and then, Jaggers would lean towards her and bellow something in her ear, provoking a startled smile and an involuntary rapid eye movement as she frantically scanned the room for a means of escape. Johnny couldn't help smiling. God, Jaggers. He was scary and energetic enough at the best of times, but at a party, having ingested a skipful of drugs and alcohol, he was positively possessed.

There was a touch on his arm from behind. He turned and there was Juliet. She smiled at him and said something, but he couldn't hear it over James Brown. He bent down to her and she pulled his head towards hers and repeated her line, shouting in his ear.

"Where've you been? I've been looking all over for you."

Her lips brushed his cheek and ear and her perfume finished the job. His inclination to sarcastically suggest she hadn't been looking very hard disappeared immediately and he smiled and shrugged. He bent towards her, for another voyage through her perfume cloud, and shouted his reply, "Sorry, got stuck with Dr Death."

He was just about to suggest that they get a drink and go somewhere quieter when he noticed that, even though she had hold of his elbow, she was under the spell of James Brown, her body sinuously moving in time with the bass line. She seized upon his hesitation and propelled him further into the room, deeper into the maelstrom of dancing bodies. No conversation was called for. It was understood that something more serious, more pressing was at hand. At first, Johnny was a little taken aback, but initial doubt dissolved in the face of Juliet's utter absorption in the groove. She abandoned her leather jacket and beret, throwing them both in a crumpled heap into the corner of the room, and gave herself to the music with every sinew in her body. It was intoxicating to watch, thrilling to be near. Johnny was famed among his social circle for his love of the dance floor, but he felt himself a callow amateur in the face of this onslaught. Surprise was replaced first by admiration and then by fellowship as he felt they were both conspirators in some higher enterprise that only they were aware of. James Brown gave way to Funkadelic, provoking a squeal of delight from Juliet. She grabbed his arm, face alight with a smile, and pulled him down to her.

"This is brilliant," she shouted, aglow. Before she let go, she kissed him on the cheek and then span away, twirling in her own pirouette, before coming back to resume the bump and grind groove opposite him.

Just for a second, Johnny floated outside of his body to observe what was happening dispassionately. It made no sense. A few minutes ago, she had been engaged in something inexplicably serious with Gordon outside on the icy pavement. Now she was kissing him and dancing with a joyous sort of freedom. Who was she, really? What was… But the questions evaporated into the ether as he floated back into his own body and let himself be carried on the same ecstatic wave as her.

The dance continued for another ten minutes, more real than any amount of awkward party conversation, and then the song changed. Their eyes met, and an unspoken agreement was signalled by a mutual wide smile. She collected her beret and jacket and followed Johnny out into the hall.

It was immediately quieter there, and cooler, and there was a sense that they had both re-entered earth's atmosphere. Johnny turned to Juliet, sweat pouring down his face, dark patches forming on his shirt. She seemed untouched by her exertions on the dance floor, her dark, glossy hair impervious to sweat, her face with the faintest glow.

"We need to talk," Johnny barked at her, his voice unadjusted to the quieter environment. A few other people in the hall looked up at this interruption, smiled and looked away. He repeated it, more quietly this time. "Sorry, but we do need to talk."

She nodded. "I know. But I need to drink as well."

"Me too. Wait here. I'll go and get something and we can talk upstairs."

"Upstairs?"

"Quieter. More private. I'll just be a sec."

He turned and immediately, she called to him, "Hey, Johnny."

He swivelled. "What?"

"Cold. Something cold." She smiled at him, a dazzling, warm smile, and he was caught in the headlights of that smile, like a quivering, nervous deer. He found himself frozen, his mouth slightly open, an uncertain look on his face. And then, like a yawn, her smile was contagious and he found himself returning it.

"Cold, yeah," he said, ticking off the request with his index finger held out high in front of him. He turned again and pressed on to the kitchen, determined to get the drink and come back before he embarrassed himself any further.

25

They both perched on the bed, one at each end. It was a relief to be out of the noise and press of the party below, but the cool quiet of Johnny's room generated its own kind of pressure. Here, there was no one else to look at, no one else to speak. The silence, and the far away thump of the bass, added to the growing sense of expectation and awkwardness. Johnny took refuge in his fiddling with his cigarette, matches, and drink, averting his eyes from Juliet.

"I like your room," she said. It sounded like a scream, so intrusive was it.

Johnny looked up. "Huh?"

"Your room, it's nice."

She looked around it again, as if to double-check.

"Great stereo."

Johnny's eyes followed hers all around the room, as if it were the first time he'd been there.

"Oh, yeah. Cost a fortune, actually. Great thing about getting paid, you know?"

Silence flooded the room again. Juliet shifted on the corner of the bed and reached down for her can of lager. Johnny finally lit his cigarette. The flare of the match, the creak of the bed, the hiss of the ring pull.

"So, what were you talking to Gordon about?" Johnny's studied, casual delivery sounded like an accusation.

"Gordon? When?" Juliet's confected puzzlement sounded like a deception.

"I saw you outside. When Gordon left." For some reason, Johnny was most concerned that Juliet not be caught out in a lie, so he wanted to make it clear exactly what he knew.

She flashed a look at him. "You saw us? How come?"

He nodded towards the window. "I looked down after he stormed out. And you were down there chatting like old mates. It looked pretty intense from up here. What was that all about?"

She flushed and took another pull on the can.

"I was in the hall when he came downstairs. He looked terrible and stormed out of the house. I shouted after him, you know, I asked if he was alright but he ignored me and just kept on going. So I went out after him. That's all."

She stopped and looked at him, his face set, shrouded in blue-grey cigarette smoke.

"Why did he stop?"

"Stop?"

"Stop and talk. I watched you, remember."

She snorted. "You as well? Seems like everyone's watching me."

"What do you mean?"

"Forget it, it's nothing. Can I ponce a Silk Cut?"

"Don't change the subject."

"Look, I just went out after him and, I dunno, he must have changed his mind because he came back. I asked him what the matter was, and he said the police were going to be asking him more questions because of you."

"Me?"

"Yeah, he blamed you. Said he had to get back home before the cops got there. I grabbed him and tried to get him to say why it was your fault, but he just brushed me off and stormed away. So, I came back to find you, see if you were alright, and then we danced. Remember." Her face, which up to that point had been solemn, broke into a smile. It was like the sun coming out from behind a cloud. "It was brilliant. You're a great dancer, you know."

Johnny laughed. "Well, you… You're…" He trailed off, still smiling. "So, you came back to see if I was alright?"

She moved closer to him on the bed and laid her hand on his knee. "The thing is, Johnny, I really like you."

He stammered, "Well, I really…"

She interrupted him by laying her finger across his lips to stop him talking. Then she reached out and took the lit cigarette from his fingers, dropped it in the ashtray and pulled him towards her. Her hand found the back of his neck and she pulled him into a kiss. They dissolved into each other and the kissing spread like an oil leak, slippy and viscous and prolonged. She pulled away to look at him, her smile now a shared secret delight.

"You taste of Silk Cut and Sam Smiths."

He laughed. "Every girl's dream. Well, at least in my fantasies."

"And mine."

She pulled him back to her, but he stopped her.

"Just a sec." He got up, went over to the door and turned the key. "We don't need any more visitors," he said.

His heart was pounding against his chest as he crossed the bedroom floor again and reached for Juliet's hand. She grabbed it, pulling him down towards her on the bed, and they merged in a flurry of kisses and grabbing at buttons and zips and clothing that was unsympathetically tucked in.

They were interrupted by a variety of incongruous noises. There was a battering on the front door, a slam and a volley of raised voices from down below them. The music suddenly cut out, the thumping bass lines disappearing to be replaced by part silence, part buzz of conversation. Johnny and Juliet sat up immediately, pulling hands away from each other as they hastily rummaged with their undone clothing.

Through the mutter of conversation downstairs came a man's voice, an authoritative bellow that silenced everyone. "Stay where you are. Nobody move. This is the Drug Squad."

26

Earlier, Brooks and Marsh had shivered on the black, vinyl seats of Brooks's Ford Capri, parked away from the street lamp opposite Johnny's house on East Mount Road, but close enough to be able to watch the entrance to the street and the door to number forty-eight. The car was pillar box red, and stood out among the other beige vehicles that lined the street. They had to regularly lean forward to wipe spy holes in the mist that covered all of the windows. They were both swaddled in warm coats, and wore scarves and gloves, but this was insufficient protection against the bitter cold.

"Clive, come on. Can't we just put the engine on for a bit, to clear the windscreen? I'm nithered in here. Can't feel my toes."

"No, we bloody can't. We'd stand out like a sore thumb, lights blazing, exhaust belching fumes out. Stop moaning; we won't be much longer."

Paula scoffed. "Stand out? This is a bright bloody red, boy racer's car, parked in a snow-covered road in York. Every Tom, Dick and Harry has stopped to have a look at it when they walk past. They see us in here with the windows steamed up and they draw their own conclusions."

Clive turned and gave her a beaming smile.

"I know. Bloody marvellous this car, int' it? Best I've ever had."

"Not exactly discreet, though, is it? You know, for surveillance work and that."

"Well, Obviously, I don't usually use it for that. And this is all very unofficial."

Paula shifted in her seat. "Yes, I know it is. Are you sure we should be doing this, Clive?"

"Course we should. When we go in there, after the DS lads have put the fear of God in 'em, Jewell will be shitting himself. Whatever it is he's not telling us, we'll find out in five minutes."

"Yes, I know all of that. But what about Grayson? Have you run this past him?"

"Don't be daft. Course I haven't. He doesn't need to know owt about it. As far as he's concerned, this will be stuff we've got from our interview with Jewell earlier, right? The DS lads won't say a word. And there'll be nowt on paper, because nothing'll happen tonight in terms of arrests."

Paula frowned. "Nothing? Then why are they doing it? I know you've got a mate in there, but I thought they'd want some kind of result."

"They do. And they'll get one, but it'll be information, that's all. And they'll follow it up in January when this lot are back in town after Christmas. They'll know who's worth following up and who's not. And from what I saw in The Acorn, they won't have much. There's no serious players among this lot. Harmless, the lot of 'em."

Paula looked across at him in the driver's seat.

"Is that why you're wearing that ridiculous outfit? Blend in at a trendy party?" Her grin widened and she dissolved into a giggle.

His face fell and he looked down at his clothes: double denim, flares and a round-collared open-necked shirt, all swaddled by an enormous, dark Crombie overcoat.

"What? What's wrong with it?"

She shook her head. "You're about three years out of date. Clothes and hair. Have you not heard of punk, Clive?"

"What, safety pins and all that? No, thank you."

"You don't need safety pins, but shorter hair would have been a start."

He looked in the rear mirror, and smoothed his hair, which fell in a slight wave onto his shoulders.

"And no flares. That screams off-duty copper."

His face fell. "No flares? But what else is there?"

She patted his leg. "Never mind, Clive. It's too late now anyway. The main thing is, did you get away with it? In the pub, I mean? No one recognised you?"

"No, it was chocka. The student types getting tanked up for the party, and loads of office Christmas dos. It was wall-to-wall flares in there, I'm telling you. I blended in." He thought for a moment. "Well, with the office types at least."

"Did you get anything from your expert surveillance then?"

"Not really. I overheard a few chats about the murder, but nothing to suggest anyone knew owt about it. Just a bit of sensational gossip for most of them, over and done in five minutes. I think we can pretty much rule out Jewell."

"Rule him out? Well what the bloody hell are we freezing our bollocks off out here for then?"

"I mean rule him out of having anything to do with it. But he definitely knows something and he's holding back for some reason. And we're just about to find out what. That, DC Marsh, is why you're freezing your bollocks off. Not that you've got any, of course."

He glanced down at Paula's crotch and raised his eyebrows.

"Ooh, DS Brooks, you're such a man of the world," she retorted. "There's not much you don't know about women, eh? I'm surprised—"

"Wait a minute," Brooks interrupted. "Isn't that Simpson from the hospital?"

He leant forward and cleared the windscreen to get a better view. Paula joined him, and screwed up her eyes to try to confirm what was happening. Yellow light spilled from the open doorway of number forty-eight, accompanied by the throb of the music. A tubby, middle-aged man strode down the path to the street. He wasn't wearing a coat, just a Teddy boy suit with a bootlace tie. Over his shoulder, he had a canvas rucksack.

"Someone else freezing their bollocks off. No coat in this weather," said Paula.

"He looks like he's in a hurry, whoever he is," said Clive, as the figure started off down the street, as fast as he could, despite the pitted, frozen ruts of snow that made progress more difficult than usual.

Then a woman followed him out of the house and called after him, "Gordon."

The man turned round, saw her, and began to walk back slowly towards her.

It was then that they got their first sight of his face.

"It is him, isn't it? Simpson, I mean?"

"Yep. And that's the young doctor, isn't it? Dr Fulton."

"Bloody hell, you're right. What the hell is she doing here?"

"And him, I—"

"Shh! Listen."

The door of the house had closed again and the street was quiet. The two people were face to face opposite number forty-eight and began to talk. Brooks and Marsh strained to decipher their conversation at first, but it became easier when voices were raised and their exchange turned to confrontation.

The doctor had her hand on Simpson's arm. She spoke to him with some urgency, but they couldn't make out exactly what she had said. Simpson had no such difficulty. He wrenched his arm away from her hand.

"No! I'm not doing it."

"Gordon, I—"

"I've told you, that's the end of it. It's too risky."

With that, he turned on his heels again and crunched off down the street, clouds of frozen breath tracking his progress towards the main road.

Clive and Paula turned to face each other in the darkness of the Capri, their faces lit up only by the strangeness of what they had just witnessed. It was Clive that broke the silence.

"What the bloody hell was all that about?"

27

The question hung in the air between them for a moment.

Then Paula asked another: "Shall we go after him? Find out?"

Brooks shook his head and looked at his watch. "No, we can't do that; the squad'll be here in a while. Andy reckoned around midnight would be peak time. No, we should leave Simpson and let him stew. We know where he lives and he was due another visit anyway. We can talk to him tomorrow. It's Jewell and the girl we need to concentrate on tonight."

"I wonder whether Jewell knows about Simpson and the doc? If he doesn't, it might be good to confront him with it, eh?"

Brooks's face twisted with doubt. "Knows what? Confront him with what? We've got no idea really what we just saw."

"No," Marsh agreed, "but we know there's some kind of relationship between those two, something they've kept hidden so far."

"Relationship maybe, but it's obviously not romantic."

She glanced at him sharply. "What makes you say that?"

"Come on, he's not in her league. Nowhere near it. That's Liverpool versus York City there. It would be like you pulling me. No one would believe that."

He waited for it to sink in, watching her in the cold shadows of the car, her mouth screwing up into an ever tighter circle. Then he elbowed her in the arm and burst out laughing.

"Sorry, Paula, only joking. I know you wouldn't touch me with a barge pole because I'm not what you're looking for; that's alright."

She stiffened next to him. "What do you mean?"

"Look, I know you like girls. That's alright, that's none of my business. I like you. You're going to be a good copper, and when you loosen up a bit, you're a bit of a laugh. I just wanted to get it out of the way, that's all. So we don't have to worry about that stuff getting in the way. We need to make sure nothing gets in the way of the case, you know."

"Does everyone at the station know about this? Are people gossiping about me? Bloody hell, Clive."

"No, of course not." He hesitated. "Well, when I say no, obviously, I mean yes."

Marsh spluttered with indignation in the darkness next to him.

"Look, don't get the wrong idea. You're not the centre of the universe. It's been mentioned and then people moved on. Just forget about it; everyone else has."

"Really? Even Jacko? I'd have thought he'd be perving about nothing else. He hates me; he's made that very clear."

There was a pause.

"Or maybe it's not me he hates, maybe it's just women in general. And he's not the odd one out, Clive; he's pretty typical of men, as far as I can see."

"Come on, that's a bit harsh. Jacko's alright, he's just a bit old-fashioned, that's all. He thinks women should be at home in the kitchen and all that. You should just ignore him when he goes into one."

"And you reckon that's alright? Honestly, Clive, I'm dreading having to pair up with him on this case. You and the gaffer are alright, but Jacko really gets on my tits."

"Just let it go, Paula. Grayson's got Jacko's number and Jacko knows it. Grayson wants a result and he won't let Jacko bugger up the team by acting like a caveman." He looked down at his watch again. "We haven't got time to put the world to rights; the DS'll be here any minute. When they go in, we'll follow behind 'em. We'll give 'em five minutes to sweep up, and then I'll take Jewell and you isolate Fulton. Push her about Simpson; she should be off her guard when she knows you know something. I'll squeeze the young lad and threaten him with a conviction for possession. He won't know that's a load of bollocks. He'll be shitting himself."

"Yeah but Clive, what about—"

Brooks interrupted her as a stripe of headlights rounded the corner and pointed straight at them, the white beam slicing through the darkness. An unmarked police van crunched to a halt right in front of the Capri.

"Ey up, they're here. Come on, look sharp."

They both swung open their doors and stepped out tentatively into the snow, the icy cold sharply pressing against their faces.

"Christ," gasped Brooks, "I thought it were cold in the car. It's Baltic out here."

He stamped his feet in the rutted snow, sending diamond chips into the air. Two men jumped out of the front of the van and shuffled towards him, wary of the ice. They looked more like most of the punters who had been in The Acorn earlier, rather than policemen, but the Drug Squad ploughed a specialist furrow and were a breed apart. A few paces behind them were a couple more in uniform.

"Clive," said the first man, as he approached, "nice night for it."

He had shoulder-length, dark hair and a Zapata moustache. The trendy badges on his flak jacket sparkled in the streetlights.

"Alright Andy. This is DC Paula Marsh."

Andy and his companion both nodded curtly in her direction before Andy jerked his head towards his companion.

"Stuart Long. He works most of the raids with me."

That was all that was needed as far as introductions were concerned. Both parties were eager to get on with the job and get back somewhere warmer.

"So, do your lads know the score with this? For you guys, it's an information-gathering exercise. Nothing more than a few cautions, if at all, and a bit of a bollocking all round. As far as I can see, this lot are strictly kindergarten. Paula and I will target our people of interest individually. Alright? We don't need anything written down officially yet, except any names and addresses you might be interested in."

"It's completely off the books, Clive, don't worry."

"Thanks, Andy, I owe you for this."

Andy smiled. "That's right, Clive, you do." He turned back to his team. "Right, let's get on with it. You know the drill: no one leaves without my say-so."

He led the way to the house, ID cards at the ready, and hammered on the door before opening it and striding into the hall. Once across the threshold, his ID card held high above his head, Andy bellowed, "Stay where you are. Nobody move. This is the Drug Squad."

28

The party was very definitely over, that much was certain. After the initial shock of the police entrance, there had been a flurry of activity from a few isolated knots of party goers, settled in various spots in the house. There was a panicked scrambling as addled brains engaged in survival mode, eyes desperately scanning the boundaries of where they were sitting, and decisions were hastily made. The two toilets in the house became the focus of a sudden upsurge of interest, as all manner of contraband was smoothly flushed away to safety, into the drains. In other spots, windows were opened onto the freezing December night air, and, after a quick look to check the coast was clear, handfuls of kit were dropped into the gardens and backyards below: ripped packets of rizlas, tobacco, weed and pungent lumps of resin decorated the dazzling white surface of the ground below.

Then they waited, sucking on cigarettes, legs jiggling, and sipping drinks. One or two had tried to slip away, but found their way barred by police officers who had been stationed on the door, and they apologised, and shuffled back into the rooms they had just vacated.

At the top of the house, Johnny and Juliet brushed themselves down, disposed of the evidence and came to join the action downstairs. The silence that flooded in, in the wake of the music being cut, seemed more intrusive than the pounding soundtrack it had replaced, with the buzz of subdued conversation punctuated by the bark of the lead officer issuing orders. They arrived at the top of the first flight of stairs and looked down into the hall. Various people were being searched, seemingly randomly, by two plain-clothes officers, who were indistinguishable from most of the people at the party. One person he vaguely recognised but could not put a name to, stood at the bottom of the stairs. Halfway down the stairs, he looked up and caught Johnny's eye. A broad smile broke out on his face. Instinctively, Johnny returned the smile. There was after all, a sense of camaraderie among them all, even strangers, at being subjected to this unwanted intrusion.

"Mr Jewell. Good evening. If you could just wait there, please?"

Johnny's smile vanished as he realised who it was. DS Brooks's smile did the impossible and got bigger.

Behind him, Juliet reached for his arm. He turned and she muttered to him, "I'll just wait down here, OK?" before continuing down the stairs. As she went to step around Brooks, he reached out his hand and rested it on the top of the banister, blocking her way.

"And Dr Fulton. What a pleasant surprise. Fancy seeing you here. But don't go anywhere please, Dr Fulton. My colleague will want to talk to you."

He jerked his head along the hall. Paula flashed her a smile that hovered somewhere between professional and threatening. He removed his arm and, gesturing up the stairs, said to Johnny, "Shall we revisit your room, Mr Jewell? We had such a pleasant chat last time." Without waiting for a reply, he exerted gentle pressure on Johnny's arm and propelled him up the stairs, following one step behind him.

He'd only climbed a couple of steps when a voice called him. "DS Brooks?"

He turned to see Andy at the foot of the stairs, beckoning him down. Clive turned back to Johnny.

"You go on up. I'll be right there," he said before continuing down to Andy, who gave him a conspiratorial smile. He leant in close and lowered his voice. "Was that Juliet Fulton? The girl in the leather jacket? And jeans? Tight jeans?"

"Yeah. What about her?"

Andy rubbed his hands together. "I think I'll interview her. She was gorgeous."

Clive lowered his voice. "Fucking hell, Andy, behave yourself. I need Paula to talk to her. It's important."

Andy's face turned into a picture of innocence. "Of course it is, Clive. And Paula can talk to her, obviously. But this needs a senior man, don't you think? I might have to take her in and get her phone number. After all, I'm doing you a favour, remember. You owe me one."

Clive scowled at him. "Don't fuck this up, Andy. I mean it."

Andy watched him turn and march up the stairs to find Johnny. He smiled to himself. The world was full of opportunities for a man in uniform.

"Of course not, Clive, old pal. Of course not."

*

Gordon shivered in his thin blue suit as he picked his way along Blossom Street under a black, star-studded sky. There were fewer people and cars around now. The pubs had chucked out long ago, and those that had missed the last buses were straggling along on foot. He cursed silently. Why had he come out on a night like this without his coat? He shook his head. Vanity, that's why. His parka just did not go with his Teddy boy gear and he looked a nob when he wore the two things together. He could never quite work out what real Teddy boys used to do in the winter, other than just brave the cold but he knew that that was one of the things he did not do. Brave things. Anything. If only he had stayed at home in the warm, with his pictures and his music and his book. He should know better by now, but the idea of going to a party with girls had been too appealing. And that lad Johnny, he had seemed keen as well. Yes, he should have known better. Fucking Johnny was just like all the others, looking out for himself. All he wanted was to pump him for some information. And Johnny was clearly not convinced by his explanations about the other night. But, fucking hell, dobbing him in it with the feds. There was really no need for that.

They would definitely be round to see him, there was no doubt about that; the only question was when. Knowing his luck, they would abandon their usual idleness and come out tonight or tomorrow, so he had to get back as soon as he could to deal with stuff. He went through the list in his head, partly to take his mind off the biting cold:

Get rid of his drugs.

Store his photos somewhere else for a while. At work maybe.

Talk to H and straighten things out.

Deal with that bitch doctor.

The sooner he got back home, the better. Get out of this cold and get on with the job. But there, up ahead, the last number six bus, steaming and wheezing, pulled out from his stop and laboured towards the city walls, the warm promise of the yellow lights fading as the bus receded into the distance. Damn! He stopped dead in his tracks, watching the bus turn the corner and disappear. Then he looked around, stamping his feet and blowing on his frozen fingers as he did so, in the vain hope that another bus might be coming to rescue him. The road was empty, a line of amber street lights distinguishing it from the pavement in a dazzling white blankness. His eye was caught by an illuminated sign above head height, a little way down the street. *Holgate Cars* it said, and a blue Cortina, its engine running, belching clouds of exhaust into the air, stood invitingly below it. Gordon swivelled and looked back at the bus, now a tiny blob as it rounded the bend and disappeared from view. He reached inside his suit for his wallet and checked it. There, nestling in one of the folds were the crisp notes Johnny had handed over an hour or so earlier.

"Fuck it," he muttered and walked over to the car. A word to the driver before slipping into the back seat and slamming the door. Grateful for the warmth, he sat in the shadows of the back, and the car pulled away smoothly into the night.

*

Paula waited in the hall, watching everyone who came along in the hope of being allowed out. One by one, they were sent on their way, after a nod from the plain-clothes guys, and a stern look from uniform on the door. There were only a handful left by this stage, apart from the five that lived there, but she still hadn't spotted the doctor. She was getting increasingly worried. When Clive finished with Jewell, he'd come down expecting a report from her about her interview with the doctor. She'd look completely stupid if she had to confess that the doctor had somehow given her the slip. She frowned. Fulton had definitely not come past her, and she would have to do that to get out of the house. Unless there was another door at the back, leading out of the kitchen to a yard or something. Her heart sank. If that were the case, Fulton would be long gone by now and she would have to tell Clive she'd messed up. "You're going to be a good detective, eventually." That's what he had said earlier. She shook her head. It hadn't taken her long to ruin that reputation, had it?

She slumped into gloomy introspection, rehearsing what she would say to Clive when the shit hit the fan, but then looked up when a faint movement caught her eye. Half-hidden by the curve of the hall wall was Dr Fulton. She was stock-still, as if she had tried to sneak out and then had seen Paula still stationed by the front door.

"Dr Fulton?" asked Paula, her confidence returning by the second. "Don't be shy, Dr Fulton. You can't sneak out without me noticing, so you might as well have a chat and then you can get home. I imagine it's been quite a trying night for you. Not the wild, drug-crazed party you were evidently expecting, eh?"

Juliet returned the smile. "I think we both know that it was what you were expecting, not me. And as for sneaking out, well I think the party's over, isn't it? It's just time to go home, that's all."

Paula's smile straightened. "Not quite. Come through here. I won't keep you long."

She opened the door to the second living room off the hall and ushered her in with her eyes. She followed and closed the door. Inside the room, the main light was on, revealing the aftermath of a party that had still had a long way to run when the music stopped. Several overflowing ashtrays, half-full glasses of wine and cans of lager were placed around the room and there were balloons and tinsel, with branches of holly and greenery hung above the door and any flat surface, with fairy lights threaded through them. Under the glare of the central light, the decorations all looked a little shabby, a little silly. The magic that had flickered in the shadows of the room when dimly lit had drained away, leaving a plain stage suitable for a blunt interrogation.

"Sit down, Dr Fulton," Marsh began, indicating a woolly, brown easy chair in the corner. "Now, what brings you here tonight? I didn't know you knew Mr Jewell. When you were interviewed at the hospital, you gave the impression that you were the new girl and didn't really know anyone at the hospital."

"That's right. I've only just got to know Johnny. Er, Mr Jewell. He only invited me yesterday."

"And Mr Simpson, do you know him?"

Juliet frowned. "The porter, you mean?"

"That's right."

"No, not really. I mean, I know who he is, but that's about all. I was surprised he was here, to be honest."

"Oh, why's that?"

"Well, he's a bit old, and he looks a bit weird."

"So, you don't really know him and you've not seen him socially before?"

Juliet scoffed. "Socially? I know I'm the new girl, but I'm not that desperate."

DS Marsh smiled at this, a sympathetic, understanding smile, before moving up a level. "It's just that, it didn't really look like that when you were with him outside."

Juliet's face fell for a millisecond. "Outside?"

"That's right, Dr Fulton, outside. We saw you with Simpson outside the house before he stomped off down the road. He didn't look very happy. But then neither did you. So, let's stop playing games, shall we? There's all kinds of things we know, and you need to stop digging a hole for yourself. It's not the only lie you've told us, doctor."

Juliet shifted uncomfortably in her seat. She looked down at her lap, playing with her interlinked fingers. The self-assurance that usually marked her interviews with the police seemed to have evaporated. When she spoke, she seemed to be muttering to her knees.

"He… he tried to get me to go back to his place. Got angry when I said no. I couldn't believe it; I've barely spoken two words to him before tonight at work, and he's acting as if I'd been leading him on."

"So, he propositioned you, is that what you're saying, doctor?"

"Yes, he did. Started pawing at me. Disgusting. I hate men like that, who think they're owed it. And him in particular."

DC Marsh frowned. "You're saying he grabbed hold of you, doctor? Outside, in the street? But—"

There was a knock on the door, which opened immediately. Andy took a step into the room. "OK, DC Marsh. I'll take it from here."

"Oh, but I…" she began, but then stopped. It wasn't what she had been expecting but arguing with a more senior officer was never a good look, she decided. She stood up, folding her notebook. As she passed Andy in the doorway, she stopped and lowered her voice. "Sir, I think DS Brooks is expecting me to put certain questions to her."

Andy closed the door. He was standing very close to her. When he spoke, his voice was also low, so Paula had to move in to hear him.

"I think Clive needs you upstairs. At the top. He's with Jewell. I'll deal with this."

He held her eyes in a steady look, his mouth set in a straight line, towering over her.

She lowered her eyes, took a step backwards.

"Sir," she mumbled as she turned towards the stairs.

"Top floor," he called after her. He watched her climb the stairs, savouring the tight denim of her jeans, and his straight mouth eased into a smirk. Then he went back into the room with Dr Fulton and shut the door behind him.

*

Paula climbed up the stairs, simmering with rage. It seemed like no one took any notice of her. She made herself calm down one stair at a time and by the time she had reached the second floor, she had achieved some kind of equanimity. She was about to finish her journey up to the top floor and Johnny's room when a voice called to her. from an open doorway.

"Have you finished with Dr Fulton then?"

She turned to see one of the young women who lived in the house, standing at an open doorway.

"What?"

"Fulton. What did you make of her?"

Paula narrowed her eyes. "It's Helen, isn't it? You were here when we called earlier."

"Yeah, that's right."

"Why are you so interested in Dr Fulton?"

Helen snorted. "I wouldn't trust her as far as I could throw her."

Paula thought for a moment. Clive could wait.

"Why is that then? What's she done to you?"

"Me? Nothing, I've only just met her. It's just a feeling. I'm sure I've seen her somewhere before, and I'm sure her name's not Fulton."

"Sorry, miss, but it's not much to go on, is it, a feeling?"

"Well, she's definitely not keen on talking to you lot. She tried to sneak out a minute ago."

"I know. It was me who stopped her. Anything else?"

Helen shrugged. "No, sorry. I know it sounds a bit mad. Maybe it's just me. Just forget it."

Paula suddenly felt sorry for her. She seemed a little defeated somehow.

"No, you were right to mention it. Listen, if anything more definite comes to you, ring me. Alright?"

She handed Helen a card with her number on it and then turned and carried on up to Johnny's room. Before she knocked, she looked down at Helen on the landing. It wasn't much to go on, that was true. But Helen's instincts resonated with her own. Paula hadn't believed a word Juliet Fulton had said to her either.

29

Jaggers, Helen, Mark and Kate sat around the kitchen table under a fug of cigarette smoke and gloom. They were surrounded by the detritus of the party: half-empty bottles and glasses, a few paper plates smeared with leftovers and studded with dog ends. Under the harsh central light, the tinsel and paper chains were drained of the patina of magic they had possessed only an hour earlier. Everything seemed tainted and everyone was weary. Even the gently steaming cups of tea were more of a booby prize than a comfort. The last guests had been released fifteen minutes earlier, and most of the police had left soon after that. In the quiet that remained, they were left contemplating the reality of their evening: a drug squad raid, an enforced finish and possibly some arrests. It had not been the Christmas party they had all been looking forward to. And still they were waiting.

"How much longer are they going to be up there?" asked Jaggers, reaching for his mug of tea. He took another sip, grimaced and then slammed it down on the table. "Bugger this tea, I need a proper drink."

He leant back in his chair and filled a glass from the wooden barrel.

"I mean, are they talking to him about the murder again? What's happened since this afternoon to make them come back again?" said Kate. She looked around the table, seeking answers.

"I dunno. I think maybe he was going to buy some weed from the weirdo guy at the hospital," Helen interjected.

"You don't think he's going to get busted for that, do you?" said Jaggers, aghast. "Christ, what a terrible week he's had. Poor old Johnny."

"Funny, they didn't seem to arrest anyone at all," said Mark. "Just took down a few names and addresses, but they didn't take anyone away. They've spent much longer talking to Johnny than anyone else."

Helen suddenly stood up and started pacing around the table. "How much longer are they going to be with him?" she blurted out, her voice breaking. She turned away, dabbing her eyes.

The others exchanged glances. This was not the cool, sardonic Helen they were familiar with.

They had no chance to follow up this train of thought, because the sound of people coming down the stairs filtered through to them. With a scraping of chairs, they all got to their feet and hurried to the bottom of the stairs to see DC Marsh and DS Brooks leading Johnny down.

Helen caught sight of him partially hidden by the two leading police officers.

"Everything alright, Johnny? What's going on?"

The sight of his friends forming a welcome party squeezed a rueful smile from him.

"I'm OK, Helen. Really, just a few more questions, that's all."

DS Brooks stopped at the bottom of the stairs, his casual wear jarringly at odds with the official nature of the visit.

"Mr Jewell has just been cooperating with our enquiries. We've got everything we need. For now."

Jaggers' impatience fizzed over to boiling point.

"For now?" he exploded. "What do you mean, for now? This is harassment. Haven't you lot got anything better to do, rather than wasting money breaking up parties and arresting people just for a bit of weed? What harm does it do? Why can't you arrest some proper criminals?"

Brooks bristled. It was an argument he had heard all too frequently before and it infuriated him.

"What's your name, young man?"

"Agnew. James Agnew." Jaggers spat out the words.

"Well, Mr Agnew. The law is the law, no matter who it is. And the last time I looked, possession of cannabis was illegal. So, yes, we will go after people who break the law."

"But, officer, do you really think any harm was happening here?" asked Kate, her tone markedly more reasonable than Jaggers'.

Brooks took a deep breath and replied with the air of someone whose patience was being tried.

"We're conducting a murder inquiry, miss. It doesn't get more serious than that."

Kate shook her head. "It seems murder only matters if you're a respectable member of the community. And a man."

DC Marsh replied before Brooks could. "What do you mean by that, miss?"

"Well, you've not done much about all the women who've been butchered, have you? But I suppose prostitutes don't count for much in the eyes of the police. Or not as much as eminent surgeons."

"That's right," burst in Jaggers. "Why don't you catch the fucking Ripper, before anyone else gets killed?"

Johnny looked out from behind Brooks and Marsh at the foot of the steps.

"Jaggers," he said quietly, "this is not really helping."

Jaggers turned to him. "Come on, Johnny man, this is outrageous."

"Not now, Jaggers, eh? It's been a long night," said Helen.

Jaggers went to speak and then thought better of it and lapsed into a simmering silence.

Brooks turned to the others. "Where's Dr Fulton? Still with one of the other officers?"

"She's gone," said Helen.

It was hard to tell who was more surprised, Johnny or DC Marsh.

"Gone?" they both said simultaneously. Johnny's face betrayed a touch of hurt. Marsh's a touch of annoyance.

"Yeah, I saw her leaving with the main guy, just after I spoke to you upstairs." Helen nodded at DC Marsh.

"But he'd only just started…" Marsh began. She stopped abruptly.

"She say anything?" asked Johnny.

"Not to me. She just left with the main guy."

Brooks nodded. Marsh frowned. Johnny kept his mouth shut. If nothing else, he thought he would try to preserve some dignity, at least until he was safely on his own in his own room.

Brooks and Marsh continued to the front door. Marsh opened it and Brooks turned back to the others.

"Listen to your friends, Mr Agnew. And Mr Jewell, we'll be in touch."

The door was a black rectangle, and a chill wind knifed its way into the hall, before Brooks slammed it shut behind him. Inside, they made their way back to the kitchen in silence. Outside, Brooks and Marsh picked their way over the rutted ice back to the Capri. They clambered into the car and slammed the doors, shivering.

Brooks fired the ignition and waited for the heating to crank up. He looked across to his partner.

"What do you think?" he said.

"He was right, wasn't he?"

Brooks was blank. "Who was?"

"That lad, Jaggers. Mad, but right. We should have caught that bastard by now."

Brooks sighed. "Not about that, you daft sod. Jewell. What do you think about Jewell?"

"He's telling the truth, I reckon. He's a nice lad. His story made sense and he's shitting himself now he thinks you might tell his parents about his naughty habits. Not to mention lying in a murder inquiry. He came clean straight away."

"And Simpson?"

"He's in big trouble, I reckon. We need to bring him in. But what about Fulton? I don't get why your mate just let her walk."

"It's amazing what a pretty face can do."

Paula stared at him. "What? You mean he was chatting her up? That's outrageous."

"Look, he probably got her phone number, that's all. He might be thinking with his dick, but he's a good copper. He'll have his reasons. But we can follow all of that up tomorrow. It's late and we're both shattered. They can wait until then, I reckon."

Paula fumed silently.

Clive revved the car and the first stirrings of warm air registered in the cabin. He indicated and eased the Capri out into the street and down the road.

"I'll drop you back home."

The car steamed its way into the icy darkness down the deserted main road. As they turned the corner, Paula noticed the huddled figure of a woman with striking blonde hair, back from the main road at the entrance to an alley. Despite the freezing temperatures, she wasn't wearing a coat, and looked as if she had just come out of a sweaty club. In the wing mirror, Paula glanced back at her, to see a car pull up. The woman bent down to talk to the driver through the passenger window, then got in the car, before it drove away in the opposite direction.

"Oh and Clive," Paula said.

"Yeah?" he replied without taking his eyes off the road.

"He was definitely right, that Jaggers lad. The mouthy one. And I'm not a daft sod."

She turned away from him and pressed her forehead to the side window, rubbing away the condensation for a better view. White snow, illuminated shop fronts, ancient stones, a woman on her own, a gaggle of rowdy lads, festooned with tinsel, all slipping by as if on a conveyor belt. She breathed out, a heavy sigh, and the outside world blurred in a spreading fog.

30

Johnny turned to climb the stairs back to his room, but the others would not let him.

"Come and talk, Johnny. Tell us what happened," said Jaggers, an unusual softness to his voice.

"I'm really tired. I need to go to bed."

"Five minutes, Johnny. That's all. Come on."

He hung his head on the stairs momentarily, his front foot suspended in the air in front of him, about to scale the next step. Wearily, he submitted, and walked through the knot of his friends to the kitchen. They followed and all of them sat in their familiar positions around the table.

"So, what happened? What did they want?" asked Mark.

"They're very clever, the police," Johnny began.

Jaggers raised his eyebrows and was about to comment, but saw everyone else's glowering faces and thought better of it.

"It was all very subtle. They've got enough to charge me with possession. I mean, obviously, they haven't, 'cos I got rid of it all, but they're not really bothered about that. The main copper, Brooks, he said that they knew that I was holding something back about what happened at work on the night of the murder. My choice, he said. Tell us everything, or get a record." He laughed and shook his head. "Some choice. Anyway, I told him. All about Gordon disappearing and me lying about it and not quite knowing why. So now they've got that on me as well. Lying to the police in a murder inquiry. He almost wet himself, Brooks. He couldn't believe his luck."

"So what are they going to do now?" asked Kate.

"Dunno. I asked them, but they've got no reason to tell me. Information is a bit of a one-way street as far as the police are concerned. I reckon they'll pick up Gordon and give him the third degree. Looks bad for him, whether he did it or not."

"Bastards," muttered Jaggers. "They'll stop looking now. They've got a result that kind of makes sense, even without any evidence."

"But are they going do anything about the dope and the lying?" Helen interjected. "I'm not that worried about Dr Death, to be honest."

"Nah, I don't think so. That's small beer next to a murder charge."

"I wouldn't put it past them," snorted Jaggers.

Johnny suddenly felt bone-achingly weary. It had been a long, long day and he wanted to bury himself in his bed and escape. He stood up.

"Listen, I'm shattered. I really do need to go to bed. I'll feel more like talking about it tomorrow."

"We're off tomorrow, remember?" said Mark.

"Yeah, me too. Just as well – I'm really in no fit state to go to work."

"No, I mean we're off home. For Christmas. We'll clear up in the morning and then get a train."

"I'd forgotten all about that. Are you all going?" Johnny asked.

"Me, Mark and Jaggers are going tomorrow," said Kate. "You're Christmas Eve, aren't you, Hel?"

She nodded. "Yeah, seat's booked on the two o'clock."

Johnny took it all in. "Well, let's do a late breakfast tomorrow and a blitz on the house before you go, yeah? Goodnight."

He left the kitchen to a chorus of, "Night"s and slowly climbed the stairs to the top floor. His room was warm and welcoming after the icy cold of the stairs and corridors, the gas fire still hissing softly at one end of the room. He closed the door behind him and leant back against it and exhaled, a long, low whistle of a breath. Gathering himself, he went over to his desk under the window and sat for a moment, lit by the yellow cone of light from the anglepoise. Although he was exhausted, and wanted nothing more than to climb into his bed, he knew he wouldn't be able to go to sleep for a while. He just needed some time to process everything that had happened. He listed it, like a scribbled aide memoire: a Drug Squad raid; Dr Death – what had Gordon really been doing when he disappeared? Who was the other guy he'd overheard? If it wasn't Mike Hutchinson, who was it? And why had Juliet said so definitely that it was him?

Juliet. He glanced over at his bed. It had only been a few hours ago when they had been there together. That first kiss had been everything he had hoped for. But now? Where was she? Why had she just disappeared like that? He had been certain she'd stay and they could continue what they had finally started. Maybe she was just playing him. After all, he'd seen her outside with Gordon and her explanation was a bit thin in the cold light of day.

His train of thought was interrupted by a light knock on his door. He turned, puzzled. The tap came again, followed by a low call. "Johnny? It's me, Helen. Can I come in?"

Her voice was quiet but insistent, as if she did not want the others to hear, but neither did she want Johnny to ignore it. Instinctively, he called back, "Course. Come in. It's open."

As soon as the words left his mouth, he felt deflated. He really didn't want to see anyone just then, but he couldn't do anything about that now.

The door opened a crack and Helen put her head around it.

"Sorry, I just wanted to talk. Just for a bit."

He smiled at her. "No problem. Come in, come in."

She slipped through the gap and closed the door, before perching on the end of the bed.

"You sure you're alright? It's been a hell of a night," she started.

"Wasn't the night I'd been planning, that's for sure."

"You think the police were satisfied with what you told them? They won't come back again, will they?"

"I suppose that depends what they get out of Gordon."

"Do you think it was him? Would be ironic wouldn't it: Dr Death, a murderer?"

He laughed. "That's the point, isn't it? That nickname is a joke, a piss-take. Everyone thinks he's a bit weird, a bit pathetic. And he is, I reckon. I can't see him as a murderer." He thought for a moment. "Mind you, I didn't see him as a dealer either. That came out of the blue. So, you never know. Seems like we never really know who people are."

He looked up at that point and their eyes met. Helen held his gaze for a fraction too long and he looked down.

"Like what's her name, you mean? Juliet? Were you expecting her to hang around?" she asked the top of his head.

A wry smile appeared on his face.

"She was giving me some pretty clear signs that she likes me. So yeah, I was kind of expecting her to be here. Maybe the thing with the police freaked her out. I dunno."

Helen bent down and picked up a pen that was at her feet. She twirled it between her fingers.

"What do you know about her? Really."

"You don't like her, do you?"

"What I think doesn't matter, does it? It's what you think that counts."

He was silent.

"But no, I don't like her much. I'm sure I've seen her somewhere before. And she was a bit frosty with me. And..."

"What? You got something to say?"

She shook her head. "No, not really. Except that I'm glad you told the police about Dr Death."

"Really? Why?"

She looked at him again, his face framed in lamplight and the glow from the gas fire.

"Because it means that at least you're safe. The police know, so now no one will want to shut you up and stop you talking. It's too late for that. When are you back at work?"

"Day after tomorrow."

She stood up, the pen still twirling between her fingers.

"OK, I'm going to bed. I'll let you get some sleep."

She stepped towards him and bent down. She put her hand on his neck and kissed him lightly on the cheek. He caught a shadow of perfume mingled with cigarettes, alcohol and his own scent.

"Goodnight," she said. "See you in the morning."

He stared after her, strangely disturbed, but not knowing why.

"Night," he called, just as she closed the door behind her.

The room felt her absence. There was darkness in the corners that crowded in on the yellow light from the desk lamp, and the reddish-blue light from the fire. There was a heavy silence in the room, underscored by the incessant hissing of the gas. He sat at his desk, turning things over in his mind.

It was some time before he turned the light off and went to bed. In the darkness, it was even longer before he finally fell asleep.

31

Juliet closed the door of her room, taking care to ease the latch into place without a click, and leant back against it, her head held back, her eyes closed. She exhaled without a whisper, a long, drawn-out expulsion of air and tension from her body. At the end of the breath, she opened her eyes. The clock by her bed shone out in the darkness. 2 a.m. There might still be the odd night owl among the nurses who was still up and she did not want to attract any attention. The last thing she needed after the night she had just had was a little tap on the door from a concerned neighbour. She walked across to the window and pulled the curtains across tightly before turning on the bedside lamp and easing herself down onto the mattress.

She sat forward and put her head into her hands. *Oh, Johnny, Johnny, Johnny.* She had not been expecting that at all and she had come so close to ruining everything. It had started by chance and then he had accidentally led her to Mike Hutchinson, but deep down, she had known that was only half the story. A craving for comfort, for passion, for escape, all of those things so often denied. She shook her head in her hands, still bowed in front of her. What on earth was she going to do now?

*

It had taken Gordon a couple of hours to systematically go through the house, bagging up stuff that couldn't be easily explained away. Some of it he could stash away in the hospital until the heat had gone out of the police investigation, but there were things that he had to get rid of straight away. He stamped his feet in the snow that covered his back garden. His toes were almost completely numb now, the combined effect of melted snow and freezing temperatures for over half an hour or so. The garden barely deserved the name. It was a narrow, rectangular strip, one of several in a terrace, that led down to a mirror image of gardens from the street behind. Other people in the street had turned their plots into lush, green oases, but Gordon had left his a blank canvas. The whole space was a rectangle of lawn, with a small shed at the end where he stowed the lawn mower. There were no shrubs, no trees, no plants. The lawn fringed a patio area outside a French window from the back room. He went outside three times a year to mow the lawn and that was it.

When he had opened the windows and stepped out onto the patio, he had had that sense of moving onto unfamiliar ground. Accompanying this was the sense that he was being closely observed by his neighbours from all sides, each of them baffled by this unusual appearance in the garden. It would have been unusual in high summer, but here in the dead, short days of late December, when light was always no more than a smudge of transient grey, it was positively shocking.

Gordon kept his head down for the duration of his visit to the garden, eager to prevent any kind of eye contact that would confirm his paranoid certainty that he was being scrutinised. He constructed his bonfire quickly, building it carefully with kindling wood, bought from the garage round the corner, scrunched-up sheets from the *York Evening Press*, and a couple of fire lighters. The last thing he wanted was a damp squib, and the one thing he remembered from his childhood, apart from casual neglect and belittlement, was how difficult it was to construct a coal fire when your mother was relying on you to do it successfully.

He reached into the bin liner next to him and arranged on top of the pile a handful of black and white photographs. A flickering match was held to the edges of the crumpled newspaper until the flames began to lick around the ball that made up the base of the pile.

He stopped to admire his work briefly, before reaching back into the bin liner for more fuel. The prints curled and blistered, bending and arching as if writhing in agony. Each handful chipped away at his sense of wellbeing. He hated destroying these prints. They had been for his eyes only and were things of beauty, but he had no choice. In the eyes of the world, these pictures were proof positive of his depravity. No one would understand, and the police would seize on them with something like joy, so he continued to feed the fire until the bin liner was empty, a flapping, black shroud against the snow, and tears rolled down his cheeks, glittering in the frozen air.

32

There was something about working on a Saturday during a case that Grayson enjoyed. The police station was always quieter, and so was the hospital. Fewer outpatient clinics, he supposed. He liked the idea of being able to go about his business without being observed.

"Alright, morning everyone. It's Saturday, and we've all got things we'd rather be doing, so let's make a start, shall we? Sooner we're done, the better."

The buzz of conversation had subsided as the team hauled themselves into work mode, looking up at Grayson with some sense of anticipation.

"We'll start off by sharing what happened in the various interviews you all did yesterday. You can kick off, Jacko."

Jacko looked as if he had had a heavy night. His shirt collar was askew and the bulky kipper tie looked as if it had evaded all of his attempts to tame it into submission. For Jacko, working on Saturday meant there were fewer people around to be offended by his professional dress and demeanour.

"I paid a visit to Sutherland's gaff, with a forensic team. We're still waiting for the results but the interviews were revealing. Two dolly birds there: one a legit lodger, the other supporting her mate at this difficult time."

Jacko raised his eyebrows as he spoke and did air speech marks with his fingers around the word "support". He had clearly been unimpressed with their story. Sitting to his right, Paula scowled, but said nothing. Grayson was in no mood to listen to Jacko's ramblings.

"Let's cut to the chase, Jacko. Did you get anything of significance out of them?"

Jacko sat up, chastened.

"Well, I did actually, boss. There was an unofficial arrangement from what I could see. Dirt-cheap rent for nurses – and they were both nurses – for extra 'services rendered'." The mimed speech marks returned.

"Let's not be coy, Jacko. You're saying that his lodgers slept with him for a cheap rent."

"That's what they said. Eventually. But not just the rent. He was a very senior figure, Sutherland. Lot of power with the powers that be. They were scared that if they said no, then they'd be out of a job."

"But these girls are not in the frame for the murder? You're not saying that?"

He shook his head. "Nah. They weren't at all upset he was dead, but they would never have killed him. Too scared for one thing. And I got the impression that although he was using them, there was something about him they quite liked."

This time, Paula couldn't control herself.

"Liked? Come off it, Jacko, that's just an old man's fantasy. How could you like someone who was abusing you like that?"

He barked back, "My fantasies are a lot wilder than that, I can assure you. All I'm doing is reporting what they said and my impressions."

Grayson raised his hand. "Alright, alright that's enough. Anything else?"

"Well, the lodger, the blonde one, said she thought that he was a bit worried. He had been a bit snappier than usual, and she heard some pretty tense phone calls late at night, when he thought no one was listening. She felt that he was being threatened by someone, but that he was also confiding in someone else."

"Any names? Any visitors to the house?"

"She was a bit vague about that. She mentioned some senior colleagues visiting, but she had no idea who they were. In her words, they were too far above her pay grade to register. But she also mentioned..." He paused and began to flick through his notebook. "Ah, yes, that's it, some other, 'more junior' people from the hospital. People she recognised, but didn't know their names."

Grayson thought for a moment. "Forensics? When can we expect them?"

"Maybe this evening. Tomorrow morning, latest."

"OK. Good work, Jacko. Now, Clive, Paula. What did you get from Jewell?"

Clive and Paula exchanged a glance. Grayson had eyes like a hawk.

"Come on, out with it. What've you two been up to?"

"Well, we went round to Jewell's yesterday. Right student druggy den it was. Anyway, we were a bit suspicious, and we went back. He's changed his story."

Everyone in the room sat forward. There was a collective sense in the team that this was something important.

Grayson was in no mood to milk the drama. "What's he saying now?"

"The alibi he gave Simpson has gone. Simpson disappeared during the shift right across the time when Sutherland was killed."

"Disappeared?"

"Jewell says that, according to Simpson, he was arranging some kind of drug deal. He asked Jewell to lie for him, and he went along with it because he didn't want to dump him in it. He thought Simpson was a bit of a loser and would never be involved in summat like murder."

Grayson laughed and shook his head. "He'd be surprised. So, why did nice, trusting Mr Jewell change his mind?"

"Two reasons. First, he overheard Simpson talking to someone in the hospital, someone involved in the drug thing. Nasty piece of work, according to Jewell. That's when he realised that it was more serious than he'd thought."

"And the second reason?"

The glance passed between Clive and Paula again. It did not escape Grayson's attention. Clive continued. "We, well I to be fair, I suggested that unless he told us everything, then we had enough on him to charge with possession. Him and everyone else in the house."

Grayson's reply was quiet and cold, deadly in its sense of menace. "You did fucking what?"

"Er… I told him—"

Grayson interrupted, abandoning icy quiet for full-throated fury. "I know what you fucking told him," he exploded. "I'm neither deaf nor stupid."

Clive lapsed into a silence and began to examine the things on his desk.

Grayson, wrestling for self-control, found the quiet button again.

"And you, DC Marsh, you were involved in this pantomime, were you?"

Paula jumped, not expecting the question. "Yes, sir."

"I had high hopes for you, DC Marsh. High hopes."

"Sir."

She hung her head and shot a glance at Clive.

Grayson turned his attention back to Clive.

"And will all this stand up? Is it admissible?"

"Yes, sir. Or, we can make it admissible, at any rate. He's coming in at lunchtime to make a statement. I reckon he'll say and sign anything we tell him to."

Grayson leant back in his chair, his hands steepled together. He looked closely at the two detectives and then around the rest of the team. Without warning, he sat up straight and banged both hands down on the top of his desk in a repeated rhythm.

"Well done, you two, well done. We've fucking got him."

*

Juliet sat on the edge of her bed and surveyed the chaos in the room. The leather jacket that she wore the night before, pocket linings turned inside out, had been hurled in fury at the wall. The panic attack was ebbing now, and she was able at last to face the situation calmly, knowing beyond doubt that in the confusion of last night, she had made a mistake even more serious than snogging Johnny.

Not that that wasn't really rather nice. Indulgently, she smiled at the memory. He did have the most beautiful eyes, and he was a rather lovely kisser, with a tongue that seemed less like an assault weapon than usual. With some men, a kiss was more of a violation than a mutual pleasure. It also helped that he smiled and listened as much as he talked. Another time, another place perhaps. But not now, not here.

She forced herself to file the memory and face the mistake that could not possibly have any upside. Her bag. When she had finally fallen asleep last night, she had plunged into a troubled oblivion, disturbed by scenes involving a strange cast of characters from the hospital. But it was not so troubled that it woke her up. She slept on until after nine, but the second she woke, the relative peace sleep had brought her was instantly dispelled by a lurking sense of dread. Something was wrong, but she couldn't put her finger on what. Not the narrow escape with Johnny, because an escape, no matter how narrow, was still an escape. No, it was that something was missing.

And then it slapped her across the face. Her bag. After a frantic interlude of desperately throwing things around the room, she had finally come to the acceptance that somewhere along the line, she had lost her bag. Then came the chilling realisation that that could have the most serious consequences imaginable. She forced herself to go through the events of yesterday, starting from the last time she could remember having the bag.

She'd taken it, against her better judgement, as she'd hurriedly left her room for the party, knowing her chequebook was in it. And she had it when she arrived at Johnny's house, she was sure of that. And when she was being interviewed by that police officer? No, she couldn't remember with any certainty. There were only two explanations possible. Either she had just laid it to one side in Johnny's room. Or Dr Death had somehow got hold of it, the old opportunist picking it up thinking it might come in useful.

She would try him later, when he came in for his shift, but she had already decided that Johnny's room was the more likely location. She would have to go back there before anyone opened up the bag, but the thought of facing Johnny, with all his questions and his hurt, beautiful face, was almost too much to bear. But it had to be borne, she knew that. She would just have to steel herself. After what she had already done, that was something she was getting used to.

33

It was midday when Johnny finally woke up, roused by a distant bang. He stared at the clock through sleep-bleared eyes for a moment or two, not quite believing what he was seeing. Midday? How had that happened? He sat up and was immediately thankful that his hangover was not as bad as expected. The arrival of the police the night before had curtailed the drinking, and he had spent a fretful night, tossing and turning, brooding on the events of the evening before finally falling into a troubled sleep at about four in the morning.

The usual shroud of cold hung over his room and spurred him into action. He pulled on his clothes and made his way downstairs to the kitchen. The further he went down, the more oppressive the silence became and the stronger the stink of stale beer and cigarettes. The usual Saturday-morning sounds were all missing. No radio, no low hum of conversation nor clatter or scrape of cutlery on plates disturbed the chill stillness.

He swung open the kitchen door, but there was no one there. There was a sink full of washing-up to be done, but the rest of the kitchen was clean and tidy, with several bin liners stuffed with bottles and plastic glasses tied up and leaning against the back door that led to the yard. Even the table was clear of its usual landscape of breakfast jars and crumb-strewn breadboard. In the middle of the acres of space presented by the cleared table was an A4 sheet of paper.

He snatched it up, frowning, and read the message, scrawled in black felt pen.

> *Johnny,*
> *Sorry, couldn't wait any longer. We've got to get to the station. We've left you a bit of washing-up to do. Put bin liners out for Christmas Eve – there's a collection. Hope you're OK after last night. Don't work too hard. Think of the double time! We'll all be back for work at the end of next week. Happy Christmas!*
> *Mark, Kate, Jaggers xxx*

He looked down again at the note in his hand, and thought again. He went to the bottom of the stairs and called up, "Hel? Helen?" There was no answer. Maybe she'd just popped out for a bit. She would have left a note if she'd gone out on any kind of outing. He went back to the kitchen and put the kettle on for coffee and then sat with it at the table, waiting for his toast to pop. He sipped the scalding coffee and let the reality of the new day wash over him.

He scraped his toast with butter and Marmite, and took his first bite. The crunch echoed in his head as the still silence of the house pressed upon him. There would be no socialising today, neither comfortable and quiet nor wild and disorderly. He was alone, although Helen would surely reappear before long. But then, when she had left for home on Christmas Eve, he would be entirely alone. It was the first time he had really confronted the realities of his choice to work over Christmas, and given the oppressive quiet that seemed to lay so heavily on the house, being out at work had become a little more attractive. He would still have to return to an empty, freezing and silent house in the early hours of Christmas Day and Boxing Day, but with a bit of planning, perhaps he could make that bearable, if not actually appealing.

He continued to attack his toast and coffee and his mind turned towards what he was going to do that day. Maybe he should be bold and make a surprise visit to the nurses' home and call on Juliet. They could talk about what had happened at the party, and she would be able to explain why she had had to leave. She would be relieved that he had made the effort to come and see her, and all would be well. He took the last bite of his toast and wallowed in his visualisation of that reunion. This picture of a tearful encounter that ended with them in each other's arms came to a close with the old house creaking and sighing as joists invisibly flexed and settled, windows rattled, and floorboards shifted, like a giant shifting in its sleep.

But what if she wasn't there? Or worse, she was but couldn't mask her irritation that he had called without invitation. What if there was no convincing explanation for her disappearance the night before? That would just add fuel to the fires of doubt that were raging in his mind.

Just as he was about to start to turn the whole conundrum over in his mind again, he was suddenly pulled up short. A memory of his conversation with the two police officers the night before elbowed its way into his consciousness and washed over him like a bucket of cold water.

The police. It was all coming back to him now. They had made it very clear to him that he had to appear at the incident room in the hospital today to make a statement at 1 p.m. He looked at the clock again. 12.20 p.m. Christ, he absolutely, definitely couldn't be late. These people had his balls in a vice and he didn't want them to start squeezing. He ran back upstairs and hurriedly brushed his teeth, simultaneously examining his clothes for stains. Satisfied, he grabbed his coat and scarf and hurtled back down to his bike. He hauled it out into the street, slammed the door and launched himself into the icy air and down the road.

*

Jacko hammered on the door again, his breath steaming into the air. He was still furious that his work interviewing the lodgers at Sutherland's house had been completely overshadowed by Marsh and Brooks, and their dodgy revelation about the lad Jewell and Simpson. He waited for a few seconds before turning back to DC Marsh, who stood behind him on the path that led to the pavement.

"You have another go, Paula. I'm just going to have a look round the back."

He stepped away from the door into the untouched snow on the tiny front lawn. A couple more steps took him to the window. He leant forward, shading his eyes and resting his head on the pane. The curtains were closed but there was a small gap in the middle. Jacko squinted through it, but stepped away after a few seconds.

"Nothing in there. No sign of life at all," he said to Marsh. "Could still be in bed, I suppose."

Paula, equally furious at Jacko's silence in the car, and his general cold and silent tactic, didn't answer.

The door of the house to the left of them opened and an elderly woman with a tight perm and a pinny poked her head around the door. "Are you after Gordon? I think he's out."

"Is that Mr Simpson? Do you know him then?" Jacko asked.

She looked at both of them, uncertain.

"Who are you two?"

Jacko rummaged inside his coat and pulled out his warrant card.

"Police, love."

She took a step out of the door. "Police? What's he done then?"

"Done? Why do you think he's done summat?"

She gave him a withering look of pity. "Well, you haven't come round to give him a Christmas card, have you, love?"

Paula looked around Jacko's shoulder. She wasn't sure whether he was deliberately blocking her, but that's what it felt like. "Why do you think he's out?" she asked.

"Heard the door bang. Early. I thought summat were up, mind. He had a bonfire this morning. Still dark, it were."

"A bonfire?" Paula cut in, interested. "Where was that then?"

The neighbour's withering look returned. "In the bloody garden, yer soft 'apporth. Where do you think?"

Jacko and Paula exchanged a look. Jacko's expression and raised eyebrows indicated that he shared the neighbour's appraisal of Paula's qualities.

He turned back to the neighbour. "And your name is?"

"Ramsbottom. Mabel Ramsbottom."

"Could I come in, Mrs Ramsbottom? We need to have a look at that bonfire."

She hesitated. "Ooh, well, I don't know. I don't want the neighbours thinking you've come round for me."

Paula gave her her warmest smile. "I'm sure you'll put them straight on that, Mabel, eh?"

"Aye, come on in then. But be quick. I'm baking mince pies this morning and I need to get on with it. Our Julie's popping in later wi' the kids."

Jacko followed her through the open door, Paula a couple of steps behind him. He turned back to her.

"No, Paula love, you wait by his front door, just in case. I'll only be a minute."

Paula scowled at him but bit her tongue and returned to hammer on Gordon's door again. She was certain by now no one was in, but she imagined the door was Jacko's face and she attacked it with renewed vigour. As she waited, feeling more than ever a spare part, she looked back along the terrace of houses and the street opposite. It seemed that Mabel Ramsbottom was not the only curtain twitcher in the neighbourhood.

34

By the time he skidded to a halt in front of the bike shed, Johnny had lost most of the feeling in his hands, and his face was raw from the icy slipstream his bike ride had generated. He really must get better prepared for this journey. The sky was already darkening and the thick cloud promised more snow. He blew on his hands and massaged some life back into them before stowing his bike and locking it in the rack.

He cast a quick glance over at the nurses' home and momentarily entertained the idea of dropping in on Juliet, but, checking his watch he realised he was already late. Maybe he could do it after he'd given his statement to the police.

Once he was in the building, he hurried along to the Friends Meeting Room, passing through the main reception area on the way. As he approached, the strains of a brass band sprang up and a version of 'O Little Town of Bethlehem' filled the corridors. He turned the corner to see the Salvation Army brass band established in the corner opposite the reception desk, with the non-musicians taking full advantage of the extra numbers to shake collection pots vigorously under the noses of the steady stream of visitors.

He navigated the milling crowds, body swerving those that lingered to listen to the band and donate to charity, and was relieved to hit calmer waters in the corridors where the crush had thinned out. He arrived at the door of the Friends Meeting Room. Underneath the permanent sign was another, Blu-Tacked to the door: North Yorkshire Police Incident Room. He knocked and waited, giving his clothes a quick check and brush down.

The door opened and a fug of cigarette smoke seeped out. Holding the door was DS Brooks. He smiled, opened the door wider, and beckoned Johnny inside.

"Ah, Mr Jewell. We thought you weren't coming. Come in, come in."

"Yeah, sorry I'm late," he mumbled.

He stepped inside. There was a rank of desks lined up in the middle of the room, each one carrying a stack of card files, a phone and an ashtray. Five of the desks were occupied by a variety of policemen and women who looked up vaguely as Johnny came in, before turning their attention once again to their work. Some were in the middle of phone calls; others were reading or writing on documents.

At a desk apart, focused exclusively on Johnny, was DI Grayson. Clive walked Johnny over to him.

"This is Detective Inspector Grayson. He's in charge of the investigation. This is Johnny Jewell, the porter. He's come in to give his statement after our little chat yesterday."

Johnny nodded and waited. Grayson glowered at him, his face set, before suddenly standing up.

"Good afternoon, Mr Jewell. We'll do this next door, shall we? I'm sure you don't want every Tom, Dick and Harry listening to your change of mind. Bit embarrassing, eh?"

Johnny began to answer, but Grayson marched away. Johnny trailed after him with Brooks bringing up the rear. Grayson opened a windowless side room, which was little more than a cupboard with a desk laid out with two chairs on one side and one on the other. He and Brooks sat down on one side and Grayson indicated to Johnny the remaining seat. He sat down, pulled his chair up to the desk and tried to look like a model citizen who was keen to do his civic duty.

"Now then," Grayson began, "why don't you start by telling me why you've been such a silly cunt, and why I shouldn't throw the fucking book at you for fucking wasting police fucking time in what is, after all, a fucking murder inquiry?"

*

Johnny found himself in the corridor, the door of the incident room firmly closed behind him and his ears still ringing from Grayson's bollocking. With each step he took, the humiliation of the last half an hour receded in his mind and he was able to think rationally about the consequences. He was fairly sure that the police had no real interest in him and their threats about the Drug Squad raid last night were just that: threats that had served their purpose. But if they weren't interested in him, what was equally clear was that they were interested in Gordon. Very interested.

He found himself at a crossroads at the end of the corridor. The left turn would take him to the main entrance and home, the right towards the wards. He hesitated, troubled by his conscience. Maybe he should just take a quick detour to see if he could find Gordon. He wasn't exactly sure what he would say to him, or even where he was, but at the very least, he might bump into Juliet. Or Gloria. She would definitely know where they were. Nothing went on in this place that escaped Gloria's attention. And they really did need to talk. He was decided. The right turn it was.

The corridors were still full of visiting relatives, and there was an air of busyness about the entire hospital. Even if he came across Gordon or Juliet, they were likely to have their hands full with work, but he only really needed a minute or two. He buzzed into ward thirty-six and made his way to the main desk. All the visitors were with their relatives, so in the reception area there was space and quiet. He saw Gloria sitting behind the desk, hunched over something she was intently reading. As Johnny drew up to the desk, he greeted her.

"Hi Gloria—"

He didn't get a chance to finish. Gloria jumped and cried out, a pen tightly gripped in her hand. "Jesus wept, Johnny, you frightened the life out of me. Don't creep up on people like that. Cough or whistle or something."

"Sorry, Gloria. Just testing whether you were on top of ward security. I could have been a serial killer or anyone walking into your ward."

She narrowed her eyes at him, lips pursed tightly together. "That's not funny. Not in the present circumstances."

"Sorry, didn't think."

She scanned his appearance.

"What are you doing here in your civvies anyway? Coming in on your day off – you're getting as bad as Dr Death."

He looked down at his clothes. "Oh, no. It's a long story. But, speaking of Gordon, have you seen him? I just need to have a word with him."

"He's not been up here. Probably skiving somewhere, as usual."

"What about Juliet? Dr Fulton? Is she on duty?"

Gloria gave him a look that was half-amused, half-disapproving.

"Juliet, eh? I hope your intentions are honourable, young man."

Johnny arranged his features into a picture of innocence. "I just wanted to check something with her."

"We're very busy, Johnny, and she is on call. I'd just leave it if I were you. She could be anywhere."

His face fell. This was a waste of time. He should have just gone straight home. He was about to turn on his heels when he caught sight of what Gloria had been reading. On the desk in front of her, below the level of the reception counter, lay a copy of *The Daily Mirror*. It was covered in biro scrawl, but he could still make out the headline: *Who is The Ripper? Another Victim Found.* Underneath, there was a silhouette of an identikit man surrounded by the photographs, familiar from previous stories, of the women he had killed.

Johnny reached down and brought the paper out, laying it on the counter. He shook his head. "When are they going to catch this bastard? How many more does he have to kill before they do anything?"

"They're not bothered about catching him as long as it's girls on the game. And as for this lot." She picked up the paper between her thumb and finger as if it were contaminated, "It's just a story to them, titillation before you get to the bloody Page 3 girl." Her voice was flat and she exuded a heavy exhaustion.

Johnny pressed on regardless. "I just don't get what drives someone to do this kind of thing. What kind of man can behave like this?"

Gloria smiled wearily. "Open your eyes, Johnny. There are a lot of men round here with the same attitudes. Whoever it is, he'll be someone's husband, or father, or son and everyone will be shocked and tell us how nice and normal he was. But you're right about one thing."

"What's that?"

"It's definitely not a woman who's doing this."

Johnny looked at her, frowning. "Are you alright, Gloria? Heavy shift?"

"It's been a long night, that's all. I'm fine." She produced a thin smile and then seemed to summon her usual spirit as the smile broadened into a warm glow. She patted his arm. "Go on Johnny, you get yourself home. It's your day off; you don't want to be hanging around here."

"Yeah, you're right. I'll see you next week."

He turned to walk away. After a few steps, she called out to him, "I'll let Dr Fulton know you were asking for her."

When he turned back, she was beaming at him, the newspaper still in her hand. Johnny could see that the silhouette representing the Ripper had been scored through, over and over again with the point of the biro, until the picture had been completely disfigured. The image lingered with him as he left the ward and made his way to the exit. Did all women feel like this? Was this small act of revenge what every woman wanted to do? How could they possibly trust any man with all of this going on? As he trudged through the snow to the bike sheds, he felt the troubles of a world darker than he had suspected weigh heavily on his shoulders.

*

Just at the same time, in a room not very far away from the Friends Meeting Room, Mike Hutchinson sat in his office at the back of the hospital pharmacy with his ledger open in front of him on his desk. The only other things on his desk were a plastic desk tidy, holding a variety of pens and a stapler, an empty coffee cup, now cold, and a triptych photo frame. Two sections of the frame held photos of two young children, about five or six years old, a boy and a girl, smiling and showing a random collection of wonky teeth and gaps. The third section was empty. His office looked out onto one of several courtyards created by the grid of corridors. The sky was darkening outside, and he could see across the snowy expanse, some straggling shrubs and, behind them, a patchwork of yellow lit windows.

He was an unlikely visitor to the hospital on a Saturday. The pharmacy was open and available at the weekend, because illness didn't take regular holidays, but it was generally staffed by nurses and pharmacy officers on a rota basis. When he had arrived that morning, Carol, the nurse on duty had jumped out of her skin, before recovering her poise.

"Morning, Mark. Well, we are honoured. What are you doing here on a Saturday?"

He had been expecting that kind of reaction. He gave her a cheery smile and a rehearsed reply. "I've got a ton of paperwork to go through before the holiday. Deadlines. If I don't do it now, I'll have to come in after Christmas. And I've got the kids on Boxing Day."

He continued towards his office. When he got to the door, he turned back. "You couldn't do me a coffee, could you, Carol, love?"

"Of course I can. You get yourself settled down and I'll bring it through in a jiffy. There's not many that would be coming in on their day off, I can tell you."

"Well, it's all got to be done, and no one else is going to do it. Thanks, Carol. I'll just get on with it then. Sooner I start, the sooner I'll be gone."

He slipped into the room, hung up his coat and, waiting until Carol had gone to the kitchen, went back to his desk and unlocked the set of drawers underneath the desk top. It slid out silently and he flicked through some of the hanging files, removing his secret ledger and a handful of card files. He sat down heavily at the desk, opened the ledger and began to read.

And now he had finished making sure that the record of drugs in and drugs out had been aligned in the official dispensing file. He had his own records in his own ledger and in the files, he had records of his own customers: names, phone numbers, dates, orders. He had often thought of encrypting it, of devising a simple code, but he had never got round to it. Firstly, he couldn't decide how, exactly, to do it. And then, when it had become clear just how simple the scam was, he had got a little cocky and felt that it really wasn't worth the effort. But just at the moment, it was probably a bad idea to have them in his office when there were police just yards away conducting a murder inquiry. He collected them up, straightened them out on the top of his desk, and then slid them into his leather briefcase. He would squirrel them away in the garage until the whole thing had blown over.

He sat back in his chair, a frown appearing on his face. The documents were the easy part. It was the people, as ever, who were the problem. Greedy, cunning people with little in the way of brain power or morals to hold them in check. Dangerous people, in short. Perhaps he should pay one of them a visit before he left. He straightened his desk, put the coffee cup on the side where Carol would deal with it, and got his coat and case. Yes, just a quick visit. After all, it was on his way to the car park. He looked again at the photographs on his desk. It had all been for them; everything he had already done had been for them. And so would this last thing be, just for them.

And that would be the end of it.

*

The door buzzer cut through the background roar of the open incinerator. Dave Henderson cursed and closed the door, pulling the handle to seal it tight. The noise level dropped immediately so that the buzzer, when it sounded again, was angry and impatient.

"What does he want now?" he muttered. He put down his gauntlets on a shabby little desk and glanced over at the back of the room, at an open door that led to the storeroom. With a surprising turn of speed, he hurried to the door, took a brief look inside and then shut it. He locked the door, slipping the key into his overall pocket, before returning to the main door.

When he opened it, the cold air flooded in and there, standing under the covered walkway, a straight, black, wet line in a sea of snow, were two porters with a trolley. Dave towered above the pair of them.

"Oh." He frowned, paused and then recovered his poise. "What can I do for you two wrong 'uns?" he said.

The first of them replied: "Got a nice delivery for you here, Dave, lad."

He reached into the trolley and pulled out two transparent bin liners, one after the other, that were stained with blood and other fluids and which contained an indeterminate selection of body parts and tissue. The bags were heavy and each one landed on the floor with a disturbing squelch and thump.

"Got a nice bit of liver here for you. Lovely. Have you had your dinner?"

Dave looked at him askance. "It's about time you thought of some new jokes, eh?"

"The old ones are the best, though. Eh, and look at this."

He reached down into the trolley and hauled out a brown paper parcel a yard and a half long. It took him two hands to lift it.

"Got a leg for you here. Weighs a bloody ton, it does."

Dave leant over and took the package from him.

"Theatre been busy then?"

"Aye. Christmas rush."

The second man, who had been silent during this exchange, came to the door and tried to poke his head inside. Dave blocked his way.

"Lovely and warm in there, Dave. Nice little spot you've got for yourself here."

To emphasise his point, he began to stamp his feet and rub his hands together. His breath steamed into the air above his head.

"Just leave the bags there. I'll deal with 'em."

The two porters exchanged a glance. They double-checked the trolley and left the two bags at Dave's feet.

"They're all yours. Merry bloody Christmas," said the second man bluntly, before turning back to the main hospital building. They walked side by side with the empty trolley between them.

"He's a bloody miserable bugger. He never lets anyone in that room of his. Guards it like Fort Knox. Got a telly in there and everything. Little bed as well."

The other shook his head. "Takes all sorts, I suppose."

Dave stood and watched them go. When they disappeared into the main building, he took a quick look round, hauled the bags in and shut the door.

*

It was the middle of Saturday afternoon and darkness was beginning to gather over the hospital. The incident room bore all the signs of a long day: the ashtrays were overflowing, coffee cups had multiplied and bins and desk tops bore the brunt of all-day snacking. Anyone entering the room for the first time that day would have been slapped round the face with a heady cocktail of stale grease, smoke and body odour. The team was tired and everyone had begun to think of getting home, some to their families, others to a lonely night in on their own in front of the telly.

Simon Grayson strode into the room from the side room with Clive Brooks a pace behind him.

"Alright, listen up everyone. Let's just go through what we've got so far and then see where we think that takes us."

There was a scraping of chair legs as everyone sat up straight, stopped writing in mid-sentence and cut short conversations.

"Alright, let's start. Jewell we can put to one side now. His story finally makes sense and we've put the fear of God in him. He'll think twice before parking on a double yellow line in the future, that one. The significant thing about his new statement though is that it drops Gordon Simpson right in the frame. No alibi for the time of the murder. Involved in dealing drugs, possibly to Sutherland among others. Jacko and Paula went to pay him a visit this morning but he's disappeared. Jacko, just fill us in, will you?"

"Yes, guv." Jacko consulted his notebook. "We talked to his next-door neighbour. She said he'd been burning a pile of stuff in his back garden early this morning and that he left just after that and hasn't been back since. She seemed to think he was a harmless soul. Few friends, but he was quiet enough and helped her out when she needed it. Cleared the snow from her path, did bits of shopping for her, that sort of thing."

"Adolf Hitler was nice to old people. Quiet neighbour as well. His mother probably loved him," said Brooks.

"Exactly," Grayson replied. "Did you get anything from the fire?"

"Not really, guv. Except that there must have been a lot of it. Two bin liners worth, I'd say."

Paula butted in, "I've checked the shift rotas. He's due back in on nights tomorrow. Starts at ten."

"Good. Get a warrant to search his house in the meantime, just in case. Now, according to Jewell, there's another person involved. A man. He overheard him and Simpson talking together a couple of nights ago. Bit of a gangster, according to young Johnny, but he'd be scared of Winnie the Pooh, that lad, so we can't be sure."

"Do they know they were overheard? Gordon and the other bloke?"

"Gordon does. Not sure about Al Capone."

Grayson stopped for a moment, frowning. "Hmm. Anything from Sutherland's dad, Jacko?"

He shook his head. "Nah. Straightforward identification, that's all. Nothing really on his history that flagged up any alarms. He was sad about it, but I got the impression they were not close. Almost estranged, from what he said."

"And the forensics on Sutherland's house?"

"Still waiting, guv. Hopefully by the end of the day."

Grayson turned to look at the board behind him and then back to face his team.

"So what do we think?"

There was silence. Then Clive began. "Simpson supplies drugs to Sutherland – probably others in the hospital as well. Knows that he's the subject of sexual assault allegations. Maybe there's a bit of blackmail thrown in. Sutherland is bumped off by Simpson because he knows too much."

Grayson shook his head. "But Simpson was pretty small fry, as far as Jewell says. A bit of weed and speed and not much else. And he doesn't strike me as someone who would murder. But then again, he had the opportunity; he has no alibi for the window of death."

"And he lied, guv," Paula interjected. "And murderers, usually men, don't have two heads and wear black hats. They're often as ordinary as Simpson."

Jacko snorted at this, shook his head and looked away, a big smile on his face.

Grayson glared at him. "Well, Jacko? Got something to say?"

"Come on, guv, we don't need this women's lib claptrap from Marsh. It just gets in the way of the evidence."

Paula shifted uncomfortably in her chair and waited for her boss to agree.

"Jacko, we need to keep an open mind. Paula's right; just because he's small fry doesn't mean he couldn't have done it. Motive and opportunity – they're both there."

"But no evidence, guv," replied Jacko. "Not a scrap."

Grayson thought again for a moment.

"Could we get a confession, if we brought him in and put the thumbscrews on him? What do you think?"

Jacko smiled broadly.

"Is the Pope polish, guv? Just give me a couple of hours with him."

Clive and Paula exchanged a look.

"OK, let's hope he shows up for his shift. We'll bring him in then." Grayson turned his attention back to Clive and Paula. "What about the doctor? Juliet Fulton? Let's not forget her. You two had some doubts about her, didn't you?"

Clive thought about his answer carefully. "Yeah, we need to talk to her again. I'll pay her another visit in the nurses' home and I think I'll check out what happened at the hospital in Leeds."

The phone on Jacko's desk rang. He snatched it off the cradle. "Incident room."

He listened intently as the others watched and waited. His face creased into a frown and he took up his pen. "Say those names again… You sure about this?" He scribbled down a few notes as he spoke. "OK. Thanks for that. And you'll send all of that over, will you? Monday? Yeah. Cheers." He put the phone down, looked down at his pad and looked up at Grayson and the team. "That was forensics. Fingerprints from Sutherland's house."

Grayson waited a second before losing patience. "Come on Jacko, spit it out."

"Clear dabs all over the shop there. Matches for Simpson, Fulton, and Wilson."

"Wilson? Who the hell is Wilson?" asked Clive.

"You know, what's her name. Gloria."

"Gloria?"

"Yeah, the flighty nurse with the big tits."

Before Paula could protest, Jacko pressed on, his imagination lit up by the germ of an idea. "Bloody hell, do you think Sutherland was giving her one as well?"

35

Gordon shivered as he slipped out of a side entrance from the main building. He gave a glance each way along the covered walkway and then rushed across to the door of the incinerator. It was four in the afternoon, Saturday, and the hospital was full of staff and visitors so he needed to be quick and careful. He knocked and slipped inside though the crack of the open door.

Inside, he garbled his story to Dave, who listened with one eye on the door.

"So what are you going to do? You can kip down here tonight, but that can't go on much longer."

Gordon looked defeated. "I dunno. I just need a bit of time to think, that's all. I thought maybe you might have some ideas, Dave. Fucking Johnny Jewell has dropped us right in it."

Dave looked up sharply. "No, mate. Dropped you right in it. Nothing to do with me."

"Come on. You don't want the coppers poking their noses in here, do you?"

His eyes travelled around the room, taking in the trellis work of pipes, the battered metal cages lined up against the walls, and the incinerator itself, radiating heat and a dull roar of noise. He made sure they rested on the storage cupboards in the corner and the door leading to a side room.

"And why would they do that, Gordon?" His eyes narrowed and his voice took on a tone that, along with the accompanying pause, was dripping with threat. "Unless you're going to do something silly."

Gordon looked hurt. "No, of course I'm not. What do you take me for? We've always been in it together, you and me. Ever since Blackstone. The Blackstone boys, remember?"

"Long time ago now. We've all moved on since then. But what exactly did Jewell tell the police?"

"Nothing," Gordon protested. He saw Dave's expression flicker. "Nothing much. Just that I was not on shift with him because I was meeting my supplier. I told him I just did a bit of minor dealing. To the students and that."

"And when the police pull you in and start being nasty to you, what are the chances you'll tell them who your supplier is, eh?"

"I won't say anything, Dave. I swear."

"You know you're not good when people turn violent. You don't like it. Blackstock boys, remember? And it's all this lot of coppers have got: a bit of violence. They've been nice to you so far, but that's just the way they start."

The colour drained from Gordon's face, leaving a greasy pallor.

"Look, this is what we'll do." Dave's voice was warmer now, reassuring and authoritative. "Tomorrow, you should go back home and whenever your next shift is, you should come into work. When they come for you, you say that you panicked. Admit to the dealing thing. Like you say, just a bit of dope. When they ask you who the supplier is, you say you just have an arrangement to pick up the stuff and drop off the cash, but that it's all done anonymously, for security."

"But they'll do me for that. I can't do prison, Dave, I can't." There was panic in his voice and his eyes began to sparkle.

Dave leant over and patted him on the shoulder.

"Gordon man, trust me. You'll get a suspended. First offence. But at least you're out of the frame for Sutherland. You would go down for that, and for a long time."

Gordon wiped his eyes and took some deep breaths.

Henderson continued. "There, that's better. Now, you stay here tonight and we'll go over your story, so you know what to say, alright? But listen. You can't leave that room." He nodded towards the door in the corner. "This place is busy during the day and anyone could come down with stuff to get rid of. I'll keep the door locked. If anyone knocks, you ignore it and lie low. If the door opens, it'll just be me. You can't have the radio on, and you can't be walking around. Just for tonight. Tomorrow, you can go."

"Yeah, alright. Thanks, Dave. Can you get me something to eat? I'm starving."

"I'll just go for a little walk and I'll bring something back with me. Now, let's get you in that room."

He walked over to the far side of the room, picked up a set of keys and unlocked the door. Inside was a windowless cell, more like a cupboard than a room. There was a single bed on one side, a tiny portable television at the foot of it and a side table with a travel alarm clock and a few books and magazines on it.

"See? Like a bloody first-class hotel, isn't it? Make yourself comfortable and I'll be back in about an hour. Now, do you want a coffee before I go?"

"Oh, yeah. Cheers, Dave."

Henderson went back to the main room and switched his kettle on. From his perch on the bed, Gordon could hear the rattle of cups and cutlery. Henderson called out, "How do you have it, Gordon? Milk? Sugar?"

"Milk and two sugars please, mate."

He reappeared with a steaming mug and handed it to Gordon.

"There you go. Now, you drink that and relax and I'll be back in a jiffy. And remember. Don't leave the room."

"Alright. Thanks, Dave."

Dave made to leave. At the threshold of the door, Gordon called him back. He could no longer hold on to the question that continued to trouble him, like a wasp banging up against a window indoors. "There's one thing I just can't get my head around."

"What's that?"

"Who killed Sutherland? If it wasn't you, who could it have been? Because they're still out there, aren't they? And if they've done it once, there's nothing to stop them doing it again."

The two men looked at each other across the room, the noise and heat of the incinerator a constant presence. Dave opened his mouth to speak, but paused. He thought again. "You don't need to worry about that, Gordon. Leave it all to me."

He turned, closing the door behind him. There was the sound of the main door opening and the scrape of keys as it was locked from the outside.

Gordon lay back on the bed, drank his coffee, and began to think.

*

After the heat of the incinerator room, the icy sharpness outside came as a shock. Dave shivered and pulled his brown overall tightly around his body as he hurried along the walkway to the hospital entrance between irregular heaps of grubby snow that had been shovelled away from the path. He slowed down once inside and made his way steadily to the canteen, head down and eyes averted. He threaded his way through between members of staff, and, nearer the wards, knots of visitors, oblivious to the glitter and tinsel that festooned the corridors.

He looked up only when he opened the canteen door, to scope out the best place to sit, away from tables of colleagues. He queued up, bought a cup of coffee, some sandwiches and chocolate, displaying an expression just on the polite side of a scowl and with the minimum of chat, and then retired to the corner table he had lined up. He wouldn't have to worry about any members of staff joining him, although there may be one or two who would be surprised to see him there and remark on it to their companions. They would take it no further than that, however, and Dave took quiet satisfaction from the results of his studied campaign over the years to be thought of as a harmless loner.

Because now he had to think and interruption would not help. He sipped his coffee and replaced the cup in the saucer, his eyes covertly scanning the room. No matter how he looked at it, one solution kept presenting itself to him above all others as the only realistic way out. If only Gordon hadn't run to him in a panic. He shouldn't be surprised about that; he'd done that ever since he had first met him, all those years ago in Blackstone. The Blackstone boys. He suppressed the murmur of a smile. No, it would do no good to get sentimental. He knew Gordon too well for that and it was inevitable that he would crack under pressure. Then the whole house of cards would come tumbling down and he was not going to let that happen.

Sutherland had presented an opportunity. Now, it was just a matter of timing. He knew what he was going to do. It would be easy. In the darkest hours, when corridors were deserted and people could move undetected in the shadows, anything was possible. He spent his time savouring his coffee with a growing sense of satisfaction as his plan took shape and solidified in his mind.

When he had finished, he gathered up the food for Gordon and slipped out of the canteen. No one noticed him leave. When they next looked up and over at his table, they would see it empty and struggle to remember who had been there. He slid through the network of corridors, leaving barely a ripple in his wake and arrived at the door to the incinerator room, keys in hand. He slipped inside and the door closed behind him.

*

It didn't take Gordon long to think. He'd known Dave too long to have any surviving illusions about him. Blackstock had brutalised everybody who had passed through its doors, but some more than others. And what about Sutherland? Dave denied it, but he couldn't see who else it might have been. Maybe Sutherland was cutting up rough about how much he was having to pay, and had seen an opportunity for a little blackmail of his own. He would certainly waste no tears on him, though it was a nice little income stream where the tap had suddenly been turned off, but that was more disappointing rather than dangerous.

No, it was clear to him that he would have to slip away later. He couldn't spend the night there. And with a bit of preparation, maybe the danger of being done for supply would fade if he could point the police in the right direction. An hour. That's how long Dave had said he would be away. He'd better get started.

He went over to the desk and examined the top and the noticeboard. The board raised a smile as he recognised some familiar photographs. Well, who would have thought Dave would be such a sentimentalist? And there, on a hook screwed into the corkboard was a chunky bunch of keys. He fanned them out and went through each one until he found the correct type. Then he started on the lockers, systematically trying each key in turn. After five minutes, he had all three of them open. He stepped back to take it all in and smiled. Yes, that should do the trick. He opened his shoulder bag, concealed under his overall, and pulled out his camera. Twenty minutes later, the lockers were closed, the keys returned to their hook and Gordon was sitting on the bed, reading Dave's copy of *The Daily Mirror*. Dave would be surprised when he returned to find that stupid old Gordon had finished the crossword he had started. Some things you just couldn't predict. All he had to do now was wait.

36

When Helen got back, the house was in darkness. She opened the front door and called out, "Hello. Anyone at home? Johnny?"

There was no reply. She listened for a moment, standing in the cold, gloomy hallway, but all that came back was the creak of the house shifting and breathing and the hum of the fridge in the kitchen. Johnny must have already gone. She switched the light on and hung her coat and scarf on the stair post and made her way to the kitchen holding a crumpled piece of paper. Light flooded the room and she could see the clouds of her breath that steamed into the air. Shivering, she filled the kettle and switched it on. While she waited, she took in the rest of the kitchen and felt an itch of irritation as she realised that he hadn't finished the clearing up that the rest of them had started. Sometimes, she could have cheerfully strangled him. He was selfish and lazy and, too often, just didn't pull his weight in the house. Even more irritating, he seemed to think a dose of smiling charm could instantly make everything better.

She finished making coffee and sat at the table, hands wrapped around the mug for warmth, still thinking of Johnny. She was annoyed with herself. She spent far too much time thinking of Johnny, while he didn't seem to think of anyone except himself. Oh, and that doctor, the fragrant Juliet. If only she could remember where she had seen her before, then she might be able to get to the bottom of the uneasy feeling that bubbled up whenever she thought of her.

She looked at the flyer she had placed on the kitchen table, and smoothed it out. It was printed on cheap matte paper, a washed-out violet colour, with smudged type:

End violence against women.
Reclaim the Streets.
Another victim while police do nothing but
tell us to stay indoors.
Curfew for men, not women.
Protest Saturday December 22nd
St Helens Square, York, 5 p.m.

She wondered how many people would be there at such short notice. She had only found out about it at the station when she had gone to see Jaggers, Kate and Mark off earlier that morning. The woman who had thrust the flyer into her hand as she left the station had just said, "It's for the student in Leeds. Tell as many people as possible. We can't just let everything carry on as normal." When Helen had asked, "Will you get anyone there at Christmas?" the reply had been short and blunt: "Fuck Christmas"

She finished her coffee and went upstairs to her room. She only had an hour before she would have to get going for the demo. She turned on the gas heater, which lit with a hiss and a crump as the spark caught, and settled down to read in the armchair opposite the flames. The room began to gradually warm up as the flames turned from blue to orange, a little more with every turn of the page, but then, without warning, the fire sighed and the wall of flames collapsed, guttered and then, finally, disappeared. Unlit, the grey plastic seemed ugly and useless.

"Damn," she exclaimed, and putting the book down, rummaged in her pockets for a new ten-pence piece for the meter. She tried several times, going through the same pockets in desperation, before she turned her attention to her desk and bag. The result was the same. Nothing. She slumped back down in her armchair and fought back tears. There was an icy chill in the air and the prospect of spending the night there on her own suddenly seemed very daunting. Why on earth hadn't she gone back home today, the same as Kate, Mark and Jaggers? She knew the answer, but didn't want to admit it to herself. The chance to spend some time in the house, at Christmas, alone with Johnny. Was that really what things had come to: hanging around mooning after a man, fantasising about what could happen? What had she been thinking of? Did she really think he would creep up to her bed after a night shift at murder central?

She was so annoyed with herself, she couldn't settle to her book. Besides, the brief flurry of warmth had already seeped away through the rattling window panes. She should have taken a leaf out of Johnny's book and fiddled the meter so she could recycle a ten-pence piece, like he and Jaggers did. A thought occurred to her. There would be a coin in his room, next to the fire, ready for more recycling. The idea raised a smile to her face. That was what Johnny was worth to her: ten pence.

She clambered up the stairs, two at a time, and opened the door of his room, directly above hers. She hesitated on the threshold, peeking around the door as if a monster was lying in wait for her. She looked around slowly. There were odd socks on the floor with a random collection of discarded clothes competing for space with last night's ashtray, half-empty glasses and cans. The blinds were up, showing the now dark sky and the street lamps opposite. She turned the light on, went across to the window and closed the blinds. Even under the unforgiving glare of the light, and its exposure of the mess, the room had an appealing atmosphere, with an underlying smell of patchouli and old joss stick, familiar yet forbidden at the same time.

Helen forced herself to attend to business. That way, it felt less wrong to be in Johnny's room, like a spy. She got on her knees in front of the fire and searched for the coin, finally finding it in the loosened compartment of the slot meter. She seized on it in triumph, holding it up before slipping it in the pocket of her jeans. Mission accomplished. Flushed with success, she looked around the room in what she intended to be a final sweep before going back downstairs. Her gaze settled on Johnny's desk and without thinking, she took a couple of steps towards it. Her hand grazed the desk top and she began to pick up individual items to examine one by one. A zippo lighter. That week's *NME*. A frisbee. An old copy of *Songs of Innocence and Experience*. A photograph from sixth form with a group of long-haired hippies. She smiled. Was that tall guy at the end really Johnny? And a diary.

She hesitated. Then looking round a couple of times, she picked it up and went to lie down on the bed. She propped herself up with a couple of pillows and turned the diary over and over in her hands. It was A5 size, with red hard covers. Finally, she opened it and saw it was a week to view and felt a pang of disappointment. Not enough room for pouring out your innermost feelings and desires. She hovered over the first page, from January 1979, before beginning to read. Appointments. Shifts at the hospital. Gigs. Parties. Visits back home. On one double-page spread, she saw her own name and felt a little shiver of excitement, but was deflated when it was just a note of when she was away. More air leaked out of her balloon when she saw that there were similar entries for the others in the house. Just as well there was no room for secrets, desires, or feelings as Johnny clearly didn't have any.

She closed the diary and admitted defeat, leaning back against the pillows and closing her eyes. *My God*, she thought, *what am I doing? Getting flustered by creeping around, sneakily reading the diary of a man with the inner life of an accountant.* Immediately, she felt guilty. Anyone reading her own diary would draw similar conclusions. She knew deep down that she, like Johnny, was more than the sum of her appointments and domestic practicalities.

She shivered lying on top of the bed. The cold had seeped into her bones. She should go back to her own room, use the coin she'd found, and warm herself up before going out to the demo, hopefully with a modicum of self-respect left intact. She luxuriated in one last stretch on the bed, throwing both arms out as wide as they would go. At the end of her stretch, her left arm came down by the side of the bed. Her right hand scraped against the wall, and then fell into the space between the bed and the wall. Her fingers touched leather and closed around a strap. She sat up, curious, and pulled the strap towards her. It was a small shoulder bag, black leather, with a chrome clasp.

She held it in both hands and examined it. She opened the clasp and pulled the leather flap back. Inside, the purse was full of the usual things: lipstick, mirror, brush, notebook, chequebook, perfume, some receipts, and a slim wallet. She fished out the wallet and began to go through it. The first card she pulled out was some kind of identity document for Dr Juliet Fulton, the photograph of a beautiful young woman, unsmiling, in white overall with a stethoscope around her neck, confirming her identity.

So, she'd left her bag last night. She must have forgotten it in all the confusion of the drug squad raid, and the police interviews. Except that Juliet Fulton had not been interviewed, she had just slipped away quietly, without a word of goodbye. Serve her right if she was inconvenienced by leaving her bag behind. She was not proud of her instincts right at that moment, but they were too strong to resist. She'd keep hold of Dr Fulton's bag, just for the moment.

She went up to her room, opened the chest of drawers, and hid the bag under layers of clothes. Then she lit the fire and got ready to go out as quickly as she could, shivering in the chill air. Her eyes flicked from her full-length mirror to the drawer and back again throughout the procedure. Finally, satisfied, she left, giving the drawer one last glance. The bag and its contents would be waiting for her when she got back.

37

It was completely dark as Helen picked her way through the streets of the city. By the time she got to the main shopping areas, snow had given way to a glistening, patchy slush that reflected the Christmas lights lining the streets and decorating every shop window. The centre of York was thick with shoppers in the last, frantic push for presents. Soon, in the next hour, they would be replaced by drinkers, diners and revellers of all kinds, as the shops closed, but for now, everyone seemed to press on towards their various destinations with a grim determination to achieve their goals. Their heads were down, their faces set, oblivious to the beauty of the ancient streets they walked through. As Helen walked down Davygate towards St Helens Square, the sound of a brass band playing carols got louder. She walked past the queue for Betty's and rounded the corner. One half of the square was taken up by the Salvation Army band and their tin-rattling followers. The other was a small gathering of the Reclaim the Streets protestors, with their banners and placards. There were about thirty of them, straddling the pavement on the far side of the square.

Helen looked across at them as she approached, scanning the faces for anyone she recognised. There were a couple of familiar faces, but no one she was on speaking terms with. The clock at the top of one of the stately buildings in the square made it a few minutes after five. The demo had only just begun and at the moment Helen joined the group, the Salvation Army were the dominant force. The brass band was powerful, the choir resonantly in tune and the crowd was with them.

Helen attached herself to the closest edge of the knot of protestors. She took the placard that was proffered by a smiling activist and waited to see what would happen next. At the front of the group, a young woman was dwarfed by the drum she had slung over her neck in front of her. The woman next to her, who Helen recognised as one of the organisers, gave a signal, and the drummer began to beat out a rhythm. This was the signal for pre-arranged chanting to start up, in time with the drum beat. Helen joined in, glad of the opportunity to blend in to the mass, shaking her placard in time.

The Salvation Army pressed on with their more traditional fare. The atmosphere among the crowds, both those passing through and those who had stopped to listen and put some coins in the collection boxes, began to falter. Faces turned towards the demonstrators, scowling at the disruption. A few boos sprang up, gradually growing into angry jeers and fist shaking. There was a cacophony of noise: brass band, chanting, drumming, heckling. Helen shifted uncomfortably from foot to foot, scanning the square, and then looking across the group to see if there was any reaction to the crowd's hostility.

And then she saw her. She froze, and half-hid behind her placard. On the far side of the group, chanting slogans at the top of her voice, was Juliet Fulton.

38

In that same instant, it came back to Helen. It had been gnawing away at the back of her mind, ever since the party when Johnny had introduced her to Juliet. Her face had been strangely familiar, and yet she hadn't been able to pin down why. Now, the association made the memories flood back in. Juliet had been a constant presence at all the women's demonstrations and protests she had attended over the last couple of years, in Leeds as well as York. She did not remember her as a main player, an organiser or driver of events, but as someone, strikingly beautiful, who was always there, to one side and never taking the lead at the front. Helen even remembered thinking about her at one of the rallies, that it was useful to have someone so attractive there, simply in order to counter the tiresome old stereotype of the butch lesbian feminist with hairy legs and sack-like clothing.

She chanced another glance at her from behind her placard. Yes, there she was, chanting and whooping, seemingly oblivious to Helen's presence. That decided it for her. She really couldn't bear the idea of meeting her here, with the stilted chat that would inevitably follow. She lay her placard down on the pavement, and without a word, slipped away into the crowd, her hat jammed down on her head, her collar up and her scarf wrapped high around her face, under her nose. She had no idea whether Juliet could see her escaping, but she didn't care. If it came up in any later conversation, she would just smile and lie. She was good at that when she had to be.

She picked up speed, fearing a tap on the shoulder at any moment, and skirted the window of Betty's, past the usual long queue of punters waiting for a table, still with her head down. Without warning, an arm shot out in front of her.

"Hello, fancy seeing you here."

Helen stopped as if stung and looked up, confused. There was a young woman standing in front of her, smiling. Helen stared at her, frowning. She had a familiar look but she couldn't place her, and she was acutely aware that Juliet Fulton was behind them and could be watching the whole thing. She really just wanted to get away. The thought of her flashed a look of distress across her face. The woman in front of her reached out to touch her arm.

"Are you alright? Sorry, I didn't mean to shock you. You just looked like you were carrying the troubles of the world on your shoulders."

Helen returned her smile uncertainly, but didn't reply.

The woman explained, "I'm Paula. The police officer. I've been to your house, remember? We spoke at your party last night."

Helen shook her head. "Last night? No, I don't..." She trailed off and looked at her again. "Oh, yes, I remember now. Your clothes are different somehow... Look, sorry, but, I don't mean to be rude..." She looked back to the square again and then at Paula. Her face was drawn with doubt and anxiety.

Once again, Paula tried to help her out. "Listen, do you want to get a coffee? I'm at the front of the queue and it seems a shame to waste it."

Helen hesitated before plunging in. "Can I talk to you about something? About what I said last night, I mean. It's been worrying me." She shook her head, embarrassed. "No, course not. Never mind, it's probably nothing."

At that moment, the black-suited queue manager oiled his way up to them, clipboard in hand.

"Table for two, madam? This way, please."

He slid into the café like a gentle breath of wind, and Paula, smiling in encouragement, ushered Helen ahead of her. The dining room was warm and bright, full of gilt and velvet, with deep pile carpets that deadened the sound of gentle conversation and the clink of cutlery on porcelain. The outside world disappeared behind the wall of plate-glass windows that curved round the room, a silent film screened for the unobtrusive entertainment of the café's patrons. From this vantage point, the Salvation Army and the demonstration in the square outside were both merely a part of an interesting tableau, drained of any deeper meaning. They sat down, Helen careful to choose the seat furthest away from the window. The table, like all the others, was covered in a crisp, white tablecloth. Two menus stood to attention in the middle of the table.

"It's posh, isn't it?" Helen asked, scanning the room. "I've never been in here before."

"It's nice," Paula replied. "I often come in as a treat after a long shift."

"On your own?"

"No, I was supposed to meet my… a friend, but she's late."

"Oh, sorry. I didn't mean to interrupt. I'll go when she arrives."

Paula smiled at her. "Don't worry, it'll be closing soon anyway. That's why we managed to get a table."

A new waiter appeared at the table and they ordered. Throughout their conversation, Helen's eyes occasionally glanced over Paula's shoulder.

"So," Paula began, "what did you want to tell me?"

Helen looked down at the table. "I dunno, I… You know Johnny had nothing to do with any of this, don't you?"

"How do you know that exactly? People are very good at lying to their partners, you know."

Helen bristled. "He's not my partner; he's just a friend. He was just in the wrong place at the wrong time, that's all."

Paula bristled back. "I hope you haven't made me buy you a posh cup of coffee just to tell me that."

"No. It's about that doctor. You remember I talked to you at the party about her?"

"Yes. You said you didn't trust her."

"It's just that, I've got a bad feeling about her."

Paula raised her eyebrows. The waiter returned with their coffee, and she poured two cups. "Yeah you said that before. I mean…"

"No, honestly. I just think she's a bit of a phoney. Like the way she was at our party on Friday. I know she was supposed to be there because Johnny fancies her, but she couldn't get away fast enough when the police arrived. And she was having some kind of a row with Dr… er, with Gordon. I'm surprised she even knows him, to be honest."

"But not surprised that Johnny knows him? After all, Johnny invited him to the party as well, didn't he? Can't imagine he fitted in that well."

"No, that was just Johnny trying to test his alibi about dealing dope. Oh…" She stopped suddenly, not wanting to remind the police about drugs.

"Don't worry. We're not interested in what you lot get up to. We're trying to catch a murderer, remember."

They sipped their coffee. Paula began again. "What about this Dr Death thing? Is that serious?"

"According to Johnny, Gordon is just a bit of a weirdo about the bodies. Everyone seems to know, but nothing happens, so I suppose they don't think it's very important. Sounds disgusting to me, to be honest."

"Me too."

Paula paused and fiddled with her spoon. "Listen, all you've told me is that Dr Fulton gives you a weird feeling. It's not much to go on, is it? But you seemed really disturbed when I bumped into you. I don't get it."

Helen lent forward and lowered her voice. "She's outside."

"Who is?"

"Dr Fulton. She's on the demo, same as I was. I knew I recognised her from somewhere. She's often at these demos."

"Well, that's not a crime, is it? She's your kind of age, an educated woman. A demo is exactly the sort of place you might find her. In fact, you might find me there one day."

Helen narrowed her eyes. "Oh… yeah, right," she stammered. "The thing is, well, I'm not sure that that's her name. Fulton, I mean. Or Juliet. Oh, I dunno." She shook her head and began to gather her things. "Just ignore it. Probably nothing. But thanks for the coffee."

Paula rummaged in her bag, and took out a notebook and a pen. She scribbled on a blank page and ripped it out.

"Here," she said, "this is my number. My home number. You think of anything, just ring me, alright? Or if you just want to talk. Anytime."

Helen took it and they both stood up to leave. They passed the queue manager and slipped out onto the pavement. The sound of the demo and the carols filled the air.

Helen waved the piece of paper at her. "Thanks for this."

"You walking back to East Mount Road?"

"Yeah."

"On your own?"

"It's busy, and there are a lot of people around."

"You really should be with someone when you're out after dark."

"Next, you'll be telling me to stay indoors at night. Come on, it's my town as well, you know."

Paula held up her hands. "OK. Just be careful, alright?"

Helen nodded and set off down the street.

Paula watched her go, a small figure receding into the distance, until she was lost in the crowd.

39

Helen turned the corner onto Blossom Street, under the huge poster warning about the Ripper. She barely noticed it these days. No one did any more. But one person was watching it intently.

Across the street, under the shadow of Micklegate Bar, a figure stood huddled against the cold, watching her. Helen could be seen crossing in front of the great, stark black and white billboard, set against a backdrop of icy, white snow, with the occasional flurry of flakes driven across it by a gust of wind. From the shadows in the distance, she looked as if one of the letters had detached itself from the hoarding and had started to walk across it, having had enough of poster duty. A slight, black figure, hunched against the cold, slowly making her way along the street, alone. She moved out of the glare lighting up the billboard and was swallowed by the darkness of a late-December afternoon.

Waiting until there was enough distance between them, the watcher slipped out from under the ancient stone walls and began to follow her, along Blossom Street and then turning into East Mount Road. At the corner, there was another pause, watching Helen fiddle with her keys before opening the front door and disappearing inside. With a bit of luck, she would be on her own.

After a minute, the watcher arrived at the doorstep and gave a firm rap of the knocker.

The door opened and Helen stood there, her coat still on, and a look of bewilderment crossed her face. "Oh. It's you. What are you doing here?"

Juliet gave a wry smile. "That's not very friendly."

When Helen did not reply, she continued, "Is Johnny in?"

Helen frowned. "No, he's not. Sorry."

"Good. It was you I wanted to talk to, actually."

"Me? What about?"

Juliet shuffled her feet in the snow on the doorstep and shivered. "Can I come in? It's freezing out here."

Curiosity got the better of Helen and she stood aside for Juliet to pass. She led her to the kitchen.

"Sit down." She gestured at the kitchen table. "I won't offer you coffee; I'm a bit busy."

They both sat at the table and Juliet scanned the room.

"You've done well to clean up after last night so quickly. Usually takes me days to get rid of the evidence."

Helen snorted. "You haven't seen the other rooms. As I say, I've got a lot to do. So, what was it you wanted to say?"

Juliet received the message that small talk was not welcome, so she pressed on. "Just that I've lost my bag. I've retraced my steps and I think the only place it could be is here. I must have put it down at the party and it's fallen down somewhere, or it's underneath something. Has anyone found anything here?"

Helen shook her head. "No, sorry. What sort of bag was it?"

"Was a small shoulder bag. Black leather."

"Anything valuable in it?"

"Chequebook. Work diary. The chequebook's the main thing. I'll need to get money out for Christmas on Monday. I mean, I can go to the bank, it's just a bit of a hassle."

"Well, sorry, but nothing turned up here."

Juliet hesitated. "Do you think I could look in Johnny's room? I might have lost it there, in all the…" She trailed off, not wanting to finish the sentence.

Helen smiled brightly at her, a brittle friendliness masking her annoyance.

"I think that would be alright if I came with you. Come on."

They climbed the stairs up to Johnny's room in silence. When Helen opened the door, they were greeted by the smell of cigarettes, weed, stale beer and young man, overlayed by cheap joss stick. A few items of clothing were scattered across the floor.

A flicker of a smile passed across Juliet's face. "Doesn't look like Johnny's had time to clear up then. Not very domesticated, that's what you were saying last night."

"No sign of a bag," Helen replied. "Looks like you've had a wasted journey."

Juliet clambered onto the bed and thrust her arm down the side. "Might have dropped down here," she said.

"Was this where you were then?" Helen asked, sitting on the edge of the bed,

Juliet abandoned her sweeps of the space between the bed and the wall and retrieved her arm. She sat up at the other end of the bed and the space between them was like no man's land in the trenches. Helen looked at her, waiting for an answer. Juliet looked at the bed, seemingly lost in thought.

"Well?" Helen asked pointedly.

"What? Oh, yes, I was. For a bit anyway. Until the party broke up."

"You left pretty quickly last night, didn't you? That Drugs Squad bloke barely had time to question you."

"He didn't really want to question me. He just wanted to get in my knickers. Men are so disappointing, don't you find?"

She ignored the question and pressed Juliet again. "Johnny was a bit disappointed you didn't hang around."

"Was he?" She shrugged. "The party was over, wasn't it? Generally, the police are not good as an aphrodisiac. They tend to put a downer on everything."

Helen scowled at her, infuriated by her coolness. "Listen, don't mess him around. He's a nice guy; he deserves better than that."

"He does," agreed Juliet, "but don't bring me into it. You obviously fancy him; why don't you just tell him and stop using me as an excuse?" She looked at the surprise on Helen's face. "Or are you afraid he'll turn you down? Best-friend material but not hot-date material. You'll never know unless you make a move. He's not going to. I think you know that."

Helen's coolness evaporated and she exploded into an angry outburst. "I think it's time you left. Your bag isn't here, if it ever was. You're a liar. I think you're lying about just about everything: your name, your job, Johnny, everything."

Juliet stood up, smiled and narrowed her eyes.

"You should do something about all this frustrated sexual tension, you know. It's not good for you. If you find the bag, let me know. I'll see myself out."

Juliet slammed the front door behind her and trudged through the snowy streets towards the city walls again. Her mind was working overtime, processing what had just happened. If Helen had her suspicions, when would she tell Johnny? More importantly, would he believe her? That, she decided, as she picked her way down Micklegate, could be very awkward. Very awkward indeed.

*

As it turned out, Helen didn't tell Johnny anything at all. There had been a vague plan for them to spend Saturday night together at home, once it had been established that the others wouldn't be there, but nothing had actually been arranged. He rang her on Saturday night from a phone box, saying that he had bumped into Bim and Fred on their way to watch York City play. He had gone along with them to the game and then they'd invited him back for dinner with Sarah and the others. Helen had turned down his idea that she come and meet them there. He had sounded a bit drunk and she didn't feel like being at his beck and call. Was she punishing him? She didn't know and, although he sounded pleasingly disappointed, he didn't seem that concerned that she was on her own at home. Maybe he thought he'd done his bit by ringing her. And on the Sunday, Helen was meeting some work colleagues for a Christmas lunch in town. By the time she got back, Johnny had left for work. This was not what she had imagined a Christmas home alone with Johnny would be like. More fool her, she thought, as her annoyance simmered away just under the surface.

40

Sunday was meant to be a day of rest, DCI Grayson reflected as he surveyed the crowded incident room. Some chance of that. The case was bubbling nicely; Grayson's instinct and experience told him that. He could smell it. They just needed some hard forensic evidence to stitch it all together, or, failing that, a bit of old-school interrogation, courtesy of Jacko. Grayson shuffled in his seat. He really would prefer not to go there, but it might prove necessary if nothing else emerged. And anyway, he reasoned, Simpson was clearly their man, so a bit of rule-bending was acceptable to his mind. It was time to unleash the hounds.

"Alright everyone, let's make a start, shall we? I know it's Sunday, I know you were all out on the piss last night, but we are very close now. We just need to close a few gaps and harvest some evidence. One last push, and we can all have a nice Christmas, without having to worry about all of this bollocks, eh?"

There was a hum of agreement among the team, as they multitasked handling coffee, bacon sandwiches and cigarettes at the same time as listening to Grayson's directions.

"We've got the warrant for Simpson's gaff. Hopefully, he'll show up today at some point. He's due on shift at 10 p.m., but whenever we get hold of him, it would be helpful to have got something from his house. Jacko, you're on that, with a forensic team. Clive, Paula, you get hold of Wilson and Fulton. We need to know when exactly they were in Sutherland's house and why they were there. What's the relationship there and why did they not say anything about it?"

There was a nodding of heads and a chorus of, "Yes, guv," from the team.

"You two do both interviews together, yeah. As close together as possible. And go hard on the pair of them, eh? No softly softly – we need a result."

Paula nodded and mouthed her, "Yes, guv," as expected, adding, almost as an afterthought, "What will you be doing, guv?"

There was a silence, and everyone who had started to gather their things and head out, stopped. Grayson saw her startled expression as she attempted to explain. "I just meant, what—"

He cut through her embarrassment. "Me, DC Marsh? I'm saving myself for Simpson. Think of me as the matador in the bull fight. I'll finish him off. Now, let's get on with it."

*

Jacko saw the curtains twitch even before he got out of the car. Clearly, Mabel Ramsbottom did not take time off from her neighbourly duties for Christmas. He went through the motions of knocking on the door and calling through the letterbox but he suspected that Gordon Simpson was long gone. He stepped aside and gestured to the uniform behind him, who neatly broke the lock with an easy swing of his battering ram.

He crossed the threshold and called out, "Mr Simpson? Police. We just need to ask you a few questions. It's time to tell the truth, Gordon, lad."

There was no response. Jacko held the rest of the team back at the door and listened intently for telltale sounds of movement upstairs, or at the back, but there was nothing. He turned to the forensic team.

"Just give me a minute or two to give the place a once over. I'll shout when I need you."

He went steadily through the house, from room to room. The kitchen revealed Gordon's passion for Pot Noodle, chocolate digestives and cleaning the fridge, but little else. He moved on to the living room. He noticed Gordon's exotic collection of books, which indicated an unhealthy interest in serial killers and Elvis Presley, but it wasn't exactly evidence. He picked up the first book from the shelf and flicked through it. *Beyond Belief – The Moors Murderers*. He turned to the front of the book and found the stamp. *North Yorkshire Public Libraries*. He smiled. Two years overdue. He was certain that would prove to be only the first of Gordon Simpson's crimes.

He noted the television. Large and colour with a VHS recorder underneath it. The kit of someone who spent a lot of time at home watching the telly. And films, thought Jacko. Specialist films. Next to it was a cabinet. He tried the door but it was locked. So that's where he keeps his tapes, then. God only knows what was on that lot. Plenty of time to find out, though, and he didn't want to keep the forensic lads waiting. He'd just have a quick shufti upstairs and then he'd leave it to them.

The bedroom was just as clean as the rest of the house, with some more padlocked cupboards. He had a quick look in the chest of drawers, and had a fumble among a lurid range of underwear and socks, before calling it a day. No point buggering up the forensics with too much hands-on stuff. He left the room and stood for a moment on the landing, scanning the space and thinking. No loft space. Good, he thought. Now for the second bedroom and that'll be that.

He reached for the door handle and turned it. The door would not open. He rattled against the handle and tried again. Still nothing. Odd for a bedroom to be locked.

"Fred," he shouted down the stairs. "Need you up here. Bring the key."

The man who had broken open the door to the house earlier, came up the stairs two at a time. The "key" was slung over his shoulder. He removed it, and took up his stance in front of the locked door.

"Better stand aside," he warned Jacko, with no expectation he would take any notice. He didn't wait to see. With a quick swing, the doorjamb splintered and the door swung open. The room was in darkness. He reached his hand around the door frame and felt inside the wall for a light switch. He turned it on and the room was filled with a bright-red light that spilled out onto the floor of the landing. Jacko frowned, puzzled, and took a step into the room. He stopped almost immediately.

"Bloody hell," he breathed. "Bloody. Fucking. Hell."

*

Gloria noticed the red Capri pull up opposite her flat. It stood out in the snow-covered cul de sac like Rudolph's nose. She knew before they got out of the car and instinctively took a quick look round her front room. She knew, rationally, that there was nothing incriminating on display, but she couldn't shake her automatic reaction that she'd missed something, or she had done something stupid and she was going to get caught. She glanced back to the window. Two people were walking towards her front path, picking their way carefully through impacted snow. She recognised them from the hospital. A tall, good-looking man and a younger woman, obviously junior. Detectives. *Alright then, detect this.* She took a deep breath and went into the hall. The second the bell sounded, she arranged her smile and opened the door.

"Hello?" she said, in a polite, quizzical tone.

"Mrs Wilson?"

"Yes, that's right."

Clive flicked open his ID as he spoke and flashed it in her direction.

"Detective Sergeant Brooks, North Yorkshire Police. This is DC Marsh. We need to ask you a few questions. Can we come in?"

Her eyes flicked to the ID photo. It could have been a picture of Father Christmas for all the notice she took of it.

"Is this about poor Mr Sutherland again?"

"Yes, that's right, Mrs Wilson. If you wouldn't mind?"

She appeared flustered. "Oh yes, of course. Sorry, please come through."

She stood aside to let them pass and closed the door behind her. Then she went ahead of them to the living room. She indicated the sofa.

"Please, have a seat. Do you want a cup of tea or something?"

"No thanks, Mrs Wilson, we're fine."

"So, how can I help you, Detective Sergeant?"

She flashed a dazzling smile at him, and got herself comfortable in her armchair, so that her dress rode up slightly, showing off her legs. She directed her interest towards him, but she was careful not to be too obvious.

Both detectives had taken out their notebooks. The woman's eyes roved around the room, taking in ornaments, furniture, a few pictures from Habitat. When Gloria answered Brooks's questions, she could feel the woman's eyes examining her in forensic detail. She could feel them burrowing into her, trying to peel back the layers, to separate the actor from the character.

"You haven't told us everything about your relationship with Mr Sutherland, have you, Gloria?"

"What do you mean? I didn't have a relationship with Mr Sutherland. Why do you think that?"

"So, you've never been to his house then?"

Gloria frowned. "No, no of course I haven't. He was just someone who I came across at work. At the hospital."

"So how do you explain the fact that your fingerprints are all over his house?"

"My fingerprints? There must have been some kind of mistake. I've never been there."

Brooks shook his head. "There's no mistake, Gloria, except the one you're making now. You're going to need a better answer than that in court."

"Court? I don't understand."

She looked from one to the other, hoping her bewilderment might give them pause for doubt. Brooks immediately threw cold water on that idea.

"Come on, Gloria, let's not play games, eh? We have people who will testify that you visited Sutherland at his home."

Gloria caught the look that his colleague flashed at him, partly masked by her poker face. She would have to change tack, feigning a lapse of memory.

"Sorry, I totally forgot about it. He had some kind of drinks party a couple of months ago. Quite a few staff from the hospital pitched up. He did it quite regular, I think, but it was the only one I'd been invited to. That's why I forgot all about it."

Brooks smiled at her. "Strange that, though, isn't it? I mean, wouldn't a consultant normally invite the high and mighty to his parties? Wouldn't you have been flattered? I wouldn't have thought that consultants mixed socially with nurses."

"No, they don't."

"So…?"

There was a pause. Gloria looked a little embarrassed, before appearing to make her mind up. "Look, you probably know by now that he had a bit of a reputation as a ladies' man. He liked to have nurses at his dos."

"So, you were there for decoration, then. A bit of romance, a bit of flirting?"

Marsh took up the questioning. "We think you were in a relationship with Mr Sutherland. Good-looking woman. Just the sort he liked."

"No, of course I wasn't. A relationship? With him? I…"

She trailed off, her expression somewhere between disgust and upset. Her hand automatically went to her chest, and she began to rub her breast bone, making little circles with the tips of her fingers, as if she had suddenly had an attack of indigestion. She was pulled out of her daydream by Marsh continuing to jab at her with questions.

"And then it all went wrong, didn't it, Mrs Wilson? And he's not used to being turned down, is he? Good-looking man. Successful. Nice house, lot of money. I bet he didn't like that, did he? Was he looking for a bit of rough? Went cold when you wanted something more?"

"What are you talking about? You can't possibly think I've got anything to do with his death? It's ridiculous; you're just making things up now."

Brooks took up the questioning again. "And what about your relationships with Juliet Fulton and Gordon Simpson? Tell us about them."

The blood drained from Gloria's face. She felt she was standing on trembling ground. With a supreme effort of will, she steadied herself and started to speak. At first, her words sounded to her ears as if they were coming from a very long distance away, but then the pounding in her head seeped away and she could hold on to her calm, even-toned explanations.

"Apart from work colleagues, you mean? Well then, nothing. I didn't have – I don't have – a relationship with them. They were just at the same party, that's all."

"And they were all there when Sutherland was murdered, weren't they? Including you. Easy to slip away from the ward on nights, I would have thought. Not exactly high security, is it? No cameras, nothing."

"All of that applies to everyone on duty that night, doesn't it? And he was drugged and put in the fridge, wasn't he? That's what I heard. How on earth could I do that on my own?"

There was the briefest of pauses, before Brooks replied. It was just enough to give Gloria even more certainty that they were just trying out explanations to see whether she would bite.

"No one said you did it on your own, did they, Gloria?"

She broke out into a broad smile. "Dear me, pet, you really are desperate, aren't you? No wonder you haven't caught the bloody Ripper yet, if this is the best you can do. You've got no evidence, you obviously can't charge me with anything, so unless you've got something proper, I'm going to ask you to leave. None of this is anything to do with me."

Brooks stood up. Marsh quickly followed suit.

"We've got all we need for now, Mrs Wilson. It's just a question of following up a few other loose ends and then we'll be back. What are your shifts over the next few days?"

"I'm on nights over Christmas. Back in this afternoon."

Marsh chipped in with a smile. "Nights over Christmas? That's a bit tough, isn't it? Have you got no family to be with, love? No Mr Wilson?"

Gloria glowered at her. "The less said about him, the better. No, I can't afford to turn down double time; I need the money. And, no, since you ask, there's no family I'm close to. So, all in all, I'll be better off at work, rather than staying in with

Morecambe and Wise again on my own. I've done that more times than I care to remember."

She stood up and led them to the door, pulling her cardigan tighter around her as the icy draft knifed into the hallway.

"Don't go anywhere, Mrs Wilson; we'll be in touch. Oh, and Happy Christmas."

Gloria did not reply, her mouth a straight line as she watched them pick their way down the frozen path to their car. As soon as the door slammed, she went to the front room and with her eyes fixed on the red Capri outside, she picked up the phone and dialled a number. At the other end of the line, the phone rang and rang.

Outside, the Capri, belching clouds of exhaust fumes into the frosty air, pulled away from the kerb.

On the phone, a voice answered. Gloria listened and then spoke.

"It's me. We've got a problem…"

*

The Capri eased its way out of the estate, where the roads were still ungritted and largely covered with impacted snow that was gradually turning into ice. Once they reached the main road, black and glistening, Clive did not need to give all of his attention to safety and was able to talk.

"What did you think, then?" he asked, giving Paula a quick glance.

"She was different somehow," Paula replied.

"I know what you mean. A bit quieter, no make-up. I dunno, a bit more serious somehow."

"It's almost like she's putting it on a bit at work. You know, good old Gloria, game for a laugh. Innuendo and slap and tickle, like she's in a *Carry On* film or something."

"Something to hide, do you reckon?"

Paula considered the question for a moment. "Not necessarily. Maybe she has to do it to survive at work. There are lots of women like that in the police. You know, they put up with the gropers and the dirty jokers because if they don't, the word goes round that they're frigid or uptight or can't take a joke."

Clive frowned and stared at the road ahead.

Paula looked at him, surprised.

"You must have noticed that at work, surely?" she said.

"Well yeah, there's a bit of that, obviously. But it's just a bit of fun, isn't it? If it were serious, people would just report it, wouldn't they?"

Paula began to reply, but changed her mind, and turned her head to stare through the fogged-up window at the blurred, icy landscape flashing by.

Clive swivelled his head towards her momentarily.

"What? What have I said wrong this time?"

"Nothing," she replied. "It's just a bit harder to report things than you think. Let's not argue about it."

An uneasy truce settled on the dark interior of the car. The silence between them began to grow, until Paula broke it.

"There was another thing," she said.

"Go on." There was a shadow of relief in Clive's voice.

"Did you notice her front room? No photos, no sign of any family, nothing. It was so…" She searched for the right word. "So impersonal somehow, like a hotel room."

Clive glanced across at her for a second.

"You're right. That's funny. Someone else mentioned that, about somewhere else. Just recently… in this same case. Now who was it…" He stared through the windscreen, as if the answer lay outside, buried in the snow drifts. He shook his head. "No, it's gone. Damn."

"It'll come back, when you're not thinking about it. So, let's think about something else. What next?"

"Back to the hospital. We'll do Dr Fulton. Before we question her, I'll double-check what happened to her training at Leeds. And maybe you could check Gloria's personnel files, double-check her family background and her record at work, that sort of thing."

"OK, boss," Paula replied in clipped tones. Clive flashed her another look. She gave him a reassuring smile, and then turned and lay her forehead on the window, rubbing away the condensation so that she could see outside. Snow, traffic, and people struggling along, with the first yellow lights beginning to show. Dark night was still a couple of hours away, but an air of pervasive gloom had hung over the late-December day since dawn. Paula shivered. In this murk, it seemed that any of the people out there, fighting against the elements, could be a killer. *No*, she thought, with a bitter, sinking feeling, *that wasn't quite right. Any of the men.*

A raucous group of women, bedecked in tinsel and freezing in skimpy dresses, suddenly spilled out of The Rose and Crown on the crossroads in front of them, their laughter and screaming rising above the hum of traffic. Christmas drinking had started early for some, and as the darkness gathered, work beckoned them, the working girls. After all, drinks had to be paid for. Paula narrowed her eyes and stared across the street at them. The laughter died down and the group dissipated as they made off in different directions, individually or in pairs, suddenly cloaked in a silent seriousness. If any man could be a killer, then certainly, any woman could be a victim.

41

They sat round the table in the side room, picking up the photos in turn for a closer look. They were large, glossy black and white prints, studded with pinholes, and as they changed hands among the team, the mood shifted into a compelling mixture of quiet excitement and disgust.

Grayson looked at his team and then began.

"Alright, everyone, listen. These photographs in front of you are evidence. Hard evidence, that Jacko discovered at Simpson's place earlier today. Put some flesh on the bones for us, Jacko."

Jacko collected the prints into a pile and knocked them together on the table. He took the last drag from his cigarette, stubbed it out in the ashtray, and looked up at them all: Grayson, Brooks and Marsh. The minions of the team were in the main room, paper pushing, typing and cross-referencing interview statements. The dreary trudge of day-to-day policing, accomplished while waiting for any new developments that their bosses chose to share with them.

"So," Jacko began, "I came across these in a room next to Simpson's bedroom. A locked room. It seems our Gordon is a keen amateur photographer who develops his own pictures. But these are definitely not snaps from Scarborough beach.

No, as you can see, Gordon's interests were a little more, um, specialist, shall we say." He paused for effect, evidently hugely pleased with himself. "There were only five pictures pinned up on the wall. But the room were set up as a dark room, red light, all the gear, everything. He was clearly at it all the time. I reckon that's what he were burning, when his neighbour saw him. Getting rid of the evidence, like."

"But evidence of what, Jacko?" cut in Brooks.

"You've seen the pictures. He was obviously taking photos of the bodies in the morgue. Exposed bodies. Bodies that he'd been fiddling with. I reckon these five are pretty tame in comparison with the ones he burnt."

Brooks looked unconvinced. "All of that is evidence of a crime. A series of crimes, probably. Just not the crime we're investigating."

"No, but could be a motive for blackmail. If someone found out about it," Jacko replied. "And that might be a motive for murder."

"Maybe. But 'could'? 'Might'? It's all a bit loose, isn't it? We'll need something more than this."

There was a pause as the team considered Brooks's lack of enthusiasm for Jacko's discoveries.

Paula Marsh, her forehead furrowed, changed the direction of the discussion. "But there are six photos. What about this one?" She stretched out across the table and picked up a larger rectangle that was a little dog-eared, covered in multiple pin holes where it had been pinned to a cork board. It was a black and white photograph of a group of school children sitting formally in two rows, one higher than the other, in the grounds of a large, brick-fronted Victorian building. She held it up between her finger and thumb, showing it to the others.

"Alright, smartarse. Five significant pictures. That was pinned up with the others, but it's not the same. Just an old, official school photo by the look of it. I dunno whether you noticed but everyone in that picture is alive and wearing clothes, whereas in the others, well…" He left his sentence unfinished, a smile growing on his face.

Paula fumed, but she wouldn't let it go. "Maybe. But it was significant to him or he wouldn't have kept it all these years, would he? But anyway, putting that to one side, I just don't get how he could be doing this, when it was common knowledge he was a bit of a weirdo about bodies, and nobody thought to report it or pick him up about it. Everyone called him Dr Death, for heaven's sake, like it were a joke or something. What's going on at this hospital that allows someone to get away with all of this unchallenged? Did no one see him with a camera?"

Jacko shook his head. "For fuck's sake, we don't need to complicate this any further. There's nothing 'going on' at the hospital more than at any other big workplace. A bit of banter, a few characters, it's all completely normal. It's like that all over. The Council, Rowntree's, even bloody North Yorkshire Police. Nobody's perfect."

He looked around the group for someone to back him up, to slap down Marsh's preposterous conspiracy theories, but eyes flicked away from him. Grayson took some comfort from that and decided to close it down. The last thing the investigation needed was another round of women's lib wars. He held his hand up to Jacko as he spoke.

"Hold on, Jacko. Paula might be right, and anyway, it's the obvious next thing to check. First, we need to break into Simpson's locker. If he's taking photos of bodies, he might well keep stuff in there. We also need to check personnel files, see what the complaints procedures are and whether there've been any complaints made. We also need to get access to bank accounts: Sutherland's, and Simpson's."

"Wilson and Fulton as well, guv?" asked Brooks. "There's something not right there, I'm sure of it?"

"Aye, them and all. And Jewell, even though he's more or less in the clear. Might as well make a proper job of it."

"It's Dr Death we need to get hold of," muttered Jacko. "Wherever he's hiding. The minute we get hold of him, with the evidence we've got, and a couple of hours of a friendly chat out of the way somewhere, he'll confess to it."

Marsh shifted uncomfortably in her chair. She glanced at Clive but he determinedly avoided her eye.

Grayson needed to move on. "Alright, Jacko. Great work. Simpson's supposed to be on shift tonight at ten. He was seen in the hospital yesterday, even when he wasn't supposed to be here, so maybe he's got a little hidey-hole somewhere on site. Though what he thinks he's doing is beyond me. He can't disappear forever."

"Proof positive that he's our man, if you ask me," said Jacko. "Sure sign of guilt. He probably snuck in yesterday just to get rid of some evidence. He'll be miles away by now, mark my words."

"Maybe, Jacko. Maybe. But let's check nonetheless. Talk to the porters. They know all the boltholes in this place. They probably know where each one of 'em usually disappears to, you know, when they need a bit of kip." He turned his attention towards Brooks and Marsh. "What about you two? Did you get anything out of Wilson?"

"Well, she's definitely hiding something. Denied being at Sutherlands, then made up some cock and bull story about a party when she realised we had fingerprints. Denied any kind of relationship with Dr Fulton, or Dr Death, for that matter. We were going to follow it up this afternoon with a few phone calls and a dive into personnel records."

"OK. Good. Let's get on with it, then. With a bit of luck, we can get this wrapped up before close of play Christmas Eve and we can celebrate with a few pints down the Arms, before getting back home ready for the big day. And that way, boys and girls, our better halves will have done all of the hard graft for us."

He beamed at them all. Jacko forced a smile despite not having another half, better or worse. Clive returned the beam, main headlights style, thinking all the while that Mary would have his balls if he turned up late stinking of ale. Paula looked as if she were sucking a lemon.

"Come on then, chop-chop." Grayson said, clapping his hands. "Let's be having yers."

They stood up and marched through into the main incident room before collecting a few things from desks and immediately dispersing to crack on. The minions barely looked up, the rattle of typing, the dialling of numbers and the whisper of shuffled papers undisturbed by the passage of their superiors. The work went on.

*

Paula looked over her shoulder to check where Jacko was. His familiar dishevelled figure was at the end of the corridor, waddling towards them. His shirt strained over his belly, and the fat kipper tie hanging just below his jowly neck swung as he walked. There was just enough time. She turned to Brooks and spoke in an urgent low voice.

"Come on, Clive, help me out here. Can't we do the personnel records? I really can't face being stuck in a room with Jacko for two hours."

"Sorry Paula, no can do," he replied. "I've got to follow up on those calls. And anyway, you'll be fine. Think of it as an opportunity."

She scowled at him. "An opportunity for what? To lamp him? Honestly, Clive, if he starts—"

She broke off, catching Brooks's cheery grin being launched over her shoulder.

"Now then, Jacko lad," he called, "you and Paula are on personnel files. Try not to add to the body count, eh? I'll see you in a couple of hours."

He turned to go.

Jacko called after him as he strode down the corridor. "Where are you going then?"

Clive called breezily over his shoulder, "Me? I've got to see a man about a dog. Be good."

He waggled his hand over his shoulder at them and carried on walking.

Jacko turned back to Paula, fuming. "He thinks he's God's gift, that one. Always slips out of the donkey work. You want to watch him, you know. Bit of an eye for the ladies, if you know what I mean. Has he tried it on with you yet?"

Paula was nonplussed. "Clive? No, he's been very helpful and respectful, actually."

Jacko's expression conveyed a not so subtle mixture of disbelief and amusement. He looked up and down the length of Paula's body.

"Aye, well. His wife will be delighted." He left a pause and then picked up the thread again. "Well, it looks like it's you and me, darling, so let's get started, eh? Personnel records are just round the corner. I've got a set of keys and we've got all afternoon."

He tossed a set of keys in the air and caught them, and then swivelled on his heels and strode out into the corridor, leaving Paula to grab her things and scurry after him as if she were his lackey. She could feel her fury rising with every step. It had not been a good start.

*

The Capri crunched to a halt in the heavily gritted car park. Clive grabbed his coat and a cardboard folder, got out and locked the door, shivering in the sudden blast of freezing air. It was good to be back at the station, although he knew he would have to field a barrage of questions about the progress of the case from all and sundry. He reckoned that he could just pop in, head down, and avoid most of the scrutiny. It was Sunday after all, so there was a good chance it would be relatively quiet. Back at the hospital, after Paula's comments about the management regime there, he had suddenly realised that he didn't want to make his phone calls through their switchboard. He may be paranoid, but he wondered just how secure it was. So, a couple of calls, and then for the real business. He did have to see a man, but it was not about a dog.

He hurried across the car park, picking his way through mounds of shovelled snow, and went in via the main entrance. His eyes flicked left and right as he made his way to the main desk. Just a couple of punters waiting, and nobody awkward lying in wait. He stopped at the reception desk and signed in, scanning the names above his.

"Alright, Fred. How's it going? Quiet Sunday?"

The white-haired officer looked up from his *Sunday People*.

"Hello there, Clive. Yes, very quiet, touch wood. What about yourself? Any nearer catching that bastard in the hospital?"

Clive tapped his nose. "Very close, Fred. Very close. Is Andy Johnson in? I need a word."

"Just missed him. Left ten minutes ago. Urgent, was it?"

Clive's attention returned to the ledger. There was Andy's name, with a signature against the time of his arrival and departure.

"Eh? No, no, it'll wait. But if he comes back, tell him I need him to give me a bell."

He strode off into the innards of the building, the doors from the entrance to the main corridor swinging in his wake. Just before the end of the corridor, he found an empty room, and, looking quickly in both directions, he slipped in and closed the door. He sat down, picked up the phone and dialled the number he'd scribbled down. Eventually, it took him to a recorded message. When he heard it, he slumped back down again. Oh well, it was always going to be a long shot, expecting to get hold of someone the Sunday before Christmas.

He cleared his throat and, at the beep, began. "This DS Clive Brooks from York Police. I need to check the records of a Juliet Fulton, who was training as a doctor at Leeds until a month or so ago, when she transferred to York District hospital. Can someone ring me back when you get this message? I know it's Christmas, but it's urgent."

He left his numbers for the station and the incident room and then hung up. He drummed his fingertips furiously on the desktop as he went through his options, frustrated at his lack of progress. Whichever way he turned, it seemed as if he couldn't get a handle on Dr Fulton. Whenever he got close, she seemed to slip through his fingers, and he knew no more about her now than he did four days ago. He picked up the phone again and dialled another number. "Come on, come on," he muttered as the phone rang unheeded. The tone changed as the answerphone kicked in, but he'd been expecting that and he was ready with his message.

"Andy, it's Clive. For fuck's sake, what are you playing at? If I were the paranoid sort, I'd think you were avoiding me. I need to talk to you about Juliet Fulton, and what happened when you interviewed her on Friday. Ring me back, urgently, or better still, come into the incident room at the hospital. This is a murder inquiry, you know."

He thought for a moment, the receiver held a couple of inches away from his head, before slamming it down on its cradle. He'd have one last try. He made his way up to the first floor, two steps at a time. He had a quick glance into the open-plan office where his usual desk was and was pleased to see it was almost deserted. Then he carried on to the other end, and another smaller room. One or two heads looked up as he entered. He asked the first one, "Which is Andy Johnson's desk? He's not in, is he? I just need to see if he's left me something."

There was a mumbled reply and an extended arm pointing to a side room. He went in and quickly went through the neat piles of folders on the desk. Despite his Drug Squad appearance, Andy clearly was very methodical. Clive nodded in approval, but his search found nothing relating to him or Juliet Fulton. *Well,* he thought, *I suppose it was an unofficial raid the other day.* Andy had been doing him a favour, so it's not surprising that there would be no paperwork. He replaced the piles neatly and left.

This whole visit had been a waste of time, he thought. He should have stayed at the hospital and interviewed some more of the porters, trying to get some info on where the best hidey-holes were for someone wanting to keep their head down. He checked his watch. 2 p.m. He still had enough time to do that if he went back straight away. He slipped past the door to his office as unobtrusively as he could, hoping he wasn't delayed any further, the faint sounds of telephones ringing accompanying him as he went.

42

Jacko had made himself comfortable: a clear desk with an ashtray, a cup of coffee and the tin of M&S chocolate biscuits he had found in someone's office. At his feet, there were two piles of folders.

He sighed. "Tell me again why we're doing this?"

Paula matched his sigh. "We were looking for bank details for the main players, which we've got, and now we're just looking for anything that doesn't seem right. You know, complaints, disciplinaries, that sort of thing."

"And why, exactly?"

"You know why, Jacko. We need some evidence. And something approaching a motive. You seem pretty convinced that Gordon Simpson is our man, but we've got nothing to suggest why."

"And we won't need anything once he's confessed, so all we're doing is wasting time when we should be tracking down Dr fucking Death."

"How? Shall we just wander around a bit and keep our fingers crossed? Until we get some idea where he might be, this is the best thing we could be doing. His confession will be a lot quicker if we can present him with something incriminating."

"It'll be quick enough anyway. I have done this before, you know. Whereas you…" He paused and looked at her closely. "You're only just out of playschool and you spend most of your time talking out of your arse."

"I know you've done it before. You never get tired of telling us about it. But one day, Jacko, you're going to get your fingers burned for beating someone up, or you're going to put away someone who's innocent."

"Get my fingers burnt? See, you're still talking out of your arse. You have no idea how things work in the real world. Most of the people we deal with are the scum of the earth, but you and your lot want to treat them like fucking royalty. Well, not on my watch, pal." He slammed his fist down on the desk. "Convictions, that's what our job's about. And I'm not fussy about how we get 'em. The sooner you realise that, and forget about all this women's lib shit, the sooner you'll make a decent copper. Now, shut the fuck up and let's get on with it."

"At last, you've said summat I can agree with," she muttered, turning back to her pile of folders. She began to go through them, checking the personal details, looking for cross references to complaints or disciplinaries, but realised that she wasn't taking in any of the details as she was still fuming at Jacko and his caveman approach to the job. She stopped and made a conscious effort to clear her mind. Then she went over the previous two folders again, just in case.

Still nothing. Surely, there must be something here on one of them? Simpson, Sutherland, Wilson, Fulton. Even Jewell. They'd got bank details and addresses, but nothing out of the ordinary apart from that. She stopped and then turned back to Jacko. She was reluctant to ask him anything. He didn't need any excuse to think that she was stupid, but he'd never think of asking a question as team work, just an admission that she was out of her depth. She swallowed her pride and plunged in.

"Have you come across Fulton's file, Jacko? I've been through my lot twice, and it's not here."

He frowned. "Fulton? No, I don't think so. Hang on." He went through his list, and then flicked back through the files. "No, she's not here."

Their eyes met and shared the doubt.

"I'll just check the cabinet."

She walked to the other side of the office, pulled the drawer open and began to flick.

"No, nothing here under F."

"Try E and G. You know what these bloody daft secretaries are like."

Paula permitted herself a smile. Whatever would she have done without him? She would never have thought of that.

"Good idea," she replied sweetly.

She didn't have to check very carefully. Both sections were clearly empty.

"Nothing there either."

They swapped frowns and raised eyebrows. Paula left space for Jacko to voice the conclusion they had both reached.

"So Juliet Fulton doesn't have a personnel file. Or if she does, someone else has got hold of it."

"Maybe it's too soon. She's only been here a month."

Jacko shook his head. "Nah. Same as Jewell, but he's got one."

"Did you look at Gloria Wilson's file?"

He rummaged in his pile. "Yeah, here it is." He handed it over.

Paula opened it and was about to read through it when something on page one caught her eye. She showed it to Jacko.

"What does this mean? 'Blue folder'." She pointed to the handwritten note in the top right-hand corner.

"Dunno. That was on a few of the others I did."

"Same for me. Shall we pull them out, have another look?"

Jacko rolled his eyes. "If we have to. In for a penny, I suppose."

They both went back to their piles. After five minutes, they had both filleted out a separate pile of about a dozen files. They swapped them and quickly flicked through. Paula's scrutiny got quicker as she went along and finally she laid the last folder down. She looked at Jacko, eyes gleaming.

"Well?" he asked at last, exasperated by her silence.

"Did you see the connection, then?"

"What connection, Sherlock?"

"These files. They're all women."

*

It was just the four of them in the incident room now. Uniform had gone home a couple of hours before, set to return the next day at 9 a.m. to try and crack this before Christmas Day, so that they could have time to relax with their families. No such luck for the detectives. If they didn't make a breakthrough soon, Grayson's boss would start to interfere, with thinly veiled threats of bringing in the West Yorkshire lot. There would be mutterings about that force's abject failure so far in the Ripper case, but that would cut no ice. There would be bollockings, fists slammed on desks, cups thrown. Promotions were at stake.

"Why the fuck does this country close down on a Sunday? Every fucking thing grinds to a halt on the fucking day of rest. Why? No bugger goes to church any more. It's like living in the fucking dark ages." Jacko's face had turned an alarming shade of purple by the end of this rant. He subsided into quiet simmering.

"Feel better now? Got it off your chest?"

Grayson's enquiry did not require an answer and Jacko was experienced enough not to try and supply one.

Grayson started again. "You're absolutely right of course, but there's nowt we can do about it, so let's not give ourselves heart failure. We've made some progress today and we'll just follow up the loose ends at nine sharp tomorrow morning, when people are back at work. Let's just go through it."

"Clive, you're going back to Leeds General HR department, yes? Paula and Jacko, you are going to follow up on the Blue Files, find out if there is anything we should know about there. And by tomorrow, the banks will finally reopen and you can all check those bank accounts. With a bit of luck, something will come out of all that lot, and we will be able to get hold of Wilson, Fulton and Simpson. Once that happens, the whole pack of cards will come tumbling down."

He surveyed the other two, a broad smile on his face. Behind the smile, he knew that they didn't believe him. That was not surprising, he didn't believe him either, but it was enough to witness all of them playing the game for the sake of team morale. But then, Marsh pushed against it a little harder.

"But guv, I just don't get where they've all disappeared to. Why can't we get hold of them when we need to?"

"The hospital's a big building with lots of nooks and crannies. And all three of 'em are due on shift tonight. Keep the faith, Paula. They'll turn up."

"Well we've talked to Wilson, I suppose," she conceded, "but not Simpson or Fulton. There's something not right there. No personnel folder is ringing alarm bells for me."

"Me too, Paula. But we'll deal with it tomorrow, alright? Go home, the pair of you and get some rest. Big day tomorrow."

They gathered their things up, bundled themselves into outdoor coats and left together. Paula, bringing up the rear, took a final look at the pinboard. The photo of Sutherland stared out at her, from the centre of a spider's web of connections and possibilities that ensnared Gordon Simpson more than the others. Dr Death. She shook her head. Something was missing, but try as she might, she couldn't summon up anything that might be the key to unlock this door. She flicked the light switch, and the board with its matrix of photos and connecting lines disappeared into the darkness.

43

Johnny scanned the restroom. It looked like there was almost a full crew on tonight: Pat, gold medallion nestled on the black mat of chest hair, carefully arranged in the open neck of his unbuttoned overall; Les, the shop steward, his overall straining against his swelling belly as he yawned convulsively; and Sid, his ginger-toupeed head buried in the latest copy of *Variety*. All were sitting on the jumble of chairs that ringed the room. Johnny looked at his watch. 10 p.m. The night shift had started and the afternoon team had slipped away, one by one, as their replacements had each arrived. Les, recovering from the exertions of his yawn, copied him and held his own watch up for inspection. He stood up and the others followed his lead, apart from Sid, who was buried in his paper.

"It's gone ten," said Les. "Time we made a start, gentlemen. But where the bloody hell is he?"

"He'll be here," pronounced Pat, combing his hair with precision. "He's just a bit late, that's all."

"He bloody better be," Les rumbled. "We don't want to be a man down on this shift, I'm telling you. There'll be a few treats tonight and we need the manpower to take advantage."

Sid looked up from his paper, biro poised in his hand.

"Not like him to be late, though. Specially for a night shift. You know how much Gordon likes nights."

There was a general ripple of amused recognition at this.

"You're not wrong there, Sidney old boy," agreed Les. "So much so that he came in yesterday."

Pat stopped, his comb hand frozen over his head, face aghast.

"On his day off? Jesus wept, man, I knew he was weird, but that is criminal. Hasn't he got anything better to do?"

There was a pause. Everyone silently knew the answer to that question, and after a moment of human sympathy, everyone felt a flicker of relief that, even in their darkest hour, there was somebody there who was weirder than them.

Les lowered his voice and leant in towards the group. "I heard that he didn't even clock in and out. Just turned up, out of the blue. And even then, no one could find him. Didn't answer his bleep, didn't come down here to the restroom. He was just helping out round the mortuary and the incinerator the whole shift." He let this information settle on the group and then came back. "Apparently, the police were looking for him earlier."

"The police?" Johnny blurted out.

They all turned to look at him.

"Ah, JJ. Welcome back, you dozy bugger. I thought you'd gone to sleep, you've been that quiet," said Pat.

"What did the police want with him then?" he said, his voice bright and brittle.

"Oh, I expect they were asking him to make up a four on their police darts team. They've heard how good he is for t'hospital."

Johnny's face was a picture of confusion. "Darts?" he said helplessly.

Pat pulled a gurning face. "Der… come on Johnny lad. They wanted to ask him some more questions; there has been a murder, remember."

"Oh yeah, of course." He turned to Les. "Who told you that then? About Gordon and the police?"

"Gloria, up on thirty-six. She asked if I'd seen him and said I should tell her if he turns up on shift tonight."

Pat put his arm around Les's shoulders. "You're not still sniffing after Gloria, are you, Les? Bloody hell, man, you never give up."

"We were just chatting, that's all," said Les, struggling to suppress a smirk.

Pat thumped him on the back. "Just as well, 'cos you've got no chance there. That's a woman who needs a real man, lads. A real man."

He half-turned towards the mirror and resumed combing his hair, a cocky smile spreading across his face. Les scowled at him and was about to come up with a put-down when Johnny cut across the banter.

"So, has no one seen Gordon since he finished his shift yesterday then?"

They looked around the circle, faces blank.

Les shrugged. "Dunno. When he comes in, I'll tell him you and Gloria are both very concerned about him." He winked at the group.

Pat's smile broadened. "Ooh, he'll love that, will Dr Death. Somebody who wants him. Two people want him, and they're both still alive. That'll make a nice change for him."

Les looked at his watch again. "Come on, time to make a start, Dr Death or no Dr Death. Sid, you and Johnny are on the stiffs. Gordon can spell you when he turns up. Pat, take a turn round casualty. Make sure your walkie-talkies are all on."

The others began to get ready for action. Les, suddenly remembering, raised his voice. "Eh, and make sure you bloody answer them and all. No use having it on if you're going to ignore it, eh Pat?"

Pat was about to protest when Sid, rummaging on the shelf used for the shift transfer, interrupted. "There's only three walkie-talkies here. We're one down."

Les shook his head. "That's bloody Gordon for you. He's gone off with it in his pocket, dozy sod. You and Johnny just have the one between you for now, and we'll think again when Gordon shows up." He took a final look at his crew. "Look at you lot. York's finest, eh? Alright, let's get cracking."

Pat inserted his comb in his top pocket. "And what exactly are you going to be doing, *mein führer*? You didn't say."

Les's face, pink and glistening under the strip lighting, beamed. He turned to the mirror and brushed down his lapels. "Me? I'm going to give Gloria a progress report up on ward thirty-six. Mind how you go, the rest of you."

He left the restroom and strolled out into the corridor, a bounce in his step. Through the open door, the others heard him whistling a cheery tune, which faded into the night air.

44

Sid and Johnny sat at opposite ends of the battered sofa. The first few hours of the shift had passed uneventfully. Sid continued to ring specific small ads in his copy of *Variety*, stopping every now and again to take another bite out of his canteen pizza. It was an arduous process as the stability of Sid's dentures was tested by the cardboard-like texture of the pizza.

Johnny moved in his seat and the sofa creaked in protest. The shift was only an hour old and the restroom was still a place of work, not sleep. The central neon strip light buzzed and clicked, casting a brutal white light over the room. There were a few half-hearted Christmas decorations to remind them of the season: a trail or two of tinsel, an anaemic-looking silver Christmas tree, its baubles clinging on for dear life; a wonky loop of letters spelling out *Merry Xmas* hung along the far wall. He looked across at Sid again, who had finished the battle between pizza and dentures. The pizza had won. Sid had deposited the crusts on the plate and then began to fiddle with his teeth, adjusting and extracting the debris that had got stuck. Johnny watched with the fascination of a young man who could not conceive of ever getting old. He was suddenly gripped by the need for some time on his own.

"Sid, I'm just going up to the canteen before it closes, alright? I'll only be half an hour. Do you want anything?"

Sid examined the soggy crumb he had extracted, and thought. "Some chocolate would be nice. Fruit and nut. Or Old Jamaica if they've got any left. But don't be long. I don't want to be on me own in an emergency, like."

Johnny was already at the door. "Half an hour, tops. Thanks, Sid."

He slipped out and closed the door behind him. Sid placed the walkie-talkie in the middle of the table in front of him and went back to exploring the deepest crevices of his dentures with his tongue.

*

Johnny sat alone in the shadowy canteen. His coffee was cold in front of him, untouched, and he fiddled with the bar of fruit and nut, turning it over and over on the table, all the while keeping his eye on the door and the corridor. They would be closing soon, and then the night staff would have to rely on machines or whatever they had remembered to bring in with them until they opened again for breakfast. But food was the last thing on his mind at that moment.

He'd come to sit and think. That and, with a bit of luck, come across Juliet. She had said that she was back on shift today. He really needed to talk to her. This was no time for his usual wishy-washy diffidence, the lack of decisiveness that had plagued his love life up until now. No, in the long hours of solitary silence since he had last seen her, on the night of the party, he had rehearsed his next meeting with her. First, he needed some answers. Then he needed to declare his passion. The thought made him tremble, the prospect of exposing himself to rejection gripping him with fear.

He turned the coffee cup round on its saucer. He also needed to take a walk up to ward thirty-six and have a little chat with Gloria. Where was Gordon? Why had he come in to work on his day off? Was he really trying to avoid the police? He must know, surely, that he couldn't keep that up, and that sooner or later, he would have to face the music? And, most pressingly of all, who was the mysterious man he'd seen Gordon with in the clinic the other night? Not Hutchinson, as Juliet had suggested. Johnny was sure that in some way, whoever he was, he held the key to the whole thing.

He looked up at the clock. It was just coming up to midnight and the staff behind the counter had been rattling the crockery and giving him the evil eye ever since he had sat down. It was clear they were wanting to shut up shop. He stood up, deposited the cup on the tray, picked up the chocolate and strode towards the door. It was time to have that chat with Gloria. At the door, he turned and called, "Thanks," to the woman behind the counter and disappeared into the corridor, heading towards ward thirty-six.

*

He strode along the neon-dazzled corridors. He'd need to be quick, just in case Sid got a call. There'd been precious few customers for Rose Cottage in the last few days, almost as if the Grim Reaper was having a festive holiday, but that couldn't last forever. The last thing he needed was for Sid to be on his case. He slipped in through the doors to ward thirty-six, where the light was more subdued. All the patients would be in bed by this time, most of them asleep, so he moved lightly, careful to be as quiet as possible.

He looked down towards the reception desk and pulled up short. Three quarters of the way down the corridor were Gloria and Juliet. He was about to call out to them, before he stopped himself. They were heads together, in the middle of some kind of intense conversation, Juliet with her back to Johnny. Gloria had hold of Juliet's arm and was hissing her words. Johnny couldn't quite pick up the words, but the tension was clear.

Something, a sixth sense, a survival mechanism, made Gloria stop and look up. She saw Johnny, and a look of panic flashed across her face. She bent down to Juliet and pulled her, subtly but forcefully, into an adjacent treatment room.

"Hey Gloria, can I have—" he began, but Gloria interrupted.

"Sorry Johnny, patient emergency. Resus. Come back later, eh?"

As she half-bundled Juliet into the room, Juliet turned and looked at Johnny. Her face was transfixed. Shock, fear, regret were all fleetingly present before she reassembled her features into an impassive, professional mask. Just before she disappeared into the room, Johnny caught the glitter of tears reflecting the light from the wall lamp above her head. He took a step towards them, but Gloria, standing in the gap of the door, held up her hand to stop him.

"No Johnny, not now. We've got a real emergency here. Go back to the porters' room and I'll bleep you when we've finished."

She didn't wait for an answer. The door closed and Johnny was left in the dusky corridor, completely alone. His only consolation, as the emptiness pressed in on him, was the image of Juliet's face. Amid everything else, he was left with a conviction that he had seen etched there a sense of affection, of feeling. Perhaps, he thought as he trudged back the way he had come, even of love.

45

Johnny sighed, put *Bleak House* to one side and reached for the walkie-talkie. Pressing the button, he sat up, casting his blanket to one side. It was 2 a.m.

"Porters," he said into the mouthpiece.

The reply crackled through the still air. His heart sank.

"Yeah, yeah, OK. We'll be there right away." He put the device down and called to the other side of the room. "Sid? Wake up, we've got a job on. Body."

There was no reply. He stood up to find that Sid's chosen bed for the night was empty, the blanket scrunched in a heap at the end of it.

"Christ, Sid. You pick your moments, don't you? Where the bloody hell have you got to?"

He stretched the stiffness out of his limbs and considered what he should do. In some ways, it was lucky that this could be a one-man job. He wouldn't need Sid. But sometimes, one's convenience at work, in this kind of job, came a long way down the list of priorities. He gathered up the walkie-talkie and went to answer the call, his face set, his mouth a determined straight line. It was not something he was looking forward to, something that the others had spoken about in rare moments of seriousness, but something that had to be faced.

Five minutes later, he had arrived at the paediatric ward, a gaggle of sombre-faced nurses waiting for him at reception. He pushed the iron coffin in front of him as he walked, covered in its usual lacy blanket, and waited expectantly.

The charge nurse stepped out from the group.

"She's in the side room just here. Thanks for coming so quickly."

"No problem," he replied.

The nurse opened the door and stood to one side to let Johnny pass through with the trolley. There were three beds in the room. The one on the far side had the curtains closed around it. Johnny parked the trolley parallel to the bed, removed the blanket, and opened it up, careful not to disturb the silence with a clang. He took a deep breath and opened the curtains. In the middle of the bed lay a little body swaddled in white. It was about three feet long and seemed swamped by the acres of white sheet it lay on.

He swallowed and turned to the nurse. "Who is it?"

"Sarah Clarke. Three years old."

"What..." He stopped and started again, clearing his throat. "What did she die from?"

"Cancer, poor love. Family are in pieces."

He turned back to the bed. He knew he would have to pick up the child, so neatly packaged, but he couldn't seem to make himself move.

Eventually, the nurse touched his arm. "When you're ready, love," she said softly.

"Oh, yes. Sorry."

He leant forward and scooped up the child in his arms. He was surprised how little she weighed. He placed her in the coffin, closed the lid and draped the blanket over it. His eyes prickled and he blinked a couple of times before beginning to steer the trolley towards the door.

As he got to the door, the nurse said, "Are you Johnny, the student lad?"

"Yeah, that's right."

"Will you be alright on your own doing this, Johnny?"

He thought for a moment and took a deep breath. "Yeah. It's fine. What's your name?"

"Angela. I'm the charge nurse."

He smiled at her. "Thanks for asking, Angela," he said before wheeling the trolley away through the dimly lit corridor, past the rest of the nurses who stood like a guard of honour, and out into bright lights of the main hospital.

It was two-thirty in the morning and the corridors were completely deserted as he pushed the trolley along. The only sounds were the buzz of the strip lights and the occasional creak from the trolley wheels. In every corridor, until he reached the basement, he passed pictures of the baby Jesus in the manger, surrounded by the Magi and their exotic gifts. No gifts for his passenger on her bleak journey. All thoughts of Dr Death, Juliet, even of the murder, had drained away, and faded into insignificance for him at that moment.

He stopped when he reached the mortuary. It had only just been reopened after the police had finished their forensic work and a fragment of crime scene tape was still clinging to the door handle. As he reached to turn it, everything that had happened in the last four days rushed in upon him. Four days, was that all it was? It seemed like the world was an entirely different place and he was an entirely different person. He wished he could go back, and everything would be like it had always been, but he knew that that was impossible. He shook his head, grasped the handle and opened the door.

The room was in darkness so he fumbled for the light switch. He blinked as harsh, white light chased away the shadows and stepped inside with the trolley. It was cooler inside, compared to the rest of the hospital, which was always like a moist greenhouse, no matter what the weather and he shivered slightly as he faced the bank of fridges that lined one wall of the mortuary. It was the first time he had been there since he and Gordon had discovered Gerald Sutherland. He thought of him lying in the cold, cold fridge among the other corpses, possibly even patients he himself had treated, and looked down at the trolley.

Sarah Clarke, three years old.

He could barely bring himself to do it, but he removed the blanket and carefully lifted up the lid, hoping, irrationally, that it would be empty and that Sarah Clarke was dreaming in her warm hospital bed of Christmas at home. The neatly swaddled parcel of white shroud killed that hope immediately. He reached forward to scoop her up when, just as his hands slipped underneath her, the walkie-talkie in his overall pocket suddenly blared out into the silence. He jumped back as if scalded and crashed against the table on the other wall. His heart was pounding in his chest as he wildly looked around the room. The trolley, the fridges, the table, the walls, floor and ceiling were as ever, unmoved, profoundly unimpressed and disdainful of his panic. The walkie-talkie sounded again, but Johnny had control of himself this time. He removed it from his pocket, and a dalek voice crackled into the air.

"Johnny, if you're on your walkie-talkie, come up to thirty-six when you've got a minute. Alright love?"

He sighed in relief. It was Gloria. But his ears pricked up again. It seemed to have been in stereo, with two signals slightly apart. Was that an echo? A slight delay on the signal that prolonged the message? He raised his own walkie-talkie to his mouth, pressed the button and spoke.

"I'm a bit busy right now, Gloria. I'll be..."

He stopped in mid-message and stared at the device. He

could hear an echo of his voice, his message. It was coming from the other side of the room.

The walkie-talkie crackled again and Gloria came back on. "Are you still there, Johnny? You got cut off."

He listened intently to her voice but didn't take in anything that she said. He was transfixed by the direction of the echo. He licked his lips and tried again, loudly into the mic, staring at the other wall.

"Hello?"

The echo came back, a millisecond apart: "…lo."

It was coming from the wall of fridges.

Still clinging to the walkie-talkie, he went to the fridges and, shaking slightly, reached out for the handle. He decided to try one last time. Holding the walkie-talkie to his mouth, he composed himself and said in a clear, strong voice.

"I'm not scared of you. You're all dead."

The echo came back loud and clear. It was coming from the fridge directly in front of him. He couldn't stand it any longer and yanked open the fridge door. His knees wobbled slightly and he had to cling on to the handle to keep to his feet.

On the middle shelf, right in front of him, was Gordon, walkie-talkie resting on his chest, a scalpel sticking vertically from his forehead.

46

The phone rang twice before he snaked an arm out from under the blankets and snatched the receiver up. He always slept lightly during a murder case, having learnt the hard way that unpleasant developments usually emerged under cover of darkness. "Grayson." He kept his voice low, but was careful to avoid any impression of weakness. Impressions counted. He had learnt that much during his rise up the ranks. The voice on the other end was under no such constraints. As he listened, he sat up in bed, ignoring the chilly air that scoured exposed skin.

"Yeah… What?… Where was he found?… Suicide, I suppose?"

He gripped the phone tighter. Any last vestiges of sleep were suddenly blown away and he was alert, nerve endings tingling, mind furiously churning possibilities and probabilities.

"You sure about this, no chance of a mistake?… Yeah, I'll be right there… Have you contacted the rest of the team? Straight away, please… OK."

He was about to end the call and begin his preparations for the drive to the hospital when a final question occurred to him.

"Oh, who found him?"

He put the phone down without replying. In the darkness, he looked across at the mound beside him in the bed, gently rising and falling. Johnny fucking Jewell. Again.

He shook his head and swung his legs out onto the carpet. It was going to be a long day.

*

The four of them surrounded the body that had been removed from the fridge and laid on the central table of the mortuary. Photos had been taken, surfaces dusted for fingerprints and shortly, the pathologist would supervise the removal of the body to the police lab. The initial whirlwind of activity had subsided and a calm quiet had settled on the scene. The watching detectives were anything but calm, however. Behind glassy eyes containing an empty, relentless exhaustion, they all confronted the reality of the situation that lay before them. They had royally fucked this up. The cheery confidence of yesterday, that they had their killer and that it was only a matter of time before they laid hands on him and wrenched a confession from him, all of that had gone. To be replaced by nothing more than a sinking, chilling feeling that, as the public were so quick to tell them, they really did not have a fucking clue.

Grayson's job now was to pump them up and make them think that they did. Have a clue, that is.

"OK," he began quietly, "now is not the time to feel sorry for ourselves, or to start blaming each other. Our killer has been killed. In the same manner, by the look of it, as Sutherland. So, same drill as before. Clive, you arrange the interviews of everyone who was on shift last night. No one leaves until we say so. And we need to get as many people in as we can to push through this morning. I want a plan of this part of the hospital, and I want forensics all over it. When we've got cause of death and a time window, we need to plot that against the floor plan and everyone's movements last night. We need to get some new names in the frame. There were only a certain number of people in the area of the morgue during those hours. We've got to start with them."

He looked across at the team. They were silent, eyes averted, sheepish.

"Come on, you lot, for fuck's sake. You look like you've run over a puppy. There's no point rolling over with this; we need to get some energy going again. Ideas, questions, thoughts. This bastard's not going to catch himself."

Paula voiced their feelings. "Yes, guv, but it's just that it doesn't make sense. Why would the killer of Sutherland go on to kill Simpson? What's the connection we're missing?"

"At least they are questions, Marsh. That's a start. Well? Anyone?"

His eyes scoured the other two.

"Maybe Simpson knew and he had to be kept quiet," said Clive.

"Or maybe Simpson did Sutherland, someone found out and challenged him. There's a confrontation, a struggle and Simpson cops it," said Jacko, warming to the task.

"Well, forensics will soon rule that in or out. Doesn't look like there was any kind of a struggle, but it's not always obvious," replied Grayson. He walked closer to the body. "Has anyone done this bag yet?" he asked.

"No, we were waiting for the all-clear from the forensic guys."

Grayson pulled out a pair of latex gloves from his pocket and put them on. He reached out to the canvas bag that was lying on Dr Death's chest and began to loosen the two buckles that fastened the front flap. He felt inside and pulled out the object it contained. It was a small Olympus Trip camera.

Immediately, the energy in the room changed. All four of them leant in towards the objects, eyes sharp as tacks.

"Why did the killer leave this on the body like that? He had enough time to leave a signature with the scalpel. Why not deal with the bag?"

"It was hidden, guv. Under his overall. You'd have had to have patted him down to find it," said Clive.

Grayson's brain was whirring through the possibilities this new discovery had presented.

"So the next question is, why did Simpson want to hide his camera from his killer?"

"Well, we all know what sort of pictures he liked to take," suggested Jacko.

"Maybe there's more on there than bodies," said Brooks. "Maybe he's taken photos of people who are still alive. People who are involved in all of this."

Grayson held up his hands. "Whoa, let's not get too excited. The camera isn't going to solve this for us; that's just wishful thinking. We've still got a lot of donkey work to do."

He turned to Jacko and handed him a couple of evidence bags and another pair of gloves.

"Bag these up and get them down to the lab. We need any prints off this lot and the film developed as quick as they can. Then get yourself back here for the interviews."

"Will do, guv."

Jacko struggled to put the gloves on his chubby, hairy hands, wincing as they snagged on the tight latex.

Once the items were bagged, he left, and Grayson turned his attention to Brooks and Marsh. "Still nothing from yesterday?"

"We can't follow up, guv, until nine. No one's going to be at their desk until then," said Clive.

"Do you think we should wait until we get confirmation before we interview Fulton?" asked Paula. "Would be good leverage if we knew more about her employment status and about her training at Leeds."

Grayson shook his head. "We can't afford to waste any time. Start interviewing everyone in the frame who was in the vicinity and on shift last night. Get as far as you can and then break off at nine and do the other stuff. And make it quick. The Chief Super will want my balls as soon as he finds out about a second murder over his bacon and eggs. And then I'll want yours."

Brooks looked uncomfortable. Marsh raised an eyebrow.

"Don't say a word, Marsh. Just get on with it."

47

By the time Johnny got home, a couple of hours after the end of his shift, he was exhausted. The police had been in a blind panic, completely thrown by the discovery of Gordon's body, and they had questioned him over and over again. When he was finally allowed to leave, he didn't even have the energy to try and see Juliet, to talk the whole thing over, to try and make some kind of sense of it. That would have to wait. She hadn't exactly been falling over herself to see him, even before this latest, terrible development.

Terrible development. He shook his head. How easily one slipped into euphemism when talking about the dead. Gordon was dead, killed it seemed, in the most cold and calculating manner, and he had discovered him. He shuddered at the memory, but then instantly closed it down. He must sleep if he was going to be able to make any sense of this.

He crept up the stairs, determined not to wake Helen. He really couldn't face the questions and the concern right then. That conversation, like the one with Juliet, would have to wait. As he passed her room, before turning to climb the last flight of stairs, he noticed the thin, yellow line of light at the bottom of her door. He hesitated for a second, then pressed on upstairs, treading deliberately, one stair after the other. He really must sleep.

Once inside his room, he removed his shoes and dived under the duvet fully clothed, catching his breath against the icy sheets. With a sigh, he gave himself to the darkness.

*

All of the interviews were still in progress when the clock ticked round to 9 a.m. Both Clive and Paula used that as a cue to wrap up their own. They passed those remaining onto the rest of the team and then went their separate ways. Clive found a quiet corner with a telephone and Paula retraced her steps from yesterday to the personnel department.

It was 9.15 when she knocked and poked her head around the door, brandishing her warrant card.

"DC Marsh, North Yorkshire Police."

A grey-haired woman blinked at her through wire-framed granny glasses. She was tall and stooping, wearing a floral dress engulfed by a thick, brown cardigan.

"I need to ask you some questions about your personnel records."

"Personnel records? Oh dear. Nothing wrong, I trust?"

She looked around her as she spoke, as if evidence of some past, indeterminate crime might be lurking in the corners of the office.

Paula stepped into the room and closed the door behind her.

"And you are…?"

"Brigstock. Janice Brigstock. Miss. I'm in charge of personnel in the hospital."

"Been here long, Miss Brigstock?"

"Since before it opened. I was at the old County Hospital.

Let's see, must be about twenty-five years now." She smiled uncertainly, as if she had only just remembered.

"So, you would know all about the records, then?"

"The records? What records?"

Paula gave her an encouraging smile, holding down her irritation. "The personnel records, Miss Brigstock. Janice."

"Oh, yes, of course. Silly me. Yes, I know them inside out."

Paula's eyes lit up. "Can you tell me then, what the blue folders are, and where I could find them?"

A frown passed across Janice's face. "They are nothing to do with me. Mr Edwards has those, in his office."

"And who is Mr Edwards? Why does he have these folders? What have they got to do with him?"

Miss Brigstock gave Paula a look of withering pity. "Mr Edwards. The hospital secretary, Mr Edwards. Everything is to do with him. They'll be in his office, in the Board Room."

"I need to see him, urgently."

The look of pity intensified. "You can't see him, he's not in. It's Christmas Eve; he's never in on Christmas Eve. He's got a function, up at The Manor. He's a very important man, you know."

"I'm sure he is," Paula replied sweetly, drawing on all of her reserves of charm. "So, his keys will do."

"Oh, no love. No one's allowed in the Board Room."

"Janice, let me be blunt. I don't care whether he's at a function at The Manor, or whether he's a very important man. This is a murder inquiry. The keys, please." She stretched her hand, palm upwards, out in front of her. Her sweet smile did not waver.

Janice looked at her hand, chewed her lip, and walked to her desk. She rummaged in the drawer and pulled out an ancient key ring that contained a large mortise key, like something from a fairy tale, and some cabinet keys. She deposited it in Paula's palm.

"I'll want it back. Today, please."

Paula closed her palm into a fist. "Thank you."

She turned to go. At the doorway, she remembered something. "Oh and Janice? Why doesn't Dr Fulton have a personnel file?"

Miss Brigstock pursed her lips and thought before replying. "Yes, I've asked that question myself. Mr Edwards has that, apparently."

There was a silence between them. Their eyes met, but Miss Brigstocke's expression was neutral.

"Thanks. I'll bring the keys back as soon as I can."

She slipped into the corridor, closing the door behind her.

The hospital was shaking off its night stupor and gearing up for another day. The corridor was a churn of activity: porters, nurses, doctors, consultants, cleaners, admin staff all single mindedly pursuing a determined path to the next task, the next emergency. She navigated a route through this torrent towards the Board Room, the heavy key jangling in her pocket. As she walked, she processed what Miss Brigstock had told her.

"Mr Edwards with the blue folders. Not quite Colonel Mustard and the lead piping, but it'll do for now."

*

Clive got through to the right department at Leeds General straight away, with none of the expected Christmas Eve laxity. At the sound of the call being taken, he perked up. *At last,* he thought, *maybe now we'll get some answers.* They both went through the formalities before getting down to business. The voice at the other end sounded young and bright.

"I got your message, DS Brooks. I was just about to call you."

"Good. That sounds like you've got an answer."

"I have. I don't know who your Juliet Fulton is, but she doesn't exist as far as the hospital is concerned. There's no record of anyone of that name having started training with us."

"You sure about that? And nobody else dropped out of the training programme or transferred anywhere else?"

"Completely sure. And no, we have the same cohort we started with."

"That's brilliant, thank you."

"Glad to be of assistance. Have a nice Christmas."

She put the phone down and Clive was left holding the receiver, a smile beginning to form on his lips. A nice Christmas, eh? It was beginning to look as if it might be.

48

It was lunchtime when Johnny emerged, still exhausted and battling a pounding headache. He went through to the kitchen. Helen was sitting at the table, hands in fingerless mittens wrapped around a mug, a list on a sheet of paper in front of her. She looked up and gave him an arch smile, one eyebrow raised.

"Afternoon, stranger. Mammoth sleep..." As soon as she saw his face, ashen and pained, she abandoned her usual tone of friendly sarcasm. She frowned. "Are you alright, Johnny? You look weird. You're not ill, are you?"

He sat down heavily in the chair next to her. "Any tea in that pot? I've got to eat; I'm absolutely starving."

"You pour the tea, I'll make you some toast."

She bustled around with the bread, glancing back at Johnny, whose expression was flat and numb.

"You haven't got any paracetamol, have you? I've got a shocking headache."

She rummaged in her bag that hung over the corner of her chair, relieved. He probably just had a hangover. She passed him the foil rectangle with a smile.

"Was there a lot of drinking on the shift, then? Christmas cheer and all that? Bugger the patients, let's party?"

He shook his head. "A bit. I wasn't really in the mood."

"Never known you to turn a drink down." Helen's tone was forced and brittle by now.

Johnny swallowed the pills and sat in silence, staring at his mug.

Helen sat down and the silence grew. It was broken by the sound of the toast popping. "Has something happened, Johnny? What's wrong? You're worrying me."

Johnny looked up from his tea. "Sorry, it's just that…" He stopped and took a sip of tea.

"Johnny?"

"It's Gordon. He's dead."

"What? What do you mean?"

"Murdered. Just like Sutherland. I found him, in the fridge. He had the same scalpel sticking out of his head. I was on my own, doing a body, a little kid it was. Barely weighed a thing. And then, when I opened up the fridge, Gordon was just lying there."

His voice quavered at the end and he paused, as if the enormity of what he'd experienced had come upon him for the first time.

Helen reached out and took his hand. "Oh Johnny, you poor love," she said.

She got out of her chair and knelt down by Johnny's chair. She reached out and enveloped him in a hug. She stroked his hair and held him close. He sank into her body with some relief, drinking in her warmth, clinging on as if he would never let go. They stayed like that for less than a minute. Helen moved her head away from him, and put her hand on his cheek.

"Better?"

He smiled ruefully. "Yeah, just about. Sorry, I just felt a bit overwhelmed, that's all."

She got up, went back to her seat and reached across to pat his knee.

"Come on then, tell me all about it."

He told her everything that had happened. Gordon not turning up for his shift, and not being at home when the police called. Some of the other porters gossiping that he'd come in earlier and had been seen around the morgue. He told her about the police interviews and how Grayson had given him a hard time about lying to them at first. Then he recounted the interviews that morning, after he'd discovered the body.

"They were even more shocked than I was. I reckon they had got Gordon down as the killer. If he'd been in when they went round to his place, they would have arrested him, I'm sure of it. And he'd still be alive now."

He looked at Helen directly. She had been listening intently to his story.

"I just feel terrible about it, Hel. It's all my fault."

"How do you make that out?"

"He must have told someone that he was probably going to be arrested because he had lied and didn't have an alibi. Whoever it was couldn't take the risk. They knew Gordon couldn't hide from the police indefinitely and that when they finally picked him up, he would start to talk. And there was only one way to stop him."

"But who was it? You said he had that scalpel thing, you know, just like Sutherland. Was it the same person, then?"

"Dunno. Could be. But then again, could be deliberate, trying to make it look like that." He shrugged his shoulders. "Listen to me. I sound like bloody Hercule Poirot, for God's sake. What do I know? And the police, the so-called professionals, are furious. They had Gordon down as the killer, case closed. Now they're buggered and Christmas is cancelled for them again."

"But it must be someone at the hospital, don't you think?"

"But who? The pharmacy guy, you know, Hutchinson?"

"You said Gordon had told you it wasn't him."

"He could have been lying. It wouldn't be the first time."

He reached for a piece of toast. His ravenous hunger could not be ignored any longer. While he crammed the toast into his mouth, Helen filled the gap in the conversation.

"Do you have to go to work tonight? I'm worried about you, Johnny. One of the people you work with is a murderer, and you could easily be on their list."

"That's sweet of you, Hel, but there's no need to worry. The place is crawling with police now..."

Helen picked up a knife and started to tap the blade against the pitted wood.

"Hel? What are you doing?"

She stopped and looked directly at him. "What about Juliet Fulton?" Her face was set and her voice had lost its warmth.

"Juliet? Yeah, I'm worried about her being there on her own as well. I've tried to talk to her since the party but can't seem to find her at the right time."

"That's not what I mean. I'm worried about you, not her."

Johnny looked baffled. "I don't get you."

"I don't trust her."

She saw Johnny's face slide from puzzlement to annoyance. She held her hand up defensively.

"There's just something about her that doesn't add up. After all, what do you really know about her? Why was she talking to Gordon at the party as if they were plotting something? She didn't even wait to see if you were alright after the police were finished with you."

Johnny's annoyance intensified. "None of that means anything, Helen. The party was only on Friday. Christ, give her a chance."

Helen persisted. "Who knows her at the hospital? Nobody, that's who. Why has she only been there a month?"

"For God's sake, she transferred her training from Leeds. What is the matter with you?"

"I've been trying to remember something since I met her at the party. I was sure I'd seen her somewhere before, but I just couldn't place her. And then I remembered. Yesterday afternoon at the demo in town."

"The demo? What are you on about, Hel?"

"The Reclaim the Streets demo. She was there. She's always there. I'm pretty sure I've seen her at one of the big ones in Leeds."

"So what? There's no law against it. You can be a doctor and go on marches, you know. You're not the only right-on girl in town."

"But her name, Johnny. I'm sure Juliet Fulton isn't her name."

Johnny's headache was thumping now, despite the pills. His eyes were sore and dry, and his skull throbbed incessantly. He snapped.

"Of course it's her fucking name. This is ridiculous..."

"No, Johnny, it's you that's ridiculous. She's playing you for a fool. You can't see past what she looks like. Honestly, a bit of flattery, and—"

"What?" he interrupted, a sudden revelation spreading across his face. "My God, you're jealous." He shook his head in disbelief.

"No, I just—"

"Yes, you're jealous. It's so disappointing. I thought better of you than that. I thought that you might be pleased. Stupid of me."

He trailed off. His voice had risen to a shout, but he wrapped his closing words in a fake, honeyed reasonableness, as the realisation of what he had done dawned on him.

Helen stared at him as if he'd slapped her. Her eyes began to prickle, her breath caught in her throat.

"Jealous?" she managed to say. "Really? Well, thanks, Johnny, you've made things absolutely clear." She stood up. She couldn't look at him. "I've got a train to catch. Enjoy Christmas."

"No, no, sorry, Helen," he stammered, "I didn't mean—"

His explanation was interrupted by the shrill ring of the telephone coming from the hall. They both swivelled round to look.

"You'd better get that," Helen said. "Might be Juliet."

Johnny scowled at her, but went to pick up. The phone sounded even shriller somehow in the icy air of the hall.

"Hello… Yes, speaking… Today?… Why?… Yeah, OK, I see. Yeah, two o'clock. Yeah… Bye."

Still holding the receiver, he looked back into the kitchen. Their eyes met and a crackle of feelings sparked between them. He replaced the phone and made his way back.

"That was the hospital. They want me to go in for a double shift."

"Well, that's not so bad. You obviously prefer being there to being here."

Both of them spoke looking at the floor. There was a pause as they tried to find a way back.

"You know that's not true," Johnny said quietly, raising his eyes.

Juliet looked back at him.

"No, I know." She tried to shift the mood. "They really know how to look after their staff, don't they?"

"You know what they said when I asked why? They said, 'We're a man down.' A man down. Fucking hell." He shook his head. "And we all know which man they're down."

"Gordon?"

"Yeah. Dr Death himself."

The conversation dried up. They stood looking at each other, both inhabiting that paralysing no man's land between simmering anger and regret.

"I'm still angry with you," Helen said finally. "But I have to go and catch a train."

Johnny nodded.

Helen picked up her rucksack and carried it into the hall. She put on her coat, wrapped a scarf around her neck, and hoisted her backpack over her shoulders. She opened the door. From the kitchen, Johnny could see that the rectangle of the open door was entirely filled with huge snowflakes. Helen did not look back, went out into the snow and slammed the door.

In the kitchen, the echoes of the slam vibrated through the house and then faded away. The silence crowded in upon Johnny, and he was left with his pounding headache as his head sank forward into his hands. He had never felt so utterly alone.

49

When Helen stepped out of the house, she gave a sharp intake of breath. She had never seen snow like it. The sky was full of fat snowflakes falling relentlessly on ground already covered, in some places where it had drifted, up to a couple of feet deep. The familiar landscape had been transformed into a white, featureless expanse of smoothly rounded hills and hollows, beautiful to look at but punishing to walk through.

By the time she reached the station, past abandoned cars and broken-down buses, she was exhausted and frozen. The concourse was seething with passengers, steaming, as they looked up at the departures board. Helen joined them, squinting up at the board to locate her train to Oxford. The message was clear. Every train on the board was labelled with the same word: cancelled. The sign at the bottom of the board was intended to leave a glimmer of hope. It read:

ENGINEERS ARE CURRENTLY WORKING TO CLEAR THE TRACKS. WE HOPE TO HAVE NEWS OF TRAINS LEAVING SHORTLY. PLEASE LISTEN TO STATION ANNOUNCEMENTS FOR FURTHER UPDATES.

She looked down from the board and peered over the heads of the crowd. She couldn't bear the idea of going back out into the cold so soon, so she squeezed her way between the damp coats and unwieldy cases in the direction of the British Rail snack bar. It was standing room only when she finally got there. The windows ran with condensation and the room was rank with the smell of old, damp overcoats, sweat and stale perfume. At least, thought Helen, it was warm. She heaved her rucksack from her shoulders and shuffled it along in front of her to join the queue for food. Twenty minutes later, she claimed a spare seat at the corner of a table and took a sip of her coffee. Immediately, she grimaced. The grey liquid had a burnt and bitter taste. With a bit of luck, she could catch the next train and be sitting in her parents' cosy front room in front of the Christmas tree with a drink in her hand. She settled down to wait.

*

"We regret to announce that all trains out of this station have been cancelled. This is due to the exceptionally severe weather conditions affecting the north of England. There will be no trains running until Boxing Day, when, weather permitting, a reduced service will be in operation. Please check local television and radio broadcasts for information before setting out to travel. The latest advice from the Meteorological Office is that you should only travel if absolutely necessary."

A groan ran around the station, followed by a few angry shouts.

"Of course it's bloody necessary. It's Christmas Eve, for God's sake."

Shouts of agreement followed from the crowd, with a list of culprits named and blamed. British Rail. The government. The unions. The staff dotted round the packed concourse exuded weary concern. The next half an hour would be challenging and they would bear the brunt of passengers' anger, until everyone had drifted away, grumbling with simmering discontent.

Helen hoisted her rucksack back onto her shoulders and began to thread her way through the crowd to the exit. No point hanging around. Nothing was going to change so she might as well bite the bullet and negotiate the snow drifts back to East Mount Road.

The cold hit her when she stepped outside, gnawing at her face. It had stopped snowing but a hard frost was setting in with the disappearance of the sun. It was dark and the air was full of exhaust fumes pooling around ankles in the arctic air.

Once away from the station, the snow crunched and creaked underfoot, as each step broke through the crisp crust of ice. The traffic had disappeared and there were very few people out on the streets now. Work had definitely finished for nearly everyone and it was a little too early for anyone making their way to the pub. By the side of the road, there were still abandoned cars, covered with a fresh layer of snow since she had passed them on her way out, but the steaming, broken-down buses had gone, somehow towed back to the garage for repair. None were running now, and she felt the night and the darkness closing in on her and on York.

*

Paula turned the key in the lock of the heavy wooden door of the boardroom. It swung open surprisingly smoothly, revealing a large, high-ceilinged room that smelt of beeswax and flowers. There was a polished wooden parquet floor covered in a thick Turkish rug in the middle of the room. At one end was a substantial oval table with a bouquet of lilies in the middle that were just beginning to go over. It was surrounded by chairs. At the other end, in the space of a large bay window a desk, and in between the two, a green, leather Chesterfield. The walls were hung with heavy oil paintings in gilt frames that were a mixture of previous hospital secretaries, local NHS worthies, and a few of horse racing at The Knavesmire racecourse.

She creaked her way over the parquet, with an interlude of silent sinking into the thick pile of the rug, before arriving at the filing cabinets next to the desk. She fiddled with the smaller keys on the ring and after a little bit of trial and error, opened each of the cabinets in turn. Eventually, she found them at the back of the top drawer of the third cabinet, the one closest to his desk, and using two hands, levered them out. There were about twenty of them, each one paper thin. She settled herself in the leather desk chair that hugged her like a padded suit of armour and opened the first file on the pile. To her surprise, there was only a single sheet of A4 in there, a closely typed report that was signed, *A Edwards*. Her eyes scanned the report and she began to make notes. As she did so, the ghost of a frown appeared on her face. She looked at the second file and then the third, abandoning her note-taking in favour of quickly skimming each file in the pile.

When she was finished, she stacked them in a neat pile and laid her hands flat on the top of it, trying to make sense of what she had just read. They were all the same. Each single sheet of paper told the same story. Serious allegations of bullying, harassment up to and including assault, made by female members of staff, each one investigated solely by Arthur Edwards, each one finding no case to answer. There was no sign of any other paperwork: no witness statements, no records of meetings, nothing.

Her heart was racing now and she fought to hold down a rising tide of emotions and keep calm. She was excited. She was anxious. But most of all, she was angry. The first report she had read was ten years old. How long had this been going on?

An idea suddenly struck her and she flicked through the files for one in particular. Gloria Wilson. She began to read it. It dealt with three separate complaints of sexual assault against Gerald Sutherland. They were dismissed for "lack of evidence" in each case. The last one was over a year ago.

It was all there, in the pile of folders in front of her. She knew that if she ran back to Grayson and the team and blurted all of this out, they wouldn't take her seriously. Jacko would just rant about "women's libbers" and dismiss it all as random coincidence with no relevance to the murders. Grayson would rein him in, but half-believe him. Clive, at least, might give her a fair hearing. The only thing that would convince them would be if she was clear about the facts, and that meant spending some time trawling through each folder and compiling a list of complaints, cross-referenced with details of complainant, the accused, the investigator, dates and outcomes. Dull plod work in short and just the job for a woman on a mission with an eye for detail.

She took a handful of paper from Edwards' desk, removed the top from her biro and began.

*

Helen closed the front door, chilled to the bone. She dumped her bag in the hall and bustled around, lighting the gas fires in the front room, the kitchen and her bedroom, and turning on all of the lights to dispel the gloom. It was an extravagance, she knew, but left in the house on her own, she needed to banish all of the shadows and cold that lurked in every corner.

Just as she finished, her eye was caught by the folded newspaper at the end of the kitchen table, and the large photo it carried on the front page. She unfolded it, laying it flat in front of her. A grainy black and white photo of a young woman stared out at her, under the headline, *Ripper Still at Large*. It was a picture that could be of any female student in the country. Could have been one of her friends. Could have been her. The eyes, nothing more than a blurred collection of ink spots, held her own eyes, and Helen held her breath. One woman, barely more than a girl, who would not be going home for Christmas, whose parents would be living through unimaginable pain and disbelief, in an ordinary house that would be dressed for a family celebration.

She pushed the paper away, suddenly overwhelmed with guilt about her own parents. She lived twenty miles away from this woman. It was all over the papers and the telly. Her parents would be working themselves up into a frenzy, fuelled by their ignorance of the North. To them, Leeds and York were practically only streets apart.

She took a deep breath and rang the number.

It was answered immediately. She sighed, and readied herself for the hysteria.

"Hello, Mum, it's Helen... Yeah, sorry, it's been hellish here... All the trains are cancelled, because of the snow... No, it's really bad, I've never seen so much... Well, no, I won't be able to get there for Christmas now... Mum, don't cry... I'm fine... Yeah... But Mum, that's miles away; it's a different city... No, I know... No..." She looked around the bare hallway. "No, I'm not on my own, Mum, Johnny's here... You know, Johnny, from university... Yeah, he has to work... I told you, Mum, at the hospital... No, no, he's not a doctor..."

The conversation carried on in the same vein for some time. There were tears and recriminations, before her mother had to admit that although Helen may be responsible for many disappointing things in the world, bad weather wasn't one of them. Her father, more practical, had quizzed her gently on heating, on safety and on food before letting her go, insisting that she ring again the next day, just before the Queen's Speech.

She put the phone down, having done her duty, and in the silence that followed was left staring the reality of her situation in the face. She was alone in a cold, gloomy house, full of echoes and creaks, and memories of past conversations, good and bad. The last conversation she had had there, a few hours earlier, jostled its way back to the front of her mind. She replayed Johnny's words, with a picture of his angry face fixed in her head: "…jealous… I thought better of you than that."

The sting was sharp. Hurt and humiliated, the sobbing could not be held back any longer. The house was the only witness to her tears so that when they had subsided, and she dried her eyes, and taken a breath, it was as if they had never happened at all.

She gathered herself. Time to move on.

50

Tempers were frayed in the incident room. They had spent half an hour pooling what they had found out during the morning. Every positive development seemed to be countered by a new problem and the team had begun to snap at each other, as their findings were challenged or dismissed. It felt as if they were no nearer finding someone to replace Dr Death as their main suspect. Grayson had listened patiently, allowing each member of the team to have their say unchecked, but now it was time to draw a line under sharing and begin laying down the law.

"OK everyone, that's enough. Let's just see where we've got to and then move on. We'll do facts first before we get on to wild speculation and personal theories."

He gave a quick look around the team, a half-smile on his face and an eyebrow that was deciding whether to raise itself. Bad feeling, in his experience, was quicker to dissipate when a lighter note was introduced. Despite what Jacko instinctively thought, an old-fashioned bollocking was not always the best solution.

"So, this is what we've got so far."

He stood in front of a flip chart and itemised new information as he talked it through. They listened in silence, knowing better than to interrupt him in full flow. The final list stared out at them:

- Juliet Fulton unknown at Leeds General and no personnel file here.
- Gordon Simpson died from diamorphine overdose. Awaiting further details. Approx time of death: Midnight–2 a.m., Sunday night, Monday morning.
- Gloria Wilson made several complaints re sexual assault against Sutherland. No action taken.
- About eighteen similar complaints against Sutherland (and others) investigated and dismissed in last ten years.
- Payments made to Simpson's bank account by Sutherland over the last couple of years.

"Any thoughts?" he asked, gesturing at the chart.

"The complaints, guv," Paula began.

Jacko shifted in his chair and rolled his eyes. "Here we go," he said.

"Enough," Grayson barked. "Let Marsh make her point."

"It's just that it backs up what I was saying before about the sort of place this hospital is. All of those complaints, and there's been a lot of them, they were all investigated by Arthur Edwards, the hospital secretary. Well, I say investigated; it looks to me like his investigation consisted of him saying to Sutherland, 'Did you do it, Gerald old boy?' Gerald says, 'No, just fun and games, Eddie,' and Edwards says, 'I thought so, case dismissed.'"

"You've got no bloody evidence for this, Paula, just your own hang ups," Jacko burst out.

"The personnel files, Jacko. Kept apart from the others, in Edwards' own little kingdom. There's been no investigation at all. No witnesses, no interviews, nothing. And what about bloody Dr Death? Loads of complaints about inappropriate behaviour in the mortuary, but absolutely bugger all done about it. And another thing, guv."

"Go on, Marsh," Grayson replied wearily.

"I'd need to chase it up to make sure, but I reckon if I do, I'll find evidence that a lot of staff who made complaints are moved out a few months later."

"We haven't got bloody time to have you with your head stuck in a filing cabinet; we've got a killer to catch," said Jacko, unable to maintain his silence. "On second thoughts, at least that would keep you out of the way so the rest of us can do some proper coppering."

"Alright, that's enough, Jacko," said Grayson, raising his voice. "Paula's stuff is worth investigating. It gives a possible motive to Gloria Wilson at the very least. Juliet Fulton is another story." He thought for a moment, fingertips steepled in front of his face. "Alright," he said finally, "this is what we'll do. I'll put a rocket up forensics. We need the stuff on Simpson and the photos. In the meantime, we'll haul in Gloria Wilson and Juliet Fulton again. Wilson in particular needs to account for the complaints against Sutherland."

"And Edwards, guv?" Paula asked tentatively.

"Let's not push it, eh?" He looked around the team. "Just another couple of hours, then get yourselves home. But be warned. If the phone rings for you to come in, then be ready. Christmas Day or no Christmas Day."

There was mumbled agreement and they all trooped out to get on with it in a final push before calling it a day.

Grayson watched them go and then his fingers returned to their steepled position on his lips.

And you, DC Marsh, he thought, *you just leave Arthur Edwards to me.*

51

Juliet Fulton checked herself in the mirror. White scrubs, sober, short, dark hair, no make-up, bleep and stethoscope at the ready. She smoothed down her uniform and then, satisfied, she put on a pair of latex gloves, and bent down to the chest of drawers. She opened the top drawer, rummaged inside it and slipped what she'd been looking for into the inner pocket of her uniform.

A minute later, she was walking at a measured pace through the piled-up snow towards the incinerator room. Her breath came in clouds above her head as her flat-soled shoes moved soundlessly along the walkway that was liberally sprinkled with rock salt. The biting cold seemed to sharpen her resolve to finish the task as quickly as possible and she sailed along, serene and untroubled. She paused at the incinerator room before looking both ways and tapping firmly on the door. She waited, a cover story regarding operating-theatre waste ready to use, just in case. She was confident that it wouldn't be needed, however. She had seen him leave fifteen minutes ago, his car ploughing through the blizzard and out onto the Huntingdon road.

When no answer came, she turned her key in the lock and slipped inside, closing the door behind her. Two minutes later, she reappeared. With a quick glance around her, she locked the door and was gone.

*

Helen looked around the kitchen and a wave of isolation swept over her. It was unheard of for it to be so empty and desolate of an evening, and the difference suddenly seemed stark, pressing in on her. The silence seemed only intensified by the ticking of the clock, the creaking of the house and the moaning wind outside.

She felt the need to fill the silence and hear some other voices, so she collected up the chocolates, the bottle of wine and her glass and retreated to the front room. It was altogether cosier in there. The gas fire was bright orange, and the light from the side lamps reflected from the Christmas tree, with its cheap baubles and tinsel. She poured another glass and switched on the telly. It spluttered into life, resolving itself into a shimmering haze of black and white ghosts. After a few seconds or so of adjusting the aerial, the screen crystallised into an acceptable monochrome picture and she snuggled up on the sofa, legs tucked underneath her, covered with a blanket.

Val Doonican's Christmas special. Jesus wept, how much worse could this get? She endured it for five minutes before its cloying sentimentality overwhelmed her. A quick flick to BBC 2 and then ITV provided no alternative, and she reluctantly concluded that silence was the only bearable option, even in a lonely house with dark shadows and creaking joists.

The silence pressed in on her. A whining gust of wind. The hiss of the gas fire. A creak on the stairs. She forced herself to block out the external world and, in doing so, she was brought face to face with the subject she had pushed to the margins of her mind. Johnny. She was still bruised after their row earlier. Angry and hurt. He was usually so amenable, so even tempered, so ready to chat and to listen, that his change of personality at lunchtime had come as a nasty shock. Maybe she had made a mistake and her fears about Juliet Fulton were nothing more than jealousy. She would apologise, that's what she would do. She would leave a note for Johnny, before she went to bed, so he knew about the trains and that she was still here, and then in the morning, they could talk it through and make up. It was a resolution of sorts. She reached for her glass of wine again.

52

A hum of quiet conversation hung in the air of the canteen. Seven o'clock in the evening was a relatively busy time. Patients' dinners had been delivered, and staff readying themselves for the last push on to the end of their shift had chosen this as a good time to refuel. Johnny sat at a table on his own, picking at a rubbery pizza and chips. He couldn't face chatting to anyone. The only conversations he had had with anyone there, including the police, consisted of answering questions about finding Gordon's body, and he really did not want to go through that again. It was bad enough that the sight of the scalpel sticking vertically out of Gordon's forehead would not leave him, without having to describe it in painstaking detail. It was funny how, only a couple of days ago, the very same sight had been almost an excitement, a bit of adventure. That's the effect, he supposed, of what happened when it involved someone you knew.

The staff could talk of nothing else, and an atmosphere of shock and disbelief clung to the whole building, driving away any remnants of festive feeling. The decorations and relentless enforced jollity of an institutional Christmas seemed an insult somehow. So staff huddled together, spoke in subdued tones and glanced up from their meals and looked quickly around the canteen at intervals as if scanning the tables for potential murderers.

Johnny could feel their eyes on him and thought he caught some mentions of his name. Johnny Jewell… young student lad… mortuary… again… Porter… weird… Dr Death… the police…

It droned on from all four corners of the canteen in hushed tones. Johnny took another bite of pizza and tried to block it out. Only another half an hour and he'd have to join Sid to take away the meal trolleys.

"No one talking to you, then?"

He jerked his head up. It was Juliet.

"Well, you're certainly not. Talking to me, I mean."

He even surprised himself by how bitter he sounded. He had gone over what he would say when they came across each other, but surprise had made all of his rehearsals dribble away down the plug hole. Her smile faded at the sight of his cold expression.

"I'm sorry. It's been… difficult. But we do need to talk. There are things you don't know."

"Well, you're not wrong there. It feels like there's a lot that I don't know."

He looked at her and immediately felt guilty. Her face looked drawn and her eyes were red-rimmed, as if she'd been crying. Her white uniform and stethoscope reminded him that some staff had to carry on through the events of the last few days bearing a greater weight of responsibility than others. Porters did an important job, he had realised that after the last month, but moving some bin bags full of medical waste was less stressful than having someone's life in your hands.

"Look, I really need to talk to you about stuff. I need to explain; I owe you that at least."

She looked around the canteen and noticed many pairs of eyes on them. She lowered her voice. "I don't really want to do that here. It's like being an animal in the zoo with everyone gawping at us. Come to my room. It'll be easier to talk there."

He softened. He always found it hard to be angry with anyone for long. "Are you alright? You seem, I dunno, a bit… Have you been crying?"

"Not here, Johnny. My room. Can you come now? Please."

He looked across at the clock on the wall. "Not really. I've got to get back on the trolleys with Sid. He'll be expecting me."

Juliet's face fell and Johnny cursed himself. This was an opportunity he really couldn't miss.

"He'll manage without me. Most people seem to be able to. Come on."

He got up and ushered her towards the door.

The walk to her room was awkward and silent. Neither of them wanted to embark on what threatened to be a difficult conversation, so they trudged along the corridors and out into the snowy walkways with the silence pressing down on them.

By the time they got to Juliet's room, the silence was like a scream. She turned the key and switched the light on, and they both went in. In the glare of the central light, the room seemed even barer than before. Everything had been removed, presumably into the boxes stacked by the door.

She gestured around the room. "I'd make you a coffee, but it's all packed away."

"I'm not interested in coffee. What did you want to say to me?" Johnny forced himself to be terse, hating himself for it. He didn't want to be a pushover, but he could see that she was struggling with this.

She shrugged, took a step towards him and leant forward. For a second, Johnny thought she was going to kiss him. He leant forward in anticipation and was left feeling a little embarrassed when instead, she reached for the pocket of his overall. She pulled out *Bleak House* and dangled it in front of him.

"Are you still reading this? I don't think you're reading it at all; you're just showing off, pretending you're an intellectual."

He reached for it but she snatched it away.

"I don't think that's the sort of thing that impresses my colleagues. And I haven't had a lot of time for reading in the last few days," Johnny snapped.

"Sorry, just teasing. I'm a bit nervous." She dropped the book onto the table and sat down opposite him.

"What did you want to say to me?" His voice was cold and flat.

"I know you're angry with me. I deserve that, but I just need you to know that I never meant any of this to happen."

"Any of what? I mean I suppose you're going to tell me that you never really fancied me, and you were just stringing me along, but I don't get why."

She laughed.

"Oh, you mean you don't get why I didn't fancy you because you're so gorgeous and so successful with women who always fall at your feet."

He raised his voice as his anger bubbled up again. "No, of course I didn't mean that. You don't know me very well, do you? I'm not particularly successful with women, they don't fall at my feet, and I'm obviously not gorgeous. There's no need to be sarcastic. This is difficult enough as it is. Just tell me, for God's sake."

She stared at him and shook her head. "You really are a lovely guy, Johnny."

"Oh please. Next thing, you'll be telling me how nice I am. Nice, for fuck's sake."

"Johnny, most men just wouldn't say things like that. Would be like admitting defeat or something. And nice is a very underrated quality. Particularly in a gorgeous man. I like you a lot. You should stop underselling yourself."

"It's hard to believe that. You backed out after the first kiss. Not really a vote of confidence, is it?"

"No, listen to me. I didn't mean to fall for you. I thought you could be a friend. I've been very lonely here and it was so nice to meet someone who didn't just stare at my cleavage. I didn't think anything would come of it. I've, I've..." She stopped and gulped in some air, composing herself. "I've had some bad experiences with men, so I'd kind of given up on that. But it just started to happen. I should have put a stop to it, but I didn't. That's my fault and I'm sorry for leading you on."

"But why did you have to put a stop to it? Why couldn't you have just carried on? Why can't we just carry on now? I don't get it. Haven't you just met the wrong men?"

"Met the wrong men?" She laughed and shook her head. "Do you have any idea what goes on in this place? This hospital is full of the wrong men. It's time that something..." She trailed off, unwilling to say more.

Johnny filled the gap. "What do you mean?"

"No, there's no time for that now. I just need you to listen to me. In the next day or so, you're going to hear a lot of stuff about me. Not very nice stuff. Stuff you'll find hard to believe."

"And is it true, this 'stuff'?"

"A lot of it will be. But I really want you to know that a lot of it was out of my control. I never, ever, throughout all of this, wanted to hurt you. But there's other stuff going on, bigger stuff."

"I don't suppose there's any point in asking what this bigger stuff is? Or where you're going?"

"Can't tell you, sorry. You'll know soon enough."

"You know Helen warned me about you. Said I should be careful, that you weren't what you seemed. Looks like she was right."

"Well, well. Clever girl. I saw her on Saturday, you know."

"At the demo? She said she'd seen you."

"No, no, at your house."

"What? I didn't know that. What were you doing there?"

"I was looking for my bag. I've lost it and I thought maybe I'd left it at yours after the party."

"And had you?"

"Couldn't see it. And Helen said nothing had been found. She made it pretty clear that she thought I was up to something."

"Looks like she was right about that. I should have listened to her."

There was a pause. Juliet glanced up at Johnny as if she were making her mind up about something.

"You do know she's in love with you, don't you?"

Johnny was completely taken aback, his face a picture of confusion. "Helen? No, don't be silly she…"

He trailed off, as the impact of Juliet's words began to cut through. He shook his head uncertainly. "No, no really, she's just a friend."

"Come on, Johnny, open your eyes. She won't hang around forever, though. Don't just put your head in the sand. You need to do something about it."

Johnny was speechless as he turned over what Juliet had just told him. A silence grew between them before Juliet decided.

"There's more I need to tell you. But you've got to promise not to tell anyone else."

He snapped out of his confusion, suddenly alert. "What do you mean?"

She reached out and took his hand in hers. She was gathering herself as if she were about to dive from a high cliff.

"I…"

The moment was broken by a crackling voice from Johnny's walkie-talkie. "Johnny? You there?"

He snatched it up, furious at the interruption.

"Les, I'm right in the middle of something here."

The reply crackled back. "So are we, and this is more important. Get down to casualty, pronto. We need every man standing."

"But—"

"Now, Johnny. Don't be a prick. Now."

The crackle ended. As far as Les was concerned, that conversation was over.

Johnny lowered the walkie-talkie, looked at Juliet and shrugged.

"Sorry. Got to go."

"Come back as soon as you're finished. Eight o'clock at the latest. There's more to say."

"I'll try. But I can't promise; you heard the walkie-talkie. But what about you? Aren't you on call? Your bleep could go off at any minute."

She gave a hollow laugh. "I don't need to worry about that any more. Come at eight; I'll be there. But don't be later than nine, whatever happens."

"Where will you be at nine? What's so urgent, you can't wait?"

"I said I'd go and see Gloria. She went home after the police interviewed her again. I just want to make sure she's alright."

"The police? What did they want?"

She stood up abruptly, patting his hand.

"Sorry, Johnny. You should go now. I'm in a rush."

He stood up and they faced each other. Suddenly, she held him close and they hugged. She whispered into his cheek, avoiding eye contact.

"I'm so sorry. There are a lot of horrible men in the world. Don't ever be one." She pushed him off, pointing him towards the door, and wiping away some stray tears. She gave him a false, bright smile. "Eight o'clock, yeah?"

He nodded and found himself in the corridor automatically speed walking towards casualty. He negotiated the corridors in a daze, oblivious to his surroundings, his mind racing. The wrong men. "This hospital is full of the wrong men," she'd said. But who could she possibly mean?

*

Clive was nicely settled in his favourite armchair. David sat on his lap, a wriggling bundle of seven-year-old Christmas excitement, watching the telly. On the sofa, Mary cuddled up to little Jane, who was wide-eyed and silent, entranced by the lights on the Christmas tree and quietly baffled but delighted by the amount of chocolate they'd been allowed to eat. Clive looked across and caught Mary's eye. They exchanged a smile across the heads of their children. Clive indicated his watch and raised his eyebrows. Mary took up the cue.

"OK, you two little monkeys. Bath time. Then it's new pyjamas and bed."

There was a ripple of groaning, more of a performance than a reality.

"Now then, you two," Clive chipped in, "you know Father Christmas won't come if you're not tucked up in bed asleep. Up the stairs now, chop-chop."

Mary led the way, with Clive bringing up the rear. He had just started on the first step when the phone rang. Mary glowered down at him.

"Don't they ever bloody leave you alone? It's Christmas Eve, for goodness sake. I don't care what's happened, Clive; you can't go out on Christmas Eve."

"Don't worry, love. It won't be anything, just someone returning my call."

Mary sighed and shook her head. "Oh, answer it then. I'll

get these two in the bath, but be quick. I can't do it all on my own."

She ushered the children into the bathroom and Clive turned back and picked up the phone.

"Hello, Clive Brooks."

"Clive, it's Andy."

"Andy? Andy Johnson? Where the bloody hell have you been, man? I've been ringing you all day. I've left God knows how many messages."

"I know, sorry Clive, it's been a bit awkward."

"Damn right it has. Well, now you've finally rang me back, what's going on?"

"What do you mean?"

"Juliet Fulton. The one you were supposed to have interviewed the other night in East Mount Road. You know, the one you were drooling over," he snapped.

"Look, calm down and listen. I've heard you're close to taking her in."

"How do you know that?"

"Never mind that now. Listen to me. On no account is she to be arrested."

"What the fuck?"

"Listen. Just listen."

*

Back in her room, Juliet sat on the bed and checked her watch for the umpteenth time. She couldn't wait any longer; she had to go and find Gloria and find out what had happened with the police. But she had made all the preparations and one call to the police would bring the whole thing to an end once and for all. Not even North Yorkshire Police could mess it up, surely? And once there were arrests, they would be in the clear and the police would not be interested in complications. She should know that better than anyone. She ached to tell someone, though. Someone who would be on her side. Someone she could trust. There was only one person and he hadn't turned up. And he was in danger; she was sure of that. She had decided she was going to warn him when they had talked in the canteen and she couldn't just leave it now, despite the risks to herself.

There was only one solution. She reached for her desk drawer and pulled out a writing pad and a pen. She took a deep breath, wiped her eyes and began to write.

*

An atmosphere of simmering calm had settled on the waiting room of the casualty department, but it was clear that violence could re-erupt at the slightest provocation. The two sides stared at each other across the no man's land of the ranks of chairs, surrounded by the glittering decorations that celebrated peace and love to all mankind. A couple of the porters, Sid and Fred, were strategically positioned in that buffer zone, while others paced around in front, glaring at the rival armies with well-rehearsed expressions that suggested brutal retribution would swiftly follow any further outbreaks of aggression. All of this, the threat of the imminent arrival of the police, and the prominent display of the departmental baseball bat, given an occasional swing by Les, as if in preparation for further action, had dampened down the visitors' enthusiasm for a fight. As time slipped by, exhaustion and the effects of too much Christmas cheer also helped the combatants to re-evaluate the attraction of more fisticuffs.

Johnny looked at his watch. There was only so much glowering he could do. It was the Christmas Special version of an old familiar story: a night out in town on payday ended in casualty when too much drink tipped mouthy banter over the edge. Warriors from both sides needing stitches were invariably accompanied to casualty by their mates, all cheek by jowl in the cramped waiting area. It was a recipe for permanent conflict. Often on a Thursday night, the police would call in before they were summoned, just in case. On this Christmas Eve, however, they were delayed, so the porters had to step into the breach.

It was the last thing Johnny needed. He'd already had to separate several punch-ups, hold someone down while being stitched and, at intervals, talk sympathetically to the combatants and their followers, dripping in the suggestion that calming down before the police arrived would be a very good idea. Now, as he paced and glowered, his mind was on his earlier meeting with Juliet. What was it she wanted to tell him? What did she mean by the wrong men? And what were the bad things he would find out about her? He turned it over and over in his mind, letting the tense situation in casualty fade into the background of his consciousness, but could make no sense of any of it. He really needed to see her again, or he would drive himself mad with his wild speculations.

But by the time the police arrived and the drunks had dispersed, wishing Happy Christmas to all and sundry, even their sworn enemies of a couple of hours earlier, it was already too late. It was past nine and Juliet would be making her way to see Gloria. That thought stirred more unease. What had Juliet said? Gloria had gone home after being interviewed by the police again. It didn't make any sense to him. What had Gloria to do with any of this? And what had she to do with Juliet?

He finished off taking back the meal trolleys with Sid in silence, barely responding to his animated recollections of legendary fights in casualty over the years, his mind whirling with the same questions.

They stowed the last trolley. Sid laid a hand on his arm. “You alright, Johnny, lad? You’ve barely said a word since we left casualty. Don’t let them yobbos get to you. You did very well.”

Johnny looked up as if roused from a dream. “Huh? Sorry Sid, got things on my mind. Bit of a headache as well. I think I’ll take some paracetamol and get my head down for an hour. I’ve got my walkie-talkie.”

He waved it in the air as proof, turned and trudged away down the corridor, head down, the weight of the world on his shoulders. It wasn’t sleep he needed. It was answers.

53

The house was in darkness when Juliet arrived. She knocked once and then fumbled in her pocket for a key without waiting for an answer. She stepped into the hall, closed the door quietly and called out, "It's me. Where are you?"

The reply, pained and weary, came from the front room. "In here."

She went through. The curtains were closed and all of the Christmas lights were off. The only light came from a flickering candle, which sent dancing shadows across Gloria's face, and the glowing tip of her cigarette. She was perched on an armchair, legs tucked underneath her, rocking as if she were about to spring into action. A bottle of whisky was on the side table with an empty glass next to it.

"Why are you sat here in the dark? Was it the police? Has anything happened?"

"I didn't want all the bloody fairy lights on. Not in the mood for Christmas."

"What did the police say? Why aren't you at work?" Juliet's tone, which had exuded a soft, caring concern at first, veered into something sharper.

Gloria shook her head. "Not you as well. I've had all this from the police already. They can smell blood and they won't let go."

Juliet crossed the room and knelt by the armchair.

"Sorry, I didn't mean it like that. I'm just worried, that's all." She stroked her arm. "Tell me what happened. With the police, I mean."

Gloria took a drag on her cigarette, and exhaled like a sigh, sending clouds of blue-grey smoke into the air. It wreathed around her face, illuminated by the candle that shivered in the breeze.

"They wouldn't stop going on about Sutherland. They've been through the personnel records and went on and on about the complaints I'd made about him. They made me go over it again and again, like it was my fault. All the things he did. Over and over, like they were trying to trip me up. And now I have all of those memories churning around in my head." She shook her head. "I wish I'd never bothered complaining now. Didn't do any good at the time anyway. The police couldn't give a damn about what they get up to in that hospital. And now, they're like a dog with a bone."

"What about Gordon? Surely that's thrown them off the scent. I mean, how does that fit into whatever theory they've got?"

Gloria snorted. "Theory? They've got no theory; they're just scrambling around as usual, putting pressure on and waiting for someone to crack. But I don't get who did that to Gordon and why? And what about Johnny?"

Juliet frowned. "What do you mean? What about Johnny?"

"Is he still going around asking questions? How much does he know?"

There was a pause before Juliet answered.

Gloria jumped into the space that the pause had left. "You need to do something about him, before anything bad happens."

Juliet gave a wry smile. "Before anything bad happens? A bit late for that, don't you think? Listen, I've got to get back in a minute or so. Give me a fag and a drink and let me think for a bit."

Gloria poured another finger of whisky and passed the glass, a cigarette and the lighter over to her. Juliet lit up and took a sip of her drink. In the flickering candlelight, she looked up at Gloria, whose face was drawn and pale.

"You don't need to worry about the police. I've already taken care of that and they won't be asking you any more questions. It'll all be over by tomorrow."

"And Johnny?" Gloria's eyes shone in the gloom, intense and questioning.

Juliet took a drag on her cigarette and considered. Their eyes met and the question went unanswered.

*

By the time the bottle was empty, Helen had passed the evening in front of the telly watching *The Go-Between*, the BBC's big Christmas film, and returning, at intervals, to brooding about the argument with Johnny. She swung wildly between fury at Johnny and guilt about judging Juliet too harshly. Eventually, the wine triumphed and she simply simmered gently as her bed called to her.

She settled down into it, pillows piled up and swaddled in a duvet. Her breath steamed into the air. There was a single bedside lamp that cast a pool of yellow light onto her lap and her book. The rest of the room was a darkened cave. She read, but after a while, the printed words began to slip and slide across the page, and her head began to nod, her hands relinquishing the book, which slipped from her fingers. As she fell towards sleep, a picture of Juliet Fulton at the demonstration came to her, chanting and waving a placard. The face began to melt and slip, subtly morphing into that of Paula Marsh, the detective she had met in Betty's. The book escaped her grip completely and fell to the floor with a clatter.

She sat up with a start. The bag. She had forgotten completely about the bag. She roused herself and swung her legs out from under the duvet and into the floor. The icy chill sent shivers through her and sharpened her mind. Where on earth had she put the bag? And then she remembered. It was in her drawer, under a pile of socks. She dashed across the bedroom floor, grabbed the bag in the drawer and dashed back, diving for the warmth of her bed.

She emptied it out on the duvet in front of her. It was the unremarkable miscellany of a woman's bag: lipstick, perfume, tampons, a purse. Helen was suddenly furious with herself. What on earth was she doing, rifling through someone's personal things like some kind of psycho stalker? She needed to pull herself together, forget all about Juliet Fulton and start thinking of herself for a change. Starting now.

She would put all of this stuff away, back in the bag, and try to get some sleep. She reached for the bag, which lay at the end of the bed where she had tossed it. She stretched and just managed to pinch the edge of it between two fingertips before carefully reeling it in. She gathered it into a more secure grip and scrunched up the bag into the palm of her hand, and pulled it towards her. She stopped. Then looked at the bag in her closed fist. She squeezed it and her eyes opened a little wider. She could feel a rectangle of something inside.

But that couldn't be right. She had emptied everything from it. She squeezed for a second time and there it was again: something solid and slightly yielding inside. She opened it up, holding it under the cone of light from the bedside lamp. It was completely empty. She pushed her fingers in and began to feel around every inch of the walls of the bag. Her forefinger touched metal at the bottom, in the far corner. She looked again and there it was. A hidden zip, in the long seam of the bag. She was excited now and her fumbling fingers took several attempts to hold on to the zip tag and pull. She felt inside and pulled out whatever it was that was hidden in there.

It was a chequebook. She flicked through it. The stubs showed regular withdrawals of cash, but of perfectly reasonable amounts of money. Nothing suspicious there. And then Helen noticed the name on each cheque: Juliet Macdonald. But why would Juliet have someone else's chequebook, hidden away in a secret compartment? Was it stolen? Maybe that was her real name and Helen had been right all along, but the name didn't ring a bell for her. She turned these ideas over and over in her mind, but nothing seemed to make sense to her.

She looked over at her alarm. It was nearly midnight. Soon it would be Christmas Day, but this was like no Christmas she had ever experienced before. She was alone in a freezing house, full of creaks and shadows, and for the first time in her young life, there was nothing to look forward to when Christmas Day dawned.

The thought was a sobering one and pushed her into making her mind up. It was time to stop being so silly about Juliet and the strange events at the hospital. Time for sleep.

She reached for the bag again and started to insert the chequebook into its secret pocket. It was a tight fit and she had to wiggle it around a little to get it in. Her fingers brushed against something else, something she had missed the first time around. It was a strip of card, matte on the side facing her, glossy under her fingertips.

She turned it over to inspect it, and gave a gasp when she processed what she was looking at. It was a strip of black and white pictures from a photo booth of two people. One of them was Juliet Fulton. She didn't know the other, but whoever it was was wearing a hospital uniform with a name badge. It was hard to make out the writing. She held it under the side lamp and leant forward, screwing up her eyes to see it more clearly. The words gradually took shape and formed a name. A name she had heard many times from Johnny's work anecdotes.

She brought her hand up to her mouth. Her breath caught in her throat. She turned it over again and saw what was written there, on the back of the strip. A slowly dawning fear gathered force and turned into a wave that swamped her, as connections, questions, and deadly consequences lurched through her mind.

They had kept their relationship hidden. Had they given each other alibis? She couldn't remember exactly what Johnny had said now. She willed her heart to stop racing and tried to breathe more steadily so that she could focus on the conclusion that kept forcing itself to the front of her consciousness.

Johnny was in trouble. Big trouble.

54

The next couple of hours were quiet. Johnny was bleeped to transfer a patient from intensive care to a normal ward and managed to avoid a Christmas drink when he got there. He didn't feel like drinking any more. After the argument with Helen earlier in the day, and now Juliet's weird farewell, this was a day he just wanted to be over. And when it was over, then what? Struggling back to a deserted, freezing house to spend Christmas Day alone wasn't anything to look forward to, more something to endure. But, strangely, he wasn't in the mood for company either, certainly not from the other porters. There was only one person he wanted to see, one person he had unfinished business with. Juliet Fulton. He checked his watch. It was 11.15. He wondered. Maybe she would be back by now; maybe she was still waiting out there for him. It was no use pretending; he had to know what it was she was going to tell him.

He trudged his way through the corridors, now deserted, and braced himself to cross the outdoor space to the nurses' home. Shivering, he pressed on through the relentless blizzard until he was able to dash through the doorway into the bright, breeze-blocked hallways of the home. At her door, he paused and brushed the melting flakes from his hair and his overall. As he did so, he noticed the note pinned to the door:

Come straight in Johnny. Jx

Puzzled, he tried the handle. The door opened immediately and he found himself in Juliet's room, with its disturbing trace of her scent.

The room was shadowy, the inky blackness lifted by the ghostly, silvery light that seeped in from the large window on the far side. The curtains were open, and it looked out onto the car park that was lit by a couple of street lights, harsh, icy white. Johnny felt his way across the room and stood by the window looking out on the empty scene, the snowflakes filling the window, large and luminous against the night sky. It would be impossible for anyone to leave or arrive by car without being seen from this vantage point.

He turned back and surveyed the room. A lot of her stuff had been cleared, but her uniform still hung on the door and there were a few books scattered across her desk. It felt as if she had left in a hurry, but she had made sure he could get in the room. Why? Was she coming back? Had she left him something? He scanned the whole space and his eye was caught by something on the bed. It was an envelope, like a Christmas card. In the dim light, he could just make out the writing on it:

Johnny Jewell. Porters' Room. Personal.

He sat down at the desk by the window to get the benefit of the lights outside, opened the envelope and pulled out three neatly folded sheets of white A4 paper. It was a letter, addressed to him and signed by Juliet. What more could she possibly have to say? He glanced around the shadows of the room, took a deep breath, and began to read.

Dear Johnny,

If everything goes to plan, you won't see me again. This letter is to explain, but you must promise me that you will destroy it after you've read it. I shouldn't even really be writing this down, but I couldn't tell you earlier. I waited for you but you didn't show up.

I really like you, but sometimes, things happen, and you just have to make difficult decisions. It's nothing personal, but in the end, it's a survival thing. There's too much at stake and you already know too much, although I don't know exactly what Gordon told you at the party. He wouldn't tell me. And that's a bit of a problem. Whatever happens, I will never forget you. I will do whatever Gloria asks of me – it's the very least I owe her.

He put the letter down and gripped the edge of the desk. It was as if his world had suddenly tipped on its axis. He couldn't read the rest. The silence in the room, the dark, silvered shadows clustered around him, the view of the icy wastes through the window, all of it played on his imagination. *You already know too much.* What did she mean? Had Gordon known too much as well? He thought back to the conversation he had overheard in the clap clinic about knowing too much. And look what had happened to him. A powerful sense of foreboding crept upon him. She was with Gloria right at that moment, checking up on why the police had interviewed her again. *I will do whatever Gloria asks of me.* They were both probably on their way back right now.

He had to stop and make himself think. He smoothed the letter out and laid his hands, palms down, flat on the desktop and bent his head down, breathing evenly through his nose until he felt his heart rate calm and his panic subside.

"So," he told himself, "this is nothing, really it's not, she just..."

He stopped, his rational mind jerking to a halt. Looking down, he found himself staring at a strange optical illusion: a creamy, bloodless finger hanging from the desk drawer. His breath caught in his throat, and before he could stop himself, he was reaching down, hoping beyond hope that it wasn't what he thought it was. His hand stopped short, trembling, before he stretched out and closed around the mystery object and pulled. Cold and clammy, he recoiled from it but then pulled again as he realised what it was. A pale latex glove snapped out of the drawer into his hand. He pulled the drawer open wide and rummaged inside, removing items one at a time. The second glove. A packet of gloves. A used syringe. A box of syringes.

He stopped and looked at the pile of recovered loot. Each object seemed to add to his growing unease. He shivered. Come on, she was a doctor. Why wouldn't she have these things in her room? Even as he was telling himself this, it all felt a little desperate, a little contrived, as if he were trying to convince himself. He knew what Helen would say.

As an afterthought, he reached back into the drawer and swept his hand around it. His fingers closed on a small object, glass by the feel of it. He brought it out and placed it on the desktop. A glass vial with a York District Hospital label. Diamorphine. The silvery light through the window sparkled through the glass to reveal the merest dribble at the bottom.

He suddenly felt very exposed and very alone, aware that no one knew where he was. He shuddered, thrust the letter into his pocket and slipped quietly into the corridor.

55

Fifteen minutes later, Helen was downstairs in the hall, fully dressed. The house was ablaze with light to dispel the shadows and allow her to concentrate without being disturbed by irrational fears. She held a piece of paper in her left hand along with the telephone, and with her right, she dialled the number. She could hear it ringing, its tone harsh and insistent. She looked at her watch. It was quarter past midnight. Christmas Day, she thought with a wry smile. What was she doing, ringing at this time? No one was going to answer, or worse, if they did, they'd be furious, being dragged out of bed in the early hours of Christmas Day, for God's sake, for some ridiculous theory she had. She was just about to put the receiver down when she heard, as the phone was en route to the holder, the tinny ringing tone suddenly stop and a voice begin speaking.

She wrenched the phone away from its base and brought it to her face.

"Hello?" she shouted, afraid they might hang up.

The voice on the other end sounded calm and reasonable, if a little curious. "Hello? Who's that? Are you alright? You sound a little…"

"Is that…" Helen stopped to consult the scrap of paper. "Paula Marsh? The detective?"

"Yes. DC Marsh here. Who's speaking?"

Helen wasn't sure but she thought she just caught a hint of pride in the other woman's answer, as if she was quite pleased to be called. It gave her a little boost of confidence to continue.

"It's Helen. You probably don't remember, but we met outside Betty's on Saturday."

There was the merest missed beat before Marsh continued smoothly. "Of course I remember. I asked you to ring whenever you needed to. You said you were worried about Juliet Fulton. Is everything alright?"

Helen couldn't answer. She looked around the hallway. Under the unforgiving light, her worries seemed ridiculous, her theory fantastical, something not of the everyday world.

"Look, sorry for disturbing you at this hour. Especially on Christmas Eve. It's nothing. Forget about it."

Paula cut in, a note of urgency in her voice. "You're not disturbing me. Just tell me what's on your mind. If you put the phone down, I really will be annoyed."

There was silence.

"Helen. Just tell me."

In the glare of her freezing hall, Helen took a deep breath and told her, her words tumbling out of her in a torrent, as if she were afraid that if she stopped, she would never start again.

On the other end of the phone, Paula Marsh listened. Occasionally, she asked a question to clarify, and to signal she was still listening. When Helen had finished, she waited, clutching the phone to her ear.

"Listen, Helen. I know you're worried, but it still could be perfectly innocent."

"Look, forget I rang you. I just thought you'd help, but don't worry about it. I'll go myself."

"Go? Go where?" There was a note of panic in Paula's voice.

"The hospital, of course. I can't just leave him there on his own."

There was a pause.

"You're in East Mount Road, aren't you? Forty-eight? Stay there. Make some tea. I'll be there as quick as I can."

*

Paula rubbed furiously at the windscreen in front of her, her breath steaming into the air in the car. Her ancient Mini was just not built for this kind of weather, its gentle breeze of cold air all the heating system could manage, even after fifteen minutes of precarious driving through persistent snow. Not for the first time, she cursed the girl, Helen. She was overreacting, Paula was sure of that, but Helen seemed determined to mount some kind of heroic rescue mission, regardless of the weather. Paula couldn't bring herself to let her get on with it on her own. The dreadful weather was bad enough, but more than that, Paula could not bear to think of any woman in the north these days, walking alone at night through the city. The Ripper might be celebrating a family Christmas, tucked up warm in his bed, but he might not. She knew she'd get a good bollocking from Grayson and a torrent of abuse from Jacko. From Grayson because it broke all precedents and procedures. From Jacko because it was a daft, soft-girls thing to do. Clive would get it though, and if they did finally decide to go in, she'd ring him first for backup.

Just as well she was on her own on Christmas Eve. Sandra was with her parents, and Paula had spent a solitary evening with the telly on, while going through the details of the case over and over again. No one would miss her and it was good to be doing something.

She was just about to turn into East Mount Road when she saw the snow drift. Just in time, she managed to bring the car to a sliding halt on the main road. She left the engine running and picked her way down the street to the front door. Stamping her feet, a red woolly hat jammed down on her head, her body looking as if it had been inflated because of the plump winter coat she was wearing, she hammered on the door.

The door opened almost immediately. Helen was already kitted out for an arctic hike and had clearly made up her mind that she was going to the hospital come what may.

"You got everything?" Paula asked.

Helen looked a little confused. "Aren't you coming in? I've made tea. I thought you'd want to see the bag."

"The tea was for you, to give you something to do. And I do want to see it, but I daren't turn the car off. In this weather, it might never start again. Get your coat and the bag, lock up and I'll look at it in the car."

"Where are we going?"

"The hospital, obviously. We're not going to midnight mass."

Helen peered through the snowstorm and saw, parked a little way away at the end of the road, a car that sounded like it had bronchitis, spewing fumes into the night air. She didn't need any more convincing and dashed back inside, to return seconds later with everything she needed. She locked up and slowly negotiated the pavement and road, through two feet of snow, to get to the Mini.

There was a sudden gust of wind, driving a flurry of snow from the car roof stinging into their faces. They both gasped.

"Quick, let's get out of this before I change my mind. Door's open."

They scrambled into the front seats and slammed their doors. Immediately, they felt the benefit of the shelter it gave from the wind. Paula reached above her head and switched on the internal light.

"Let's have a look at this purse then. We'll have to be quick if we don't want to get stuck before we've even started."

Helen handed it over and Paula examined it carefully. She looked through the chequebook and scrutinised the photo strip. She looked across at Helen, who had been watching her with some trepidation.

"I see what you mean. And yes, that's definitely them. Both of them. 'Me and Mum'. Who'd have thought it?"

Helen sighed in relief and a relieved smile spread across her face. Paula hesitated, troubled by Helen's reaction. It was clear to her that Helen was going to go through with this regardless. She couldn't let her do it on her own.

"What's up?"

"Give me your keys. I just need to make a phone call before we go."

Helen handed them over, and Paula unfolded herself from the tiny Mini and picked her way back to the house.

Three minutes later, she was back.

"What was all that about then?"

Paula revved up the car, sending clouds of exhaust into the air, and turned on the windscreen wipers, scattering the new accumulation of snowflakes.

"Come on," she continued, "let's get going. We can talk it all through on the way."

She manoeuvred the gear stick, a wobbling, uncertain wand, into place and the car slowly pulled away from the drifted snow into the central strip of navigable road. Wheezing and groaning, it made off down the street, trundling its way through the softly falling snow and into the darkness.

56

Gloria and Juliet. How could he have been so stupid? Thinking with his dick again instead of his brain. Helen had tried to tell him about Juliet, but he just hadn't wanted to hear it. But if he knew, then they would have guessed by now and they would not hesitate to remove the last threat to them. One more body wouldn't make any difference, not now.

He hesitated, and doubts crept back in. She had been so nice to him earlier in her room, so full of feeling and warmth. Hadn't she? How could that fit in with his fears now? But then again, she'd left him hanging for days, when she could have easily sought him out and cleared the air. Maybe the nice bit was just another act from someone he didn't really know at all, someone who was a consummate actress. And Helen, someone who was as far away from being an actress as was possible, had always been so sure about Juliet.

He leant back against the wall, his mind racing. Maybe he should just sneak away to the bike shed, get on his bike and ride home. He could lock the door, hole up on his own, and contact the police first thing in the morning. He'd get the sack, but it was a crummy job anyway, and would be worth even less if he was dead.

Opposite him, the other wall of the corridor was a bank of floor-to-ceiling plate glass windows that, under the lights, were a shiny, black mirror, reflecting him in his greying porter's overall. He was struck by his own haunted expression and by his complete isolation. The corridor formed one side of a rectangular courtyard garden, paving stones studded by low, evergreen shrubs.

On the other side of the courtyard, invisible to Johnny, two figures standing in the shadows could see him as clearly as if he were in a spotlight on a darkened stage, even though the night air was thick with falling snow. They watched Johnny straighten and start to hurry down the corridor. Immediately, they began to follow.

Johnny turned the corner and came to a crossroads. His nerves were stretched and jangling, and every sight from the corner of his eye, and every sudden noise – a pinking strip light, a sighing hum from a vending machine – screeched an alarm in his mind. He had to get out, get away, somewhere, anywhere. He hurried away, head swivelling in all directions to check that the coast was clear, and took a left. If he could get to the bike sheds and get to his bike, he could ride off the site and get on to the main road, where, out in the open, he would be safe. At the back of his mind lurked the problem of the piled-up snow in the streets, and the biting cold, but he could not think more than one step ahead at a time.

Just as he turned, he froze. Was that the sound of footsteps? He listened, his face contorted with concentration. There it came again. Footsteps and the light, quiet tone of voices. Two people and the footsteps were getting closer.

In a panic, he started again, half-running down the corridor. He got to the next corner, hid around it and listened again, struggling to quieten his panting breath. Sweat had started to trickle down his face and neck. At first, there was silence and he dared to hope that he'd lost them, but then they came again. Distant footsteps getting closer and hissed, urgent conversation. He took off down the corridor, careering through the pools of light that punctuated the dim corridors in this part of the hospital.

When he got to the next crossroads, he stopped again. He bent over, his hands resting on his knees, fighting to get his breath back.

By the time the burning in his lungs had subsided, and his breathing was a little easier, he was able to see exactly where he was. To his left, the corridor led to the incinerator; to his right, it led to the mortuary, still taped off as a crime scene. He could see, against the black rectangle of the glass-panelled door that led to the bike sheds, the blizzard that had whipped up outside. The sights in both directions produced a shiver in him that pulled him out of his exhaustion. He stood up straight and for a split second, began to relax when he heard it again. Footsteps and the quiet hum of talking. He looked again at the whirlwind of fat, white flakes outside and made up his mind. He dashed to his right, ducked under the police tape and slipped inside the mortuary, closing the door, but not tight.

The mortuary was in darkness, shrouded in cool silence, except for the hum of the fridges in front of him. The rest of the room was bare, with only a trolley on the far side of the room.

He stood by the half-closed door, straining his ears. Surely they must be going outside. The mortuary was out of action now it was a crime scene again, so no one would be coming this way, would they? Then he heard them. When he calculated they had reached the end of the corridor, he had his fingers crossed, praying they would go the other way. The first set of footsteps coming towards the mortuary pushed him over the edge. Without thinking, his wild eyes found the bank of fridges and he ran over to the doors at the far end. He took a deep breath and opened the last fridge. A dim light spilled onto the floor in front of him. He was praying that it would be empty. There were four shelves and all of them were vacant, apart from the top one, with its white, swaddled figure.

This was no time to give in to fear. He scrambled onto the shelf below, directly in front of him, gagging with disgust. He laid down flat and, turning over to face the door, he reached out and found the lock mechanism. He grabbed hold of the lock between his finger and thumb and pulled it towards him until it was almost closed. The light inside the fridge went off and he was enveloped in thick, choking darkness. He had a few seconds of respite, and almost wished that the fear would return because at least that meant he didn't have the time to focus on the appalling situation he had found himself in.

In that minute, in the absolute blackness of the fridge, his senses were at the very edge of sensitivity. The hum of the fridge was louder inside and was accompanied by strange creaks and shiftings that tortured his nerves. Out of nowhere, a memory popped into his head. It was of Gordon, on his first shift with him, only a month ago, delighting in telling him stories of the terrible, frightening sounds the bodies would make in the fridge as trapped air and fluids escaped hours after being shelved, as their bones and tissues settled. The final groans and protestations of the dead. He couldn't see the bodies, but didn't know whether that was a blessing or not. He knew they were there, lying in ranks in their carefully bound sheets, an army of the deceased, including the one just above his head on the next shelf up.

The air was cold and he shivered. Just as well they were kept above freezing, otherwise he really would be in trouble. The air in the fridge was thick with a strange cocktail of smells: chemical, metallic, disinfectant and a certain sweetness. Johnny, noticing it properly for the first time, began to gag, and had to control his breathing through his nose to subdue the rising tide of panic and, above all else, to keep quiet. He started, automatically it seemed, to try to identify each separate component of the odour, but then immediately tried to block it from his mind after the first few suggestions popped into his head. He forced himself to calm down, and made himself think that perhaps he'd just heard some members of staff walking innocently down the corridors. If he just waited for a minute or two longer, he could get out of this ghastly place, shut the door and slip away quietly, as if nothing had ever happened.

The creak of the door, the footsteps and the mumbled conversation soon put paid to that idea.

"Put the light on and shut the door. We don't want anyone coming in here to investigate."

Johnny froze, renewed his grip on the inner lock and strained to hear what was being said.

"I don't know why we've come down here anyway," said a second voice. "This is the bloody crime scene. Might have been crawling with police."

"Police?" scoffed the first voice. "You're joking, aren't yer? Lazy bastards will have clocked off long since. Couldn't catch a fucking cold, that lot."

Who were they? Johnny racked his brains to try to identify the voices, but it seemed to him that he'd never heard these people in his life before. One thing was definite though. They weren't Gloria or Juliet. These were two men. He tried again.

The voices and footsteps came closer, until they were standing right opposite the fridge he was hiding in. His hands had begun to sweat regardless of the temperature inside the fridge and he could feel his grip slipping, the metal of the lock sliding against the greasy surface of his fingertips. He clung on, willing the metal to hold fast. If it did slip, the door would open and he'd be done for. Even if it slipped just a crack, the light of the fridge would come on and give the game away. He pulled his left arm from underneath his body, moving as slowly as he could to stop the shelf creaking. He felt certain that his breathing and heartbeat could be heard in Leeds, so loud did it appear to be in this terrible, confined, darkened space, but the men outside, a mere yard away from him, seemed not to hear a thing.

His efforts to move without being discovered had blocked out the voices from outside. He cursed himself silently and forced himself to concentrate on what they were saying. He listened and as they went on, he could scarcely believe what he was hearing. By now, both arms were aching and sweat was pouring down his back, the trails like icicles against his warm skin. He grimaced with the effort to keep hold of the door, and to his horror, felt the first fluttering beginnings of cramp in his legs.

But now, the conversation just outside his cramped prison changed. Quiet restraint ebbed away and tempers became frayed. Voices were raised and there was the sound of a scuffle. Some pushing and shoving, a stumble and then a crash. Johnny had to bite his tongue not to cry out as, without warning, one of the figures suddenly crashed against the door of the fridge, Johnny's hands were thrown off the inner lock, and he was bounced up and down on the rattling shelf. He clung on and tried to move his head back towards the door.

"…just the start, unless you fucking do as you're told. There's nothing connects him with us, nothing."

"But—"

"Never mind but. Once coppers have arrested 'em for both murders, that'll be it done."

"What about Jewell?"

"Fuck Jewell, he's a woodentop; we don't have to worry about him."

"He's not stupid. We don't know exactly what Gordon told him."

There was a pause as the other man considered their options.

Inside the fridge, Johnny waited, straining to hear what would come next.

Finally, the first voice spoke again. "I don't think we can take the risk. There's only one way to make sure he keeps his mouth shut."

Outside the fridge, there was momentary silence.

Inside, Johnny was hyperventilating, sure that at any moment, the fridge door would be flung open and he would be discovered. He jabbed his fingernails into his palm to make himself concentrate and to quieten his breathing.

Outside, footsteps turned and walked away. Johnny could hear the sound of the light switch and the door closing. He waited for a minute or so, taking great deep breaths, and began to turn his attention once again to his current situation. He crawled up to the door along his shelf and pushed it. It wouldn't move. He pushed again, harder this time, rattling the shelf and mechanism of the lock and as he did so, the thought that had been lurking at the back of his brain ever since one of them had crashed against the fridge elbowed its way to the front of the queue.

The door was locked. It could not be opened from the inside. No one would be coming to use the fridge now the morgue was a crime scene. He searched for a ray of hope in the blackness that surrounded him. Oh yeah, the fridge was also full of dead bodies, merely inches away. He lay back on the metal shelf and exhaled like a steam engine. *Really good work, Johnny, old son. Really good.* That guy outside was right; he was a woodentop. A gold-plated, top of the range, real fucking woodentop.

57

The porters' restroom had a weary, half-hearted festive air that already smelt of January disappointment. The overhead strip light was off. The battered, artificial Christmas tree in the corner, wire branches bent at improbable angles and draped with threadbare vintage tinsel, twinkled with fairy lights which were echoed by a second string draped over the sink. The gloom in the rest of the room covered the shabby corners, home to discarded old trainers and pizza boxes. A paint-streaked radio dribbled out Slade's 'Merry Christmas Everybody'.

In the middle of the room, it seemed as if a modern recreation of the nativity scene had been constructed. Instead of a manger and the wise men, there was a low Formica table surrounded by four porters, lit by a lamp in the centre. They had gathered to worship, not the son of God, but the game of poker. Their faces were etched with concentration, their heads covered with paper party hats, their uniforms decorated with tinsel and baubles, their hands clutching fans of playing cards. A cloud of cigarette smoke hung in the air above their heads. Scattered around the room were empty cans of lager, and on the table, a half-empty bottle of scotch and a landslip of an ashtray.

It had been a long night. From the time of the evening meal that they had delivered to the wards, it had been a non-stop round of drinks in every ward and every department they had visited. A toast to the season at every stop had led to a raucous jollity that had now reached the stage of maudlin exhaustion when the novelty of the festive season could no longer prevent their inner fears crowding in on each man present. They were all secretly waiting for the first of them to crack, throw in their cards and slip off to their chosen place of rest.

Les, his piggy eyes even more like pinpricks than usual, took a prodigious drag on his cigarette, stopping only when the acrid chemical taste told him he had reached the filter. He eyeballed his playing companions over the top of his hand, and dropped the butt into an empty can of lager. He let fly a belch like a crack of thunder before speaking. "I'll see your two and raise you," he said, pushing three Rothmans to the centre of the table.

A frisson of excitement circled them and eyes flashed this way and that for reactions from the players. A new energy pushed thoughts of sleep away again, but as quickly as it bubbled up, it drained away again. The phone rang, shattering their silent concentration. All four players jumped, suddenly alert to the world outside of the game. They looked around the circle as the phone screeched again. Then their eyes settled on Les, who barked in impatience.

"Well answer it then. Bloody hell, it's not going to answer itself."

Sid stretched behind him and found the receiver. His jump of shock had temporarily displaced his ginger toupee, which now sat at a racy angle under his paper hat.

"Porters," he intoned.

The rest of them could hear the sound of a woman's voice raised in irritation on the other end. Sid nodded and tried several times to intervene but the diatribe continued uninterrupted.

By the end, he had moved the receiver a few inches away from his ear. Eventually, the torrent of abuse stopped and Sid seized his chance.

"Yes. Sorry about that. Yes, we will. Alright, we'll be right there."

Even on the far end of the phone line, the impact of Sid's night of festive jollity was clear as he slurred and stumbled over his words.

"No. I assure you, I've just had a couple of glasses to celebrate the season… No… Well, that's very rude, if you ask me. I think…" He stopped suddenly and looked up at his colleagues, who had been following the conversation. "She hung up. Cheeky cow, said I'd been drinking on duty."

"You have been drinking on duty," snorted Pat. "We all bloody have. She probably has and all. What did she want anyway?"

"Well, first off, she told us to switch our walkie-talkies on again. Said she'd been bleeping us for ages, mardy old bag."

"Jesus. Some people don't seem to know it's Christmas, do they?"

"And all it's for is a customer for Rose Cottage. Not as if they're going anywhere, is it? Wouldn't hurt them to wait a bit, would it?"

"So selfish. I had a bloody royal flush and all," said Les bitterly. "Come on then, lads. Whose turn is it? Sid?"

"Aye, alright. I could do with a walk. Clear me head. Who's going to join me?"

The other three quickly looked around then cast their eyes down to the floor, like school kids avoiding the teacher's raking gaze.

Pat could only do avoidance for so long before he cracked.

"Should be Johnny, shouldn't it? Where the bloody hell is he?"

"He must be lying low somewhere. I haven't seen him for hours. Lazy sod. Typical bloody student," said Les.

"Nah, there's summat up with him. He's been a bit weird tonight," said Pat.

"How do you make that out then?" asked Sid.

"When I called him JJ earlier, just to wind him up like, he didn't say a word. Usually, he goes mad." Pat waggled his head and imitated an effete southern voice. "You know, 'Don't call me that, Patrick, it's not my name'. I think the thing with Gordon has got to him."

Les stared at him. "Bloody hell, Pat, hidden depths of sensitivity. Not like you."

Sid chipped in. "Well, the thing with Gordon was terrible, wasn't it? It's a bit weird to think there's a killer out there, walking in these corridors. That's two people done in, in a few days. Who's going to be next? Could be one of us."

"Victim, or killer?" asked Les, looking round the group.

An uncomfortable silence fell upon them as they paused to consider the question. All Christmas spirit seemed to have evaporated.

Les stood up and walked over to the light switch.

"Ha! Only joking, lads. The weirdo killer's out there, not in here."

He flicked the switch and the room was drenched in harsh, white, fluorescent light.

There was a chorus of anguished groans as the rest of the group shielded their eyes.

"Come on, snap out of it. There's a body to do. Where was it for, Sid?"

"Ward thirty-six."

Les stopped, a smile beginning to spread. "Is Gloria on tonight? Come on, Sid, I'll do it with you. Christmas Day – I think I might be on a promise."

Sid got unsteadily to his feet and the two of them went out into the corridor. At the door, Les turned back.

"Don't forget to switch your walkie-talkies on. Just in case we need backup."

He turned and disappeared into the dimly lit corridor, shutting the door behind him.

In the restroom, Pat and Fred were left staring at the closed door.

"Bloody Hell," Pat said, "I've worked here for eight years and that's the first time I've seen Les volunteer for anything. Either the drink's talking, or he really is on a promise from Gloria."

Fred, a man of few words, each of them steeped in grumpiness, grunted, "It'll be the drink." It had been his only contribution to the conversation for the last hour. He switched the light back off and settled himself down on the sofa for a final sleep.

*

Johnny lay back in the darkness. He stretched, trying to keep his muscles supple in the aching cold that had seeped into his joints in the time he had been in the fridge. At least there was enough room to move. It was tight, but he could turn over and sit with his head raised slightly. He remembered once doing a body with Sid in his first week. It was of a middle-aged man, grossly overweight, who had died of a heart attack. He must have been about twenty stone and it was a real struggle to manipulate the body up and into position, and they had almost had a real disaster as the body slipped on its way to the shelf. They had been able to manhandle it back onto the shelf and in position, but it had been a close thing and only possible because the shelves were designed to accommodate outsize corpses. He was glad of that now.

How long had it been? He couldn't tell. It could have been anything from ten minutes to a couple of hours such was the effect of the sensory deprivation that had overwhelmed him after the initial surge of panic had faded. He had hammered at the door by his head, twisting his body round so that he could get as much leverage as possible. He had bellowed for help over and over again, before slumping back on the freezing metal shelf. He had wept, great, wet, gulping gasps of tears, before forcing himself to stop, suddenly, irrationally afraid he would wake the dead. Then his heart began to race and his breathing became shallow and irregular, as he teetered on the edge of a full-blown panic attack, a lurid technicolour mindscape of zombies, mummies, and worse of all the clutching, grasping figure of Dr Death, desperately trying to tell him something, to whisper a confession into his ear. With a supreme effort of will, he had grabbed both edges of the shelf, closed his eyes and laid back counting upward slowly and breathing through his nose.

And with that had come some sort of calm. He had maintained it by reciting a variety of lists in his head. The best attacking midfield players in Division One. His top ten albums since 1970, closely followed by his top ten gigs. His ten favourite Shakespeare scenes. The sexiest women in film, with a subsection of the sexiest women in rock. Greatest goals scored at World Cups he had seen. Greatest foreign players, starting with Johan Cruyff. Best ten novels, starting with *Bleak House*. He maintained his calm even as the cold began to bite and he began to lose feeling in his hands and feet.

And then, out of the blue, there came an agonised sigh and groan, and the sound of a body shifting at the far end of the fridge…

"Fuck, fuck, fuck," he whimpered.

He cringed in the darkness, trying to make himself smaller, waiting for the ghastly prospect of one of the corpses trying to make friends with him. And then, in a wave of relief, he remembered Gordon's tales from the crypt.

"It's nothing, nothing. Air escaping, bodies settling, that's all. Nothing to be scared about," he muttered, convincing himself.

The spell was broken, though. It was time to open his eyes and face up to the reality of his situation. How the fuck could he get himself out of this? He'd already realised that there would be no new bodies delivered that night, because of the police tape. But, surely, someone would come tomorrow, even if it were just the police revisiting the scene of the crime. A tiny spark of hope flickered in the dark. He was buoyed by this, somehow. He just had to work out ways of keeping warm, keeping moving and keeping sane, at least until the morning. And he would listen out for footsteps from the corridor and then bang the fridge door for all he was worth, to try and cut it short. Yes, he could probably just about manage that, despite the cold. He was young and fit and he needed to get out, if only to see Helen again and apologise to her for being such a dick.

He lay back down on his shelf, closed his eyes, and began to think. *'Life on Mars', 'Changes', 'Suffragette City', 'Queen Bitch'... 'Queen Bitch'...*

58

The car slalomed across the junction of the road, before coming gently to rest sideways against a privet hedge. The impact had been lessened by a soft bank of snow, about four feet high, that the wind had piled up against the base of the hedge. The engine continued to rev, and exhaust fumes steamed into the night air. Paula switched the ignition off, and the silence that engulfed them was both oppressive and soothing at the same time.

"This is far as we're going to get in the car, I reckon."

"What are we going to do then?" asked Helen. "We can't just give up."

"Who said anything about giving up? We can walk it."

Paula undid her seatbelt and reached in the back for her coat and scarf.

"Walk it?" Helen exclaimed. "Are you sure? Look at the state of it out there."

"Have you got a better idea? Come on, it's only ten minutes away."

Helen rubbed her window and peered out. The sky was full of snowflakes.

"You got snowshoes in the back?" she asked, raising her eyebrows.

"It's not that bad. Wrap up and let's get going."

Paula couldn't open her door because of the snowdrift. She waited for Helen to ease herself out, then scrambled across the gear stick and out through the passenger door, slamming it behind her. After the warmth of the car for the previous forty-five minutes, the freezing air came as a shock. They both prepared for the walk, fastening coats, wrapping scarves, pulling hats down over ears and slipping on gloves. Ready, they looked around to get their bearings.

Cars had been abandoned on the main road they had just left, and the side road they had ended up in. They were at crazy angles, all more or less covered by thick snow depending on when they had finally slid to a halt. The sky was starless and full of gently floating snow, lit up in cones of amber light from the lampposts that by this stage were the only indication of roads and kerbsides. The houses in this residential street were a carnival of fairy lights and Christmas trees, but both here and on the main road, there was no sign of human life. The streets were completely deserted.

Helen and Paula were unable to move, frozen by the eerie beauty of the scene.

"It would be really stunning," said Paula at last, "except that we're on our way to a mortuary to stop a psychopath. Kind of spoils it a bit, doesn't it?"

The thought of Johnny snapped Helen out of her reverie. She shivered. "What are we going to do when we get there? Find Johnny and then what?"

Paula shrugged her shoulders. "Dunno. We'll think of something. We can get through to the hospital this way."

She nodded towards the end of the street and set off walking, a slow, deliberate trudge through the creaking snow.

"What about the car?" Helen called after her. "Aren't you going to lock it?"

"No need. That car's going nowhere for a couple of days." She turned and took up her slow progress again.

Helen looked helplessly at the car and followed her, two black smudges receding steadily into the glaring white landscape, swallowed by the thickening snow.

*

The lift door sighed open, and the battered metal casket squeaked as it emerged onto the dimly lit corridor, Sid at the front and Les bringing up the rear. They were both a little unsteady on their feet and clung to the trolley as much for support as for steering. Every turn of the wheels produced a grating screech that poked a finger at Les's mounting headache.

"Bloody hell. When was the last time this thing had a drop of oil on its wheels? Disrespectful to the dead, that's what it is. Imagine, your last journey made to that soundtrack."

Sid shuffled along behind him, his flat feet slapping the lino with his familiar, shambling gait.

"There's some WD40 in the restroom. We can do it when we get back."

Les stopped dead in his tracks, and Sid, at the back, crashed to an unexpected halt.

"Oof," he exclaimed, "watch out."

Les fixed him with a steady glare.

"Is that your oil, Sid?"

"Well, er, yeah. It's for me bike."

"How many times, Sidney? You do not use your own stuff at work. It's for hospital to provide oil, not the workers. Where will it end, if we bloody subsidise them? Next thing you know, we'll be providing our own overalls and washing them."

"Just a drop of oil, Les lad. That's all. It won't delay the bloody revolution."

"Maybe not, but it won't bring it on, neither. Don't collaborate, Sidney."

He held Sid's gaze, one eyebrow raised, until there was a flicker of contrition, when he judged that he had fulfilled his comradely duties and they could proceed. They turned into the ward, the screeching trolley announcing their arrival. There were two nurses at the reception desk, heads together under the subdued lighting. The rest of the corridor was in near darkness. They both stood up, the closest one holding up her arms to them. They were both very young, barely out of nursing school.

"Shh!" she hissed. They scrambled from behind their desk and down the corridor.

"Stop, for God's sake! That bloody racket's enough to wake the dead."

"Well," replied Les, the shadow of a smile playing on his face, "that would save us porters a job, eh love?"

The nurse scowled. "Very funny. But it's not you that'll have to deal wi' patients who wake up the minute you've gone."

"There's not much we can do about a squeaky trolley, love," said Sid, appeasingly.

"No, mebbe not," she conceded. "Anyway, just keep it down. She's through here." The nurse nodded in the direction of a side ward. "Mrs P from Poppleton, poor old soul."

"Bloody hell," exclaimed Sid, "I thought she shuffled off days ago."

"We were all expecting her to, but she fought like a tiger. Some of 'em do, you know. You can't always tell which ones are just going to slip away, like, and which are going to cling on."

"Well, that's a relief," said Les.

"What do you mean?" asked Sid.

"It's just that Dr Death had given her the black spot. Reckoned she'd be next. Good to know he hadn't lost his touch at the end."

The three of them stood awkwardly in the corridor, as if waiting for something. Eventually, the nurse lost patience.

"Can you just get on with it, lads? It's been a long night."

"Sorry, love. I was just waiting for a word with Gloria," Les replied.

"You'll have a long wait then," she said. "There's been no sighting of Gloria since she went off with the police. We've been short-handed up here ever since. And that bloody new doctor's disappeared, as usual."

Sid's ears pricked up. "Fulton? Pretty young lass?"

The nurse snorted. "Aye, that's her. All she does is smile at the other doctors and before you know it, she's wriggled out of any work. She might be pretty, but she's bloody useless. I've never seen her do a damn thing since she's been here."

Sid turned to Les. "That's the one that fancies young Johnny."

The nurse interrupted before Les could reply. "Johnny? That nice student lad? Tell him to leave well alone there. She's playing him." She thought for a moment, a smile growing on her face. "Mind you, I wouldn't mind. He's a lovely-looking lad. Always friendly and all. Send him up here and get him to ask for Mary. I'll sort him out."

Les had finally lost patience and cut across her. "Yes, this is all very interesting, and I'm sure you'll both be very happy, but what about Gloria and the police? What did they want with her?"

"Dunno. But I can tell you this much. When she walked off down the corridor with 'em, she looked as if she had the worries of the world on her shoulders. Never seen her like that before. She's gone off sick."

"It'll be the drink," Sid volunteered. "That and the festive season. She's on her own and Christmas can be a terrible time. Same happened to that Kathy Kirby. Her agent told me. The hits dried up, people abandoned her, she turns to the bottle for comfort and the next thing you know, she's in The Retreat, strapped down and pumped full of sedatives. Terrible loss. I had her booked for a tour once, you know."

The nurse stared at Sid, her mouth hanging open. She looked across at Les, who gave her the tiniest of winks.

"You're probably right, Sidney. But come on, let's get this job finished."

He allowed Sid to push the trolley into the side room first, hanging back to exchange a look with the nurse. He waggled his index finger at his temple and shook his head sadly.

A few moments later, the trolley emerged, announced by the screech of the wheels. The same nurse was there waiting. She lowered her voice. "Don't forget, lads, the mortuary's out of bounds. Police. You've to take it to casualty and an ambulance'll transfer it up the road to Clifton."

"Aye, will do lass. And Happy Christmas to you." Sid gave her a cheery smile, adjusting his dentures, his party hat and his ginger toupee in that order.

The nurse produced a glassy, fixed grin in response.

"Yes, same to you."

She watched them creak down the corridor towards the door. Her smile evaporated as she tracked them receding into the shadows, paper hats at rakish angles and tinsel glinting in the night lights. She shook her head as her colleague joined her.

"Bloody hell," she muttered, "Mrs P's last journey with that pair as a guard of honour. Poor old soul. Happy bloody Christmas."

59

When Clive got to the bottom of the stairs, the little red light pulsing in the chilly darkness of the hallway came as an explanation. The phone had woken him from an uneasy sleep, and once awake, he could not get back, troubled by the unanswered questions in the case. He stopped in front of it and listened to the house, sharpening his ears against the cloying hiss of silence, dampened by the thick covering of snow outside. Nothing. Mary and the kids fast asleep.

His finger hovered over the button and he winced as the message began, a bellow in the silence. "You have one new message." He listened, his eyes flicking up the stairs all the while.

At the end of the message, he went through into the front room and opened the curtains a crack. The snow had finally stopped falling and the familiar landmarks of his close were disguised as thick, white sculptures, all smooth, round edges and jelly-mould shapes. He could just make out a flash of red, under the street light, of the Capri, but that too was encased in a plump, white shroud.

He shook his head. "Shit," he breathed. He went to the kitchen and sat at the table with a glass of water. He needed to think. He looked at his watch. It was 1.15. The message from

Paula jabbed away at him, forcing him to acknowledge that he was just delaying the inevitable. The hospital was a fifteen-minute walk from here. Twenty minutes, maybe, in all of this snow.

"Shit," he said again. He couldn't leave her to do this on her own. He stood up and wrote a note to Mary, which he left on the kitchen table. If he was lucky, he'd be back before they got up, he told himself, but he knew that he was about to ruin their Christmas Day. Oh well. Being married to a copper, a detective with ambitions, was never going to be easy; she knew that when she took him on.

He put on his walking boots and heavy winter coat and slipped out into the snow. The door clicked gently into place behind him and he set off, leaving a trail of footprints, dark dashes in the pure, white, undisturbed snow, like a sentence to be completed later on a blank sheet of paper.

*

By the time Paula and Helen arrived at the hospital, they were both frozen to the core. Their footwear was soaked through and their feet had lost all feeling. Once they had negotiated casualty, they found themselves in a dimly lit corridor, and the heat of the hospital, always set at the top of the thermostat, had forced them to remove gloves, unzip coats and wince as feeling began to return to their extremities, causing toes and fingers to throb.

They stopped to adjust their clothes and for the first time since they had left the car, they were able to talk to each other about what they were going to do. The journey had been a head-down slog through the deep snow.

"So what now?" Helen asked. "Johnny could be anywhere in the building. And we need to find the other two."

"Let's not worry about them yet," Paula replied. "We need to make sure Mr Jewell is safe and well. I reckon the porters' room is our best bet. They'll know which of them is on a job. If he's not there, they're more likely than anyone to know where he could be."

"Come on then," urged Helen, "let's go. We can't hang around hoping everything's alright. We need to find him."

Now the trek to get to the hospital was over, the reality of the situation crowded in on her and a sense of panic began to rise. Without waiting for an answer from Paula, she pressed on down the corridor. A few minutes later, they were both standing outside the restroom. Paula found her warrant card and knocked sharply on the door before swinging it open.

A fug of cigarette smoke billowed out. The room was completely in darkness. Paula held her card out in front of her and shouted, "Police!", switching on the main light at the same time. The room was flooded in a blinding, white light and two figures struggled to their feet from makeshift beds on opposite sides of the room.

"What the hell…" grumbled Pat, rubbing his eyes.

"DC Paula Marsh, North Yorkshire Police. We're looking for Mr Jewell. We understand he was on duty tonight."

"Johnny?" Pat stammered, "Yeah he's been on this shift. But none of us have seen him for hours. What's going on?"

"You haven't seen him for hours?" Paula responded, her voice rising. "When exactly? Where could he be now?"

"Dunno. Before midnight, maybe. He's been funny all shift."

"What do you mean?"

"You know, quiet like. Not like him at all. Is he in trouble?"

"No, we just need to find him. And we need your help. Where might he be? Come on, think. You porters know the hospital like the back of your hands. Where would he go?"

Pat screwed up his face, trying to come up with a reasonable answer.

A voice came from the other side of the room. Fred, having leapt out of bed at the disturbance and then sat back down again, had had enough of his sleep being disturbed.

"Try the mortuary. Every bloody thing ends up at the mortuary these days. Oh, and the nurses' home, where that doctor friend of his kips. He might be there."

"Dr Fulton?" asked Helen, her face ashen.

"Aye, that's her. Nice-looking lass."

"Can you show us? It's urgent," asked Paula.

"Yeah. Give me a minute," replied Pat, who was fumbling with the laces of his shoes.

"Come on, come on, hurry up," said Helen, already moving out into the corridor.

Pat finished tying his laces, picked up his walkie-talkie and set off, Helen and Paula at his side. In the restroom, Fred lay back on the sofa under the blazing fluorescent light.

With a heavy sigh, he hauled himself up again and went to the light switch. He turned it off, returning the room to its cavern-like darkness.

"Bloody hell. Do I have to do everything myself?"

*

The lights in the hospital blazed through the night. They were a welcome sight and Clive accelerated as he picked his way along the path leading to the main entrance, piles of recently shovelled snow on either side spoiling the pristine covering on the manicured lawns beneath. The main entrance was locked, and there was a sign directing out of hours callers to the casualty entrance at the side. He looked over and could see a couple of ambulances steaming in the night air as they trundled along the drive. Nothing stopped those guys; weather, plague or famine, they would be out doing their job regardless. Bit like the police.

The entrance to casualty was awash with melted snow, and the linoleum floor was treacherous, despite the best efforts of the cleaners to keep it safe. There were a handful of cases in the reception area: a few drunks, some domestic violence victims and an elderly man, slumped in a chair surrounded by medics. Cardiac arrest. Clive shook his head. Christmas Day. *Don't die today, mate.* They were all surrounded by death, and one thing Clive had learnt as a detective was that death did not respect any calendar, any festival, or any anniversary. It was a twenty-four seven, relentless operation.

He went up to the desk to sign in. Fire regulations. The man holding the fort gave him a cheery smile that complemented his party hat and tinsel accessories. Clive returned it while signing the book.

"Alright? Aren't you one of the detectives that's been working here?"

Clive didn't look up. "That's right. DS Brooks."

"What's going on? You're the second of your lot in tonight. Or should I say this morning. Happy Christmas, by the way."

Clive looked up. "Who else? Are they still here?"

"Yeah. They only got here fifteen minutes ago. It was that young girl and someone I've never seen before. What's going on?" The man leant forward and lowered his voice. "Has there been some kind of breakthrough in the case? Are you going to make an arrest?"

"Where did they go?"

"Huh? Oh, mortuary, I think."

Clive dropped the pen and set off down the corridor.

The man stared after him and then shouted at his retreating back, "There's something else."

Clive stopped and wheeled round to face him. "Well?"

"Some stuff was couriered over for your lot tonight. Went to the Meeting Room. Must be important on Christmas Eve. The girl didn't seem very interested, though."

Clive thought for a moment. He came back past the desk and took the corridor going in the opposite direction.

The man on the desk watched him go, his Christmas smile souring on his lips as he muttered, "Yes, thanks for your help. And Happy Christmas to you too."

*

Johnny blew on his hands and rubbed them together. He was beginning to feel light-headed and so, so cold. It had seeped into his bones like an ache. He tried to keep moving, but he was tired and flexing his muscles was dispiriting as it seemed to have little effect. He had exhausted all of his lists, but the thought of just lying there with no distraction was unbearable. He could feel himself nodding off and suddenly woke with a jump. Shit. He absolutely could not fall asleep. That sort of thing happened to people in the Arctic and they never lived to tell the tale. He vaguely remembered a documentary about one such expedition where hypothermia brought on unconsciousness, and then found himself teetering on the edge of despair. This was not going to be as easy as he thought.

How much longer did he have to wait? The time! Of course, he needed to know the time. He felt for his wrist watch and held it up to his face, but in the choking blackness of the fridge, he might as well have been wearing a blindfold. Then he remembered. He had a lighter in his pocket. And cigarettes. He could spark the lighter, read his watch and have a cigarette. There had been nothing in his life up to this point as exciting as this. Something to do, an appetite to sate.

He felt down his uniform, patting it as he went. In his left-hand pocket, he found his packet of Silk Cut, nearly full, and a lighter. In the right, his hand brushed against a solid block that filled the pocket. For a second, he was puzzled and then he remembered. *Bleak House*! *Thank you, Charles Dickens. Saving me from a grizzly death in a hospital fridge would be, surely, your greatest achievement.*

What was he talking about? His mind was beginning to wander, slipping into surreal flights of fancy. He clenched his right hand into a fist, digging his nails into his palm and banging his hand on the metal shelf that gave a dull clang in response. *Keep it together, Johnny old son. Concentrate.*

With trembling fingers, he tried to pull a cigarette from the packet. Two fell to the floor, victims of his numb fingers, but he clung on to the third. He sparked the lighter, lit the cigarette, and inhaled a deep lungful. He checked his watch: 2.30 a.m. He manoeuvred the book on his chest and opened it. The glowing ember at the end of his Silkie wasn't quite enough for him to read by. He sat up, hunched against the shelf above his head, and leaning against the door, he found his place, clicked the lighter on and began.

*

Les's headache had put down strong roots by this stage and every squeal from the trolley's wheels was painful. They both trudged through the darkened corridors, one at each end of the trolley, without speaking. Alcohol, exhaustion and a night shift of relentless, enforced festive jollity had left them running on empty now they had entered the final few hours. Sid, who was at the front of the trolley, was virtually asleep and was being pushed by the trolley rather than pulling it himself.

He was jerked out of semi-consciousness by an abrupt stop. He opened his eyes fully to find they were at a T-junction at the end of a corridor. The left turn went to casualty, the right to the mortuary. He turned back to face Les.

"We've to take her to casualty, remember. Morgue is closed off," said Sid, puzzled by the wait.

Les did not reply, but instead, shared a long, meaningful look with Sid before he eventually realised that an explanation was required.

"It's further. We'll have to wait there for an ambulance."

The thought settled in Sid's mind and began to grow. He raised his eyebrows and nodded his head.

"Fuck it," Les pronounced finally. "We'll slip in, bung her in the fridge, and scarper. No bugger'll know. I need my beauty sleep."

"Fair point," Sid conceded. "And Mrs P's not going to tell anyone."

The trolley squeaked into motion again and swung right down the corridor. The screech of the wheels, as regular as a heartbeat, announced their passage to anyone else who might be lurking and listening.

*

Johnny rested the book on his chest and thought. His head had started to spin and he began to doubt what he'd been reading. His mind began to slip into a jumbled recollection of the story. It was wild. So Krooks, some minor character with a weird name, falls asleep in his grimy garret and is found the next day, a pile of smoking ashes. Spontaneous combustion, apparently. Was that even a thing? That you could just go to bed and without warning, without knocking over a Dickensian candle or letting your old pipe fall onto the bedcovers, you could just catch fire and burn like a candle. And that would be that. Just fall asleep and... Johnny's eyes began to close and his head lolled forward, but then he jerked upright.

He half sat up, his head wedged against the shelf above. He'd chain-smoked three cigarettes in a row and now he felt sick and dizzy. The air was thick and he was struggling to breathe. The thought crawled into his brain and squatted down there. Maybe the oxygen was running out. Was the fridge sealed? And if it was, how much air was in there? It was a pretty big space, almost the whole wall of the mortuary, so surely enough to last more than a couple of hours. Just as well the other occupants weren't using up any of his air supply. He wished that one of them would spontaneously combust. It would use up oxygen, but he would give anything to feel warm again. He really couldn't do this any more. He had to get out.

He twisted round on his shelf to face the inside of the door and flicked his lighter on so that he could inspect the lock mechanism, but immediately froze, ears pricked. A noise. He leant his head right up against the door. There it was again. Footsteps.

For a second, he waited and listened, afraid of who it might be. Then he changed his mind. It was hardly a decision, more an emotional response, born of desperation not to let slip this chance of escape into the warm. He banged on the door with all his strength, bellowing at the top of his voice.

He drew all his might into one last effort. In the confines of the fridge, scraping against the shelves above and on each side, he tried to lever himself into position to shoulder the door, but slipped and only succeeded in head butting it. A searing pain jagged through his skull and he cried out. Immediately, the door swung open and two pairs of hands hauled him out. He crashed onto the floor of the mortuary and his head smashed against the steel leg of the central table where he lay spreadeagled, gasping for breath. The harsh neon lights dazzled him. He cried out and shielded his eyes, but through his fingers, he could see, upside down, two pairs of shoes next to him. Then he saw blood oozing thickly between his fingers. He tried to speak, but somehow couldn't form any words. Hands, clad in cream latex, grasped him roughly at the shoulders and the feet and he was suddenly airborne and weightless. Then, just as suddenly, he was dumped onto a hard surface and the walls and ceiling began to move around him. There were voices but he couldn't make out what was being said, and as he stared up at a doorway and then a ceiling, moving past him, his eyes began to close and the darkness reclaimed him.

*

Clive went straight to Grayson's desk. The two large, brown envelopes in the middle of it were clearly new additions. He ripped open the first one and pulled out the contents: a couple of pages of A4 stapled in the corner. The forensic report on Gordon Simpson. He scanned it, flicking through the pages. Cause of death was confirmed as diamorphine overdose, just like Sutherland. Unlike Sutherland, there were significant traces of a sedative in his blood and stomach. Time of death was Saturday between 11 p.m. and 3 a.m. Saturday? But that meant he'd been dead for over twenty-four hours by the time he'd been found. Had he been in the fridge all that time? Clive shook his head as he tried to work out the implications of this. They would have to completely review who had been in the vicinity during that time window. They might have missed the key person completely. He turned his attention back to the report. The scalpel in the skull, like Sutherland, was decorative, carefully kept vertical in the flesh on top of the head. No prints on anything.

He opened the second, fatter envelope and emptied it, a pile of black and white photos spreading across the desk. A note on the front of the envelope identified them as coming from the camera found with Simpson's body. He reached for the photo on the top of the pile, staring in disbelief. It was a photo of a photo. An old school photo, pinned to a cork board, showing rows of school kids. Two of them, standing next to each other, were ringed in a biro circle. He brought it closer. One of them, a shy, uncertain smile on his face, looked vaguely familiar. The boy on his right scowled at the camera, eyes alive with suppressed fury, his mouth a thin, straight line of malice. He looked up. There it was again, pinned to the overview board. It was the same photo Jacko had found in Simpson's own dark room.

He flicked through the rest. They showed open lockers containing cardboard boxes. One such box had been opened and revealed a plastic bag full of white powder. He stopped at the last photograph and held his breath. It took him a moment to decipher what it was and then, finally, he got it. It was the incinerator, door opened, and a raging fire inside.

He collected the photos in the envelope, left it on Grayson's desk and slipped out into the corridor. The incinerator, as they had discussed just hours before in that very room, was next to the mortuary. He set off at a brisk walk. By the time he had reached the end of the corridor, he had broken into a run.

60

Pat had left them at the end of the corridor leading to the mortuary, pointing them in the right direction before returning to the peace and quiet of the porters' restroom. Paula and Helen ducked underneath the crime scene tape at the other end and then, Paula, taking the lead, held out her arm to stop Helen in her tracks.

"What…?" Helen began.

Paula raised her finger to her mouth and lowered her voice. "Look."

She pointed down the corridor. It was shrouded in darkness, except for a triangle of light that spilled out from the open door of the mortuary.

"Shit," whispered Helen, "do you think there's someone in there?"

"Dunno, but someone has been down here. More than one person by the look of it."

"How do you know that?"

Paula pointed. Along the corridor, in the light from the morgue, was a trail of shiny, wet footprints.

"Come on. Stay behind me."

Paula crept to the door, pushed it tentatively, then strode into the room, raising her voice as she did so.

"Police. Stay where you are. Put your hands in the air."

There was no one there.

"They've gone," said Paula, "but someone was definitely here. And only a few minutes ago."

Helen repeated her quizzical look.

"Do you know everything?"

"The room's still warm. In this weather, with the door wide open, it wouldn't take long for this room to lose all of its heat."

"But that means that whoever it was, they must be very close."

"Exactly. And..."

Paula stopped mid-sentence. She looked at Helen and they both raised their eyebrows. Someone was running at full pelt down the corridor outside. They both flattened themselves against the wall as the footsteps got closer, and then the door slammed fully open again, striking the wall of the mortuary with a bang.

Helen jumped in shock and cried out. Paula prepared herself to wrestle whoever it was to the floor. She stopped herself just in time.

"Clive! Thank God for that."

He registered the two of them and scanned the room.

"You've not found him, then?" he asked.

"No, we only arrived here about a minute ago," said Paula. She gestured around the room, finishing pointing at the open fridge door. "It was just like this when we got here."

Clive's gaze rested on the door.

"We'd better check inside. Just in case." He turned to Helen. "You might not want to see this, miss"

A look of horror flashed across her face. "You mean... Johnny might..."

Paula lay her hand on Helen's arm. "He might," she said gently, "but more likely, he's not."

Clive opened the first fridge door, in the corner of the room, as wide as it would go. There were four shelves, and each one was occupied by a white, swaddled corpse. He moved to the next door and repeated the process. Each opened door revealed all four shelves occupied. He stopped at the final door. He poked his head tentatively through the space, so that it was just inside the fridge. Then he withdrew it and turned to look at the two women, his face screwed up and a puzzled expression on his face.

"There's a smell," he began.

"Oh God, that's disgusting. Is it the bodies?" asked Helen.

"No. It's… cigarette smoke. And look."

Clive bent down and reached inside the fridge. He brought his hand back out and showed what he had found. A pile of dog ends and two untouched cigarettes.

All three of them looked baffled.

"Who the hell is smoking inside there with a crowd of dead bodies? This is…"

They didn't find out what Paula thought this was, because the conversation was interrupted by an eerie squeaking sound coming from the corridor. All three of them froze, their eyes flashing wildly from one to the other. Clive motioned for them to be silent and they waited as each screech, a couple of seconds apart, got louder. When it seemed as if the squeaking and grating was virtually in the room, suddenly, it was.

Sid shuffled into the room, head down, pulling the trolley behind him. The first sight they had of him was of his battered paper party hat, a flash of his bright-ginger toupee and the glitter of tinsel worn as a tie. Helen gasped out loud at this fresh hell of walking zombies. Sid looked up, roused from his sleepwalking, and saw the three of them in the room and all of the fridge doors wide open. He smiled at them instinctively, a naive, welcoming smile.

Clive shouted at him, holding his warrant card out in front. "Police. Stop there!"

Sid's smile faded. "Police? That's a bit over the top, isn't it?" he said. "We were just too tired to take it to casualty. Isn't that right, Les?"

He looked behind him at the rear of the trolley. There was no one there. Clive dashed out to the doorway and saw the tubby figure of Les, creeping away stealthily.

"You! Get back here. Police."

Les stopped and reluctantly turned around. He smiled apologetically and came back to the mortuary.

"Sorry. Didn't think you needed me."

"What the hell do you think you're doing?"

"Just delivering a body. We could take it to casualty if you like? It's no trouble; it's on our way back."

They were all in the room now. Two police officers, two porters, a civilian and the body of Mrs P from Poppleton, all in front of a bank of open fridge doors, five of them staring in at the inhabitants, stacked like Egyptian mummies.

Sid broke the silence. "Er, if you don't mind me asking, why are the police here? It's Christmas Day. There hasn't been another murder, has there?"

Helen gave another strangled gasp. Paula put her arm around her.

"Come on now, Johnny will be fine, I'm sure of it."

Clive decided to take charge.

"Never mind Johnny Jewell," he began, "the question is, who the hell has been inside that fridge smoking cigarettes? And where are they now?"

They all looked around blankly. These were questions whose answers resolutely evaded them. Then Sid delivered his verdict.

"Well that's obvious enough," he said. "It's Johnny."

"How do you make that out? Could have been anyone," said Clive.

"No, look. There's his book."

He pointed to the floor underneath the central table. Paula bent down and, holding on to the table leg, reached for the paperback. She pulled it out and showed everyone else. *Bleak House*.

Helen gaped at her. "Your hand. Look at your hand."

Paula frowned, puzzled, and held up her hand, trying to process what the red, sticky mark on it was.

"That's blood. Oh God." Helen's hand went to her mouth.

Clive bent down and checked the bottom of the table leg. "Yeah, traces of blood here. Listen we need find Jewell as quick as we can."

Paula looked inside the book, flicking through the pages. "This is definitely Johnny's book. Look, his name's inside it." She raised it to her nose and sniffed. "And it stinks of fags."

Clive checked it. His face was a picture of confusion.

"So he was inside the fridge smoking cigarettes? But why? And why the blood, just there on the table leg? It doesn't make sense."

Paula looked again at the blood on her fingers. "But more importantly, where is he now?"

"I think I can help you with that."

The new voice made them all jump and they whirled round in the direction it had come from.

There, in the open door way, was Juliet Fulton.

*

The warmth of the incinerator room came as a comfort to Johnny after his hours in the fridge. His shivering had calmed down but his brain seemed scrambled and his head shrieked with pain. He could hear groaning and then he realised that that was him. Voices seemed to come from miles away but he was dimly aware that there were people around him. Pairs of legs came in and out of his field of vision as he lay on his back. Conversation faded in and out and it was hard for him to follow, but he forced himself to concentrate. Somewhere, deep inside his consciousness, he knew that he had to stay awake, he had to try to focus on what was happening around him so he lay back and stared up at the ceiling. It was a tired white, with flecks of brown congealing in a spreading stain, and peeling in flakes like dandruff. His head dropped down and his eyes came to rest on a noticeboard. There was a black and white school photograph of children sitting in rows. It reminded him of something from an old history book. Two figures were ringed with pen, one a face that caused his gaze to linger. Was that really Gordon? Gordon when he was younger? Hard to imagine Gordon ever being a kid at school. Hard to imagine… But Gordon was dead… Hard to imagine him being anything.

The voices cut through again.

"…no need for us to do this."

"…too risky… What he knows…"

"…no part of this… This is different…"

"…don't fucking let me down now… I won't let you…"

"…no… I won't say a thing… Walking away…"

The voices faded away as a wave of exhaustion crashed over him. If he could just sleep, just for half an hour, everything would be alright. He closed his eyes, but almost immediately, he could feel someone bending over him, talking softly close to his face.

"…everything's going to be alright, Johnny… Just let me take this off… Under the blanket… Yes, just like that… Good… Well done…"

He felt the weight of a blanket and snuggled into it gratefully. Then opened his eyes again. To the side, he saw a pair of hands, wearing cream latex gloves, reach for something. What were those things called again? It was on the tip of his tongue, but he just couldn't… Just couldn't… Yes! That was it. Syringe! That's what it was, a syringe, for… for… injections…

He lay back under his blanket, a great sense of achievement washing over him. Now he could sleep, at last…

*

They arrived outside the door to the incinerator. Clive looked back to Sid and Les.

"Do you have keys for this?" he asked.

Les raised an eyebrow and a knowing smile, and began to fumble with the prodigious bunch attached to his belt. "We've got keys for everywhere."

Clive raised his hand, and then put his finger to his lips, gesturing to the others. He reached for the handle and gently turned it. It was open. He pushed against it and the door opened silently, the constant hum of the incinerator spilling out onto the walkway. They all piled into the room, Clive at the front, and were met by a horrific scene. On the floor in front of them was the crumpled body of a man, still and silent. Johnny was lying flat on a trolley, under a blanket with his bare arms out on top. A trail of blood covered one side of his head, coming from a deep gash on his forehead, wet and red. A second man was standing over him, a loaded syringe in his gloved hands.

Helen, just behind Brooks, screamed, "Johnny! Wake up, Johnny."

The man with the syringe looked up, panic-stricken.

Clive shouted at him, "Police! Walk away from the trolley. Now!"

The man stared back at him and his eyes flicked back and forth around the room, weighing up the numbers of new arrivals and the routes of escape. He held tight to the syringe and then saw again, as if for the first time, the body on the floor.

Clive repeated himself. "Drop the syringe and walk away from the trolley. Do it now."

The man smiled, held his hands and the syringe in the air, and said calmly, "Thank God you've arrived. I only just managed to get the syringe out of that maniac's hand. I think Johnny's alright, though."

"This is your last warning," Clive said. "Drop the syringe."

"You've got this all wrong, honestly," he replied. "Look."

He dropped the syringe on the floor. Clive and Paula rushed towards him, Paula carrying a pair of handcuffs.

"Put your hands out, please, sir," Paula ordered.

He did as he was asked and Paula snapped the cuffs on him, one hand at a time.

"What's your name?" Clive asked.

The man stared back at him, hatred in his eyes, and remained silent.

"Your name?" Clive barked at him.

"This is Dave Henderson. He's in charge of the hospital incinerator," said Juliet. She had hung back slightly and was standing just in front of the door. Henderson turned his unblinking gaze on Juliet, clenching and unclenching his fists. Brooks nodded and continued with the charge.

"Dave Henderson, I'm arresting you for the suspected murder of Gerald Sutherland and Gordon Smith. You don't have to say anything..."

Helen wasn't paying attention to anything Clive was saying. As soon as Paula had finished cuffing the suspect, she led him away from the trolley to the other side of the room. Helen immediately stepped forward to take his space so that she could see how Johnny was. She took his hands in hers, leant forward and kissed him lightly on the cheek.

"My God, Johnny, you're so cold."

She stood back to look at him. He was awake, but could hardly speak. His eyes flickered up at her.

"Helen… Sorry, I should have…"

"Shh. Don't speak now. Everything is going to be alright. You're safe." She caressed his cheek and then looked to the others. "He needs to go to a ward and be checked out."

They all looked at Juliet. She shrugged her shoulders. "Don't look at me. I think this is where you guys come in," she said, nodding at Les and Sid.

They shared a glance, eyebrows raised, resignation on their faces.

"Well, it is for Johnny," said Sid.

"Aye, I suppose so. Always the bloody workers pay the price," replied Les. "Come on, Johnny lad," he continued, "let's get you to casualty. Some people will do anything to skive off work, eh?"

There was a flicker of a smile from Johnny and then they pushed the trolley out into the corridor. As they passed Juliet at the door, they stopped to manoeuvre the trolley through carefully. A pained look passed across her face at the sight of the livid gash on Johnny's forehead and she instinctively reached out her hand to his face to comfort him. Then they moved on, out into the corridor. The squeak of the wheels persisted, fading as the trolley got further away.

Helen glared at Juliet and then looked out through the open door, watching the trolley as it receded into the distance. "Can I go down with him? Just to see if he's alright?" she asked, looking between Clive and Paula.

"No, we need you here for the moment," Clive replied.

"He's in good hands, Helen. He'll be fine, I'm sure," said Paula.

"That's more than we can say about this guy," said Clive, pointing at the figure on the floor. He had not moved since they had been there.

Paula looked across at Juliet. "You need to look at him. If he's still alive, we..."

She stopped, staring across at Juliet, who was in the doorway, standing apart from everyone else. Her right hand was held up in front of her, and she had a horrified expression on her face. Her doctor's coat, newly laundered and dazzling white, was stained with a vivid splash of red, and her right hand was marked with fresh blood. She muttered, shaking her head. "I've got blood on my hands."

There was silence, as they all shared glances before their attention rested on Juliet.

"It's from Jewell's wound," said Clive finally. "Here, wipe your hands. You'll be OK."

He handed her a roll of tissue from the side and she began to clean herself up, rubbing vigorously.

"What about him?" asked Paula.

Juliet thought for a moment, with one eye on Clive, still trying to rid herself of all the blood.

"Well?" Paula insisted.

"I think you'd better ring for a doctor, just in case," Juliet said finally.

"This is ridiculous," Helen burst in. "You're a bloody doctor; you should look at him. Do something useful for once." She turned to Paula. "What are you waiting for? You should arrest her now. We agreed that she's been lying all the way through."

Paula took a step towards Juliet and was about to recite the familiar form of words when Clive interrupted.

"Paula, there's no need for that now."

"What do you mean? Didn't you get the message I left on your answerphone?"

"Yes, I did. But that wasn't the only message I got. Andy Johnson got back to me."

"Yeah? So what?"

He pointed at Juliet Fulton, her bloodied hand stark against her white scrubs.

"Paula, this is DC Julie Macdonald. Drug Squad."

61

Grayson took another puff on his Havana and rolled the single malt around in its heavy glass, enjoying the way the light reflected through the amber liquid. Taking a drink in his office on duty was unusual for him, but it was Christmas. And it had been a rather special day. It was the best Christmas present he could have possibly hoped for. There were a couple of irritations of course. At first, he couldn't decide which he was most annoyed about. Either that his Christmas Day had been disturbed by Clive Brooks's phone call, or that he hadn't received the call in the early hours of the morning when Brooks was on his way to the hospital. He would have liked to have been there to make the arrest.

But once he had got over that, and the story had emerged, what a result it represented. This would show those bastards at West Yorkshire who were always so full of themselves, despite the fact they still hadn't a clue who the Ripper was. It meant he would not have to ask awkward questions of Edwards. And they could quietly forget all about Marsh's theories about cover-ups and sexual assaults involving senior staff at the hospital. Nothing good would have come out of that little lot. He smiled. Perhaps something good might come out of it, if he played his cards right.

No, they were left with two murders cleared up in a matter of days, with lots of evidence and forensics to back it up. A narrative and motive that made sense. No point looking for complications where none existed. And, yes, it was a little irritating that Henderson had confessed to one murder, after a bit of persuasion from Jacko, but not the other, but he was just an awkward sod, playing some kind of power game with them. Well, let him try. No jury in the country would let him get off both murders, he was sure of that, given what they'd found: syringes taped underneath the bed in his hideaway incinerator room. A bottle of chloroform. Cupboards full of heroin. That was a lot of evidence. Cooperation from Mike Hutchinson, recovered from Henderson's assault on him, with details of their drug-running operation, and his own refusal to go along with him in the attempted murder of Johnny Jewell, in return for a lesser charge.

Drugs, that was one thing. But the fucking Drug Squad was quite another. They were a law unto themselves. Could one of them not just have had a little word with him? Tipped them the wink about their undercover officer? Admittedly, it had worked. Julie Macdonald had intel on the business being run out of the hospital pharmacy using Henderson's contacts. But talk about last minute. They were just about to arrest her and take her in for questioning for the murders. He laughed. That would have been embarrassing.

It had been an explosive meeting with the team earlier, but to be honest, that had not been a surprise, given what had been bubbling under since the investigation began. The team had actually done really well in the end, but it had been touch-and-go at times. Paula Marsh was going to be a bloody good detective, he was certain of that, but only if she learnt her lesson from this, her first big murder case. She had been brave and decisive to follow up the phone call from Jewell's flatmate, even though it broke all the rules going along on her own.

She'd been lucky that Clive Brooks had got her message and had the balls to leave the family home in all of that Baltic snow to back her up. He liked that, respected it. For a team to work, they had to have each other's backs. Judging by the meeting earlier, the only way Jacko would have Marsh's back would be so that he could put a knife in it.

He took another sip of the whisky. Jacko was a good copper as well, but times were changing and he wasn't changing with them. Marsh was right to challenge him when she did, and she showed some bottle to stand up to him, but now, having got their man, she needed to stop and let them all enjoy their victory. Thinking back to the meeting, it was not going to be easy, that much was clear.

*

"So we're just going to leave it then? Is nobody else worried about the loose ends? Just me?" Paula appealed to all of the team.

"Maybe the fact that it is just you might tell us something. Have you thought about that?" said Jacko.

"Of course I have. But it just doesn't make sense. Why would Henderson cough for Simpson's murder, but not for the first one, Sutherland? He was shouting the place down about it. And what about all the complaints of sexual assault and the cover-up? There is something going on in this hospital, I know there is."

Jacko sneered. "You know it, do you? Women's instinct? Like you knew Juliet Fulton, or Macdonald, or whatever her name is, was involved. That was a bit embarrassing, wasn't it?"

Paula flushed a little.

"Embarrassing? You obviously don't know the meaning of the word. What was it you said about Henderson, with his girlie pics on the noticeboard? 'Sound as a pound'. Yes, that was it. You should apply for a transfer to West Yorkshire. They could use someone like you on the Ripper case."

Jacko pursed his lips and simmered. "At the time, he had an alibi. No one knew he was skulking around in the incinerator room all night, running his drug business. No one ever saw him." He shook his head in defeat. There was no use trying to defend it.

Paula carried on. "Alright, I got Fulton wrong, I admit it. But the rest of it is there in black and white. And what about Gloria Wilson? Grudge against Sutherland. Didn't tell us about the party at his house."

Clive Brooks interrupted. "Paula, there's not one bit of forensic evidence linking Gloria to either murder. She has alibis for both. Jacko's right; we just have to drop it now. We've cracked it. We've got two murders cleared up. Let's leave it at that."

"What, you as well?" She shook her head.

"Look, you were right about something going on here at the hospital. But that was the drugs ring, and the connection between Gordon Simpson and Dave Henderson. Nothing to do with sexual assault."

"But what's Henderson's motive for killing Sutherland?" Paula persisted.

"We're not 100 per cent clear. Maybe Sutherland had had enough of Henderson having something over him, knowing about his addiction. Maybe there was a bit of blackmail going on, you know, threats to expose him, that sort of thing."

Paula smiled. "Of course, there's not one bit of forensic evidence to link him. Funny that."

Grayson, who had been listening to the discussion without comment, had heard enough.

"Not yet," he said, with the faintest of glances towards Jacko. "But something will turn up." He smiled at Paula. "It always does."

*

Juliet had waited until Helen had left, lurking on the outside of the ward for the right time. The full story hadn't yet been transmitted on the hospital gossip telegraph, so she was spared awkward questions and hostile stares from any passing nurse. Then she slipped into the private room. Johnny was unconscious, fully wired up, with a bank of instruments bleeping softly around him. She crept up to the bedside and looked down at him. His breathing was regular, his face serene: even features, smooth skin, apart from the livid gash on his temple. Looking over her shoulder at the door, she opened the bedside cupboard and began rummaging through it, until she found what she was looking for. She stood up and flicked through the pages of *Bleak House*. A frown began to spread across her face. There was nothing. Holding the book open, she shook it, but she already knew the letter was not there.

She put the book back and began to go through the pockets of his jeans, her eyes flashing all the while between the door and the bed. Again, nothing. She put them back, closed the door and thought. Maybe the letter wasn't too serious. She could pass it off as the ramblings of a woman in love. And she was a police officer, after all. And perhaps she was, improbably, in love. She shook that thought out of her mind and looked back to the door. She should go. The letter wasn't there and there was no point opening herself up to awkward questions.

Johnny's chest was gently falling and rising under the blanket, and a regular, reassuring, soft bleep underscored the scene. She would just stay for a few minutes more, just so someone was with him. Taking his hand in hers, she gently lowered herself into the bedside chair and let the atmosphere of quiet, calm care wash over her. At first, it was soothing. But then, eventually, doubts and fears crept back in. What had she done? And what more might she have to do, before all this was over?

62

It was Boxing Day before he came round. Johnny was sitting up in bed in the overnight stay ward of casualty. His left temple carried an ugly slash of black stitches and the mustard-coloured stain of a powerful antiseptic. The other seven beds in the room were all empty, the patients there when he had first been admitted having been discharged. There was a vase of flowers next to his bed, some oranges and a box of Milk Tray that was already half-empty. Helen sat on a grey plastic chair by the bed. She nodded towards the chocolates.

"I can see you're on the mend then."

He smiled at her. "The nurses told me I'm probably being discharged this afternoon. Just waiting for the ward round."

"You look a lot better than you did yesterday. You're going to have a scar. Very sexy. When I came, you were totally out of it."

"I don't remember much about yesterday, to be honest. In fact, I'm in the dark about most of it, apart from the fact I was pretty lucky in the end. And I've got a weird memory of you being there in the middle of the night and talking to me at some point."

"Yeah, I was."

"What were you doing in the hospital in the middle of the night? Why aren't you back home with your mum and dad?"

Helen filled him in on the gaps in his understanding of the story. He heard about the train cancellation, her finding the photograph of Gloria and Juliet, ringing Paula Marsh and coming to the hospital in the dead of night.

"So you came all this way in the middle of a blizzard just on a hunch?"

"It just rang alarm bells for me. I never trusted that doctor from the start." She gave Johnny a look. "Not because I was jealous of her, just because she was lying."

He immediately looked sheepish. "Sorry, I was out of order when I said that. I—"

She leant forward and laid a finger across his mouth. "Shh, not now. Just listen. When I showed Paula the photo, she thought you might be in danger, but to be honest, I think she was more worried about me wandering around on my own in the middle of the night."

Johnny thought for a moment, taking in what Helen had told him. "But in the end, it wasn't her, was it? Or Gloria. So who was it?"

"Dave Henderson, the incinerator guy and Mike Hutchinson. Head of the hospital pharmacy. He's still in intensive care. Henderson tried to blame him, but there was loads of evidence against Henderson himself. And when we all got to the incinerator, he was just about to inject you with diamorphine. Just like he did the others. If we'd been a minute later, we would have been too late, you would have been…" Her voice quavered and she hesitated, unable, it seemed, to say the next word.

Johnny reached out and took her hand. "But I'm not. Dead, that is. All thanks to you. And I'm so sorry, Hel; I should have listened to you from the start. I've been a bit stupid. About a lot of things."

There was a flurry of activity at the entrance to the ward, and a nurse bustled her way in. Johnny let go of Helen's hand and leant back in the bed. Helen took a step backwards.

"Sorry. I'm afraid you'll have to leave now. The doctor's on his rounds and needs to give Mr Jewell a final check before he can be discharged."

"So will it be long then? Shall I wait?"

"No love, best not. He might be kept in after he's been looked at. And anyway, the police are wanting to talk to him."

"The police? What now?" asked Johnny.

"They've been desperate to have a word since yesterday. Now you've woken up, they'll be back knocking on my door."

"They'll just want to hear your version of the story, that's all," said Helen. "Just a formality."

The nurse hovered by the bed. "So, if you could let us have the room, please."

Johnny turned his most charming smile on the nurse.

"If you could just give us a minute."

She glowered at him before thawing a little.

"Thirty seconds," she replied, looking at her watch fob. "I'll be outside."

She slipped out into the corridor again.

Johnny sat up again and reached for her hand. He pulled her towards him, and they sank into a kiss. He didn't know whether it was thirty seconds or not, only that it wasn't long enough. Finally, they pulled apart.

"We have a lot of things to talk about, but let's leave that until you get home. I'll be waiting for you."

*

It was DS Brooks who came to interview him. Although Johnny was able to fill in the gaps of his story, recounting his suspicions about Juliet Fulton and Gloria and his panic-stricken dash to the mortuary and the fridge, he could not shed much light on what happened next. Brooks pushed him to try and identify who it was who had taken the lead, Henderson or Hutchinson, but it remained a blur to him. Brooks didn't seem particularly interested in Gloria, or Juliet come to that. In the end, it was Johnny who learnt more from Brooks than the other way around.

"The Drug Squad? An undercover officer? That can't be right, she..." Johnny trailed off, thinking. "So that's what she meant."

"What?"

"She said to me last night that I would find out stuff about her that wasn't very nice. Must have been that."

He went quiet, thinking what a fool he'd been. He had never really known her, and she had played on his ego. He'd been flattered and went along with the whole thing. And yet, last night, she had seemed genuinely upset, as if she really felt something for him. Maybe she was just a really good actress.

*

"So all in all, it's a great result. Better and quicker than any of us could have hoped for. Well done, Simon, fantastic work."

Edwards beamed across the Persian rug that separated the pair of leather sofas and raised his glass to Grayson opposite.

"You sure you won't have a drink? Surely, you deserve to celebrate a double-murder conviction, don't you?"

"No, really, not for me, thanks. I am on duty, after all." Grayson gave a faint smile, radiating a cold, polite restraint.

"Oh come on, Simon, don't give me that. The rules can be broken every now and again, surely?"

"No, I don't think so. The rules have been broken far too much here as it is."

He fixed Edwards with a penetrating stare. It was met by a frown.

"I don't follow you, Simon."

"You know precisely what I'm talking about. I don't know exactly what has been going on here, but we've uncovered enough to know that it stinks."

"Simon, come on. You're a man of the world. Boys will be boys, you know."

"No, you listen to me now. I'm giving you a heads-up here. You need to clean up the mess that you've presided over and you need to put things right. You need to make sure that nothing like this is allowed to happen again, and that you've sorted out your HR procedures and your records. And have a quiet word, unofficially of course, with your senior consultants. Because believe me, Arthur, if we were to come in and investigate certain allegations, then there is absolutely no way you could survive it."

Edwards sat up straighter in the sofa, put his glass down on the table and tried another tack. The backslapping camaraderie of the beginning of their meeting had disappeared. When he spoke, his voice had an air of menace.

"Be careful, Simon. You had been in line for a nice little promotion, out of the firing line. Don't mess that up."

"I'm fully expecting that promotion, Arthur. You seem to be under the misapprehension that you've got some leverage. I hold all the cards here. We've already got a paper trail and some evidence. All of that can be picked back up again the minute we come back in to investigate. Of course, it doesn't have to be that way, if you want to look forward to the next honours list."

The colour drained from Edwards' face. He took another sip of scotch and looked round at his office as he thought. Finally, he sighed. "Alright, what do you want me to do?"

*

During the days that followed Henderson's arrest, it was clear to Paula that she had been kept out of the preparations to charge him. The police station was a whirlwind of activity, with Grayson, Jacko and Clive together or separately disappearing into interview rooms, or crossing the end of corridors deep in conversation. She was not invited. She thought, just for a moment, of storming into Grayson's office and demanding to know what was going on, before the thought evaporated as quickly as it had formed. It was a stupid idea which would only confirm all of Jacko's prejudices. She'd had high hopes for Clive, and had thought that Grayson was one of the more reasonable senior officers, but they had both been persuaded by the prospect of a double result. Shouting her mouth off would not help them change their minds. So she sat at her desk, ignored, and used the time to follow up some ideas of her own, in an attempt to tie up some nagging loose ends.

Towards the end of the second day, when the loose ends had transformed themselves into something more compelling, her concentration was interrupted by the sounds of celebration from the corridor. She looked up from her files. The door crashed open, and a ragged knot of detectives spilled into the room, whooping and cheering. Jacko was at the head of the group, his eyes sparkling.

"We've got him. Henderson's being charged with both murders. Confession and new forensics."

A great cheer went up from the staff at their desks, and the new arrivals were back-slapping and punching arms.

Grayson moved through the group to the front.

"Well done everyone. It's been a great team effort, and its one in the eye for those fuckers at West Yorkshire. We'll be in The Arms in about half an hour, and I'm buying the first drink for everyone, just as a thank you. I know it's been difficult for many of you what with Christmas and families, but it's one more bastard off the streets."

There was a cheer from the whole room. When the noise had settled down, with Grayson raising his hands to them to get some quiet, he said, "Make sure you finish off what you're doing now, and then come down and join us. We don't want to leave the shop unattended, do we?"

The group of detectives turned on their heels and made off in the direction of the pub. Everyone in the office watched them go and continued the excited hubbub of conversation until eventually, it tailed off completely, and they gradually returned to their work. Paula had observed all of this rather than choosing to be a participant, but then she too resumed her work, reading through the next file on her desk.

"You going to come along for a drink, Paula?"

She looked up, distracted. Clive was there, a friendly smile on his face.

"Not sure." She gestured at the files on her desk. "Got a lot to do."

"Come on, this is your result as much as anyone's. Your first murder case and a probable double conviction. That's something to celebrate, isn't it?"

"Doesn't feel like it, to be honest. You've all been very keen to keep me away the last couple of days."

Clive pulled up a chair and sat in front of her desk. He lowered his voice. "That's for your own good, Paula."

"I'm sure Grayson didn't want me to see the 'new forensics'. Or clock the bruises on Henderson's face."

"Listen. You've got years ahead of you. You'd be better off not getting a reputation for being awkward and then you can show 'em all what women detectives can do. You've got to play the long game."

"I can't face going to the pub. Jacko's bad enough sober, but with a few pints down him? No thanks, I'll give that one a miss. He'll just rub it in and be full of himself."

"Look, come for one and stick with me. I'll keep him in line, promise. Just one. Go on."

She hesitated. Clive had been good to her. He'd taken her seriously, helped her out, tried his best. He was doing all of that now, she knew. She didn't want to throw it in his face.

"It's not just Jacko, it's the case. I just can't get excited about Henderson being charged."

"Paula, don't waste time feeling sorry for him. Have you read his file? He's an absolute scumbag."

She gave a hollow laugh. "Are you joking? I know it inside out. Yes, he's a scumbag, but there's just one problem."

"What? I don't get it."

"He didn't do it, Clive. Do you hear me? He didn't do it."

Her voice had begun to get louder and several people at adjacent desks looked over.

She lowered her voice. "At least, he didn't do the first one. Sutherland."

The frown on Clive's face began to settle.

"You mentioned his file," she continued, "and it's all in there. And in Gordon's. And…" She looked around the office before finishing. "And Gloria Wilson's."

Clive was bewildered. "What do you mean?"

"You know we found out that Gordon and Henderson met at the old Blackstone children's home, when they were young?"

"Yeah. That's what linked them together. Good friends from that terrible place. Miracle that anyone survived it by all accounts."

"And you know that Henderson was damaged goods. Had a string of convictions from the age of about fifteen for violence. Really weird, chilling stuff."

"Yeah, I said, he's a scumbag. Don't waste your time on him."

"And that Gordon Simpson has never been in trouble with law. Not even a parking ticket."

"Yeah," Clive replied hesitantly. "I don't see where you're going with this."

"I did a bit more digging about why he attended that particular home. He was an only child. No father ever on the scene. Mum was a prostitute on heroin. Overdosed when he was seven years old. He was found in the flat on the estate when neighbours got worried. When the police forced entry, they found him. He was sleeping in his mother's bed. She was in it, naked, the syringe still on the floor. He'd been there for two days."

Clive's face fell. "Fucking hell," he breathed.

"The real miracle is that Simpson didn't turn out any weirder than he was. But there's more. Do you know who else he met at Blackstone?"

Clive grimaced and shook his head.

"Gloria Wilson," said Paula, holding his eyes in a steady gaze.

"What? But…"

"Orphaned when she was eleven. Car crash. Bit of a tearaway in her teens, apparently. Got in with a bad lot. Heroin user, abusive partner left her pregnant, kid taken into care and then adopted. Julie Macdonald."

Clive shifted in his chair. "Paula, all of this is really good work, but it doesn't change anything."

She stared at him. "How can you say that? It's worth pursuing, isn't it? She's linked to Sutherland. Her daughter, who she kept quiet, is also there conveniently."

He held his hands out, patting the air down in front of him. "Whoa, whoa, slow down. Her daughter is a police officer. They were asked to keep it quiet. This is just getting a bit wild, A bit far-fetched. A bit…" He searched for the right word. "A bit obsessive."

Paula glowered at him. "Obsessive?"

"No one is going to open this up again to investigate a police officer. No one. Especially when we've got a confession."

She knew it was true but she couldn't bear to let it go. This wasn't why she joined up. She opened her mouth to fight back, but Clive interrupted her sharply.

"Drop it. Now. That's enough."

Her eyes dropped back down to her desk. She picked up the nearest file and began to flick through it. Inside, she was raging, but she knew she couldn't say any more. If not even Clive was buying it, then no one would.

Clive's voice was more soothing next time he spoke, as he stood up to go. "Look, finish up here, and come down to the pub. Just for one drink. Trust me, it's for the best."

She manufactured a smile for him. "Thanks Clive, you're probably right. I'll just do this last bit and then I'll pop down for a beer. See you down there."

Clive nodded. "Good girl."

She watched him go, her smile fading.

After five more minutes of staring at the file, she looked around the room at the people who were left. Five women, heads down, typing. She banged the file down on her desk and followed him. What was the point?

63

By the time Johnny returned to work, the snow had disappeared, apart from the grubby hillocks of old slush and ice that studded the dark, glistening pavements. It felt good to be back on his bike again, with blood coursing through his veins as he sped along the line of the city walls that stood on top of neat green banks. The sun was out, the air was mild and the shocking events of the previous week were safely consigned to history. He had survived.

He swung round into the hospital entrance and made for the bike sheds, where he glided to a halt, swinging his leg over the handlebars. He locked up and headed for the restroom to get changed. He was back on the middle shift and had no idea who would be on the team, though he knew they'd be full of questions for him. They may even have some fresh answers, news of things that may have emerged in the few days he'd been away. He shivered as he skirted the incinerator room and then saw the police tape still around it and the door to the mortuary. It could have all been so different if not for Helen.

Helen. Notwithstanding the failed attempt on his life, the last few days had been most memorable for the beginning of a romantic relationship that seemed to be working. This seemed to Johnny to be the strangest thing of all. It was lovely, and he could not think why he hadn't seen her like that before. Perhaps it would have happened anyway, if Juliet Fulton, or whatever her name was, hadn't suddenly appeared in his life. The fleeting thought of Juliet cast a chill shadow. He frowned as he strode down the corridor, struggling to work out why she brought out such difficult feelings in him.

After he had clocked in, still troubled, he got to the restroom and opened the door to be greeted by a chorus of cheers.

"Ey up, Johnny lad. How are you going on?"

"He's back, lads and just as handsome."

"Einstein has returned."

"Einstein? Nah, Sherlock Holmes, this lad."

Johnny held up his hands. "Alright lads, all very funny. Good to be back, though."

The bantering went on for a little longer. Eventually, Les called a halt to it and allocated the tasks of the shift, going round the team one by one. He left Johnny until last.

"You'll be floating today, Johnny, just to ease you back in gentle like. Make the most of it though, cause it's back to full throttle tomorrow."

"Thanks, Les," he replied.

The others drifted out of the restroom to their jobs and Johnny was able to get changed on his own. He opened his locker and rummaged around inside, looking for his overall. He frowned, seeing the pile of crumpled stuff that had been hurriedly shoved in. Usually, his overall was hung up, and clean items delivered to the restroom every week. He reached down for it and put it on, smoothing the creases. A faint air of stale cigarette smoke clung to it. He would just have to grin and bear it, and try and get a new one from the laundry later.

He transferred the packet of Silk Cut and lighter from his coat, slipping them into the left-hand pocket. Then he noticed, on the floor of the locker, his copy of *Bleak House*, open and crumpled. It all must have been chucked in there on Christmas Day, after he had been taken to casualty. He put it into the other pocket, hoping he might have a chance to make some progress with it, if he had a reasonably quiet shift. His fingers brushed against something at the bottom of the pocket.

It was the letter Juliet had left for him in her room. He had stuffed it into his overall when he couldn't bear to read beyond the first two paragraphs on the Christmas Eve shift. And then, with everything that had happened, he had forgotten all about it. He sat down on the sofa, turned off his walkie-talkie, smoothed the letter out, and began to read.

> Dear Johnny,
> If everything goes to plan, you won't see me again. This letter is to explain, but you must promise me that you will destroy it after you've read it. I shouldn't even really be writing this down, but I couldn't tell you earlier. I waited for you but you didn't show up.
> I really like you, but sometimes, things happen, and you just have to make difficult decisions. It's nothing personal, but in the end, it's a survival thing. There's too much at stake and you already know too much, although I don't know exactly what Gordon told you at the party. He wouldn't tell me. And that's a bit of a problem. Whatever happens, I will never forget you. I will do whatever Gloria asks of me – it's the very least I owe her.

He put the letter down and smiled to himself, embarrassed. He must have been in a right state the first time he had read this. It was a leap of imagination to think this had been written by someone planning murder. But even looking back on that time now, he shuddered. He had been alone in an eerie, darkened room, worried about a murderer and needing some kind of explanation about Juliet's behaviour. And then, right on cue, he had seen the ghostly finger of the latex glove and found the used syringe and empty diamorphine bottle. At that moment, he would have believed anything. He turned back to the letter.

> The real reason for this letter is to warn you. You must leave the hospital as soon as you read this. Go home sick and wait. Only for a day or two, and then you'll be safe. But I'm getting ahead of myself. I need to tell you our story, so you've heard it from me. Then you can make your own mind up.
>
> Yes, I am a police officer. I work for the Drugs Squad, based in Leeds. I was chosen for the undercover operation at the hospital because we had a lot of intel to suggest that a big drugs operation was centred there: a combination of redirecting drugs from the pharmacy, and a hub for stuff imported from Europe. By the time I met you, I was pretty certain that Dave Henderson was working with Gordon Simpson and it was just a matter of time before we busted them – probably a day or two. Mike Hutchinson was the surprise, and it was you that pointed me towards him. But then the murders happened and the investigations got in each other's way. It all got very complicated for a day or two.
>
> One of the reasons they allocated me to the role was that my mother worked at the hospital. Gloria is my mother. No one else at the hospital knows that, so don't tell anyone. The other nurses think Gloria is on her own with no family. And so she was for too many years. I was taken into care when I

was a baby and eventually fostered and adopted. My new parents moved to Edinburgh soon after. I went to university in Leeds and stayed there after I'd finished. I made contact with Gloria again about a year ago. She has had a very hard life and has made something of herself after a short-lived abusive relationship with my father, a man I have never met and never want to. He may be dead for all I know. I hope he is, for what he put my mother through. Violence, repeated rape, heroin addiction. She escaped from that nightmare, only to step into another one. It seems that the wrong men are everywhere and everyone just accepts it.

The Squad thought it would be helpful to work at the hospital with my mother to keep an eye on me. She covered for me and made sure I never had to take charge of anything needing medical expertise. The extent of my knowledge runs to opening a packet of Elastoplast. They thought I could get away with it because I would only be there for a few weeks. They were nearly right. I had confronted Gordon about the whole thing and managed to turn him. He'd had a hard life himself and was totally messed up. A combination of the threat of prison and the offer of a way out in return for cooperation convinced him. He really needed to get away from Dave Henderson, who is a nasty piece of work. Pure evil. Gordon was desperate and pretty brave to go for it.

I think he will be arrested soon, either for the drug scam or for Gordon's murder, or both. But you must be very careful on nights. If Henderson thinks that Gordon told you stuff, he will come for you as well, I'm sure of it. He's a complete psycho. Keep your head down, don't go anywhere on your

own, and go off sick. At least for a couple of days. He'll be in custody by then.
I shouldn't be telling you any of this and I'm sure you can see why I've asked you to destroy this letter, but I'm worried about you. This hospital is dangerous and you're in the firing line. I won't see you again, but I won't forget you. Make sure Helen doesn't forget you either.
Juliet

*

Johnny bundled his bike into the hall, hung his coat up on the end of the stairs and made his way to the kitchen. Helen got out of her seat and met him at the threshold. She embraced him and leant forward for a kiss.

When they parted, she said, "So, how was it? Did it all go alright?"

"Yeah, it was fine. They were all taking the piss as usual, but it was good to get it out of the way."

"So, just a normal day then. No murders? Nothing weird happened?"

He gave a half-smile and looked away from her. "No, nothing. All normal."

64

New Year's Eve, and for the first time in many years, Gloria was spending it with family. She stepped from the shower, reached for a towel and began to dry herself. The air was thick with steam. When she had finished, she dropped the towel and stood in front of the mirror, reaching out to wipe away the condensation. Her reflection emerged in the hole in the fog, lines of moisture dribbling through it. She noted, as she did every day, the small cross, like a tattoo, in between her breasts, where the skin lay close to the bone, and reached up to touch it, her fingers tracing the raised edges. Nobody else had ever seen it, only her. And him, of course, but he really didn't matter any more.

As she stood there, cooling in the swampy, perfumed air, she went over it again, the details still vivid so many months later. She stopped and took a breath. No matter what she did, she could never be free of it. Not even now.

In the mirror, her reflection was fading back into the mist. All she had was her memory of that night.

*

It had been an unremarkable night shift in a hot, sultry summer. She'd seen Sutherland earlier. He wasn't even the consultant on duty that night, just on the prowl, but she was ready for him when he appeared at the end of the corridor, pacing towards her, a half-smile on his face as if he were on the edge of making a joke. The two pretty young nurses had been dispatched on an "urgent" task. They didn't need it to be explained twice. Both of them had experienced Sutherland's attentions and were in no hurry to repeat the experience.

"Mr Sutherland. What can I do for you?"

Sutherland radiated oily charm. He was a good-looking man, tall, powerfully built with well-groomed, silver-grey hair set off by a warm tan. His leather brogues clicked on the tiles as he walked, and a cloud of expensive cologne clung to him. His coat was a shimmering, unblemished white and from the breast pocket, a black Montblanc pen protruded, next to a scalpel, its blade sheathed in a plastic cap. His eyes raked down the length of Gloria's body.

"Good evening, Gloria, my sweet. Normally, you would be perfect, but actually, it's one of your juniors I'm after."

"They're busy, I'm afraid."

"I'm sure they could do with some help," he said, his smile continuing to beam out, his eyes scanning the corridor for any sign of them.

She leant across him and lowered her voice. "You really don't want to do that."

He raised his voice, "I can't see what—"

"Mrs Armstrong," she continued, "shat the bed. Poor old soul. She's not long for this world."

Sutherland took a step backwards.

"Ah. Yes. Of course."

He looked at Gloria again. Crisp, white uniform. Bright-red lips. Hint of cleavage. Shoulder-length, blonde hair.

"Never mind." He smiled. "You'll do, Gloria. Come."

He turned on his heels and marched back down the way he had come.

Gloria, nonplussed, called after him. "What is it?"

He stopped and turned impatiently.

"No time for explanations. Come with me; I need a nurse."

"But the ward. I can't just—"

"Leave it to the other two. I don't need you for long. Come on."

She looked back down the empty corridor. Jill and Margaret would be sitting in a store cupboard, among the packs of bed pans, calculating when it would be safe to come out. Probably better all round if she went along with Sutherland, no matter how repulsive he was. At least that would lead him away from the ward. Honestly, it was so pathetic, seeing a grown man turned into a dribbling infant by the sight of some blonde hair and a nice figure. She'd had enough of her own experience of that, thank you very much.

She turned to face him, recalibrating her smile as she did so. "Lead on, Mr Sutherland."

He returned the smile. "There, that's a good girl. Follow me."

So she did, half a pace behind him, struggling to keep up, as he motored through the corridors. After ten minutes of near silence, they finally came out at the bottom of a set of stairs, into a corridor that seemed familiar somehow.

"Isn't this the way to the car park?" she asked. "And the nurses' home? What are we doing down here?"

"Believe me, I'd love to be going to either of those places, I really would, but I've got work to do. It's just round here."

He led the way right, away from the door to the outside world, and Gloria, still baffled, followed him. She looked at the signage on the walls.

"But this is the mortuary, isn't it?"

"Don't worry, we're not going there just yet. Too much living still to do, the both of us. Plenty of time for the morgue when we're old and past it, eh? It's just here."

He led the way past the mortuary for a few yards until the corridor turned a corner. There, tucked away, where the passage reached a dead end, was a door bearing the sign, *Gerald Sutherland, consultant.*

Gloria stopped, puzzled.

"I didn't know you had an office down here," said Gloria. "I thought consultants on call used their common room."

"Most of them do," he said, his smile broadening, "but I'm a little different, a bit more important, as it were."

He produced a key from his trouser pocket and bent forward to unlock the door.

"I thought you needed help with a patient, Mr Sutherland. I don't understand what I'm doing down here."

He opened the door and ushered her in, closing it behind them.

"I just need a hand. I've got a lot of paperwork I need to catch up on."

A look of annoyance flashed across her face.

Sutherland's voice hardened. "Look, this is an opportunity for you. I have a lot of influence. If things work out, I could be very good for you."

Gloria cursed herself for making her irritation so obvious. It wouldn't do any good to make a scene. The only thing that men like Sutherland understood was compliance, and, even better, gratitude. She would just keep her head down, do what he wanted, and then she could go.

"So where are the files? Shall I make a start?" she asked.

"Over by the desk."

She looked round the room. It was a cross between an office, a sitting room and a hotel room, with a single bed in the far corner. She walked across to the desk and began to look at the neat pile of papers. Then Sutherland was right behind her. A hand squeezed a buttock and he pressed himself against her. She went rigid and tried to move away but she was trapped against the desk. She steeled herself, and keeping her voice as light as she could, said, "No, Mr Sutherland, I don't think this is a very good idea."

He ignored her, moving harder against her and reaching round to squeeze her breast. He whispered in her ear, "Don't play hard to get, sweetheart. Look at you, you're gagging for it. You all are. I've seen you flaunting your tits, wiggling down the corridors."

She pulled away in a panic and her voice hardened. "Get your hands off me. If you touch me again, I'll scream the place down. I'm warning you."

Sutherland dropped his hands, stood back and laughed.

"Go ahead, scream all you want. Who's going to hear you down here, you silly bitch?"

Gloria's eyes darted around the room and over Sutherland's shoulder. She tried a different tack.

"You're making a big mistake if you think I'll stay quiet. I'll finish you if you go any further. Let me out now, and you can save your career. We'll say no more about it."

He smiled and stepped closer to her. His face was an inch away from hers. She could smell his breath, onions and cigarettes, and his sweat mingled with aftershave. He laughed again. "Stay quiet? Who, exactly, are you going to talk to? Edwards, maybe? You've got no idea, have you? He doesn't give a fuck about you, you stupid tart. He knows exactly what goes on here, and he helps himself more than anyone. You make a complaint, it'll be internally investigated, filed and forgotten about. And you'll be dismissed for something six months later."

Gloria's face fell as this reality struck her. She was gripped by an overwhelming sense of powerlessness that battled with her rage. All of the fight seeped out of her, and she began to sob quietly.

Sutherland smiled sweetly at her. "There, there. It's much better to accept it, isn't it. There's a good girl. And really, if you let yourself go, you'll enjoy it. I'm very good at this."

He pulled her towards him, his hand around her neck underneath her hair. His other hand cupped her breast again.

The raw fury in her erupted. She wrenched herself free and showed him her nails: long, pointed, scarlet. "You touch me again and I'll make a mess of your face, you bastard. Everyone will know."

His smile vanished. With his left hand, he grabbed her neck, while his right hand fumbled around in the top pocket of his white uniform. He pulled out his scalpel, and showed it to her, an inch away from her face.

"No," he said, his voice chilling in its quiet calm. "You won't. And no one will know. Only you and me."

Ten minutes later, he had finished. Gloria was limp and lifeless. Her mascara streaked down her cheeks. Her uniform had been cast aside, her underwear discarded on the floor, but he had been careful not to tear anything. She lay quietly, holding her breath, restraining the gasping, choking, sobbing that would come later, when she was safely alone. She looked to the side, not wanting to catch his eye.

Sutherland adjusted his trousers and then bent down to pick up her bra and knickers. He smiled, held them to his face for a moment and then tossed them over to her.

"Clean yourself up and get changed. Then show me. We can't have you going out there and letting yourself down, can we? Beautiful woman like you. Use the bathroom."

She gathered up her clothes, keeping her head down, and hurried to the bathroom, shutting the door behind her. Inside, she washed her face, dried her eyes and sorted out her make-up as best she could. There was always a lipstick in her uniform pocket. She thought of it as part of her essential kit to face the world, like putting on armour. She studied her reflection in the mirror and took a deep breath. A smooth face, dead eyes, and turmoil behind them.

She did not look at him as she left.

At the door, he said her name.

She turned, a heavy weight pressing on her.

He patted the scalpel in his top pocket.

"Not a word, Gloria. Just remember."

She turned away from him and walked down the corridor, past the mortuary and out towards the main body of the hospital. As she walked, she began to practise her smile. She could cry later.

*

She could have managed it all. She could have survived. After all, she'd done it before, a long, long time ago. She had filed complaints, but pursued them only half-heartedly, knowing from bitter experience that this was not a woman's world. And then she had kept her head down and buried the memory as deep as she could. She had planned to move away and start again somewhere, but then Julie had arrived on her doorstep one night and her world had been turned upside down.

For a while, she had floated on a wave of an unfamiliar emotion. What was it? Love, she supposed, but she wasn't sure. But almost as quickly as it had arrived, this blissful, late flowering of happiness was threatened. When Julie had told her how Sutherland had cornered her, one night shift, and how she had only just escaped with a bruised arm and a ripped uniform, the rage of all of her past, long buried, erupted.

She was talked down from immediately confronting him by Julie, and in the process, Gloria told her daughter, her precious daughter, a story she had never told anyone before. And during that long night of anger and tears, a plan began to emerge, a cold, rational plan, born out of the heat of visceral emotion. The more they talked, the clearer it became how easy it would be. Sutherland, thinking himself an irresistible alpha male, would not be surprised when mother and daughter offered themselves to him, in the quiet dead of night at work. It stimulated his appetite for the exotic, in his room by the mortuary, with the piquancy of a little light bondage thrown in. She could still see the horror pass across his face as the needle slipped into a vein in his exposed, naked arm, securely fastened to the bed. He had found the latex gloves exciting. They had found them useful. The scalpel in the head was a last-minute flourish to confuse the police. Julie's idea. Julie who did the deed.

And Julie had done it all for her. Her daughter, who could not bear the idea of what her mother might do if she had said no, knew that the only way of saving her was to use her position at the hospital. It provided mutual alibis, and a certain security. For who would believe an undercover police officer could possibly be involved in murder? Certainly not the police, who, as Julie confirmed, were famous for protecting their own.

She shuddered at the memory. The warmth of the air in the bathroom had drained away with the bath water and the steamy atmosphere, and she was left staring at herself in the clear mirror. Her reflection stared back at her, naked and unhidden, like the truth she could never completely escape from. With a heavy sigh, she shook herself free from the past, and slipped into her robe. *One day at a time*, she told herself, rehearsing a smile, *one day at a time*.

*

A few hours later, after an expensive dinner, a few drinks, and a film on the telly, midnight was approaching. Juliet wondered about her parents in Edinburgh and what they would be doing right at that moment. Probably their usual house party with the comfortable middle classes in Morningside. Or maybe just a dinner for a few friends. Would they think of her? A difficult adolescence, punctuated by sex, drugs and self-harm for her, and shouting, tears and accusations of ingratitude from them, had left its scars on both sides. Gloria's love – raw, unconditional and unconstrained – had come to her like a life raft.

Gloria interrupted her thoughts. "Get the champagne ready, love. We don't want to miss Big Ben, do we?"

There was a pop, a surge of bubbles and two glasses were poured. They each took one, clinked them and waited. When the final bong sounded and the sound of raucous celebrations flooded into the room, they both took a sip of their drink. Gloria put down both glasses and folded Juliet in a bear hug.

"Happy New Year, darling."

"Happy New Year, Mum. Here's to 1980."

Gloria had tears in her eyes, and her voice quavered. "I'm so pleased you found me. I… it's been very hard."

Juliet pulled her into another embrace.

"Hush now. It's alright. Everything will be different now. You're free. And we're together. You don't have to worry any more."

She looked over Gloria's shoulder at the celebrations on the television and her smile faded. Her hands were clasped around Gloria's back, stained by the red light from one of the tiny bulbs on the Christmas tree. She shuddered. *Out, damned spot. Out.*

Sometimes, the sea seemed more appealing than the raft.

65

January, 1980. So this was The Eighties. It felt significant to Johnny, as if he was on the cusp of his real adult life. At the beginning of the Seventies, he'd been twelve years old and still had one foot in childhood innocence. A different kind of cusp, he supposed. It was his birthday in a week's time, when he would reach the ripe old age of twenty-three. The idea both fascinated and appalled him. It seemed so old somehow, and old was never a good thing.

His reaction summed up his general mood. The initial buoyancy of surviving the murders at the hospital had deserted him, and he felt like a sodden piece of flotsam stranded on the beach after the tide had gone out: abandoned, deflated, dissatisfied. He couldn't understand it. He should be full of the joys of spring, striding forward eagerly to new and exciting things, but everything seemed stale and uncertain.

Helen had noticed his low mood. She put it down to a delayed reaction to the horror of the events over Christmas, a realisation of just exactly what had happened and how close he had come to dying. Taking bodies to the mortuary was distressing enough, as part of his job, but finding people he knew killed in macabre circumstances in the dead of night was quite another.

She was right of course. She always was.

Occasionally these days, they slept apart. Sometimes, if she had a big day at work, or Johnny was on nights, he crept up to his old room and slipped into his own bed as if he were slipping back into his old life. In the dark coolness of his room, unaccountable to anyone, he worried that, actually, he preferred it. When this thought first occurred to him, he hastily put it to one side, and buried himself in any other distractions. There were plenty available to do the job for him. When Jaggers, Mark and Kate returned after Christmas, they were keen to be regaled with tales of the Great Hospital Murder Mystery. When they found out about Helen and Johnny's new romance, they were even keener for details.

Soon, their interest moved on. Life settled into a comfortable rhythm of parties, dinners, work and culture: gigs, films, books. There was always something Very Important to chew over with Helen, friends, a bottle of wine and a pack of cigarettes as midnight approached. Most of the time, this was more than enough. But always, just at his back, was a nagging thought that something was missing.

Those nights in his own room were also when he considered the part Juliet had played in all of this. He had read her letter over and over again and still wasn't sure what to make of it. The opening had been enough to make him convinced that she and Gloria were about to kill him, but when he read the rest of it, that was clearly not the case. Even the beginning of the letter seemed innocent now and he had jumped to the worst possible conclusion, his jangling emotions and the macabre atmosphere in the hospital leaving him prey to irrationality. What had she meant, *I'll do whatever Gloria asks of me*? Who were 'the wrong men'? Every time he turned these questions over in his mind, his confusion and dissatisfaction only grew.

Paula Marsh had kept them up to speed about developments in the case. Henderson had been charged with double murder and drug trafficking. He had withdrawn his confession, but they were pretty confident of getting a conviction. Hutchinson had been charged with supplying drugs and the police were expecting a lighter sentence, or even a suspended one because of his willing cooperation with the investigation and the crucial nature of his evidence. Helen had even met her for a drink a couple of times. They seemed to get on very well. She had also told them more details about Gordon, his childhood and his time in Blackstone. That had shaken Johnny. He already had trouble shifting the image of Gordon's body in the fridge from his mind, but now it was compounded by the chilling picture of a seven-year-old Gordon being found sharing a bed with his dead mother. Dr Death – that nickname seemed particularly cruel now. On many occasions, he found himself wishing that he had handled things differently. If he had had a more sympathetic conversation with Gordon at the party that night, maybe he would still be here. Gordon's weirdness with bodies, his obsession with taking pictures of them, all of that would still have had to be dealt with, but you can't atone for your mistakes if you're dead.

But life went on and as time passed, he was able to store his troubled thoughts and questions at the back of his mind.

It was late January and he had just finished an early shift at the hospital. Everyone on his crew had got changed and had left. The new crew had arrived and had dispersed to their various jobs in the hospital, leaving Johnny on his own in the restroom. He had hung up his overall and was sitting down on the sofa, lacing up his trainers. It was Friday and his last day at work for three days. When everyone in the house got back from work, the weekend would begin: house dinner tonight with friends, a gig on Saturday at the De Grey Rooms and then on Sunday, a walk on the moors to set up a lunch in a promising-looking pub in the middle of nowhere. It would be nice. And then, they could do the whole thing again the next week. And the week after.

He shook himself. *Stop being so fucking gloomy, for God's sake.* Life was good. Life was…

The phone in the restroom rang, wrenching him out of his introspection. He stretched out from the sofa and picked up.

"Porters," he said.

A voice replied: a soft Scottish accent. He couldn't quite place it but it derailed him anyway. Something in the tone, something in the timbre, even through the crackle of the line.

"Is that Johnny?"

That voice. He swallowed.

"Yeah, this is Johnny. Who's that?"

He knew the answer before it came.

"It's Juliet."

There was a pause. The static on the line filled the silence.

"Listen, can we meet up? There are things we need to talk about."

The static swamped him again. His mind raced as all of the questions he had suppressed came crowding in, jostling for answers. What did they need to talk about? Why now? Where was she? Maybe she really did like him and now she wanted to do something about it. Or maybe she was worried about him because, now what was that phrase she had used? Ah yes, that was it, worried because he "knew too much". Or was it…

"Johnny? You still there?"

He opened his mouth to speak, lips dry, heart pounding. A picture of Helen formed in his mind's eye, as if she were waiting with Juliet for his reply. He cleared his throat. Only one of them would hear it.

"Yes, I'd like that. Where shall we meet?"

Acknowledgements

With many thanks to The Creative Writing Programme, Kemptown Bookshop, Brighton and the South East London Writers' group for all the encouragement and constructive criticism.

About the author

Rob Barron was an English teacher and Deputy Head in London. Since retiring in 2017, he has published several novels, including *Zero Tolerance,* a satire on contemporary immigration and education policy, and the first two books in a YA fantasy trilogy: *The Watcher and The Friend* and *A Cold Wind Blows.* He is a graduate of the Creative Writing Programme based in Brighton.

Follow Rob's work on www.growl.blog and www.rjbarron.co.uk.